THE SKY-LORD'S RETURN

THE SKY-LORD'S RETURN

SECRETS OF SAEMAR
BOOK TWO

TUPPENCE VAN DE VAARST

To Rose

Our Lady Pellalindra

A LIBRARY

Thalion! On your right!"

Thalion acknowledged Kishtar's shout with a short nod. He couldn't let himself be distracted. He kept his sword up and ready, never looking away from their opponent.

Kishtar charged forward, and their opponent laughed mockingly, circling away from Kishtar and heading toward Thalion. Thalion knew what she was doing. She was trying to isolate him, so that she could eliminate him and then deal with Kishtar at her leisure. Well, it wasn't going to work!

He took a half step backward, allowing Kishtar to catch up. Step by step, they drove their opponent back, never allowing her to separate them as she wove back and forth. Finally, Thalion caught her sword in his, allowing Kishtar to present his sword at her throat.

She dropped her weapon in surrender, and it bounced off the packed dirt of the indoor practice salle. "Well done! It doesn't seem I have any more to teach you about fighting together."

Thalion smiled as he leaned down to pick up her sword. He handed it back to her hilt-first with a little bow. "It's only because we have the best teacher, Aunt Gwyn."

"Flatterer," Gwyn shook her head, dislodging a strand of her severe white-gold bun. She wore chainmail armor under her green and gold livery, which Thalion could never remember seeing her out of. No one would believe she was almost fifty years old.

"It's not flattery if it's true, Aunt Gwyn," Kishtar batted his eyes at her.

Gwyn aimed a mock blow at his head, and the young man ducked. "Save the flirtation for girls your age, boy."

Kishtar grinned, unperturbed by her response. "But Aunt Gwyn! You're the most striking woman there is!"

Thalion couldn't stifle his laughter. Gwyn certainly was as attractive as any noble lady. But even if she hadn't been a combination of aunt, guard, and teacher, she was also very happily in a relationship with their other bodyguard, Evalynna.

Gwyn gave Kishtar a mock scowl. "Impudent rascal. Why we kept you, I'll never know."

"Because you love me, Aunt Gwyn," Kishtar's smile never faded.

"Rascal," Gwyn muttered again. She turned to glare at Thalion, who was trying desperately to keep his laughter under control. "Something funny?"

Thalion shook his head, but chuckles escaped despite his best efforts.

Gwyn shook her head in mock disgust. "Go get cleaned up, you two. Can't have the two lordlings disgracing Ninaeva by smelling like a workout."

Kishtar clapped Thalion on the back as they moved to the stone wall to remove their armor. "Good work, little brother."

Thalion grinned at the familiarity as he removed his gauntlets, although he and Kishtar were by no means related, and no one would ever think that they were. Kishtar was tall, with blue eyes and dirty blonde hair that he kept slightly unkempt. Thalion stood shorter, and his dark hair hung in tight curls. Most of all, however, his skin was a dark brown, unlike almost anyone else in the entire kingdom. "Same to you, big brother." He and Kishtar finished disarming and left their weapons and chainmail in a neat pile on a low wooden bench for the servants to collect and clean.

"You know what this means, right?" Kishtar asked as they exited the salle, heading down one of the stone corridors of Ilhelm Castle. Woolen tapestries hung on the walls, this particular set depicting the legend of the stardrop flower of the Ninaevan mountains, one of Thalion's favorites. The silver flowers twinkled in the torchlight of the corridor, almost providing illumination of their own.

Thalion glanced suspiciously at Kishtar. "What?"

"If we can beat Aunt Gwyn, then we can do anything!" Kishtar exclaimed triumphantly. He beckoned for a servant as they reached the entrance to the bathing chamber and asked them to fetch a change of clothing for himself and Thalion.

Thalion looked doubtfully at Kishtar as they ducked inside the room. The servants had already prepared the granite tubs, and hot water steamed from them, obscuring everything except the huge fireplace that roared in the corner. "Anything?"

"Anything," Kishtar nodded emphatically. He quickly stripped and sighed blissfully as he climbed the steps into his tub.

"Even beat Prince Andreas?" Thalion followed Kishtar's example and stepped into his own tub, his muscles relaxing as the hot water soaked his body.

Kishtar snorted. "Prince Andreas may be a good swordsman, but he's only ever been trained by the fancy court duelists like Lord Kamian. We've had expert instruction."

Thalion wasn't certain of that. Prince Andreas had won the last tournament they'd all participated in, after all. Then again, if he and Kishtar ever teamed up against the prince, the best fighter in the world could be taken down by two mediocre fighters. It was one of Gwyn's favorite lessons.

Thalion closed his eyes and settled back in the spacious tub, submerging himself so that only his face remained above water. The two versus one fight had been the finale of a long series of exercises and sparring matches. Gwyn never went easy on them, for all that they were nobility. Then again, with the way she treated Thalion's mother, that was hardly surprising.

"Gwyn said you'd be here."

Thalion's eyes flew open, and he yelped and curled into a ball underwater, trying to cover himself. "Niara!"

His sister rolled her eyes. "Relax. I can barely see anything with all the steam you two have in this room."

Despite her words, Thalion remained hidden in the water, blessing his dark skin for not showing how flushed he was.

"Would you like to see more?" Kishtar's voice was bright. Thalion turned his head to glare at him.

"Give up, Kishtar," Niara said in exasperation. "That's never going to happen."

Kishtar laughed. "But you're so fun to tease!"

"Men," Niara sighed. "Mother sent me to tell you that lunch is nearly ready, and to remind you that we're expecting the MacTirs for dinner."

Thalion groaned. He had completely forgotten about the MacTirs.

"Like they're going to bother you," Niara said, frowning at him. "Dinah will be flinging herself at Kishtar, and Niall's going to try to get my attention while being a pompous ass to Mother and Father. We're the ones who are going to have to deal with them, not you."

Kishtar chuckled. "Dinah is certainly persistent."

"Are you encouraging her?" Thalion asked in disbelief.

Kishtar grinned. "Should I not be? She's certainly pretty enough. And imaginative. And flexible."

Niara's eyes widened. "I don't want to know how you know that," she said, backing out of the room. "Food! Soon!"

Thalion didn't relax until the door had shut behind her. He exchanged a look with Kishtar, who shook his head with a rueful expression.

"Sisters," Thalion said.

Kishtar laughed. "You realize if she was the teasing type, she'd be barging in here more often, right? You're lucky you've got a sister like you do."

Thalion grumbled, but he knew Kishtar was right. He raised an eyebrow at Kishtar, changing the subject. "Have you and Dinah really…" he flushed.

Kishtar snorted. "I know better than to go that far with a noble lady! Especially one with Niall for a brother! He won't let Dinah go to anyone except a landed noble. My title means nothing to him."

Thalion nodded. Despite the questionable circumstances of his birth, Kishtar did have his father's noble title, mostly thanks to Thalion's mother's insistence. Lord Torainn had not been landed, however, and so Kishtar had grown up a ward of Ninaeva.

"But she still…"

Kishtar smiled smugly. "Oh, she can't resist me. She caught me alone last time we visited Dunbarrow."

"Kishtar!" Thalion sat bolt upright in the tub. "She didn't! What did you do?"

Kishtar's smile broadened. "Well, I couldn't disappoint a lady now, could I? I gave her a few kisses and left her wanting more."

"You'd better hope Niall never finds out," Thalion warned, wavering between shock and admiration. "I don't know whether he'd force you into a marriage or try to kill you."

"Well, that's why we're brothers! You'll stand by me, right?"

Thalion groaned, and Kishtar laughed. He splashed a handful of water at Thalion. "Come on, we'll be late. You don't want your sister to peek in on us again, do you? Or worse, send Gwyn?"

Thalion shuddered and pulled himself out of the tub. No, he did not want to do anything that would result in their fearsome bodyguard being sent after them!

***

Lunch was not served in the great hall today. On most occasions, Thalion and his family ate there, so that the people of Ilhelm Castle could see them and talk to them in a more informal setting than a petitioners' court. Today, however, with visitors arriving, Thalion's mother decreed a private lunch for just family in the smaller dining chamber. Small did not mean poorly furnished or uncomfortable, of course. Carvings decorated the rich oak furniture, and more tapestries hung on the walls, these ones brightly colored depictions of the eternal battle of Mazda and Manyu.

Just family included Gwyn and Evalynna, as well as Kishtar, none of whom were Ninaevan by blood, and Gwyn and Evalynna weren't even noble. No one at Ninaeva cared about that, though.

Thalion knew most other noble estates had very different opinions.

To his chagrin, Gwyn had beaten him to the small dining room. She grinned and raised her soup spoon in salute at him as he and Kishtar entered.

His father looked up and smiled. "Gwyn has been telling us about your morning workout. Seems you're doing quite well."

Thalion smiled back into the eyes so like his own. No one could ever doubt he was Nazir et-Alim's son. Aside from the dark skin, they had the same black hair, the same dark brown eyes. Nazir had no aptitude for fighting, however, preferring scholarly pursuits. It was a measure of his love for his son that he still praised Thalion for something he found incomprehensible.

Thalion shrugged as he sat down, trying to conceal the warm pride his father's words brought. "Well enough," he said, attempting modesty.

Kishtar had no such reservations. "Together we are unbeatable!" he exclaimed as he sat down next to Gwyn. "Together we are a match for the prince and all his knights!"

Vinet raised an eyebrow at Kishtar's exuberance. "Well, you might have a chance to test that theory against the prince, but let's leave the knights out of it, shall we?"

Kishtar nodded sheepishly, and Thalion's mother gestured for them to start serving themselves chunks of bread and bowls of thick stew spiced with rosemary and sage. Even though it was Mazda's Rise, the warmth of the stew provided a welcome contrast from the chill in the air.

Lady Vinet et-Alim of Ninaeva resembled Niara so strongly that it was a very good thing she had acknowledged her daughter before Thalion's birth. Both had slender forms, with the same red-brown hair and the same bright green eyes. Vinet wore her hair braided in a crown around her head, a style her daughter copied. As Vinet turned her attention to her son, Thalion thought, not for the first time, that she and Niara could be mistaken for sisters instead of mother and daughter.

"Well, at least you cleaned up." Vinet smiled warmly, taking any disapproval out of her tone. "Just please don't challenge Niall when he arrives. I don't want another bruised ego."

Thalion exchanged a guilty look with Kishtar as he started eating. Two years ago, when Thalion had just been introduced to noble society, he and Kishtar had entered a tournament at Dunbarrow, one that Niall was certain he would win. Thalion and Kishtar had knocked Niall out of the very first round, and Vinet had thought it prudent to leave the party early before Niall lost his temper.

"I don't think Niall would ever challenge one of us again," Kishtar said. "Not until he'd improved in skill. And with all the troubles in his territory..."

"Indeed," Vinet dipped her bread in her stew. "Don't bring those troubles up while they're here, either, or to him or Dinah while you're on tour. Niall doesn't want it known that he needs royal authority in order to keep his own lands in check, and we are not going to be the ones to mention it. The last thing we need is our closest neighbor angry at us."

Niara nodded solemnly, but Kishtar rolled his eyes. Vinet fixed her gaze on her adopted son. "That includes you, Kishtar," she said firmly.

When Vinet used that tone, her children, even the ones not hers by blood, listened. "Yes, Aunt Vinet," Kishtar promised. "No annoying Niall."

"And if you must flirt with Dinah, do so discreetly. At least while you're under this roof."

Thalion blinked. Then again, he shouldn't have been surprised. His mother knew everything about everyone. Or so it seemed.

"Do I have to go on the tour, Mother?" Niara ate her stew with a studied air of indifference, a contrast from the suppressed hope in her voice.

Vinet smiled sympathetically at her daughter, but her tone remained firm. "Yes. You're the heir of Ninaeva. People need to see you, and you need to start making allies of your own."

Unspoken was the reason behind that. Vinet could not remain in the public eye for much longer. Soon, within the next few years, she would have to step down. Otherwise, someone would remark on the fact that she looked exactly the same at fifty as she had at twenty.

Vinet, Niara, and Thalion all had elven blood, a fact that they kept secret from the rest of Saemar. They could not afford anyone else to find out.

Niara reached up to make sure her crown of hair covered her ears. Of the three of them, Niara was the only one who'd inherited visibly pointed ears.

"I understand that, Mother," Niara said. Thalion could hear the strain in her voice. "I just… I hate the lying."

"I understand too, daughter," Vinet's voice was gentle. "Nevertheless, you must go. For all our sakes." She ate a spoonful of her stew before continuing. "I can hardly send one of my children off without the other to guard their back, can I?"

"I'll watch Thalion's back," Kishtar volunteered.

Vinet raised an eyebrow. "I'm sure you will, Kishtar, but Niara is going with both of you."

Niara's shoulders drooped a little, but she nodded.

That wouldn't do. Thalion poked her under the table, and she looked up at him, frowned, and poked him back. Thalion grinned.

Niara shook her head, but Thalion could see her lips twitch. "Is Niall accompanying us on the tour, or is he returning to Dunbarrow?" Hope filled his sister's voice. For reasons of her own, Niara disliked Niall intensely.

"Unfortunately, yes," Vinet said. "It is in his interest to make the entire circuit and maintain the illusion he has complete control of his lands. He'll be with you all the way to the coronation—"

She stopped abruptly. Her eyes went black, staring out into nothingness, and her hands clenched the table.

Thalion's eyes widened. "Mother?"

"Vinet!" His father sprang to his feet and grabbed Vinet's shoulders. Instead of shaking them, however, he held her close and started whispering in her ear.

Gwyn stood up as well, and Thalion could tell she was searching for danger as Evalynna moved to guard the door. He got out of his own chair, Kishtar a heartbeat behind him. What could he do? What was going on?

He saw Niara staring at their mother for a long second. She then took a deep breath, rose to her feet, and deliberately walked over to stand beside their parents.

"Niara, don't," Nazir said, holding out a hand. "You'll—"

"I know," Niara interrupted. She took Vinet's hand. Instantly, her face took on the same far-away gaze.

The visions! Thalion realized abruptly. Although he'd never had them, Niara had described them to him once. He'd never seen his mother have one, though. Not like this.

Niara had done the right thing. After a tense heartbeat lasting an eternity, Vinet blinked, sighing as she relaxed into Nazir's arms. Niara stumbled, and Thalion nearly tripped over his feet as he rushed to support his sister.

"Vinet?" Nazir's voice was low. "Vinet, is everything alright?"

Vinet nodded wearily. "That was…interesting."

Nazir snorted, but Thalion could tell his father was relieved. "What was it? Was it connected to our conversation?"

Vinet frowned. "I…I don't know. I don't see how it could be." She exchanged a glance with Niara.

"It was here," Niara said. "Here at Ilhelm. It had to be."

Thalion glanced in confusion between his mother and sister. What had they seen?

Evalynna moved away from guarding the door to return to the table, checking in on each of her charges before meeting Gwyn's eyes. Gwyn moved over to stand behind Vinet and Nazir, still on alert.

"What was here?" Nazir asked.

"There's a secret entrance below the castle," Vinet said. "I know exactly where, although I've never even heard a rumor of it before. And it leads…to something. Something that we're going to need."

Thalion felt Niara shiver in his arms, and he was a hair's breadth from demanding why they would need it. His father silenced him with a look.

"Then we will open it," Nazir said firmly. He paused. "Is there anything else?"

"I don't know," Vinet said. "It was…far vaguer than most of my other visions. There were feelings, more than anything."

Niara nodded in agreement.

"It's been a long time since your last involuntary vision," Nazir said quietly.

Thalion frowned at the expression on his mother's face. He couldn't quite read it. There was fear, acceptance, knowledge of… something, and love.

"I know," she said quietly.

Thalion didn't interrupt as his parents stared at each other, seeming to speak without words.

Finally, it was Gwyn who cleared her throat. "Well, if there's no immediate threat, then we'd better finish our meal before rushing off to discover a secret passage," she said practically.

Kishtar laughed uneasily as he returned to his seat, returning his eating knife back to his place setting. Nonetheless, it broke the tension, and they returned to their food, quietly speculating about what they might find.

The fresh air of Mazda's Rise still held a faint chill to it, but after the harshness of Manyu's Time, Thalion breathed it in eagerly. Beside him, he noticed Kishtar and Niara doing the same thing. None of the three of them liked being cooped up indoors.

His mother walked with a sure step, leading them deeper into the castle compound. She nodded acknowledgment to servants and guards who bowed in respect or saluted her but didn't let anyone distract her.

Thalion watched her carefully. He had never been certain whether the visions his mother and sister had were a blessing or a curse. But regardless, he would never have to deal with them. When he hadn't had a vision by the time he was thirteen, Vinet had exclaimed in relief and given him to Gwyn to teach. Not that he'd minded! He'd much rather be a master of sword than some sort of mysterious magician-witch.

Vinet stopped abruptly, causing the whole group to halt behind her. Thalion blinked in confusion. They were in the very back of the castle garden, near the grove of willow trees at the edge of the lake. Nothing behind the willows but a wall of solid rock boulders that towered as high as the central keep. He should know. He'd hidden in the trees often enough as a boy.

"Behind there," Vinet said in a firm voice.

Gwyn raised an eyebrow. "Vinet, are you sure?"

"Absolutely." Vinet wrapped her green wool cloak tight around her. "The boulder will lift up, but we'll need strong men to do it. That's where it is."

Gwyn sighed but didn't argue. Instead, she strode off, waving a hand and shouting orders to one of the guards at the entrance of the garden.

Thalion exchanged a look with Kishtar and went to sit at the edge of the lake. This might take a while.

To his surprise, Nazir came over to sit beside them on the pebbled shore. Thalion smiled a greeting to his father.

"What do you think is behind the wall, Uncle Nazir?" Kishtar asked.

Nazir shook his head. "I never try to predict what she sees. If there's something beneath the castle, that is a surprise to us all."

Thalion frowned, struggling to remember his history lessons. "Great-grandfather built this castle, didn't he? After he convinced the clans to unite under him."

Nazir nodded, without mentioning the fact that it hadn't actually been his great-grandfather. It was still necessary to keep up the fiction that his grandfather had been the lord of Ninaeva, instead of an elven Eye of the Lady.

Thalion's frown deepened. "Was there some reason this site was picked? Was it a meeting place for others beforehand?"

"That would be a reasonable assumption, regardless of whether there is a record of it," Nazir said. "But I believe you are right. Maybe there is something from the previous generations here."

Thalion could see the excitement in his father's eyes, and he concealed a smile. His parents shared a passion for the past. He enjoyed a good story, but the present seemed so much more exciting.

Nazir sobered. "I've been meaning to talk to you, son," he said.

The wind rustled through the willows as Thalion glanced up. "About what?"

"This trip." Nazir placed a hand on his son's shoulder. "Thalion, be careful."

"Be careful of what?" Thalion asked. "We're accompanying the prince on a tour of the kingdom. There won't be any danger, will there?"

"More than you think," Nazir said. "And not just for you. For your sister as well."

Thalion blinked and looked over to where Niara and his mother stood, talking quietly by the gray stone boulder. "For Niara?"

"Thalion, neither you nor Niara are fully..." Nazir sighed, "accepted among certain circles of the nobility."

Thalion nodded impatiently. He knew that, of course. Niara was a bastard, and Nazir was a commoner with rumors of demon heritage, which made Thalion suspect as well.

"Maybe they will avoid the topic, seeing as you're in the prince's entourage, but do not provoke them, Thalion. Do not react to the insults. You are representative of Ninaeva, and we cannot afford to give credence to their rumors." Nazir looked at him seriously.

"Rumors?" Thalion frowned in confusion.

Nazir's lips tightened. "That we are becoming barbaric and degenerate, and that the regent should send royal troops to administer justice like they do in Dunbarrow."

"They say that?" Thalion blinked.

"Not in our hearing, but we have friends," Nazir nodded. "Dunbarrow has been under direct royal control since Conn MacTir's death. Even though Niall is fully an adult, he cannot hold the lands on his own. This gives the crown a great deal of power there. Power that Ninaeva cannot afford to give up."

"Because of Grandfather," Thalion said. The scandal that Vinet's father was not the former lord of Ninaeva but, in fact, an elf would shock the nobility to the core.

"The prince could disinherit all of us," Nazir said. "And since your Aunt Nimue is content at the convent, he would be free to bestow the title and lands on whomever he thought appropriate."

Thalion bit his lip. "So, what am I supposed to do?"

"Make friends," Nazir said instantly. "Niara will be doing the same. Make yourself respected by the prince and his court, and they will have no reason to speak out against you, and thus the nobility who think you should be disinherited will have no voice in the discussions."

Thalion nodded seriously. "I can do that."

Nazir smiled. "Good," he paused. "One other thing. For both of you," he looked at Kishtar to include him in the conversation.

"What?" Kishtar perked up.

Nazir lowered his voice. "Watch over Niara."

"Niara's perfectly capable," Kishtar tossed one of the pebbles from the shore into the lake, causing the water to ripple in symmetrical circles.

Nazir shook his head. "Not in this instance. You know the rumors, that the prince is searching for a queen this tour. Well, the rest of the nobility and their children will be pairing everyone off as well. Your mother receives several invitations a year for Niara's hand, but she's refused them all, saying it is Niara's choice. Someone will likely press his suit during this tour. And you need to be there for her, to back her in whatever decision she makes."

Thalion blinked at the intensity of his father's voice. "You think someone might get aggressive about it?"

Nazir shrugged. "There are ruthless men among the nobility. Niara is heir to wealthy lands, regardless of her questionable heritage. Someone may decide that her lands are worth more than her 'no'."

Thalion nodded. "I promise, Father," he said.

Nazir sighed in relief. "Good," he said. He glanced at Kishtar.

"Me too!" Kishtar exclaimed. "I'll defend Niara to the death!"

Nazir smiled. "It's too bad she doesn't find you attractive."

Kishtar made a face, and Thalion suppressed a laugh. "Uncle Nazir! She's like my sister! My annoying older sister!"

"Just watch out for her," Nazir said again. He rolled some of the gravel they were sitting on, considering. "And…maybe keep her away from the prince. The last thing we need is the prince deciding she's a suitable queen."

Thalion chuckled at the idea of his sister ever being queen, but he sobered at the serious expression on his father's face. "If you think it's best," he said.

Nazir nodded. "I do." The noise of dozens of feet interrupted him, and he turned his attention to the entrance of the garden. "It appears the workers have arrived."

Thalion scrambled to his feet and went to join his mother and sister as the workers set their equipment in place. They illustrated their faith in Vinet by not questioning her assertion that something existed behind the wall. They simply began their work.

Thalion observed, impressed. The contraption consisted of multiple pulleys and levers, far more complicated than he'd ever seen. The men knew exactly what to do with it, though. Inch by inch, they shifted the rock, pulling it further out into the garden.

Thalion's eyes widened as the opening behind the boulder slowly came into view. He could only see pitch blackness, but a tunnel obviously stretched into the rock.

"That's enough for now," Vinet said, her voice trembling with excitement. "Someone get me a torch."

Quickly, a torch was passed forward, but Gwyn took charge of it before it got to Vinet. "I'll go first, my lady," she said seriously.

Vinet rolled her eyes but didn't argue, just beckoned impatiently. Gwyn smiled and stepped warily into the opening, followed closely by Vinet and Nazir.

Thalion was right behind them. He wasn't about to let his parents have all the fun, after all!

He gasped as his eyes adjusted to the dark, his elven heritage allowing his sight to stretch far into the cavern. A huge staircase with steps as tall as his knee led down into the darkness. Strange geometric carvings in the stairs glinted in the light of Gwyn's torch. He sensed more than saw Niara join them before they began to descend into the depths.

They had gone maybe ten, fifteen ells down into the ground when Gwyn stopped. Thalion blinked. Where once had been a huge door, now a giant slab of stone simply lay on the ground.

"Careful going around it," Gwyn called. "I don't want anyone to slip."

Thalion didn't want to slip, either. He made it onto the stone, then turned to offer Niara his hand.

His sister smiled sweetly at him as she took it. "Why thank you, little brother," she said.

Thalion gave her the best mocking bow he could on the huge stairs. "My pleasure, big sister."

She laughed, and her voice echoed down the passage. Her eyes met his, bright green piercing through the dark.

That was the other reason his father wanted him to protect her, Thalion realized. Niara looked so much more like an elf than their mother. Whoever she chose as a husband had to be completely trustworthy. If someone tried to coerce her into a marriage, she needed all the support she could get. *But that means...Mother and Father don't consider the prince trustworthy. What does that mean?*

They passed two more destroyed doors, then the stairs abruptly ended and they were walking on level ground. Well, level underground. Thalion wasn't certain how that worked.

The passage widened until they stood at the entrance of a huge cavern. Thalion swallowed. The dim light of Gwyn's torch illuminated only one path, an old stone bridge right through the center of the cavern. On either side of the bridge, a long abyss stretched into darkness.

Gwyn squared her shoulders. "Follow behind me," she ordered. "I don't want all of us on that bridge if it proves to be unstable."

"It's stable," Vinet said quietly, but she followed Gwyn's instructions. Thalion wondered how she could be so calm about it. He was of Gwyn's opinion. Something that old should not still be standing.

Thalion thought it an eternity before his turn came to cross the abyss with Naira. The limited light from the torch on the far side of the chasm made its depths appear bottomless. An illusion, or so Thalion kept telling himself. He couldn't quite get his gut to agree.

He gasped as they reached the end of the bridge, and he looked beyond the safety of the cliff. Rising huge behind Gwyn and his parents, glinting in the torchlight, was a bronze door. It stood three times as tall as Thalion, intricately carved. Thalion spotted a small dragon breathing fire, a lion, and several other fantastical beasts. No doorknob was apparent, nor any crack that appeared to be a keyhole.

"What is this?" Niara breathed. She reached forward to touch the door, letting her fingers glide over the bronze. "It's beautiful!"

Vinet shook her head. "I don't know," she said, her voice full of admiration.

"Well, we can't seem to get through," Gwyn said practically. "What now?" she asked Vinet.

Vinet stared at the door a moment longer before tearing her attention away from it. "I'll set the scholars on it, find out where it comes from, see if they know a way to open it. We'll find out what's inside."

She turned to Niara and Thalion. "When the MacTirs get here, please don't tell them what we found," she said. "And don't mention it to anyone else on the tour, either. This needs to remain a Ninaevan secret."

"Speaking of which," Gwyn said. "The MacTirs are almost due. We should get back to the surface so you can greet them when they arrive."

Vinet released a string of curses that she must have learned from Gwyn.

His father merely laughed. "Come, dear. You only have to deal with them for an evening. Then you can send your children off to suffer in your stead."

Thalion exchanged a look with Niara as they started back toward the surface. *I'm beginning to think suffer might be the right word for this tour.*

2

THE PRINCE'S BALL

My lords and ladies of Saemar! Prince Andreas bids you welcome to the Belgar Ball!"

Thalion applauded politely with the other nobles as the door to the ballroom was thrown open. The crowd surged forward, and Thalion let himself be carried with it.

The ballroom was a picture of opulent splendor. Glinting gold and silver decorations hung from every chandelier, elaborate displays of sweet-smelling pastries and fruits lined the tables at one end of the hall, and silken banners depicting the arms of Saemar hung prominently on every wall. A group of musicians in royal heraldry sat on the dais quietly tuning their instruments, ready to play at the prince's whim. The polished black marble floor where the dancing would take place shone in the light of the chandeliers, the reflections from the candles twinkling like starlight. Heat pressed from the mass of bodies around Thalion, an overwhelming sensation when mixed with the perfumes, bright gems and silks, and deafening chatter as the gathered nobility exclaimed in wonder.

Prince Andreas himself stood at the bottom of the wide stairs leading into the ballroom, his golden tunic bordering on gaudy when matched with his gold crown and silver-inlaid boots, greeting every guest personally as they entered. Thalion suppressed a sigh as servants ushered the nobility into an organized line and the crowd moved to a crawl. It would take hours for everyone to enter like this.

Kishtar rolled his eyes, and Thalion grinned at him. Niara frowned at them both.

"Lady Niara! Lord Thalion!"

Thalion looked behind him. A tall, striking young noblewoman in a long gown of russet red smiled warmly at Niara. She was not pretty, but rather handsome, with brown eyes and auburn hair braided into an intricate style.

"Lady Rian!" Niara exclaimed. Ignoring propriety, she reached out and pulled the other noblewoman into a hug. "I was hoping to see you! Are you accompanying the prince on his tour?"

Rian laughed. "Well, of course!" she exclaimed. "All three of us are, in fact. Lokrian has to show their support for the crown."

"Meaning Lady Lokris-Pythian just wants to attend a lot of parties. Hello Lady Niara, Lord Thalion, Lord Kishtar," another female voice spoke up.

Thalion smiled at the petite young woman who stepped out of Rian's shadow. Ianna could not have looked more different from her sister. Her long black hair, instead of being braided, fell back in loose waves, and her hazel eyes were soft and gentle.

Kishtar gave her an elaborate bow. "Always a pleasure, Lady Ianna."

"Hey, you watch the flirting with my sister," the young man next to Ianna mock-glared at Kishtar. It was obvious he and Ianna were siblings, though hardly anyone would suspect they were twins. They shared the same hair and eyes, but Arrex seemed to have stolen all his sister's height.

Thalion grinned at Arrex. "Hey, you know Kishtar flirts with anyone he can."

Ianna blushed, and Arrex rolled his eyes. "Yes, we know. Though he's never tried it on *me*," he said.

Kishtar bowed slightly. "My apologies, Arrex. But you know I'd prefer to dance with your sisters," he turned to Rian, bowing. "I must claim you for at least one dance this evening. Two, even, if I might be so bold!"

Rian laughed as if unaffected, but Thalion caught the faintest blush on her cheeks. He suppressed a smile. Kishtar had that effect on women.

As if he heard Thalion's thoughts, Kishtar turned back to Ianna. "And of course, I would not neglect you. May I claim the first dance of the evening, Lady Ianna?"

Ianna flushed but nodded.

"Well, since we're all arranging dancing partners already, I may as well ask you for a dance, Lady Niara,"

Arrex's tone was casual, but Thalion caught more than a hint of hope in it. He glanced up sharply.

Niara didn't appear to hear anything unusual in Arrex's voice. She curtsied slightly. "Well, of course! I'll be a bit better at it than when you were trying to teach me in Ninaeva."

Arrex smiled, but it seemed to Thalion that Niara had not given him his preferred answer. Or maybe he was just being paranoid.

"Thalion," Kishtar hissed. "You're supposed to ask the ladies to dance too."

It wasn't much of a whisper, as both Ianna and Rian suppressed giggles.

"Ah, right!" Thalion flushed. He bowed awkwardly to both of the Lokrian ladies. "I hope both of you will do me the honor of a dance tonight, as well."

Rian bowed her head in acknowledgment, and Ianna curtsied low and bowed her head. "It would be my pleasure," Ianna said softly.

A noble behind them coughed, and Thalion looked forward guiltily. The line had moved without them, and only one group now stood between them and the prince.

Only a few moments passed before the group moved on, and Thalion, Kishtar, and Niara stepped forward. Thalion gave his best bow, perfectly in sync with Kishtar and Niara.

Prince Andreas nodded in acknowledgment. "Lady Niara, Lord Thalion, Lord Kishtar, a pleasure to see you again."

Thalion rose from his bow as Niara answered, being the highest ranked among them. "Thank you for inviting us, your highness," Niara said smoothly. "We will be delighted to accompany you as you tour Saemar."

Prince Andreas smiled. "Well, I doubt all the events will be as marvelous as this one, but that can hardly be helped," he said with casual arrogance. "I hear your mother is planning something extravagant for Dragon's Day."

Thalion stiffened but managed to prevent a frown. His mother and father were hosting Dragon's Day together. The prince surely knew that.

"My mother and Lord Nazir have been planning the event for months," Niara said, without reacting to the slight. "They are looking forward to hosting you."

"As they should," the prince nodded firmly. "We will speak more during our travels. In particular, Lord Thalion, Lord Kishtar, I hope that you will spar with me at some point. I must know the strength of my nobles."

Thalion concealed his uneasiness. Niara was heir to Ninaeva, not him. But perhaps he represented his sister in this matter. Most noblewomen, including Niara, were not warriors.

"We would be honored," Kishtar said, bowing smoothly.

The prince gestured in dismissal, and Thalion gave a breath of relief as they stepped into the ballroom proper.

Niara brought a hand to the hair covering her ears, a gesture Thalion knew she did when she was nervous or trying to conceal her tension. "Well, that was interesting," she said.

"He slighted Father," Thalion said in a low voice.

Niara shrugged, but Thalion could see her lips tighten in displeasure. "That's hardly surprising," she answered, her voice equally soft. "Most of the nobility don't like him."

Thalion didn't need her to explain why. A commoner, a foreigner, a stranger, should never have been able to marry one of the highest-ranking noblewomen of Saemar. He had tainted their supposedly pure bloodlines.

He glanced down at his dark skin. There would never be any concealing his heritage.

Kishtar elbowed him in the ribs. "Stop brooding," he said. "Those who matter like Uncle Nazir. You should find someone to dance with. It'll take your mind off things."

Niara rolled her eyes.

Kishtar turned his gaze to her. "What? It does!"

Niara shook her head, then peered over Kishtar's shoulder. "Mazda's light," she whispered.

Thalion's lips twitched as he saw Niall and Dinah MacTir approaching. Dinah was looking exceptionally pretty tonight, her black curly hair tamed only by a silver circlet glinting in the light.

Thalion nodded a greeting as the two approached. Niall nodded in return.

Niara smiled charmingly, completely different from her initial dread. "Lord Niall, Lady Dinah. I see you've managed to get past the gauntlet," she said, gesturing back toward the doorway where a line of nobility still waited to enter.

Niall frowned. "That will not happen in Dunbarrow," he said firmly.

Thalion caught himself just before he heaved a sigh. This had been the pattern the entire journey to the capital. Whatever topic was brought up, Niall brought the subject back to Dunbarrow and his lordship. Just because he was lord in his own right...

"You two will fight in the tournament at Dunbarrow, right?" Dinah asked. "It falls on Ululu, you know, so there will be a great tournament in Mazda's name."

Thalion exchanged a look with Kishtar. Was it really such a good idea to fight in a tournament hosted by Niall MacTir?

They couldn't refuse a direct invitation, though. "We would be honored," he answered for both of them.

Niall nodded. "Then at least someone from the north may claim victory," he said, "since I am prohibited from fighting in my own tournament for some Manyu-cursed reason."

"Niall!" Dinah hissed. "Language!"

Niall shrugged but didn't apologize directly. Instead, he waved a hand at the door. "Well, at least the line of sycophants is coming to an end."

Kishtar perked up. "That means the first dance will be soon. Excuse me, I must find my scheduled partner." He bowed low to Dinah. "I shall claim you for a dance later tonight?"

Dinah batted her eyelashes, a flush rising to her cheeks. "Perhaps," she said.

Kishtar grinned, entirely unperturbed. "I shall find you, then. Lord Niall." He nodded, then moved through the crowd to where the Lokrians were standing.

Niall raised an eyebrow, then turned to Niara and bowed. "Would you do me the honor of the first dance, Lady Niara?"

Thalion could almost feel Niara's suppressed sigh as she curtsied. "I would be delighted."

A bell chimed, and the prince strode out into the middle of the ballroom. The chatter of nobles stopped as all attention centered on the prince.

He was certainly the picture of royalty, Thalion had to admit. His raven-black hair was a stark contrast to the gold crown on his head, and the opulence of his outfit now appeared to simply match the splendor of the ballroom. He smiled as all eyes fastened him.

"Lords and Ladies of Saemar," Prince Andreas said, his voice pitched to carry across the ballroom. "Welcome to my Belgar Ball. On this festival of fertility, the start of my tour through Saemar, we carry that fertility with us to ensure growth and prosperity for the kingdom. I know many of you will join me on this tour, and I hope the same fertility and growth will carry with you back to your lands." He raised both hands. "And may that strength carry into your warriors, so that we may bring Tigri back into the fold!"

Thalion suppressed a shiver. The war had started again a few years ago, and the prince had been at the forefront of the campaign. His mother had kept Ninaeva out of it as much as she could and talked little about the war except to tighten her lips and shake her head. The only reason Prince Andreas was not on campaign this summer as well was because of his coming of age.

Niall nodded approvingly. "Bring those Tigrian bastards under control," he muttered.

The prince nodded at the crowd. "But I have delayed your entertainment long enough. I shall now pick my partner for the first dance!"

Thalion nearly laughed at the wave of excitement that went through the assembled noblewomen. Only Niara seemed unaffected.

The prince strode toward the crowd purposefully, as if he already had someone in mind. There was a ripple of disappointment when people saw who he was heading to. Tall and intimidating, the regent had somehow managed to blend in unobtrusively at the edge of the crowd. His wife and daughter stood next to him, his wife with a satisfied smirk on her face. But Thalion dismissed both Lord and Lady Auriel in a heartbeat as he glimpsed the vision standing next to them.

She was gorgeous. Her golden hair tumbled in long waves down her back, held in place only by a simple silver band. Golden embroidery decorated her sky-blue dress, a perfect match for her hair. She cast her eyes modestly down as the prince approached, but even from where he stood, Thalion could see their piercing green.

"Is that Serana?" he whispered under his breath.

Niara glanced at him in amusement. "Lady Serana Auriel, daughter of the regent, yes."

Thalion watched, mesmerized, as Prince Andreas approached Serana and bowed, offering his hand. She accepted it with a curtsy, and the two of them moved to the center of the dance floor.

That was the signal for the rest of the nobility. Couples detached themselves from the crowd, moving to take their places for the dance. Thalion hardly noticed as Niall led Niara off. He was still staring at Serana.

Dinah sniffed, and he jumped guiltily. No one was approaching her for a dance. He should have already asked…

"Ah, would you care to dance, Lady Dinah?"

Dinah sniffed again. "I suppose," she said.

Thalion's body remembered the proper motions to lead her onto the dance floor, but his mind was still in a whirl. It had been three years since he'd last seen Serana Auriel. She mostly kept to the capital, living with her father and mother in the palace. If the prince was at an event, she was sure to be there, but since the prince had been on campaign the past few summers, she had barely been seen at any of the balls of the nobility. When had she turned into such a beauty?

He managed to bow politely to Dinah at the end of the dance, but she stalked off, clearly not impressed with his performance. Thalion didn't care. He watched as the prince escorted Serana back to her parents and bowed. Another young noble immediately came up to her and asked for the next dance.

"Having fun?"

Thalion jumped. He'd been so absorbed in observing Serana, he hadn't noticed Kishtar approaching. "Ah—"

Kishtar followed his gaze and grinned. "See something you like?" he asked.

"I..." Thalion's cheeks heated as he stumbled for words.

Kishtar's grin broadened. "You should ask her for the next dance."

Panic rose up in him as his eyes found Serana again. She moved as lightly as a butterfly on the dance floor, laughing as her partner spun her around. He could never match her grace. "I...no," he said. "I'll just watch."

"Thalion!" Kishtar exclaimed. "You like dancing! Why wouldn't you ask her?"

Thalion's cheeks heated even more. "I..." he shook his head. "Kishtar, she's the daughter of the regent! I can't..."

Kishtar snorted. "And you're the son of Lady Vinet et-Alim, member of the Regency Council, currently Lady of the Regency Council, and Lady of Ninaeva. Your point?"

He shook his head again. "I'm going to go find some refreshments," he said, trying to walk away.

"Oh no you don't," Kishtar stood to block his path. "Why are you intimidated by a pretty girl?"

"Pretty?" Thalion stared at him. "Kishtar, she's not just pretty, she's gorgeous!"

Kishtar grinned. "So you *do* like what you see. I can see how she feels about you, if you like."

"No!" Thalion threw up his hands in defense. "Don't you dare!"

Kishtar's smile didn't fade. "What? It would only be a simple question—"

"Kishtar!" Thalion exclaimed, then subsided as several other nobles gave the two of them questioning looks.

Kishtar eyed him, then shrugged. "Suit yourself. I need to go fulfill my obligation to Dinah to dance with her. You should dance with Rian, at least. You promised her." He nodded over Thalion's shoulder.

Thalion turned around just as Rian approached them.

"I heard that," Rian said, smiling. She extended her hand to Thalion. "Are you ready?"

Mazda bless Rian. She always knew how to take charge. Thalion bowed, and they moved onto the dance floor just as the musicians began another number.

He danced with Ianna immediately afterward, leaving him no time to think. He caught a glimpse of Niara dancing with Arrex. Serana had disappeared at some point, and he fought down a surge of disappointment. He left Ianna with her sister and took the opportunity to grab a glass of wine from a passing servant. This was obviously a planned break in the dancing, as nobles moved about, chatting. Thalion caught a glimpse of the prince and Arrex standing next to each other, heads together as they talked in low voices.

That's right, Arrex has been on campaign with the prince the past few years, Thalion remembered. Of course, they would be sticking their heads together.

He smiled as Niara approached him through the crowd. She looked slightly frazzled to his eyes, though he doubted anyone who didn't know her well would notice. "Having fun?"

He concealed another smile as she took a deep, exasperated breath. "How's Ninaeva, Niara, how are your parents, oh, I'm sorry, your mother, he's not your father, is he, how rude of me, dance with me now that I've reminded you you're a bastard and see how much favor I'm bestowing on you…"

Thalion couldn't restrain a chuckle, and she glared at him. "You've just been hanging out with our friends," she accused. "All the second sons decided to approach me. Prigs."

Thalion tried to hold back his laughter and only ended up coughing. Niara rolled her eyes at him as he recovered.

She stiffened, and her 'formal' mask appeared on her face. She nodded to someone behind Thalion.

He turned and froze. Serana Auriel stood in front of him, her hand resting lightly on Kishtar's arm. Her green eyes were even brighter this close.

"Lord Thalion, Lady Niara, you remember Lady Serana, don't you?" Kishtar said, ignoring Thalion's reaction. "She has not been at court the past few years."

"How could I forget you," Niara said warmly. She curtsied. "It is good to see you again, Lady Serana."

"And you, Lady Niara," Serana's voice was low and musical as she returned the curtsy.

Thalion thought he had his breath back before she spoke to him. "I remember you as well, Lord Thalion. You have not forgotten me, I hope?"

Words. Breathing. "I—of course not. I could—" he coughed, then swallowed. "I could never forget you, Lady Serana."

She smiled, and Thalion felt his breath freeze in his lungs. He nearly jumped as the musicians struck a chord.

"That's the signal for the next dance set," Kishtar said. "Pray excuse me, Lady Serana, I am engaged with Lady Ianna. I shall see thee anon," he bowed politely and disappeared.

Thalion stared after him in shock. What was he thinking, bringing Serana here and then just leaving? The only way to be polite about this—

If they hadn't been in the middle of a crowded ballroom, Thalion would have rushed after Kishtar and punched him. He had done this purposefully. Politeness would force Thalion to ask Serana for a dance.

As if to emphasize the point, Niara nudged him gently.

Thalion cleared his throat and bowed. He felt so awkward compared to her. "May I have this dance, Lady Serana?"

She curtsied and accepted his hand. "I would be delighted."

Her hand rested as a feather in his as he led her onto the dance floor. He couldn't breathe. What was this dance? Where were they supposed to stand?

He cursed Kishtar again as he realized that this was not a set-dance like the rest of them had been, but a couple's dance. How could he survive this?

He placed his arms in the proper position around her as the music started. She smiled at him, and he caught his breath.

She moved gracefully with the music, and Thalion strove not to disgrace her. He soon had the measure of the dance, though. Kishtar was right; he did enjoy dancing.

"Ah, so how have you been since we last saw each other, Lady Serana?" he managed. "It's been…three years?"

She nodded as he twirled her around. "Likely. I have been involved in other pursuits the past few years."

"Other pursuits?"

She nodded again. "My mother felt there were certain areas of my education that were…lacking," she said.

Thalion blinked. "I don't think you could ever be lacking in anything," he said without thinking.

She flushed. "Thank you, Lord Thalion."

Heat rose to his own cheeks. "What were you studying, if you don't mind me asking?"

Serana waited a full measure of the dance before answering. "Politics. Deportment," she finally said.

Thalion frowned. "You don't sound like you enjoyed those lessons."

"I didn't!" Serana flushed and clapped a hand over her mouth. "I mean…the lessons were necessary and useful information. I was pleased to have them."

Thalion couldn't suppress a grin. "I hear Lady Pellalindra speaking."

"Don't tell her," Serana whispered. "She gets so disappointed."

"Your secret is safe with me, my lady," Thalion smiled conspiratorially. "They sound like dull lessons to me too," he whispered.

She giggled.

Thalion led her around in another spin. "So what do you enjoy?" he asked.

To his surprise, her grip tightened on his hand, and she hesitated before answering. "Well, dancing," she said. "This is very fun."

"Well, yes, but these events don't happen the entire year," Thalion said, curious now. "Surely there're other things you enjoy."

Serana flushed deeper. "Well, what do you enjoy?" she asked.

Thalion raised an eyebrow at the evasion but answered anyway. "Well, Kishtar and I practice swordplay quite a bit," he said. "But I also enjoy history and riding. As well as chess and tree climbing. Unless I fall off a tree. Though that hasn't happened in a few years." He was rambling, but he couldn't seem to stop himself. Especially as Serana's smile grew genuine.

"I enjoy chess too," she ventured.

He returned her smile. "You're accompanying the prince on his tour, right? Perhaps we could play a game sometime."

Her smile broadened. "I'd like that," she said.

The music came to an end, and Thalion bowed as Serana curtsied. He took her arm again and led her off the dance floor.

"Can I get you some refreshment?" he asked, remembering his manners. "Or escort you anywhere?"

"Ah, I think my mother has already found me."

Thalion followed her gaze to where Lady Pellalindra was making her way through the crowd. He bowed as she approached. Although she was no longer a member of the Regency Council, her son having taken her place a few years ago, she was still the regent's wife and a political influencer in her own right. "Greetings, Lady Auriel," he said.

She smiled at him. "Lord Thalion. I trust your mother is well?"

Why did they never inquire about his father? "Both my parents are well, thank you," he said.

Pellalindra's eyes flickered. "That is good to hear. I look forward to seeing them again this tour."

Thalion blinked. "You are accompanying us, Lady Auriel?" He had been under the impression that the tour was mostly going to consist of the younger lord and ladies.

She nodded. "I am going to chaperone my daughter."

Thalion glanced at Serana, who lowered her eyes to the floor, flushing. A dozen questions flew through his mind, but all of them would have been impertinent. Why did Serana need a chaperone? Niara didn't. If Serana did, then why couldn't it be her half-brother? Lord Percival was going on the tour, even though he was a member of the Regency Council.

Pellalindra cleared her throat. "Well, we'll all have time to chat later. All summer in fact. Serana, dear, please come with me. The Jyrian ambassador is here, and he expressed a desire to be introduced to you."

Serana gave Thalion an apologetic look, and he smiled, trying to say that he bore her no ill will. He bowed slightly as the two women left, Pellalindra still talking to her daughter. He gazed after them.

"Was that so hard?"

Thalion glared at Kishtar. "You set me up," he accused.

"Absolutely," Kishtar grinned. "But you seemed to manage just fine."

He turned to gaze at Serana again. She was curtsying as her mother introduced her to an older gentleman. "She's wonderful."

Kishtar chuckled. "You certainly think so."

Thalion narrowed his eyes, but Kishtar only chuckled harder. "Shouldn't you be flirting with Dinah, or Ianna, or whoever your next target is?"

Kishtar shrugged. "They come to me, usually. I just take advantage of it."

Thalion rolled his eyes. He scanned the ballroom again, searching for Serana. Instead, he saw his sister, hemmed in by two lords standing far too close to her and talking intensely.

"I think I should rescue Niara," he said. "Want to help?"

Kishtar followed his gaze and grinned. "Oh, absolutely," he said. "I'll ask her to dance. You can follow your lady love."

"Kishtar!" Thalion exclaimed, but Kishtar was already striding toward Niara. Thalion brought his hands to his face. He was flushing. He shook his head. Unconsciously, he turned his head, searching for Serana.

She was dancing with the prince again. He sighed. This was going to be a long summer.

3

LOKRIAN

Mazda's light, they are a loud group. Thalion glanced over his shoulder to fully appreciate the size of the tour. There had to be well over a hundred people. Then again, over a dozen young nobles meant guards and servants, and the numbers added up quickly. He, Kishtar, and Niara had brought the least number of people, and even they had six guards, a maid, and a manservant. Evalynna remained home with Gwyn, but she had trained all their guards personally. Two of the guards were with the carriage, where the two servants were riding, while the other four rode directly behind the three nobles. The MacTir party was behind the Ninaevans, and the Lokrian party just ahead. Somewhere in the middle of the line of carriages was the prince, the safest of all of them. Thalion had been unable to find out where Serana rode.

They caused quite a commotion whenever they rode into a town or village. Guards went ahead to warn the villagers, of course, and generally a line of people gathered on either side of the road hoping to catch a glimpse of their new monarch. The prince usually indulged them, riding to the front of the procession to wave. The people loved that.

Thalion blinked at the sight of the prince himself riding forward to join them. He managed a semblance of a bow from his saddle. Kishtar did the same, while Niara contented herself with a polite nod. "Your Highness," she said.

"Lady Niara, Lord Thalion, Lord Kishtar. I hope the journey is treating you well?" the prince said in greeting.

Niara answered for all of them. "Well enough, Your Highness," she said. "Then again, we are used to traveling at much greater speeds than this. This is practically a holiday for us."

The prince laughed. "Ah, Ninaevans. Always off to see the world."

Niara smiled coolly. "You know our reputation well."

"I would have to, with your mother on the Regency Council," the prince said. He changed the subject without missing a beat. "I have been informed that I am to dance with all the eligible ladies at every event. At Lokrian, of course, the first two dances will go to Lady Rian and Lady Ianna, but after that I shall dance with you, should you accept."

Thalion fought to keep his eyebrows from rising at the arrogance of the prince's invitation. He glanced at Niara to see how she was taking it.

Her expression remained smooth. "You plan far in advance, your highness. We are still two days' travel from Lokrian."

"Ah, but Lady Rian has been filling my ear with her plans for the event. A masquerade, I hear. So I am determined that I shall know who I am dancing with at all times."

Thalion was very grateful that the prince wasn't looking at him. It was all he could do to restrain his chuckles at how affronted the prince was.

Niara nodded, as cool and regal as any queen. "Then you may count on me as your third partner, your highness."

"Excellent," the prince turned toward Thalion and smirked. "Unfortunately, you won't be able to conceal your identity at a masquerade, will you?"

Thalion stiffened but forced himself to shrug. "A benefit and a curse," he said.

"Benefit?" the prince raised his eyebrows.

Thalion quickly pushed down a flash of anger. "The benefit of knowing who I am," he said. "At a masquerade, it can be so easy to forget."

The prince narrowed his eyes. "As you say. I look forward to seeing what sort of costume you manage."

Thalion grinned. "I look forward to seeing yours as well, Your Highness."

"Hmph." The prince cast his gaze on Kishtar, dismissed him as unimportant, then spurred his horse ahead. Thalion felt a surge of triumph at being able to appear unaffected by the prince's tactlessness but that didn't stop his hands from shaking with anger.

"The nerve," Niara whispered. "The very—that was the most graceless invitation to dance I have ever received!"

Kishtar snorted. "It wasn't even an invitation," he said. "He just demanded."

Niara glared at him, then turned to Thalion. "But to you! That was just rude!"

Thalion shrugged, his own indignation fading in the face of Niara's. "It's hardly the worst thing people have said to me," he said.

She shook her head. "He's the prince. He should know better." She sighed. "So, what did you pack as your costume, anyway?"

"A cat. Figured I'd honor Ninaeva if I can't disguise myself." Ninaeva's sigil was a golden mountain lion, but it was close enough.

Niara nodded, an abstracted expression on her face, her thoughts clearly already elsewhere. Thalion rolled his eyes.

Kishtar groaned. "We're coming up on another village."

Thalion grinned. Kishtar hated the procession through the villages and towns. He said he felt like everyone was watching him. "They're not staring at you," he said. "They're staring at Prince Andreas, and maybe me."

Kishtar shuddered. "I still don't like it."

Niara held up a hand. "Wait."

Thalion followed her gaze. Where people usually lined the streets, a group of bedraggled and worn smallfolk huddled together. He frowned. Several of them had injuries, and the houses…some of them bore the marks of recent fire. The prince and several of the other nobles had ridden up to the townspeople.

He exchanged a glance with Kishtar and urged his horse forward.

"Thalion!" Niara whispered.

Thalion ignored her. Whatever else was going on, these people had suffered some sort of tragedy and needed help.

The prince looked up at their approach, and his eyes glinted with satisfaction. "You're here, good. These people have suffered a bandit attack. We are going to hunt the culprits down and bring them to justice."

Thalion blinked. They were going? In person? He swallowed as he observed the other nobles gathered around the prince. Niall, Arrex, and Percival. All lords who had done a great deal more fighting than him or Kishtar.

The prince seemed to sense his hesitation. "They're bandit scum," he said. "You cannot be afraid of them. Wasn't your father a great general, Lord Kishtar? He would agree that such an attack needs to be made."

Thalion squared his shoulders. "Just let me get my armor," he said.

The prince snorted. "While the bandits get farther every moment?"

Thalion was sorely tempted. He wanted to prove himself to Prince Andreas, to ride out and show him he was as good a noble as any of the other men here. But a shadowy figure of Gwyn stood behind him, ready to deliver a ringing blow to the ears if he dared go looking for a fight without his armor.

"The bandits can wait five minutes," he said, trying to make his voice sound firm. "Your highness," he added belatedly. Before he could mess things up more, he turned his horse and headed for the Ninaevan carriage.

To his relief, Kishtar was by his side. They passed Niara as she headed toward the square, obviously unable to restrain her curiosity about what was going on.

It took only minutes for Thalion to slip his chain shirt over his head and belt a tabard over it. He hesitated, then donned his metal helm as well. Gwyn truly would kill him if she'd thought he'd been that stupid. He made certain his sword was fastened securely to his belt, then grabbed his shield. Kishtar did the same.

As they rode back to the group of noblemen, Thalion saw Niara dismount from her horse. One of the villagers took it, and she started walking toward one of the houses.

"Niara?" he called.

"They're wounded," she called. "I'm going to see what I can do."

He hesitated, then nodded. He couldn't stop her, anyway. And the bandits weren't likely to come back and attack the place they'd just raided.

The prince rolled his eyes. "Foolishness," he said. He turned to one of the villagers, barely acknowledging Thalion and Kishtar's return. "Show us where they went."

The man was ragged and had a bandage wrapped around one arm, but he seemed healthy enough otherwise. He bowed and headed off into the woods, the prince, Arrex, and Percival right behind him.

"Rearguard?" Thalion asked Kishtar.

Kishtar nodded. They waited until the prince was about thirty feet ahead of them, then started off, keeping their distance.

To Thalion's relief, at least some of the regular guards were accompanying them. The prince hadn't just decided on vengeance without a plan. He recognized two of the guards as their own from Ninaeva.

One of the guards noticed him watching and grinned at him. "Lady Niara told us to go with you," he said. "Gwyn would be proud of you, my lord."

Thalion smiled, feeling a bit more confident. "Thanks."

They fell silent, listening to the horses' hooves as they walked through the forest. Thalion's neck prickled, on high alert as he expected an attack at any moment.

Kishtar shook his head. "This is madness," he whispered. "How are we going to find them? They're not going to attack a group like this—"

A yell from the prince's group cut him off, and the prince and his immediate entourage went charging into the bushes. Thalion blinked, then jerked his sword out of its sheath. To follow, or not? Which was the better idea?

"Thalion!"

Kishtar's warning was all that saved him. He turned, instinctively raising his shield as he did so. The arrow bounced harmlessly off the metal. He heard his horse whinny beneath him. "Kishtar! Forward!" He shifted his weight, and his horse moved obediently into a trot toward the forest. He tightened his grip on his sword.

Another arrow flew over his head and he cursed. As he burst into the undergrowth, there was a cry of fright, and a dirty man dropped his bow, scrambling out of the way.

Thalion stared at him. The bandit appeared starving and cold, dressed in little more than rags. He didn't even look tough enough to put up a fight.

"Saemarian bastards!"

The shout took Thalion by surprise, and he barely turned in time to see the figure flying from the trees toward him. He tried to keep his balance, but the man hit him with such force that all he could do was brace for impact as he was flung out of the saddle. He winced as he hit the ground hard, the man directly on top of him. The man's weight made it impossible to scramble to his feet, and he saw the glint of steel in his hand. He twisted desperately, crying out in fear as the man stabbed at his side. The knife glanced off the chainmail.

"Thalion!"

He heard Kishtar's shout but couldn't look around to see what was happening. The man was raising his arm again, this time for a strike at his neck. He did the only thing he could think of and brought his leg up, kicking as hard as he could. The man fell forward, unbalanced, and Thalion twisted out from underneath him, grabbing his sword as he did so. The man scrambled to his feet just as quickly, and Thalion eyed him warily. The odds had shifted in his favor. The man had a dagger, and he had a sword.

The man realized this as well and backed up a pace, his eyes wide with new fear. "Drop your weapon and your life will be spared," Thalion ordered.

The man hesitated, then began to lay down his dagger. As he did, the prince burst into the fray, cutting him down with a single sweep of his sword. The man fell, blood spurting from his neck where the prince's sword had cut.

Thalion choked as bile rose up in his throat. He held it back as best he could as the prince rode toward him, a huge grin on his face.

"That was the last of them!" he exclaimed. "Well done, Lord Thalion! You kept him from escaping!"

Thalion forced himself not to look at the dead man on the ground. He bowed instead, not trusting himself to say a word.

"Your horse is still in good shape, I see. We're taking the prisoners back to the village. They must see the execution of justice."

"Yes, Your Highness," Thalion choked out. He turned, feeling unsteady. His horse was standing by a tree as calm as could be.

The prince let out a wild laugh and rode away. "For justice!" he called.

Thalion's vision spun as his eyes found the dead man on the ground. He couldn't hold it back any longer. Desperately, he leaned on a tree and retched, all the contents of his stomach rebelling against the sight.

A hand rested on his shoulder, but he couldn't focus to see who had come to comfort him. Only when his stomach was empty could he straighten enough to see Kishtar standing there, his face pale. Thalion winced. "You must think I'm a fool."

Kishtar shook his head, but another voice spoke. "It's your first combat, my lord. I'd be surprised if it was otherwise. Here. You'll feel better."

Thalion blinked as the Ninaevan guard stepped into his line of view and handed him a water-skin. He took a grateful swallow. "He was surrendering," he whispered.

The guard's eyes narrowed. "I saw. Poor bastard never stood a chance. Ill-trained, ill-fed…probably refuse from the war with Tigri. We're close enough to the border."

"But the border's days away!" Kishtar protested.

The guard shrugged. "Desperate men."

Thalion glanced at the man on the ground and shuddered. He turned to his horse. "Let's get back."

There was a group of men standing bound in the center of the road when they reached it. The guards formed a circle around them. All of them were just as bedraggled as the man Thalion had fought.

The prince rode up to the group of prisoners and sneered down at them. "Better start moving, scum," he said. "Unless you want to taste my blade?"

Thalion swallowed again as the prisoners flinched back. They started moving down the trail, closely flanked by the guards. The prince followed closely, urging them to greater speed, causing the prisoners to stumble over themselves. One of them fell to the ground, and Thalion's breath caught in his throat. The figure was a boy! He could have barely been twelve!

He didn't think as he found himself moving forward, blocking the guards moving to haul the boy to his feet. He crouched down beside the boy, wincing as he saw tears leaking down the child's face.

"Leave the scum, my lord," a hard-faced guard said.

Thalion glared up, trying to put all of his authority as a nobleman into his expression as he could muster. The guard blinked but didn't retreat.

"Are you giving Lord Thalion orders?" Kishtar's voice was light. "I'd be careful about that if I were you. I hear the prince is renowned for his desire for discipline and authority."

Thalion caught his breath as the guard backed off, surprise in his eyes. "I...just make sure he's there for the prince's judgment," he said harshly, before moving to follow the rest of the prisoners.

Thalion cast Kishtar a look of gratitude. Kishtar merely shook his head as he crouched down beside him. "Don't thank me yet. What are you going to do with him?"

Thalion turned his attention to the boy lying on the ground. He had stopped crying and was regarding him warily, like a rabbit about to flee.

He mustered a smile. "What's your name?"

"Mar," the boy said, barely moving his lips.

Thalion nodded encouragingly. "I'm Thalion," he said. "Where are you from?"

The boy blinked, obviously startled. "Fensdale," he said, naming a town just over the border. He stared at Thalion. "What 'bout you?"

Thalion let out a breath, relieved at the boy's question. "Ninaeva," he said. "To the north. Why are you here, Mar? Why aren't you at home?"

Mar's eyes filled with tears. "Got no home," he whispered. "The soldiers came…" he swallowed, getting himself under control. "Got no home," he repeated.

Thalion exchanged a glance with Kishtar. *This boy's no bandit,* he thought. *And if Saemar destroyed his home…well, Saemar should give him a new one.*

Kishtar nodded, easily following his thoughts. Thalion extended a hand to Mar. "Come with me," he said.

Mar regarded the outstretched hand warily, but took it, allowing Thalion to help him to his feet. His eyes widened as Thalion led him to his horse, and he let out a small yelp as Thalion lifted him up in front of the saddle before mounting himself.

"Don't worry," Thalion said encouragingly. "You're safe now."

Kishtar snorted softly but luckily didn't make any further comment. Thalion refrained from rolling his eyes as he realized that the rest of the guards and prisoners were long gone. Of course, the prince hadn't even noticed the boy in the middle. Or cared.

He chatted encouragingly with Mar as they made their way back to the village. It was only when Kishtar held up a warning hand that he stopped.

The prince had gathered the prisoners into the center of the village square, all lined up with their hands bound. Guards surrounded them, watching their every move. Thalion caught his breath. What was going to happen?

"My people!" the prince called. "Behold the men who ravaged your village! They have committed dreadful crimes! Such atrocities cannot be permitted in my kingdom!" His steely eyes swept the assembled smallfolk. "Let this show you that justice is swift." He nodded to the guards. "Execute them."

The royal guards near the men didn't hesitate. Ignoring the frantic protests from the men, they killed them, one by one. Thalion heard Mar start to cry out, and he covered the boy's mouth, overwhelmed by a flash of panic. He couldn't let the prince see the boy!

He swung off the saddle, dragging Mar with him. Kishtar was a half-step behind him and moved to flank Mar. "The carriage," Kishtar said.

Thalion heard a horrified feminine gasp and saw Serana at the edge of the village square. He blinked. Where were her guards? Her mother? *Mazda's light, she's just seen...*

He felt Kishtar shove him. "Go to her," Kishtar said. "I'll look after Mar."

Thalion couldn't help himself. After glancing to make certain Kishtar and Mar were out of sight, he walked quickly toward Serana as she turned away from the scene of carnage, her shoulders shaking.

"Lady Serana," he said in a low voice.

She shuddered. "Lord—Lord Thalion." She straightened. "I— forgive me."

He shook his head. "There is nothing to forgive," he said. "This is... this is not something you should have to see."

"How could he do such a thing?" Serana whispered. She didn't seem to have heard his words. Her eyes were still full of the memory of the blood and bodies.

Thalion searched for words. The men had been bandits, but at the same time... "The prince thought it was justice," he said, his words sounding lame to his own ears.

"Justice?" Serana whispered.

Something compelled Thalion to explain, though he couldn't say whether it was to Serana or to himself. "They attacked this village," he said. "They're defenseless. They stole what these people need to survive, but…" he swallowed. "They're from Tigri," he said. "Where our soldiers have done the same to their homes. I don't know…" he stopped, seeing Serana's face grow pale.

"No, continue," she whispered.

Thalion looked at her helplessly. "What Prince Andreas did was harsh," he said. "I cannot…I don't know what I would have done. But according to the law…Prince Andreas saw them in action. He was within his rights."

Thalion felt the pain in Serana's eyes as if he was his own. "I'm glad you don't think you'd be able to do the same," she whispered.

He blinked in surprise. That wasn't exactly what he'd said, but she was right. He didn't think he could ever act so harshly, so swiftly.

"Thalion!"

He spun around at Kishtar's shout. Kishtar was walking toward them, Niara leaning heavily on his shoulder.

Thalion's eyes widened as he started forward. "What's wrong? Niara?" he asked.

"I—" Niara stopped, and Thalion could see the exhaustion and fear flickering in her eyes. "I—my pardon, Lady Serana."

Serana had followed him. "Are you alright, Lady Niara?" she asked.

"Just tired," Niara said, waving a hand. "Please, I just need to get to the carriage."

Thalion put his arm around his sister so that she could lean on him instead of Kishtar. He turned to Serana. "Serana, I…I wish you hadn't had to see that," he managed.

She gave him a tremulous smile. "Thank you," she whispered. "Perhaps…perhaps you can explain it more to me? At Lokrian?"

He nodded, and she curtsied before moving away.

Niara let out a hiss of breath, and Thalion focused all his attention on his sister. "Are you alright?" he whispered. "What did you do to yourself?"

Niara shook her head. "Not here. Carriage."

Thalion bit his lip as he half-carried his sister to the Ninaevan carriage and helped her inside. "Niara, what's wrong?"

Niara shook her head, curling up in her seat. "A vision," she said.

"I...I saved a boy, and then..." She shook her head, her eyes wide with fear.

"You saved Nico?"

Niara's eyes flew open, and Thalion felt his heart leap out of his throat as he saw Mar curled up in the corner of the coach. Mar ignored their reactions and leaned forward, utterly intent. "I saw him get stabbed! I thought..." his voice shook. "But you saved him? He'll be alright?"

Niara looked at Thalion, questions evident in her expression.

"Niara, this is Mar," he said, explaining hastily. "He was...he's from Tigri. But he has no home left."

"I see," Niara said. "How do you know Nico? And yes, he will be fine."

A shadow flashed across Mar's face. "We used to meet in the forest," he said. "I didn't know what was going to happen, I swear!"

"I believe you," Thalion said hastily.

Niara regarded Mar thoughtfully. "You don't have a home, you say?" she asked.

Mar shook his head, his expression mournful.

Niara put a hand on the boy's shoulder. "I understand," she said softly. "Would you like to stay with us for a while? We can't replace your old home, but we might be able to offer you a new one."

Tears suddenly poured down Mar's face, and he flung himself forward into Niara's arms. She held him as he shook like a leaf, gently stroking his hair.

"Ah, Niara?" Thalion whispered. "Just so you know..."

She looked up, not releasing the boy.

Thalion took a breath. "The prince doesn't know about Mar," he said. "I don't know if he didn't notice, but...he definitely doesn't know I took him here rather than to..." he swallowed, unable to continue.

Niara's eyes flashed, and her expression hardened. "Then we'll just have to make certain he doesn't find out," she said. Her arms tightened around Mar.

Thalion remembered the guard's hard gaze. If no one else, he would have noticed Mar's absence from the bloodbath. And if he reported to the prince...

Don't borrow trouble, he scolded himself. His lips tightened as he regarded the boy shaking in Niara's arms. *Besides, it's worth it.*

The bruise was a dark blue with bits of purple and green around the edges, visible even against his dark skin. Thalion winced as he poked it experimentally. In the heat of the moment, he'd thought his chain-mail had deflected the blow. Well, at least he wasn't bleeding.

"Thalion—Mazda's light!"

"You could knock," Thalion said in annoyance as Kishtar entered his room.

Kishtar ignored him and strode over to stand by his side. "That's nasty. Was that the guy who tried to wrestle you?"

The image of the man bleeding out on the ground flashed through Thalion's mind, and he firmly shoved the thought aside. "He tried to stab me."

Kishtar's eyebrows rose. "Good thing you were wearing your armor, then."

Thalion nodded, sobering at the thought. If he hadn't been wearing his armor, the knife would have cut right through his tunic and into his side. "I'll have to remember to thank Aunt Gwyn when we get back to Ninaeva." He reached for his tunic, uncomfortable looking at the bruise any longer. "So what are you doing here? You're ready for the masquerade, I see. What's your mask?"

His friend struck a pose. His tunic was of russet orange trimmed with gold, and cut to expose a good deal of neck and even some brown chest hair. A similarly colored band held Kishtar's hair in place, and his mask was held loosely in one hand. "I," said Kishtar, "am the greatest of tricksters, the master seducer, and the bearer of secrets. Master Fox, at your service." He gave Thalion an elaborate bow.

Thalion couldn't help but laugh. He buckled his belt over his tunic as he looked for his boots. "Modest too. Though what do secrets have to do with foxes? I've never heard that one."

A wicked grin spread across Kishtar's face. "Well, it's true in this case. I have a secret you'd dearly love to find out."

Thalion paused in the middle of pulling on one of his boots. "What do you mean?"

Kishtar leaned back against the wall and winked. "I know how you're going to recognize your lady love tonight."

"Kishtar!" Thalion exclaimed. "She's not—I'm not—we're not—stop laughing!"

Kishtar only laughed harder. "Who's not?" he asked. "You seem to know whom I'm talking about. Who do you fancy?"

"Kishtar!" Thalion felt the heat rising to his face. He finished pulling his boot on, then folded his arms across his chest and glared at his friend.

"But I can't tell you if I don't know who she is!" Kishtar exclaimed, wide-eyed with innocence. "I'd hate to give you false information and see you courting the wrong lady!"

Thalion stared helplessly at him. "You wouldn't!"

Kishtar spread his hands. "Well, if you just tell me which lady you want described, then there won't be any mistake."

Thalion felt his face heating even more. "How do you know what she's dressed like?"

"How do I know what who is dressed like?" Kishtar's grin was impudent.

"Mazda's light!" Thalion burst out. "Kishtar, you know I'm interested in Serana!"

Kishtar laughed. "I just had to get you to admit it!"

Thalion shook his head, trying to sort his feelings out. "Mazda's light, Kishtar," he cursed again.

"Hey, you had to admit that you like her," Kishtar's voice was unrepentant. "If you don't know that, then any chance you have of seducing her is lowered."

"Seduce?" Thalion's eyes widened. "Kishtar, I don't want to seduce her! I want to—" he cut off. *What do I want?*

Kishtar stared at him, his expression entirely serious. "You want to…" he encouraged.

Thalion caught his breath. "I barely know her yet," he said, almost pleadingly. "I don't know what I want yet."

"But you like her," Kishtar stated.

Thalion snorted. "Didn't you just get me to admit that?"

"Yes, yes," Kishtar stopped, giving Thalion an approving gaze. "You're certainly dashing enough to sweep her off her feet."

Thalion looked down at himself. His tunic was pure black, trimmed only with a light silver design on the hem and collar. His breeches were also black silk. He'd managed to tame his unruly curls enough to tie them back so that no stray hairs would get caught in his mask. The cat mask itself rested on the bed. "You think so?"

Kishtar nodded. "I say so," he said. "You will turn the eyes of many fine damsels tonight, and leave them all envious as you ignore them for your lady love. Come on, grab your mask."

Thalion obeyed without thinking, tying the mask securely in place before following Kishtar out the door. They were nearly to the great hall when the lilt of music made Thalion stop in his tracks. "Kishtar! You said you'd tell me what Serana was wearing."

Kishtar simply laughed and tugged Thalion's arm, leading him through the open door and into the great hall.

Rian had certainly outdone herself for this event. Lanterns of colored glass hung on every wall, illuminating the room with an eerie mix of colors. To one side, tables with refreshments were set up, light snacks to satisfy anyone's hunger. A group of musicians sat together at one end, each with their own mask, presumably to blend in with the general atmosphere. At the rear of the hall, the doors had been thrown wide open to the garden, where more colored lanterns hung, illuminating the night. The sweet perfume of flowers drifted in on the gentle breeze, a welcome relief from the otherwise hot and humid air. Dozens of people milled about, eating and gossiping as they waited for the ball to properly begin.

Thalion followed as Kishtar tugged his arm, leading him around the edge of the hall. He caught more than a few whispers as he passed and tried to act as if he didn't hear them.

"The man in the center of the floor is the prince," Kishtar whispered. "Any guesses as to his partner?"

Thalion looked to where Kishtar was nodding. The man in the center could be no one other than Prince Andreas. He wore a burgundy tunic trimmed with gold, and his mask even had a crown on it. The music struck up, a warning for the dancers, and he bowed to his partner.

"He's not being very subtle," Thalion whispered.

"He doesn't have to be. His partner?"

Thalion turned his attention to the woman the prince was dancing with. Tall and slender, she held herself with an unconscious air of authority. Her dress was of dark blue with a wavy hem, and her mask was a simple stylized blue. She stood close to the prince, even leaning against his chest as they waited for the dance to start. "If this is the first dance, that's Rian," he said. "But she's…" he stared. As he watched, she whispered something in the prince's ear, causing him to chuckle and draw her into a close embrace.

"She's flirting?" Kishtar asked. "Using the anonymity of her mask to let her do so openly?"

Thalion blinked. If that was flirting, then praying at a temple made you a priest.

"Anyway, you guessed. So, next lady." Kishtar nodded at a young woman standing by the refreshment tables.

Thalion rolled his eyes before he remembered Kishtar couldn't see. "You can hardly expect me to not recognize my own sister." He relaxed as he saw her. Mar was safely in her rooms, then, being taken care of by the maid. It had been the safest place they could think of for the boy on short notice.

Kishtar laughed openly. "No, but I had to try! Like her costume?"

Thalion had to admire his sister's style. Her dress was of pure gold and decorated in a way that made it gleam and sparkle when she moved. He gasped as her face turned toward him. Her mask was of a golden cat. "She didn't."

"She did," Kishtar seemed extraordinarily pleased with himself. "I wonder if anyone will guess the connection."

As if she noticed their gaze, Niara started moving purposefully in their direction. To Thalion's disappointment, however, she was intercepted by a tall man in a wolf mask, who then escorted her onto the dance floor.

"Three guesses who that was," Kishtar said in a low voice.

Thalion snorted without answering. The only noble who'd dare wear that mask was Niall MacTir.

"Anyway, that's not part of the game," Kishtar said.

"Game!" Thalion exclaimed. "Kishtar, you said—"

Kishtar shushed him with frantic hands. "Hush, don't give anyway my identity like that! Mysterious fox, remember?"

Thalion subsided but crossed his arms over his chest. "I will if you don't start talking," he threatened.

He heard Kishtar sigh. "Fine. See the lady next to the purple lantern, opposite the refreshment tables?"

A gorgeous figure dressed all in white stood quietly at the edge of the room. Her golden hair was covered by a white veil, and her mask was a simple white cloth over her face. His breath caught. It could only be her.

"See, I told you I knew what she would look like."

Thalion tore his gaze away from Serana and turned back to Kishtar. "Kishtar, thank you," he said earnestly.

Kishtar shoved him in Serana's direction. "You can thank me by going and dancing with her," he said. "Go!"

Thalion stumbled toward the vision in white. She looked up as he approached, and he nearly froze. Somehow he kept walking until he was by her side and offered her a bow. "Would you care for a dance, my lady?"

She gave a small laugh as she took his hand. "Of course, my lord."

Thalion felt a surge of gratitude that she hadn't immediately called him Thalion. It was bad enough that his identity was obvious to everyone in this crowd of anonymity.

He heard a few quiet murmurs as he led Serana to the dancing and couldn't help but smile. *We must make quite a sight together, dark and light, white and black...*

Serana reached out to place a hand on his waist, and he let out a pained gasp as she touched his bruise. She jerked her hand back. "What did I do?"

He shook his head and took her hand, guiding it to a point above his bruise. "A bruise. It's nothing."

"You're bruised?" Serana pulled back to look at him. "Was it during that bandit hunt?"

Thalion cursed to himself. This was not what he wanted to talk to her about. "Yes," he admitted reluctantly.

A distressed gasp escaped her lips, and Thalion pulled her closer as the music started. "It's not that bad. Really."

"But you were hurt!" she exclaimed.

Thalion had to chuckle as a wave of pleasure swept over him. She cared enough to be distressed that he had been injured. "It's nothing, really," he protested again. "See?" he swung his arm out, and she followed instinctively in a twirl that ended with Thalion bending her over his arm briefly. He winced at the strain it put on his side and blessed that she couldn't see beneath his mask. "See? I can still do that."

She relaxed in his arms. "I see."

He couldn't resist twirling her around again. She laughed delightedly, the sound of tinkling bells, and he saw people look their way. His side protested, but he ignored it. It was just a bruise, after all.

He watched her, enthralled, for the rest of the dance. How could she be so graceful, so beautiful?

He bowed as the dance ended, then offered her his arm. He didn't want to let her go quite yet. "Would you care for a stroll in the gardens, my lady?"

To his delight, she accepted his arm as she rose from her curtsy. "It would be my pleasure, my lord."

Eyes bored into his back as he led her into the gardens but refused to turn around. Let people wonder what lady Thalion et-Alim was walking with.

Serana gave a gasp of delight as they entered the garden. "Oh, it's beautiful!"

Colored lanterns hung every dozen feet or so, giving off just enough light to see. Small tables had been set up with light refreshments for the guests, a handful of whom were wandering around, chatting idly. Most impressive of all, however, were the flowers. Somehow someone had coaxed the giant, white, day-blooming lilies to bloom and glow in the moonlight.

Feeling bold, Thalion led Serana over to one of the vines and plucked one. Feeling even more daring, he gently tucked it behind one of her ears.

Her hand came up and lightly brushed his as she touched the flower. "Thank you," she murmured.

Thalion had to smile. "It suits you."

Her shoulders moved in a shrug, and Thalion frowned. She seemed stiff, not quite as at ease as she'd been in the ballroom.

"Is something the matter?" he asked, careful to keep his voice quiet.

She shook her head. "It's nothing, I'm just…oh, Thalion, how awful it must have been!"

The distress in her voice made any resentment he might have felt with her using his name vanish. He gripped her arm, trying to be reassuring. "I'm fine," he whispered.

She shook her head again. "I know, but…how could you bear seeing those men killed like that?"

He shrugged helplessly. "It wasn't nice." He looked down as her hand squeezed his arm.

"Tell me what happened."

He hesitated, staring at her.

"Please," she whispered. "Thalion, I…I need to know."

This was not the conversation he'd wanted to have with her, but he sighed in resignation. He glanced around and saw a bench a little way off the main patio. Serana followed willingly as he led her toward it.

They sat down, and Thalion tried to cast his mind back to the earlier events. It was hard, with Serana sitting right next to him. He could feel the warmth from her body, a contrast to the chill of the night. Even her mask could not conceal her beauty. He wanted to…

He shook himself. *Mazda's light, Thalion, you were about to lean forward and kiss her! Only you're still both wearing masks, and you don't even know how she would feel about being kissed!*

"Thalion?"

He shook his head at the concern in Serana's voice. She couldn't know what he had just been thinking. "I'm fine," he said again.

He looked down as she placed a hand on his arm. "What happened?"

Thalion forced himself to focus. "Well, we rode into the village," he said. "The prince had already heard of the attack when Kishtar and I rode up, and he said that we needed to do something about it. We stopped just long enough for Kishtar and I to get our armor, and then rode after the bandits."

She nodded, encouraging him to continue.

"Well, we found them. Kishtar and I had been riding rearguard, and an archer started shooting at us. The rest were all involved up ahead, so I rode toward the archer, and then was jumped by someone in the trees." He frowned, trying to remember. The events had all happened so fast.

"I got out from under him, and he realized he was overmatched and started to surrender. Then the prince…" his voice trailed off.

"The prince?" Serana's voice seemed tight. "What did you do?"

Thalion shrugged, wanting to banish the memory of the sight. "He killed him," he said softly. He felt himself shudder and cursed inwardly. Now Serana would think him weak.

Her hand tightened on his. "Was it awful?" she whispered.

There was no scorn in her voice, only sympathy. He risked looking up before he remembered that neither of them could see each other's face. "I'd never been in a fight before," he risked admitting. "I didn't expect the…the blood."

Her hand tightened again, then relaxed. "Like the men he brought back," she said. "Thalion, I…did they deserve that?"

That question had been plaguing Thalion the entire day. He stared at her, helpless to answer. "I don't know," he said.

"I was hoping you could answer that for me," she whispered, her shoulders slumped.

His mother and father had had him read all kinds of Mazdian texts growing up, saying that they would teach him 'moral lessons.' At that moment, Thalion was grateful for that teaching. "The Mazdian texts say that it is Mazda's place alone to judge," he said. "To do so is to put yourself in Mazda's shoes, an act of great arrogance and pride. So how could I know?"

"The Mazdian texts say that?" Serana's shoulders straightened.

He nodded. "Have you not read them?"

She shook her head. "My mother..." she swallowed and started again. "My mother said I had more important things to think about, that I should leave religion to the priests." She tilted her head. "But I always heard your mother was not..." she paused, stumbling over her words.

A chuckle escaped him. "Did you hear someone call my mother a heretic?" he said, daring to put a teasing lilt in his voice.

She mumbled something.

He squeezed her arm and settled back on the bench. "My mother is not your typical Mazdian, true, but she is very devout in her own way," he said. "My father even more so. But both of them believe it is up to the individual to learn the teachings of Mazda for themselves."

"And one of those is not to judge?" Serana asked.

"According to the first book of the prophet Jaasen," Thalion said, drawing on the memory of his lessons.

"I've heard of Jaasen," Serana said, her voice soft. She paused. "If we are not to judge, then is what the prince did wrong?"

Thalion felt uncertainty rise up within him again. "I don't know," he said. "Just because you're not supposed to judge, doesn't mean you're not supposed to protect yourself. And Mazda is a harsh god, at times. He scorches as well as protects. And the bandits did raid and kill. But..." his voice trailed off, thinking of Mar. If he hadn't seen him, Mar would have been swept up with the other bandits and executed alongside them.

"After their homes had been raided from them." Her voice sounded almost defiant, daring him to disagree.

He shrugged again, helpless. "I know," he said. "And Serana...there was a boy with them. He could not be blamed for the actions of his elders."

"A boy?" Serana's voice was horrified. "Thalion, he didn't..."

Hastily, Thalion placed a hand over hers. "He's safe now. We're going to take care of him."

He felt Serana relax again. "Thank Mazda," she whispered. She regarded their joined hands but didn't try to pull away.

"I am sorry I don't have answers for you," Thalion squeezed her hand. "It's good to think about these things, though. If you think and doubt, then you are in no danger of becoming what you fear most."

She chuckled softly. "Another Mazdian teaching?"

He shook his head. "No, that's my father."

"Your father," Serana whispered, without a hint of judgment. "I would like to meet him one day. He does not often come to the capital."

"Well, you'll see him on Dragon's Day," Thalion said. "We'll be in Ninaeva."

"I'm excited for that," Serana's squeezed his hand. He tried to release it, but she held on.

"Serana..." he whispered.

She paused. "I didn't tell you my name."

He felt himself flushing and spared a moment to be grateful for his mask. "You didn't have to."

"I..." she swallowed. "Thalion, what do you think of the prince?"

He blinked. Why would she ask him that? "I—"

"Where is she?" The harsh voice rang through the patio. "It's time for the seventh dance."

Thalion jumped, and Serana flew to her feet. "Mazda, I forgot!" she exclaimed in a rush of breath. "Thalion, forgive me!" She dashed away, leaving him sitting on the bench in bewilderment. He watched as she flew toward the door to the ballroom, dropping a low curtsy to a figure standing in the doorway before he swept her inside.

The prince and his schedule of dancers. It must be Serana's turn.

He sat back on the bench and tried to think over the conversation, but kept getting distracted. She had been so concerned for him, so gentle. She barely needed to know about Mazda's teaching of not judging, because he couldn't imagine her judging anyone harshly. And she was so beautiful.

His skin tingled as he thought of her again. In his mind's eye, her mask slipped away, and her green eyes smiled at him. Her golden hair fell over her shoulders, concealing both their faces as he pulled her in for a kiss.

4

THE TOURNAMENT

The imposing gray mountains came into view first, the final sign that the party had reached the north. The Ninaevans and Gray Mountaineers of the traveling entourage felt comfortable again, but the southerners, especially those from Lokrian and further south, complained constantly about the chill in the air.

Thalion sighed as they crested one of the rolling green hills to see the dark fortress of Dunbarrow seated on a tall hill several miles away.

Kishtar laughed. "Not looking forward to the tournament?"

"Are *you* looking forward to a MacTir tournament?" Thalion asked incredulously.

Kishtar merely grinned, sitting astride his horse with the ease of long practice. "Well, since Niall won't be fighting in it for some odd reason…"

"He won't be fighting in it because he's running it. It would be too easy to cry foul if he happened to win the tournament he was running." Niara drew her horse alongside Thalion, so the three of them rode slightly apart from the rest of the party. "I thought you liked tournaments?"

Thalion hesitated. "I don't know about this one," he said. "There's something…" he shook his head, unable to verbalize his concern over the clatter of horse's hooves and the creaking of carriage wheels along the dusty road.

"Is it Serana?" Kishtar asked.

Thalion glared at Kishtar, but it was too late.

"Serana?" Niara asked. "Have you and she been getting close, brother?"

Heat rose to his face. "I…"

Niara grinned and glanced over her shoulder, to where Thalion knew the Duskryn party rode three carriages behind theirs. "You have been dancing together a great deal. In fact, I don't think there's been a single ball since Lokrian where you've failed to dance with her."

"Oh, he likes her," Kishtar confirmed, ignoring Thalion's glare. "He's purely infatuated with her if you ask me."

"Kishtar!" Thalion exclaimed, staring at his friend in betrayal.

Kishtar laughed. "It's not as though you haven't been obvious about it."

Thalion wanted to sink into the ground. He wasn't ready for his sister to know!

"Is it serious, then?" Niara raised an eyebrow.

Thalion flushed, and he tried to speak casually. "I…I think so." He was prevaricating. The past month of balls had taught him that whatever he knew about Serana, he wanted to know more. He had never met another woman like her. She was compassionate, kind, smart, funny, lovely…and there were hidden depths that he guessed no one, not even her mother, was aware of. He wanted to know everything, to be taken into her confidence and accepted into her heart.

Niara pursed her lips. "It would be a good match," she said.

Thalion fixed his gaze on the brown ears of his horse. Of course, her mind had immediately jumped to marriage. It was what was expected of young nobles.

But then she shrugged. "Well, you know Mother will never make any arrangements for us, so we're free to make our own choices. I like Serana, though. She'd make a good sister."

Thalion looked up to see if his sister was teasing him again. She appeared completely serious, though she was smiling.

Marriage? He had to admit the thought had crossed his mind. How could it not have? Although the focus was on the prince's choice for a wife, all the other young lords and ladies were using this trip as an opportunity to make a choice for themselves. Thalion was willing to wager that every young noble on the tour had received lectures and orders from their parents about suitable marriage partners. *Except us. Mother would never lecture anyone about suitable partners.* But was he ready for marriage? He was eighteen, not too young to be married, but certainly younger than most of the other noblemen here.

But what about Serana? She had to be searching for a husband. Or rather, her mother was. At all of the balls, she had been in the background, scrutinizing Serana's partners, and occasionally subtly interjecting herself when she thought one partner was monopolizing her daughter. Thalion had been victim to that himself at the last ball. The only partner never interrupted was the prince.

That thought sent chills down Thalion's spine. What if Lady Pellalindra had plans for her daughter? What if she would refuse any suit other than the prince's? Then he shrugged the thought aside. There were plenty of other noblewomen for the prince to choose from. Rian, for one, was making it clear that she would do whatever the prince asked of her. And then there was Ianna, Dinah, and even Niara, not to mention any of the other noblewomen in the land. Lady Pellalindra could hardly be certain the prince would choose her daughter.

But would she find me acceptable? an insidious voice asked. *After all, your father is hardly the exemplar of nobility that Lady Pellalindra strives for.*

"Lady Niara! Lord Thalion! Lord Kishtar!" The prince's voice jolted Thalion out of his thoughts. He looked up as the prince, Niall, and Percival came riding up to their group. They pulled their horses to a stop as the royal party drew up alongside them.

Niara nodded a polite greeting. "Your highness, Lord Niall, Lord Percival."

The prince grinned at Thalion. "Well, Lord Thalion, shall I finally see if the tales I've heard of your prowess are correct! You will be fighting in the tournament, of course?"

Thalion exchanged a wry glance with Kishtar.

"We would not miss it," Kishtar said smoothly.

"Excellent," the prince seemed satisfied. He smiled slyly. "Care to race to Dunbarrow, then?"

A race? Thalion exchanged another glance with Kishtar, then glanced at Niara. She shrugged infinitesimally.

"Why not?" Kishtar answered for both of them. "Is there a prize?"

"Choice of horses from the MacTir stables?" The prince raised a questioning eyebrow at Niall.

Niall appeared about to protest, but then he relaxed. "Not any currently claimed by my immediate family."

"Agreed," the prince nodded shortly. "Care to send us off, Lady Niara?"

Thalion saw Niara's lips tighten, and he braced himself for her reaction. "Am I not invited to this race?" she asked.

Thalion exchanged a look with Kishtar. As soon as all three of them had been able to ride, they had been racing their horses through the fields outside Ilhelm. Thalion could only beat his sister half the time, and he was one of the best riders in Ninaeva.

The prince seemed nonplussed. "Well, if you wish it," he said. "We shall simply have to find someone else." He glanced around. "Lady Serana!" he shouted.

Thalion instinctively turned his head to meet Serana's gaze. She rode several yards behind them, in quiet conversation with her mother. At Lady Pellalindra's nod, she rode forward to join them. "Yes, your highness?" she asked softly.

"We are all racing to Dunbarrow. We would appreciate it if you gave us the countdown, unless you would like to join us as well?" the prince raised an eyebrow in Niara's direction.

Thalion saw the astonishment in Serana's face as she regarded Niara. She glanced at the prince, then Thalion, then down at her saddle. Thalion frowned. Had that been envy on her face?

"I would be delighted, of course," she said. "Just let me know when you are ready."

The prince looked around. "Everyone prepared?"

Thalion adjusted his balance, tightening his legs slightly to let his horse know to prepare to gallop. The beast whickered as if it knew what was about to happen. He nodded.

The prince gestured at Serana. She took a breath. "On my count, then. In three, two, one, race!"

Thalion shifted, and his horse bolted in response, along with everyone else's. The thundering of hooves and the wind in his face sent a surge of exhilaration through him.

He was side by side with Kishtar, a horse's length behind the prince. Niall and Percival were somewhere to his right. From her wild laughter, Niara was right behind him.

All thoughts beside the race dropped away and Thalion urged his horse forward. He felt the horse's muscles flex underneath his legs as the stallion put on another burst of speed, drawing level with the prince. He caught the prince's astonished glance, but it wasn't directed toward him. Instead, Niara was pulling ahead of them both, her hat gone, and her long hair tumbling out of whatever confines she'd pinned it up in.

Oh no you don't! The long habit of friendly sibling rivalry pushed anything else out of his mind. He wouldn't let Niara win without a fight! He snapped his reins, and his horse, recognizing the woman in front of it, surged forward again. His horse knew what this was, now. It knew there was a hot trough of mash and several carrots, and all the praise and care it could want if it pulled ahead of Niara.

"You won't win so easily, sister!" he yelled, trying to distract her as his horse slowly gained.

She glanced back, her eyes sparkling. "Are you going to stop me?"

He knew his face showed equal excitement. He leaned down as close to his horse as he could get to create as little wind resistance as possible. "Come on, boy! We can beat her! We've done it before!"

The horse heard him, and he felt its strain as it put all its effort into one final gallop. As the stone gates of Dunbarrow drew into view, he pulled ahead of his sister, galloping through the open portcullis a mere horse's length ahead of her. Two guards sprang to the side, obviously warned of their approach, as they offered no challenge or attack.

She laughed as they both reined their horses to a stop. "Well done, brother!" she exclaimed.

Thalion grinned at his sister, and then his eyes widened. Her hair, so carefully arranged to cover her ears, was flying loose, revealing two very pointed ears. "Niara! Your hair!"

She knew immediately what he was talking about. With a gasp, she pushed her hair over her ears just as the prince came pounding up, followed closely by Kishtar, Niall, and Percival.

"Congratulations!" the prince exclaimed. "I think I saw Lord Thalion was the victor?"

"By the slimmest chance, your highness," Thalion said, still breathless with adrenaline.

The prince slid off his horse and bowed slightly to Niara. "You have my admiration, Lady Niara."

She slid from her horse as well and curtsied low, her hair falling in front of her face. "Thank you, your highness."

The prince grinned at Niall. "Shall we see what Lord Thalion's choice of a prize shall be?"

"Indeed," Niall said, dark eyes boring into Thalion.

Thalion glanced at Kishtar and jerked his head toward Niara. Kishtar followed his gesture and nodded, his eyes widening.

"I will escort Lady Niara to the Keep, if that is acceptable, Lord Niall, your highness," he said.

The prince waved a hand. "Absolutely. Female fripperies to put back in place? I'm afraid your hat is lost for good."

Niara managed a chuckle. "In a good cause," she said. "Thank you for the escort, Lord Kishtar." She waited for Kishtar to dismount and turned their horses over to a servant, then walked toward the keep. Thalion relaxed.

"I shall go to greet my mother and sister," Percival said. "With your permission, your highness?"

The prince waved a hand in dismissal, and Percival rode off the way they had come, leaving Niall, Thalion, and the prince alone. Thalion took a deep breath as he dismounted, his heart returning to a normal tempo. He led his horse at a walk toward the stable, allowing it to cool down slowly from the effects of the race. Niall and the prince walked alongside him, having chosen instead to turn their horses over to one of the many servants in Gray Mountains livery that swarmed the courtyard upon the prince's arrival.

"That was fine riding," the prince said in a neutral voice.

Thalion nodded. "Thank you, Your Highness. My sister and I have often raced against each other."

"I can tell." The prince's voice held none of the congratulations from earlier. "It seems you two were carried away in the rush of memory."

The hair on the back of Thalion's neck stood up. "Your highness?"

The smile the prince gave was icy. "Make sure your stablemaster is prepared for us, Lord Niall, won't you?"

Thalion blinked at the smoldering glare Niall sent him. "Of course, your highness." Niall's back was straight and stiff as he walked off.

The prince stopped walking, and Thalion swallowed, forced by politeness to stop as well. He waited for the prince to speak, his mind reeling.

"I have seen an unfortunate pattern among you Ninaevans," the prince said. "I think you have remained isolated in the frozen north too long. You certainly forget the existence of your liege lord often enough."

Thalion caught his breath. "Your highness, I assure you..."

The prince held up his hand, and Thalion stopped, biting his tongue. The prince's eyes were steely as he continued. "You forgot my presence today, as you did in Lokrian," he said. "Surely you cannot believe I missed that bandit you let escape from justice?"

Thalion's heart pounded in his chest, harder than it had during the race. "Your highness, he was a boy," he protested. "I just..."

"That is not the point," the prince said in a clipped voice. "The point is that you ignore the presence of your liege, and your sister, heir to the lands, seems to do nothing to educate you." His voice dripped with scorn. "Dunbarrow has benefited greatly from increased royal presence. Perhaps Ninaeva would as well."

Panic rose in Thalion's chest. "Your highness, I…"

"Do not let it happen again, Lord Thalion," the prince stepped closer until his face was only inches from Thalion's. "If hierarchy is not respected, then anarchy rules. And I will not allow that to happen in my kingdom."

Thalion couldn't find the words to answer, and so he merely nodded, feeling like his throat had turned to ice.

The prince smiled. "Good," he said. "Lord Auriel will be pleased to hear it." The switch from intimidating to cheerful jarred Thalion from his stunned state. "So, what kind of mount will you claim as your prize? A stallion, mare, or gelding? I know Lord Niall has plenty of each in his stables."

Thalion stuttered over his answer, his heart still pounding with adrenaline. *I need to talk to Niara,* he thought. *Mazda's light, I hope I haven't doomed us all!*

* * *

"Lords and Ladies of Saemar, and your most Royal Highness, it is my greatest honor to welcome you to the Ululu tournament!" Niall swept his hand out to address the crowd of nobles in the yard. Thalion stood next to Kishtar, armored and ready next to the rest of the dozen or so contestants. Part of the yard had been fenced off as a tournament list, and banners decorated the fence in the red and black colors of Dunbarrow. Raised seats had been set up at one end of the fence, where the nobles who did not intend to compete in the tournament sat, dressed in their colorful finery and chatting excitedly.

"The tournament will be in two parts," Niall continued. "First, a double elimination tournament, fought with sword and shield. The two finalists will fight each other with whatever weapons they choose. Then, light refreshments, a chance for the contestants to relax a little." A chuckle swept the crowd. Niall grinned. "Finally, the event everyone is truly looking forward to, the grand melee, held in honor of the unification of Dunbarrow and the Gray Mountains! To your arms, and may the best contestant win!"

Thalion forced himself to cheer with the rest of the nobles as he moved toward the list, where a man in Gray Mountains livery held a stack of cards in his hand. The man handed two cards to Niall with a bow.

Niall took the cards with a flourish. "First pairing is Lord Thalion of Ninaeva and Lord Percival of Duskryn!"

Thalion staggered as Kishtar clapped him on the back. "Good luck!"

Thalion gave Kishtar a half-wave as he stepped into the list. He heard Niara cheering, but set it out of his mind as he sized up his opponent. Percival was taller than him by a good head, with much broader shoulders and well-formed muscles. He had also been fighting with the prince for the last few years of Tigrian war. Thalion needed all his concentration for this bout.

Percival raised his sword to Thalion, his face serious. "Good fortune."

"To you as well. Fair Ululu," Thalion saluted Percival with his own sword and waited for Niall's signal.

Niall held out a staff between them. "Are you prepared?"

Thalion nodded. Across from him, Percival did the same.

Niall raised the staff. "Begin!"

Thalion brought his sword up instantly, ready for Percival to attack. Instead, Percival watched him, only bringing up his own sword and shield into a ready position.

Thalion felt his lips tighten in a small smile. He was just as much an unknown quantity to Percival as Percival was to him.

They circled each other warily, trying to determine each other's strengths. Thalion's mind filled with Gwyn's instructions. *You're not as tall as most men,* she'd said bluntly. *But that doesn't mean you're weak. Look at me! Think of it as a strength, instead. They'll underestimate you.*

He saw the moment that Percival decided to attack. Percival's shoulders straightened as he stood tall and strode forward confidently, sword ready to strike. That moment of preparation was all Thalion needed to neatly sidestep and deflect Percival's sword with his shield. He brought his sword around for the counter Gwyn had taught him, and Percival just barely managed to bring his shield up to block. Percival fell back, his eyes filled with a grudging respect.

Sweat started to trickle down the back of Thalion's neck. It was hot this Mazda's Time, even this far north. And he was wearing all of his armor, his chainmail, bracers, helmet, and gauntlets.

Percival returned to circling, and Thalion's confidence grew. He had surprised Percival with his first maneuver. Now he would be wary.

Gwyn's voice rose up in his head again. *Once they're wary, don't waste time. Use what you know. Strike hard and fast, but leave yourself an escape. You're fast. That's your advantage. Get in and get out.*

He followed Gwyn's advice. In two quick steps, he closed the distance between himself and Percival, almost touching him. Percival was making the mistake most tall men did when fighting a shorter opponent, holding his shield a bit too high. Instead of coming up with an overhand strike the way Percival was expecting, Thalion went under, striking low toward Percival's side. Percival spun to counter, but Thalion was ready for that, spinning in the opposite direction and bringing his sword up and around to lay his blade alongside Percival's throat.

Percival stared at the blade, his eyes wide with surprise. Slowly he lowered his sword. "I yield."

Thalion lowered his sword and stepped back, nodding to Percival. "Good fight."

Niall raised his staff. "The victor is Lord Thalion!"

A cheer rose from the spectators, and Thalion heard Kishtar's cry of triumph from behind him. He managed a smile, though he couldn't bring himself to feel much triumph. Not with the prince's words hanging over his head. He walked back to where the competitors gathered at the edge of the list and gave his weapons to a young manservant. Kishtar came up to him as he was taking off his helmet and slapped him on the back.

"Well done," Kishtar said in a low voice. "I could almost hear Gwyn shouting over your shoulder that entire fight."

"She was in my head," he joked.

"Next contestants! Lord Kishtar and Lord Arrex!" Niall's voice announced.

Kishtar grinned at Thalion. "Wish me luck!"

Thalion clapped Kishtar on the back. "You don't need it. It's—"

"Skill, not luck, that wins the day," Kishtar rolled his eyes as he joined Thalion in reciting one of Gwyn's phrases. "Luck still helps!"

Thalion laughed. "Then good luck! Not that you'll need it."

His words proved prophetic. Although the fight was vicious, with neither Kishtar nor Arrex giving the other any quarter, Kishtar was ultimately victorious as he sent Arrex's blade flying across the field.

The rest of the tournament passed in a blur. Thalion won against his next opponent, and then lost against Kishtar, putting him in the loser's bracket. Kishtar then lost to the prince, joining Thalion in the loser's bracket. Slowly, the winner's bracket grew smaller and smaller, until only the prince remained undefeated.

"And now, the semi-finals," Niall announced. "The fight to determine who will challenge his highness, Prince Andreas. Lord Thalion and Lord Kishtar!"

Thalion grinned at Kishtar as they walked onto the field. "Any last words?" he asked.

Kishtar gave a flourish with his sword. "Those might be yours!"

Thalion smiled as the crowd's laughter reached him. It was music to his ears.

Niall raised his staff. "Begin!"

The dance was familiar. Without thinking about it, both of them fell quickly into the training rhythm that they had practiced so often at home. Thalion blinked as he realized they were following one of Gwyn's drills. High strike, low block, head, arm...had Kishtar noticed as well?

There was only one way to test the theory. He broke the pattern, stepping forward when he should have stepped back, and Kishtar stumbled backward, barely parrying Thalion's blow. Thalion gasped in triumph. He had him! He pressed the attack, his shield firmly in front of him until he was pressed right against Kishtar, his sword pulled back and presented at Kishtar's chest. Kishtar's own sword was too far out to be effective in any way.

Kishtar laughed as he dropped his sword. Thalion dropped his as well and pulled him into a hug. "Good fight!"

"And the victor is Lord Thalion!" Niall announced. "Lord Thalion, you have a few minutes to refresh yourself before the final bout."

Thalion nodded in acknowledgment. His eyes swept over the contestants until they found the prince. The prince was staring at him, eyes dark and unreadable. Thalion suppressed a shiver.

"Well done, you two," Niara appeared at his side with a flask of water, which he gratefully accepted.

Kishtar nodded his thanks. "Think we showed them the Ninaevans are not to be underestimated?"

"I think you did more than that," Niara said, smiling. "I think you impressed a certain lady."

Thalion's gaze immediately flickered to where Serana was sitting in the stands. She met his eyes briefly and then lowered her eyes, her face flushing. He felt heat stirring inside of him.

"You could win the tournament in her honor," Kishtar suggested. He smirked. "I bet she'd like that."

The heat cooled as panic rose up to take its place. Thalion turned to Niara. "Niara, I can't win the tournament."

Her eyes widened. "Why not?"

"Because...yesterday, after our race..." the prince's words came tumbling out. The implied threat, the threatening gaze...

Niara's eyes darkened, and she cursed.

Kishtar was quivering with anger. "That's unfair."

Niara shook her head. "Fair or not, he will be king. Mother needs us to make alliances, not enemies." She cursed again. "I should have seen this coming. We need to get Mar out of the way. Thank Mazda Ninaeva's our next stop." She shook her head in disgust.

"So what should I do? Should I forfeit?" Thalion glanced down at his hands, surprised to find that they were shaking.

Niara shook her head. "No. He wants strong warriors, he just wants to be the best. He's like Niall, the idiot. Fight, but I'm afraid you're going to have to lose."

He knew she was right, but a flare of rebellious anger stirred in his chest. He fought it down and nodded in agreement.

Niara gave him a quick embrace, ignoring his sweaty armor. "They all know you're a fine warrior, one of the best," she whispered.

"But what about the grand melee?" Kishtar asked. "Thalion and I were going to be unstoppable!"

Niara stared at Thalion, and he shook his head. "We can't win."

"Why not?" Kishtar's voice was rebellious. "If he wants strong warriors..."

Niara placed a hand on Kishtar's shoulder. "Kishtar. He will be king. Do you want to make enemies of the king?"

Kishtar shook his head and subsided, grumbling.

Niara straightened her shoulders. "That's settled then."

Thalion sighed. He would have liked to dedicate his victory to Serana. His gaze drifted back to the stands.

Niara followed his gaze. "I think I will go pay my respects to the Auriel ladies," she said lightly. "Perhaps talk about how skilled my brother is."

Thalion turned a panicked gaze toward his sister, and she managed a smile. "Don't worry, Thalion, I won't mention your interest. I'll let you do that."

Thalion flushed, but he looked at his sister seriously. "Are we going to be alright?" he asked quietly.

She sobered. "I...I don't know, Thalion," she said. A flash of fear passed across her face, and Thalion's heart sped up.

"Niara?" he asked.

She shook her head. "I'll tell you later," she said, squaring her shoulders. "You focus on the tournament right now."

Thalion sighed, but he knew from long experience that there was no changing his sister's mind when she wore that expression. She smiled briefly at him before walking over to the stands, heading straight for the Auriel ladies.

Beside him, Kishtar glowered. "I need a good insult for the prince," he said. "How about 'arrogant royal rat-catcher?'"

That made Thalion laugh a little. "You need to work on your insults," he said. Nevertheless, he was able to compose himself as Niall walked over to ask if he was ready. He straightened his shoulders as he walked back into the field across from the prince.

"My lords and ladies! For the final fight, our most Royal Highness Prince Andreas, versus Lord Thalion et-Alim of Ninaeva!" Niall dropped his staff. "Begin!"

In the first few moments, Thalion knew that he needn't have worried about trying to lose. He wasn't certain he could win. The prince was fiendishly good.

But he didn't want to go down without a fight. He twisted and parried, darting in and out, to the side and back, blocking with his shield and trying desperately to keep his sword from being bound up. How was the prince so fast?

Instinct took over and he attacked, searching for an opening. There! At his shoulder! Thalion began an overhead sweep, realizing too late that the prince's shield would be too slow to block the attack. Panic rose up. He couldn't win!

He did the only thing he could think of. Instead of bringing his sword down on the prince's shoulder, he missed. His sword flew wide, his momentum carrying it away from the prince. Too far to parry the prince's sword as it was presented at Thalion's throat.

Thalion stared at the sword, heart pounding in his chest. He dropped his sword in surrender, earning himself a dark smile from the prince.

"And the victor, his royal highness, Prince Andreas! Well fought, my lords, well fought!"

Thalion waited until the prince had lowered his sword before bending to retrieve his own.

"Well fought, Lord Thalion," the prince said in a low voice.

Thalion bowed. "You as well, your highness."

The prince's eyes flashed, sending another shiver down Thalion's back. Prince Andreas turned and walked off the field without another word of acknowledgment.

Thalion stood staring after him, fighting the rush of adrenaline. They still had the grand melee to go.

The feast hall was loud, dark, crowded, and the smell of the wood fires threatened to overpower the smell of meat and beer. Thalion's location didn't help either. As a finalist in both the single combat and grand melee, he was at the high table, on Niall's right. He was grateful he wasn't on his left. Dinah and the prince had that honor.

He and Kishtar hadn't had to worry about losing the melee in the end. The prince, Arrex, and Percival had formed a similar alliance, and the three of them fought together like they must have while on campaign. Between the two groups, they had taken care of all other challengers before facing each other. Thalion had managed to take out Percival again before the prince claimed victory, while Kishtar and Arrex had taken each other out.

He scanned the feast hall, wishing that he could have invited Serana to sit next to him. But she was seated next to her mother and brother, safely isolated from the rowdiness of the event. Niara sat with Kishtar, occasionally sending him an amused, sympathetic glance.

"You are very quiet, Lord Thalion."

Thalion forced a smile as he turned to his dinner companion, Lady Maeve, Niall's mother. "My apologies if I have not been entertaining you, Lady Maeve."

Maeve's other companion leaned forward to peer at Thalion. "No worries, lad, I've been keeping my wife plenty entertained for years."

Thalion nodded to Maeve's husband. It had caused a quiet stir when the former Lady of Dunbarrow had married her former husband's bard. Thalion was surprised that he was allowed to grace the high table. The previous times his family had visited Dunbarrow the bard had been banned from Niall's presence.

"You fought well in the tournament today," Maeve said, interrupting his thoughts. "You did Ninaeva proud."

Thalion inclined his head in thanks.

"Does your sister fight?" The bard's question was impudent.

Thalion felt himself stiffening at the bard's rudeness. "My sister has some training, but she prefers other activities," he said, forcing his voice to stay level. "Why do you ask?"

The bard grinned. "Oh, I've just crossed swords with your guardswomen a few times and thought one of them must have wanted to teach her. Tell Gwyn I send my regards. She'll know what I mean."

Thalion managed to refrain from rolling his eyes as he relaxed. Gwyn's dislike of bards was notorious. "I'll do that," he lied.

Finally, finally, Niall stood up to signal the end of the feast. "And now, my lords and ladies, let us to the courtyard! There, we shall celebrate!"

Thalion prevented himself from scrambling to his feet by a sheer effort of will. He pled a hasty farewell to Maeve and made his way through the crowd, searching for a golden-haired head. Where was Serana? She had been here only a minute ago...

She was right in front of him. He pulled up short, nearly running into her. She stared up at him, her eyes wide.

"Ah...Lady Serana," he managed.

Someone cleared their throat, and he looked up, seeing Percival standing next to her. "Lord Percival," he acknowledged. He squared his shoulders. He had come here with a plan. "Would you do me the honor of allowing me to escort you tonight, Lady Serana?"

She flushed, but there was a smile on her face. "I would be happy to." Only then did she glance at her brother, a hint of worry in her eyes.

Percival frowned as he regarded Thalion. Thalion straightened and met his eyes. *Yes, I am a suitor for your sister's hand, and I am just as eligible as any other lord here. I am a son of Ninaeva, with just as good of blood as you.*

Something in his expression must have persuaded Percival, for he stepped aside. Thalion bowed and offered Serana his arm. "My lady?"

She accepted, and Thalion led her through the crowd of people. Torches illuminated rows of tables, though how people could be hungry after the feast they'd just had Thalion couldn't imagine. Though most of the tables seemed to be for alcohol of some kind. People were already crowding into groups, drinks in their hands. Some shouts came from the rear of the great hall, though crowds of people blocked their view.

"What's going on there?" Serana asked, craning her neck to see.

"Wrestling, I believe," Thalion answered. "I heard Lord Niall mention it as entertainment."

He saw the pained expression on Serana's face before she concealed it. "But we do not need to see anything that you find uninteresting. Would you like refreshments?"

She smiled gratefully at him. "Yes, please. It was so hot in there."

"It's warmer than usual Mazda's Time," Thalion said as he led Serana through the crowd. "Lord Niall probably didn't think to tone down the usual fires."

Serana's eyes widened. "This is warmer than normal? But..." she shook her head. "Just because it's hot in here...it was so crisp outside!"

He had to laugh. "Yes, indeed, and it gets just as cold in Ninaeva, as well. Welcome to the north, Lady Serana." They reached the refreshments, and he took a jug and poured two glasses of mead. Despite his dislike of Dunbarrow and Niall, the casualness of the feast and revelry was a refreshing welcome from the balls of the rest of the tour.

"But how do you grow anything, then?" Serana asked as he handed her one of the cups. "Doesn't the cold kill the plants?"

He blinked in surprise. "Sometimes," he said. "If there's a late cold snap, or the frost comes before the harvest. But most farmers know when it's safe to plant and when they have to rush the harvest." He took her unclaimed arm and led her through the hall again until they reached the main door. Serana sighed in relief at the rush of cool air, and they stood together in silence for a moment against the stone wall of the keep, sipping their mead as the bustling noise spilled out from behind them.

"And what about flowers?" Serana asked.

The image of his favorite tapestry filled his mind, and he answered without thinking. "Oh, we have beautiful flowers up here in the north," he said. "Up in the mountain meadows, there are small white flowers we call starfire. They say that one night, a woman was up in the mountains, pregnant, cold, and alone. The snows had already fallen, and she was scared she would die up there. She called to Mazda, promising anything as long as she was warm. And Mazda sent down a blanket of stars, and she was kept warm through the night. When she rose the next morning, the stars had turned into flowers."

"That's beautiful," Serana whispered. "What happened to the woman?"

She had surprised him again. Most people only cared about the flowers. "She went back down the mountain, where her family refused to believe her tale. But she remained devout, and she founded the convent of the Sisters of Mazda. Her daughter heard the stories of starfire and became one of Ninaeva's finest gardeners."

"I like that story even more now." Serana's smile grew.

Thalion stared at her. Her golden hair fell like a halo around her head, shimmering in the light of the full moon. "I'll get you a bouquet of starfire when we're in Ninaeva," he promised. "You could wear a wreath of them in your hair. They're like you, small and beautiful, with roots as deep as the mountain. You can't get rid of starfire once it's in your meadow. It grows there forever." He gazed into her eyes, caught by the mesmerizing beauty.

"Thalion…" she whispered.

He blinked. "I…I'm sorry, Serana…I…I don't know what came over me," he stumbled over his words now. *Mazda's light! Where did my poetry go? I need it back!*

She giggled. "Moonlight and stardust?" she suggested.

He was floundering. Moonlight indeed. She practically glowed in it. Why had he compared her to a flower?

She leaned forward, her eyes twinkling. "If you bring me a bouquet of starfire, I will happily wear a wreath for the Dragon's Day celebrations."

He caught his breath. Regaining some of his composure, he swept a bow. "Then I will endeavor to please my lady." He noticed she had finished her mead, and he reclaimed her cup, holding both of them awkwardly. "So, did you enjoy the tournament?"

Her smile was polite. "Of course. It was quite enjoyable."

Thalion frowned. There was none of the genuine happiness he'd heard earlier in her voice. "You don't have to tell polite lies to me, my lady," he said. "I'm not certain I enjoyed it myself."

She turned to him, eyes wide. "But you nearly won!" she exclaimed. "I thought you would, against the prince. You were so fast, so light! The other ladies were admiring the prince, but I..." she cut off.

Thalion felt his heart leap. "But you?" he ventured.

She flushed and cast her eyes down.

He couldn't press her. He was afraid of the answer. He changed the subject. "Do the other ladies actually admire the prince, or do they just want to be queen?"

She looked up at him with an incredulous smile. "No lady would dare even whisper that question!" she sounded both shocked and delighted. She giggled. "Both, of course. Except for your sister. No one knows where her heart lies, but it certainly isn't with the prince or being queen. Or even with Lord Kishtar, though there has certainly been speculation of that nature."

Do you want to be queen? The question was on the tip of Thalion's tongue, but he forced it down.

"Thalion!" Kishtar's voice cut through his thoughts. He glanced up in alarm as Kishtar appeared at his elbow, worry clear on his face. "Thalion, Niall took Niara off on her own, and she hasn't come back yet."

Every instinct Thalion had went on alert. "Where did they go?"

"To the back courtyard, I think," Kishtar said. He shook his head. "Thalion, if he..."

"If he?" Serana glanced back and forth between them. "Is there danger?"

Thalion winced. "Only if Niara doesn't like what he has to say. And because it's Niall, she won't." He stared at her helplessly. "Serana, I don't want to abandon you, but..."

She smiled and shook her head. "Go find your sister and reassure yourself. I'm sure it's nothing. My mother's guard will watch over me fine." She gestured toward the shadows.

Thalion's eyes widened at the sight of a full-blooded elf standing in the shadows of the courtyard. Then he blinked in remembrance. He'd heard his mother talk about Saihid, Pellalindra's elven body-guard. He took Serana's hand and bowed over it, gently kissing it. "I will be back as soon as I may, fair lady."

He could see a flush on her cheeks as he rose.

"Thalion," Kishtar urged.

Reluctantly, Thalion turned, leaving Serana behind. He glanced over his shoulder once, to see her staring after him, a smile still on her face.

Once she was out of sight, worry overtook him. Why would Niara be alone with Niall? She hated him. Oh, she would never say it in so many words, but Thalion knew his sister. She despised the man. He and Kishtar shouldered their way through the crowd of the great hall, past the wrestling, to a side door near the back of the hall. They stepped through it and ran down the short passage that led to the smaller interior keep courtyard, stopping abruptly as they exited once more into darkness.

Voices echoed as soon as his eyes adjusted. "You won't even consider it?" Niall.

"Absolutely not!" his sister's voice was sharp. "That will never happen, Niall, never!"

"I'd reconsider if I were you," Niall said in a chilly tone as Thalion caught sight of them. They stood in the middle of the round court-yard, in the center of a rock garden of quartz and obsidian. Niall stood with his back to Thalion and Kishtar. Niara hadn't seen them yet, so focused was she on the man in front of her.

"You're not going to get another offer like this," Niall said. "You're twenty-six, a bastard, for all that you're heir to Ninaeva. All you're going to get is disreputable second sons, at best. I'm the only lord who will ever ask you."

"And you don't even want me!" Niara shouted. Thalion winced. His sister was angrier than he'd ever seen her. "You just want Ninaeva's lands to add to yours! To make yourself the greatest power in the north! It won't happen, Niall!"

"You dare refuse me!" Niall started toward Niara.

Thalion let out a cry of alarm and sprinted toward them. Niara turned at the sound of his voice, distracted long enough for Niall to grab her shoulders.

"Get your hands off my sister!" Rage exploded inside of Thalion as he ran forward, pushing himself between Niall and his sister. He met Niall's glare with one of his own. He felt Kishtar move up next to him, another body between Niall and Niara.

Niall stared at Thalion, his face a mask of rage. "She refused me," he said. Despite his own anger, Thalion could hear disbelief in Niall's voice.

"And showed good sense in doing so!" he exclaimed.

Niall's face darkened. "You'll stand against me?"

"I'll stand with my sister!" Thalion shouted. "And I'll stand between her and men like you!"

"Back off, Niall," Kishtar said in a low voice. "You're outnumbered. Best take her refusal gracefully."

To Thalion's relief, Niall did take a step back, glaring at all three of them. "I wouldn't wed her now for all the gold in Saemar," he spat, spinning on his heel and stalking back into the keep.

Thalion still shook with rage as he regarded his sister. "Did he hurt you?" he demanded.

To his surprise, Niara flung herself forward into his arms. He held her close as she clung to him, trembling. "Thank Mazda you came along when you did. I was about to...Mazda's light, I was going to incinerate him!" her voice shook as if she couldn't believe what she was saying.

Thalion's eyes widened. "You can do that?" he asked, horrified.

She pulled back and gave him a small smile. "I don't know. I've never tried." Despite her attempt at levity, he could still feel her shoulders trembling.

"Can Mother uninvite him to Dragon's Day?" he demanded.

Niara shook her head. "No, we can't do that," she said. "That sets a bad precedent. And will make Niall even angrier. Not that he's not angry already. I'm afraid I didn't help." Her eyes flashed. "But in Mazda's name, I wanted to wring his neck!"

Thalion gazed down at his sister in concern. "Are you sure you're alright?" he asked.

She nodded shortly. "I'm fine," she insisted as he continued to look at her. "I just…"

"Niara," Kishtar laid a hand on her shoulder. "We're here for you. To protect you. You can tell us."

Niara took a deep breath. "I'm fine," she repeated. "Two excellent brothers made sure I'm fine. We may have a permanent enemy in Niall MacTir, however."

Thalion frowned, but Niara's expression was closed. Something had happened before they'd arrived, he was sure of it. Anger stirred inside him. If he hadn't still been holding Niara, he would have charged out the courtyard after Niall, demanding to know what he'd done to his sister. He stared after Niall, rage growing.

Niara might have been right about Niall being a permanent enemy. At that moment, Thalion couldn't bring himself to care.

5

DRAGON'S DAY

Tension hung in the air. The street hummed with the quiet buzz of voices, all tense in anticipation. The only person who appeared unaffected was Nazir, who stood next to Thalion, observing everything with a small smile on his face.

Thalion grinned at his father, then returned his attention to the street. Ropes strung on either side kept the center of the cobblestone street clear but people packed either side, all eagerly awaiting the parade.

The stand for the nobility stood at the very end of the parade, at the gate to Ilhelm Castle. Next to Thalion and his father stood Vinet and Niara. Next to Niara stood the prince, although he conspicuously did not hold her arm, and instead escorted Rian. Vinet's eyebrows had risen at that slight, and Thalion knew that both he and Niara were going to have to explain why the prince was not escorting the daughter of his hostess, as well as why Niall had refused to accompany the tour to Ninaeva, sending his sister in his stead.

Dinah, at least, seemed oblivious to her brother's disappointment. She still hung on Kishtar's every word and glared daggers at an oblivious Ianna. Thalion suppressed a smirk. Kishtar's flirtations might be getting him in trouble shortly.

Thalion knew exactly where Serana was. She was on the opposite end of the stand, sandwiched between her mother and half-brother. He felt her presence as if his heart was a compass, its needle pointing straight at her.

The steady beat of drums getting louder and louder distracted Thalion from his thoughts. As the anticipation of the crowd increased, his own heart started beating faster. He gazed down the street, waiting for the parade to arrive.

His eyes widened as the first part of the parade came into view. His parents had spared no effort in creating a spectacle. Drummers filled the first few rows, pounding out a complex rhythm on the huge drums they carried in front of them. Behind them followed fire dancers, men and women dressed in bright colors dancing with balls of fire. One man took a flaming torch and swallowed it, then breathed a blast of flame skyward. Thalion gasped with the rest of the crowd, awe-struck.

"Where did you find them?" he whispered to his father.

Nazir smiled. "They're a troop from Jyria. Your mother met their leader on her last trip."

Thalion grinned. "And couldn't rest until she recruited them?"

"She's your mother," his father said, as if that answered everything.

Thalion gasped as his attention returned to the parade. Behind the fire dancers, the head of an enormous dragon appeared. As Thalion watched, more of it came into view, head swaying in time with the rhythm of the drums. The careful, critical observer could see the feet of people underneath the dragon, holding up the body and wings with some sort of contraption, but it appeared incredibly lifelike, so much so that when the head turned toward the nobles and let out a roar, Thalion jumped. He cheered with the rest as the dragon passed them, heading up into the castle.

"Well, I hope you enjoyed that," Vinet raised her voice so that she could be heard over the crowd. She smiled at the prince. "I hope you and your party will join us in exploring the Dragon's Day faire now, your highness."

The prince nodded, his shoulders tense. "I wouldn't miss it."

As if that was the signal, the crowd of nobles began to break up, small groups mingling with each other. Vinet took Nazir's arm and walked off, head held high as if she expected everyone to follow her. Gwyn appeared two steps behind them, a silent presence even in the heart of Ninaeva.

Thalion glanced around, trying to determine where Serana had gone. He caught a glimpse of her in the crowd following Vinet and Nazir, but before he could follow Kishtar stepped in front of him.

"Kishtar!" Thalion hissed, "I'm—"

Kishtar shook his head. "Your gift, Thalion. It's ready. Go get it, and then present it to her. She'll like it, I promise." Kishtar turned away, scanning the crowd. "I'm going to find Ianna."

Thalion stared after Serana for another moment, the impulse to follow her so strong it almost overrode Kishtar's suggestion. He shook himself. Kishtar was right. He'd gotten up far too early this morning to forget about Serana's gift.

It was a matter of minutes to slip into the castle and retrieve the wreath of flowers. It had been the gardener's suggestion to braid it that morning rather than the previous night so they would still be fresh when Thalion presented it to Serana.

The faire was set up in the main square of Ilhelm. Vendors and booths were everywhere, with hawkers shouting out their wares for all to hear. Thalion knew his mother had invited traders from all over the world to Ilhelm for this event. She always did, but she'd gone to extra lengths this time because of the prince. She wanted him to understand what foreign connections and alliances could mean.

Thalion wandered around the square, searching for Serana. What vendors would she look at? Jewelry? Clothing? She wasn't in any of the main booths for those items, although there were smaller stands scattered throughout. She could be anywhere.

He caught sight of Pellalindra examining a brooch, and started toward her, figuring that her daughter might be nearby. A flash of gold glinted in the corner of his eye, and he smiled as he turned to see Serana slipping into a stand. He blinked as he recognized the stand as one Niara occasionally frequented. Although it was covered in plants, it didn't sell flowers. Instead, the vendor sold herbs, some more precious than diamonds.

He made his way to the stand, staring at the wide array of items in surprise. Vines grew in carefully planned and tended patterns, and small flowers and herbs were deliberately spaced apart, none coming into contact with the other. Serana was bending over one, a vibrant orange flower with black stripes.

"Beware with that one, m'lady," the vendor said, stepping out from behind his table. "That one's deadly."

"It's Denseed, isn't it?" Serana sounded utterly calm. "I've never actually seen one before. I thought they only grew east of Tigri."

"They do," the vendor sounded impressed. "You study healing herbs, then, m'lady?"

Serana flushed. "A little," she said.

The vendor nodded. "Then you must've read Darius's *A Study of Potions, Poultices, and Poisons.* That's the only book I know that describes Denseed so thoroughly."

Thalion couldn't help himself. "If it's deadly, then why is it a healing herb?" he asked.

Serana whirled. "Thalion!"

The vendor seemed unperturbed by Serana's reaction. "Because, as I'm sure the lady knows, mixed with Riverbalm it is a cure for the deadliest of poisons. Do not even touch the flower without Riverbalm nearby, however, as one drop of the oil from the petals can kill you."

Serana stared at him wide-eyed, like she had been caught doing something wrong. He attempted a smile. "I didn't know you were interested in healing plants," he said. His words sounded awkward to his own ears.

She flushed. "I...I'm not! I mean I am, but not..." she put a hand over her mouth, cutting off her stumbling words.

Why was she flustered? Nothing seemed out of place or out of the ordinary. He took a deep breath and stepped further into the booth. "I brought you something," he said. He held out the wreath to her.

She lowered her hand from her mouth. "A gift?" she asked breathlessly.

Thalion nodded. "Starfire," he said. He paused, then took another step forward. She didn't retreat, allowing him to place the crown of white flowers on her head. He stepped back, meeting her eyes. She looked radiant.

"That's a plant with its own uses if you dabble in magic," the vendor said. Thalion jumped, startled out of the magic of Serana's face. The vendor continued as if he hadn't noticed. "Powerful protection flower, that. If you believe the stories, that is. Never dabbled in magic myself."

"Protection is good," Thalion said. "I...I hope you like them."

He glanced back in time to see a smile spread over her face. "Oh, Thalion," she said. "I love them!"

"Serana!" The sharp voice made both of them jump. Serana started like a frightened deer. "That's my mother. I need to go!" Without another word, she darted out of the stand. Pellalindra's voice immediately filled Thalion's ears.

"Where were you? You were supposed to be keeping the prince company. Instead, he's off at the swordsmiths! What did I tell you about this event?"

The vendor appeared to be busy arranging plants, but a small smile played around his face. "Trouble with the parents, my lord?" he asked Thalion. "That's always the hardest thing. Proving to each parental unit that you're worthy of their child. Such nonsense, really, as it's not the parents marrying them."

Thalion's mouth dropped open at the vendor's audacity. "It's not?" he asked weakly.

"Your mother knows that," the vendor continued unperturbed. "Then again, she didn't have parents to deal with. Some would say she was lucky."

Thalion glanced around at a loss. "Do you have any advice?" he finally managed.

The vendor laughed. "Not many would ask that of me! Me, an old bachelor!" his eyes danced. "But I've had my fun. Get the girl away from her mother. Get her to talk, and listen, boy. She'll think all the more of you for it."

Thalion blinked. "How do I get her to talk?"

The vendor shook his head "Think! I can't give all the answers. I've just seen her for a few minutes in this shop. What do you think she likes?"

It sounded like a leading question. Thalion looked around, thinking furiously. A small bush covered in tiny blue flowers caught his eye. He stared at it, an idea forming. "What does this one do?" he asked.

The vendor smiled. "Veildrops. Said to improve memory and enhance beauty. Used for disinfecting wounds, mostly. Powerful purification properties."

Thalion nodded, his gaze straying to the plant next to it. This one had no flowers, just small, green buds. "And this one?"

The vendor's smile widened. "Dreamflower. One bud in a hot drink before bed brings true dreams, or so it's said."

Thalion hesitated, torn between the two. "How much are they?"

"Normally, quite expensive," the vendor said. "But for you, I'll make an exception." He named a price that made Thalion's head spin. If that was an exception, he hated to think what the actual price was.

"I'll take the veildrops," he said. "If you don't mind, I'll send someone to collect them later and give you the money?" he made it a question. Mazda knew he didn't carry that much coin around on him.

The vendor nodded. "Done, my lord." He winked. "Now go follow that lady of yours."

A smile spread across Thalion's face. "I will," he found himself saying. "And thank you."

***

Thalion groaned as he emerged into the dim early morning light of the hallway. The next door down, Kishtar rubbed his eyes and blinked owlishly. "What are we doing awake right now?" Kishtar asked.

"Meeting Mother," Thalion answered. "When no one else will wonder what we're doing."

"But it'd be perfectly normal just for the family to get together in the study," Kishtar complained.

"But we're not meeting in the study, Kishtar," Niara interrupted their complaints as she strode down the hall. Thalion suppressed his resentment. His sister looked as wide awake and put together as if she were entertaining the prince.

"We're not?" Kishtar asked in confusion.

Despite himself, Thalion had to suppress a laugh. "Were you too involved chasing either Dinah or Ianna to pay attention to Mother's message?"

Kishtar flushed. "I was avoiding Dinah," he mumbled. "She was getting rather forward."

"Well, since her brother wasn't here, I suppose she thought she had the freedom to act like a cat in heat," Niara snapped.

Thalion stared at his sister in shock. Niara never insulted anyone. Niall must have angered her more than he'd realized.

"Sorry," Niara muttered. "Let's go." She strode on ahead of them.

A yawn split Thalion's face. "Why are you so tired?" he asked Kishtar. "You're usually up with the sun."

Kishtar waited until Niara was out of earshot before answering. He smirked. "You'll never guess what happened last night."

"What?" Thalion asked.

Kishtar's smirk widened into a grin. "Ianna."

Ianna? What does he mean—Mazda's light. Kishtar slept with Ianna? He flushed. "I thought you said you had a rule about noble ladies," he managed.

Kishtar shrugged, his grin not fading. "It'll be fine. We've worked it out."

Thalion frowned in suspicion. "Worked it out how?" he demanded. It wasn't usual for noble ladies to agree to sleep with someone outside of marriage, even with Kishtar.

Kishtar rolled his eyes. "I promised to marry her."

"What!" Thalion exclaimed. He stopped short as they ducked through a doorway, causing Kishtar to nearly run into him.

"Shh!" Kishtar's eyes twinkled. "It's a secret for now. We're going to go about it properly after the coronation. She's a darling girl."

Thalion blinked, struggling to comprehend what he was hearing. "You're going to marry Ianna?" he managed.

"Yes." Kishtar chuckled. "Now, if you want to approach Serana the same way, you just have to—"

"Stop!" Thalion exclaimed, holding up his hands. He could feel the blood rushing to his face. "I don't want to know!"

Kishtar laughed as Thalion picked up his pace, trying to make sense of his whirling thoughts. *Kishtar's engaged? To Ianna?* She had certainly been one of his major flirtations, but Thalion had never dreamed Kishtar would actually marry...well, anyone. And as for sleeping...his face flushed a fiery red, and other parts of his body react as he remembered Kishtar's quip about Serana. *Mazda's light.*

"I know what I'm doing, Thalion," Kishtar smiled, seemingly content with the world. "And trust me, it's wonderful."

His flush intensified, and he shook his head. "Why wait till after the coronation?" he said.

Kishtar rolled his eyes. "Something about the king, waiting until he makes his choice, nonsense like that. Apparently, it'd be rude to steal a choice from him."

Thalion let out a breath. "Well, congratulations," he said, trying to put as much warmth into his voice as he could. It was difficult when he wasn't certain Kishtar was making the right decision.

"Thanks," Kishtar said. "Hopefully your choice will make you equally as happy!"

Thalion felt himself flush again as they entered the garden where Vinet and Nazir were waiting for them, sitting on a bench under the willow tree by the lake. They seemed to have been involved in a deep discussion with each other, but they broke it off as Thalion and Kishtar approached. Niara had already taken her seat on another stone bench.

"Good, we'll have some privacy here," Vinet said. "Now, tell me what's been happening."

Thalion and Kishtar sat down next to Niara. By unspoken vote, his sister spoke first.

"Well, it was going fairly well," she said. She gave a brief overview of the various events they had attended. Thalion glanced at her suspiciously when her only words for Niall's event were 'a tournament.'

Vinet raised an eyebrow. "Did something happen at Dunbarrow?" she asked, her voice firm but her eyes sympathetic.

Niara didn't speak, instead looking truly torn. Thalion couldn't imagine why, unless she was afraid of disappointing Vinet.

Well, she shouldn't be. Mother has always said we have the right to our own partners. "Niall proposed to her," Thalion said. "Rather insistently. He was upset when she refused."

Niara winced. "I didn't mean to lead him on," she said.

Thalion blinked in surprise at her. "You did nothing to that arsehole," he said, not minding his language. "Niall was arrogant enough to suppose that you'd take him just because he's Lord of Dunbarrow. He didn't even bother discovering your feelings first. And if the way he threw insults about afterward is any indication, he never felt anything for you."

Niara opened her mouth, but Vinet interrupted, her eyebrows raised. "Wait. Niall MacTir wanted to marry Niara?"

Nazir placed a hand on Vinet's shoulder. "You've been expecting him to propose to her for a while, my dear."

Vinet grimaced. "Yes, I have. Marriage is about alliance for the nobility, and Dunbarrow and Ninaeva would be a good one."

Niara winced. "I don't want an alliance with Niall MacTir."

"Nor do you have to make one." Vinet's voice was firm. "Niall MacTir has grown into an arrogant ass. Or maybe he was always like that. I believe you called him a donkey in silk trousers once."

Thalion suppressed a snort at the image that conjured.

Vinet looked between her two children. "What else happened?"

It was Thalion's turn to hesitate. Was the bit about the tournament and the prince really important?

He didn't get a chance to ponder, as Niara explained the prince's actions. Vinet's lips pursed.

"Some of the Regency Council have been worried," she said softly. "Lord Dannan and I, particularly. I'm afraid this only confirms our fears."

"What fears?" Thalion demanded.

Vinet exchanged a look with Nazir. "We're about to have a very interesting time," Vinet said slowly. "The prince has grown into a man that not everyone likes, a warmongering sort that will lead the nation toward death and destruction instead of peace and prosperity. He cannot bear to hear any criticism, leaving any potential advisors burdened with the knowledge that they must guard their tongues or risk displeasing the king. And no one knows what displeasing this king will do."

Thalion shivered. His mother's words had a foreboding ring to them, almost as if she was uttering a prophecy.

"So, what does that mean for us?" Niara asked.

Vinet shook her head. "I don't know." She took a deep breath. "I pity the girl he chooses to be his queen. You don't seem to be one of his chosen candidates, though. I take it that's because of your horse race?" She raised an eyebrow at her daughter.

"I can only assume so." Niara flushed.

Vinet nodded. "Anything else?"

"Thalion's in love with Serana Auriel," Kishtar said.

Thalion's face flushed red. "Kishtar!" he exclaimed. *See if I keep your secret if you keep revealing mine!* He glared at Kishtar, and Kishtar had the grace to look abashed.

He glanced up to see his father smiling at him. "I gathered as much."

Thalion shook his head. His father always did see too much.

Vinet smiled. "And does the lady return your affections?"

Thalion felt himself flush even redder but managed to shrug. "I think so," he said. "I'm not sure her mother approves."

Vinet laughed. "Pellalindra barely approves of anything. Pay her no mind."

Thalion shifted in his seat at the similarity of the vendor's advice to his mother's.

Vinet sobered. "Do you mean to marry her?" she asked. "Feel free to say it's none of my business."

Thalion blinked. How could he say that to his mother? The one who had raised him, the one who had given him the freedom to pursue Serana of his own volition? "I want to," he said.

"Then you should know something," Vinet said. "Something Serana likely won't tell you, and her mother definitely won't."

Thalion jerked back. "Why would Serana not tell me?" he asked, insulted that his mother thought that Serana would never confide in him.

"Because she's likely promised her mother never to breathe a word," Vinet said, deflating Thalion's annoyance before it truly had a chance to grow. "It's her mother's secret, really. But it will affect Serana's future."

Thalion leaned forward, interested now. "What is it?"

Vinet exchanged a glance with Nazir. "Serana is half-elven, like me," she said. "Her father is Saihid, Pellalindra's elven bodyguard."

Thalion stared at his mother, his mouth dropping open. Serana was a half-elf?

"Wait, so Serana is not the regent's daughter?" Niara demanded.

Vinet nodded. "Yes. Which is why I told you. If you intend to marry her, Thalion, you must be prepared to protect her as well. It will be easier for her if her husband knows her secret and can work with her to protect it."

Thalion blinked. "Like Father protects your secrets," he said.

"Exactly," Vinet looked at the three of them. "Did anything else happen?"

"The bandit attack." Thalion spoke reluctantly, not wanting to relive the battle, but knowing that his parents needed to know.

"I gave Mar into Evalynna's care," Niara said. "I didn't know what else to do with him."

"No, we couldn't abandon him," Vinet sighed. "Though we do seem to make a habit of taking in refugees."

"For which I am eternally grateful, my dear," Nazir said.

Vinet smiled fondly at her husband. "Unfortunately, we need to return to playing host before everyone wakes up." She stood up. "The last thing we need to do is arouse any more suspicions."

6

THE GREAT HUNT

It was unseasonably warm, at least, Thalion thought so. The sun glinted off the lake surrounding Duskryn manor behind him. The only movement on the water was that of several swans swimming lazily, occasionally sticking their heads under the water to look for food.

In stark contrast to the stillness behind him, the bustle in front was unbearably loud. Dozens of lords and ladies were already mounted, milling around while they waited for the hunt to start. A small group of more serious hunters armed with spears and bows were already moving into the forest, ahead of the announcement. Thalion felt a brief flare of envy. They would get to hunt normally. He would have to ride with a pack of nobles and be polite to them.

"My lords and ladies! Welcome to the 379th Great Hunt of Duskryn!" The announcer bowed with a flourish and stepped aside, clearing a space for Percival and the prince to ride up to the head of the group.

Thalion's horse shifted underneath him, and he reached down to pat the horse's neck, making a soothing sound. The horse settled as Percival started to speak.

"Our prince has expressed a desire to join the serious hunters!"

Percival exclaimed. "Let all those who would follow him come ride with us!"

Thalion blinked. The last hunt he'd attended, the group of nobles had barely even seen a deer. That wasn't the point of the hunt, as far as he'd been able to determine. The point was to be seen as Duskryn basked in its self-absorbed glory.

He shook himself as Arrex, Niall, and two other noblemen separated themselves from the pack and rode over to join the prince. He raised his eyebrows at Kishtar in question.

"Go, you two!" Niara whispered. "Someone from Ninaeva needs to be there!"

Thalion heard the rest of Niara's unspoken statement. Niara hated the hunt. She'd never told him exactly why, but joining the serious hunters was not going to appeal to her, even if Niall's presence was set aside.

Thalion focused on the prince and Percival as they rode up, ignoring Niall completely. Percival gave them a sober nod, while the prince flashed a grin.

"Good to see you joining us, Lord Thalion and Lord Kishtar!" the prince exclaimed. "Now, let's ride!"

Thalion felt his heart rate leap as the prince spurred his horse forward. Instinctively, he ordered his horse to do the same, and soon the group was riding into the forest. They paused as they reached a clearing, and the baying of hounds ahead of them signaled the presence of the real hunters, hot on the trail of any game.

The prince let out a wild whoop of glee and spurred his horse forward again. Thalion moved to follow, only to find Niall had dropped back, blocking his path.

Thalion glared. "Lord Niall," he said, fighting to be polite.

Niall glared back. "Lord Thalion. How unexpected to see you joining the real hunters. Why isn't your sister here, making a spectacle of herself like she did at the approach to Dunbarrow?"

Thalion throttled down his rising anger. "Don't you dare speak that way of my sister," he growled.

Niall laughed. "Half-sister. And a bastard to boot. Don't you think you should truly be heir to Ninaeva?"

Thalion jerked back, taken completely aback. "No!" he exclaimed. How could Niall even suggest such a thing?

"Lacking in ambition as well as sense. Well, luckily for you, I've a plan that fits perfectly with that."

Thalion stared at Niall in confusion. "What do you mean?"

Before Thalion could react, Niall's hand darted out and grabbed Thalion's saddle. Thalion saw the flash of steel before he felt the saddle slip under him. His horse whinnied in fear and sidestepped, causing the saddle to fall to the side. Thalion yelped as he overbalanced, falling sideways as his saddle slipped to the ground. Training took over and he rolled, luckily avoiding any injury.

"You bastard!" he shouted at Niall as he scrambled to his feet. The saddle girth had been cut through, making it impossible to secure.

"Can't have the Ninaevan lordlings securing favor with our prince," Niall said scathingly. "Good luck catching up to the real hunters now." With that parting shot, he turned and rode away, leaving Thalion staring after him in fury.

His horse whinnied and danced, and Thalion took a deep breath before walking up to his head and stroking his nose. "It's not your fault," he said.

The horse whinnied like it understood and shoved his nose into Thalion's shoulder. *Well, I guess I'd better be getting back. I'm not good enough at bareback to hunt without a saddle.*

With another sigh, he picked up his ruined saddle and draped it across the horse's back. Using his reins as a lead, he started walking back toward the estate. *Maybe I won't run into any of the other hunters, and no one besides Niall will know. The prince might not even notice I'm not there. Kishtar will notice, but he's really the only one there who cares...* Thalion shook his head to clear it of mournful thoughts. Who cared if the other noble lords weren't really his friends? He had Kishtar. And his sister. And Serana.

The thought of Serana made his heart lighten. He would see her at the banquet tonight, though as the sister of Percival, she would be the prince's partner. Thalion would at least still be able to see her.

The sound of a bird chirping made Thalion raise his eyes, and he paused, looking around at the trees. Slowly, he turned to gaze back the way he had come. Nothing appeared familiar. He cursed. *Manyu take Niall and his blasted schemes.*

He shook his head. There was no point cursing Niall now, not until he got back to the estate. Duskryn was vast, and he was on foot.

He sighed, straining his eyes and ears to find something that was even the slightest bit familiar. *This would be easier if I had the Sight, like Mother and Niara,* he thought, a bit resentfully. *I have elven blood as well, but do I get the perks? Of course not. I'm Father's son.* He shook himself, frowning at his thoughts. Normally, he wouldn't have minded not having the Sight, and, in fact, proclaimed that he was glad of it. Niall's trick had him on edge.

He blinked as he heard a faint trickle of water. He closed his eyes, trying to picture where a river or stream might flow through Duskryn. They had crossed a stream on the way to the hunt's starting point! If he could find the stream, he could find his way back.

If you pick the right direction to follow, and if it's the same stream. Mazda's light, I wish I were in Ninaeva. Then I'd have some idea of where I was going. Thalion shook those thoughts aside. He would worry about that when he reached the water.

At least the undergrowth grew lightly in this part of the forest, just a few ferns and bushes that he could easily avoid. He made his way to the bank of the stream and took a breath, rolling his shoulders back before taking a look around.

He froze. There, on the opposite bank, was Serana. Her golden hair was bound back in a simple braid, and she wore a plain blue dress, nothing like the fancy ballgowns she'd been wearing of late. She had a wildflower tucked behind one of her ears. Despite the simplicity, Thalion thought she had never been more beautiful. She was bent over something, an intent expression on her face.

"Serana?" he managed.

She whirled to face him, and he caught a brief glimpse of her startled face before her foot slipped off the edge of the bank. Thalion's eyes widened in horror as he saw the dirt crumble beneath her other foot, and she let out a short scream before splashing into the water below.

He didn't think, he just acted. He jumped into the water himself, thanking Mazda that it was barely deep enough to come up to his chest. He half-swam, half-ran over to Serana's side, where she was spluttering and splashing.

"Serana!" he exclaimed, taking her arm and lifting her upright. "Serana, are you alright?"

She brought her hands up to her face to brush the water out of her eyes before answering. "Thalion! Don't startle me like that!"

Thalion flushed. "Sorry!" he exclaimed. "I didn't mean to." The bank he had come down was much less steep. "Here, let's get out of the water." He took her hand and led her across the stream to the bank, helping her up the bank where they both collapsed on the ground.

"What are you doing here?" Serana asked. "Weren't you with the hunters?"

Thalion glanced over at her and flushed. Her soaked dress clung to her skin, revealing curves at her hips and chest. Somehow they were more alluring now than in any of the fancy ballgowns he'd seen her in.

"Thalion?"

He blinked. She'd asked him something. The hunt! "I was," he managed. He forced his eyes away from her body and back to her face.

"Then why are you here and not with them now?" Thankfully, she seemed completely oblivious to his straying eyes.

He flushed at the memory. "I..." he stumbled over his words. He didn't want to admit that he'd allowed Niall to get the better of him. "I...my saddle broke."

"Oh no!" her immediate, genuine concern made his heart warm. "Are you alright? Is your horse?"

"We're both fine," Thalion assured her. He gestured over his shoulder. "See, he's over there, grazing happily."

Serana glanced briefly at where he gestured before turning back to him. "But how did you get here? No one ever comes this direction, especially not at the hunt!"

Heat rushed to Thalion's face again. There was no way to avoid this admission. "I got lost," he mumbled.

She frowned. "What?"

Mazda's light! "I got lost," he said again.

She stared at him, then released a peal of laughter. "Really?"

He looked away, afire with embarrassment. "It's not that funny."

A hand rested lightly on his shoulder, and he turned to see that Serana had scooted closer to him. His breath caught as her chest rose and fell with barely suppressed amusement. "I'm sorry," she said. "But you always seem so confident, so assured, that the idea of you being lost…" she giggled and clapped a hand over her mouth.

"You think I'm confident?" Embarrassment faded at the thought. He hesitated. "Do you like it when I'm confident?"

"Oh, Thalion," Serana smiled. "I like it when you're *you*. Confident or not."

The breath caught in his throat. "I like you too, Serana," he whispered. "Quite a lot."

She flushed and turned away. "Even when I'm disheveled and unkempt?"

Thalion swallowed as her words just made him look at her body again. Heat rose in his groin, and he shifted to hide his uncomfortable reaction. "Yes," he managed. "Serana, you're beautiful." He blinked as a sudden thought occurred to him. "But why aren't you at the hunt?"

She looked back at him, flushing even deeper. "I always come out here when I'm at Duskryn," she said. "This was going to be my only chance this visit."

Thalion settled back. "It's quite a beautiful spot," he said.

"True, but that's not why I come." Her voice was so soft that he had to strain to hear her.

He paused before reaching out to take her hand. She stared at their entwined hands. "Then why do you come?" he asked.

She glanced down. "Because I can be myself here," she whispered. Her gaze moved to the stream. "There're herbs that grow along the bank, if you know what you're searching for. I can pretend to be a simple wisewoman, free of my mother, of the court, the nobles, the prince..." She shook her head. "You must think I'm silly."

"No!" Thalion clasped her hand in both of his. "That's not silly," he said. "That's wonderful."

She sniffed. "I disappoint my mother every time I come out here." She met his gaze, her eyes wide. "Promise you won't tell her I was here today!"

He had to laugh. "Of course, I won't tell her," he promised.

She relaxed.

He spoke slowly. "You care a great deal about what she thinks."

"She's my mother," she said, as if that explained everything. Thalion supposed it did.

"There's another place where you could be yourself." The words stumbled out, unplanned.

She looked at him curiously.

He suppressed a curse. He hadn't meant to say it this way, but it was too late now. "In...in Ninaeva. As my wife. We're unconventional there, you can have all the interests you want. I...I love you, Serana."

She stared at him. "Are you proposing to me?"

He suppressed another curse. "Yes," he said. He stumbled over words. "I want to marry you, Serana. And you can be free at Ninaeva. Practice your herbalism, even set up as a healer if you want. Your father can even come join us, and no one in Ninaeva will think it a scandal."

She frowned. "My father?"

Thalion nodded. "There're other elves in Ninaeva," he said. "He won't even be alone."

"Wait, elves?" Serana pulled her hand away and scrambled to her feet. "Who do you think my father is, Thalion?"

Thalion rose to his feet as well, horror dawning on him. "I...your father is Saihid," he managed. "My mother..."

"That's a lie!" Serana shouted. "That's a filthy lie! My father is Lord Auriel, steward of the realm!"

"Serana..." Thalion reached out a hand, trying to calm her.

Her eyes flashed with anger. "Don't you dare spread that filthy lie to anyone else, Thalion et-Alim! Especially not my mother!" She dashed off into the forest, leaving Thalion staring after her in anguish.

"Serana," he whispered. "I thought you knew."

"Thalion! Where have you been?"

Thalion flinched away from Niara's concern. "In the woods," he said shortly. He pulled the saddle down from his horse. "This needs repair." A nearby stablehand nodded and took the saddle from him.

"Thalion!" Niara followed him as he walked out of the stable. "Thalion, wait! No one's seen you since the hunt left! What happened?"

Thalion froze as he stepped out into the sunlight. Serana was crossing the courtyard, dressed once again in a fancy gown that her mother would be proud of. She seemed to sense his gaze, as she looked across the courtyard and glared at him before turning away. He stared after her, anguish warring with pain. How had he ruined everything so completely?

"Oh," Niara made a sound of realization. "You had a fight? Well, I'm sure that everything can be sorted out."

Thalion turned his anguished expression to Niara. "No, it can't!" he exclaimed. "You don't understand!"

Niara blinked. "Why not? Of course, you can talk it over, figure out what's wrong…"

"I know what's wrong!" Thalion exclaimed. "And I ruined it, forever!" He stormed off toward the estate. He wanted nothing more than to barricade himself in his room and never come out. Blessedly, his sister didn't follow him.

He shut the door to his room behind him and leaned against it. How had he fumbled so badly? He hadn't known that Serana didn't know about her father! Why wouldn't she? Niara had known about her parentage for years!

He began to pace up and down the room. *Maybe she was just overre-*

acting because she thinks I would spread the truth about her, he thought. *But then doesn't she realize I don't care? I have a bastard sister, after all, whom I love even when she's annoying. Why would I care about her parentage? It's her I love, not her parents!*

He paced to the bed and back to the door again. *No, I don't think she knew,* he thought. *She was too shocked. But how do I tell her it's the truth? Will she even look at me again?* For it was the truth, he had no doubt of that. If his mother said something was true, he trusted that she had reason to know. And his father had known as well! That counted for even more.

He could only come to one conclusion. He had ruined everything. *Manyu curse it!* His leg banged into the chair as he paced, and he lashed out, kicking it to the floor with a satisfying clatter. He stared at the overturned chair a moment, then moved to pick it up.

I should have never mentioned her father. I should have saved that revelation for after we were married and in Ninaeva. Mazda's light, doesn't she know how beautiful she is? Or how much she's captured my heart? He swallowed hard, feeling his eyes start to sting. He loved her. And because of his foolishness, he had lost her.

A knock on the door startled him out of his thoughts. "Thalion? Thalion, I know you're in there." Kishtar's voice demanded.

He glared at the door. "Go away, Kishtar," he said.

He glared even harder as Kishtar ignored him and opened the door. He cursed himself for not having locked it.

Kishtar folded his arms. "Alright, what happened?" he demanded.

Thalion groaned and turned away, avoiding Kishtar's gaze. "I don't want to talk about it."

"Maybe not, but you're going to." Kishtar stepped forward, closing the door behind him. "You have to attend the feast, tonight, after all. The prince had enough questions when you weren't with the serious hunters."

"Manyu's curse, I don't care about the serious hunters!" Thalion exclaimed.

Kishtar's eyes widened, and Thalion felt his cheeks heating. He normally never used such language.

"Something happened with Serana," Kishtar stated. "What?"

He groaned again and sat down on the bed. "I ruined it," he said bitterly.

Kishtar sat down on the bed with him. "How?" he asked. "From what I saw, Serana was definitely partial to you."

Thalion shook his head.

"Did you tell her how you feel?" Kishtar pressed. "Sometimes women can get all nervous at the mention of feelings, though usually they adore being told someone likes them. Especially if they like him back."

Thalion glared at him. "I told her I loved her and I wanted to marry her," he said.

Kishtar stared at him. "Well, then what happened?"

Thalion threw his hands into the air. "I told her who her father was. She didn't know."

That silenced him. Thalion waited, bitter satisfaction rising up in him at how speechless Kishtar was. He had been right. "See? I ruined everything. She'll never speak to me again."

"Nonsense," Kishtar shook his head. "No, you didn't ruin everything. It was a shock for her, but I've seen the way she's been looking at you. She'll need some time to cool down and think. Then, when she realizes that you were telling the truth, you can talk to her again."

Thalion blinked, trying to ignore the hope rising inside him. "You think so?" he asked.

Kishtar nodded, supremely confident. "I've seen the two of you together. There's no other couple as suited. Leave her alone for the rest of this event, then try to talk to her."

Leave her alone? Thalion felt his heart twist. He knew that Kishtar was right, but it would kill him to sit and watch Serana from across the room, knowing she hated him.

Kishtar leaned over to whisper in his ear. "Don't worry, Thalion. I'll try to talk to her for you."

Thalion looked at Kishtar gratefully. Maybe something could be salvaged out of this.

The hall was packed full of people, all talking and celebrating the outcome of the day's hunt. At the head of the room, Lord Percival Duskryn presided over everything. At his left hand sat the prince, and at his right his mother. Seated next to the prince was Serana, her face pale and drawn.

Thalion couldn't keep his eyes from straying to the main table. Serana had seen him as he'd walked in, but she'd refused to even glance in his direction the entirety of the feast. How was he ever going to apologize if she refused to acknowledge him? *Not that I know what I'm apologizing for. For telling the truth?* He angrily pushed that thought away. He had to apologize to her. It was the only thing he could think of to make this better.

Finally, the last course was cleared away from the tables. Percival stood, tapping a knife against his goblet to get everyone's attention. "My lords and ladies! Pray join us in the gardens, where merriment and further entertainment await!"

Everyone rose, although politeness dictated that the high table leave the room first. The prince offered Serana his arm and escorted her away. As they passed Thalion, he swore that the prince sent him a smug, superior look. He clenched his hands into fists, then forced them to relax.

Kishtar clapped him on the shoulder. "Now's my chance," he said. "I'll let you know what she says."

Thalion nodded as Kishtar followed the prince and Serana out into the gardens. He waited for a few moments, then followed. It felt like his heart was pulling him to Serana, whether she acknowledged his presence or not.

The gardens were lit up against the night, servants holding trays of refreshments scattered around. A small group of musicians played some quiet music. Thalion ignored everything and focused all his attention on Serana. Her face was so pale. How could no one else notice how pale she looked?

His heart leapt as he noticed Kishtar making his way across the patio to the prince and Serana. Serana's eyes widened briefly, and she turned to the prince, pulling him away. The prince laughed and shouted at the musicians. "Let's have some dancing music!"

The prince swept Serana into his arms as the musicians struck up a dance tune. Other nobles immediately started pairing off. Thalion couldn't think, just stared at Serana. She would avoid him and Kishtar the entire night. He would never have a chance to say he was sorry.

"Not dancing, Thalion?" Rian's voice startled him out of his thoughts.

Thalion struggled to focus as he looked at the Lady of Lokrian. "I... would you care to dance, Lady Rian?"

Rian smiled. "We could, for formality's sake, I suppose. But I think both of us would rather be dancing with others."

Thalion blinked at the bluntness of her words. "Serana..." he managed.

Rian nodded. "Yes, Serana. And the prince. But since they're both occupied with each other, I suppose we can keep each other company." She curtsied. "Let's dance."

Thalion didn't know what to do. He let instinct take over as he bowed to her and led her to the group of dancers.

He didn't say anything for the first measure of the dance. As the music pulled her closer, he managed, "The prince?"

She laughed. "It's not that surprising. He's supposed to choose a bride from one of us, after all."

"And you want it to be you," Thalion said.

"What girl wouldn't?" Rian shrugged. "But what happened between you and Serana? I could see you getting close, but you've both been like ice the entire night!"

Thalion hesitated as he twirled Rian around. "I...we had a disagreement." It was as close to the truth as he could come.

"A lover's quarrel?" Rian asked. "And now she won't speak to you?"

Thalion opened his mouth but couldn't think of a thing to say.

She smiled. "What would you say to her if you had the chance?"

Thalion eyed her warily. "I would say I'm sorry," he said. "And hope she forgives me."

Rian nodded. "A worthy enough response," she said. "Maybe I can pass that message along."

Thalion stared at her. "You would?"

Rian laughed. "Of course, I would! Lokrian is friends with Ninaeva. We need to remember our alliances."

Thalion hesitated before saying, "I would consider it a great kindness if you would tell Lady Serana what I just told you."

Rian smiled. "What else are friends for? Perhaps you will remember my kindness one day."

Thalion bowed as the dance came to an end. Rian curtsied and swept away, leaving him staring after her with a feeling of foreboding. What would she ask in return for her kindness?

He watched as Rian approached Serana and drew her slightly away from the prince. They had a whispered conversation, and then Serana looked at him.

He watched, heart pounding in his throat. Rian whispered something again, and Serana shook her head. She turned back to the prince, casting one last glance back at Thalion.

His heart dropped. He had lost her.

7

LONG LIVE THE KING

Thalion looked up as Kishtar entered his room without so much as a by-your-leave. He glared at him. "I told you to leave me alone."

Kishtar ignored him as he walked up and grabbed Thalion's arm. "We're going into town."

"Go without me."

"No. We've been in the capital for two days, and you haven't left the townhouse." Kishtar tugged stubbornly on his arm. "You need some fresh air. We're going to the marketplace, where maybe you can buy a gift for Serana."

"What's the point?" Thalion asked. "She still won't talk to me."

Kishtar rolled his eyes. "She will. Even if you don't find a gift, you need a distraction. I'm not letting up until you come."

Thalion groaned but allowed Kishtar to pull him to his feet. He'd spent the last days agonizing about his encounter with Serana, trying to figure out if he could have done anything differently. Kishtar was right. He could use a distraction.

Crowds of people overwhelmed them as soon as they left the townhouse. Decorations hung half-strung on every street, music played in odd corners, and the atmosphere tensed with barely suppressed excitement.

Well, the coronation is tomorrow, Thalion thought. *Though if they knew what the prince was really like, I doubt they'd be this excited.*

The prince had stuck close to Serana's side the entire journey back to the capital, causing rumors to swirl around. And Serana had made no effort to get away from him.

Kishtar took the lead as they entered the marketplace, moving about the stalls and shops with the ease of long practice. Thalion followed without really paying attention.

"Here!" Kishtar exclaimed. He walked up to one of the booths and grinned. "I think even Gwyn would approve of one of these."

Thalion's eyes widened. The merchant had a dazzling array of armor and weaponry on display. "I thought the Jyrians mostly imported luxuries?" he managed.

The merchant heard him. "Ah, but I have made trade agreements with the dwarves of your lands!" he said. "They sell me their weapons, plain and functional as they are, and I arrange for them to be crafted into these masterpieces you see here!"

Thalion took a second look at the weapons. They were solid at the core and gorgeous on the surface. Each hilt was wrapped with gold, silver, or copper, and some were inset with gems. The armor was washed with gold or silver, and the shields were painted with intricate designs.

"You should get a new sword," Kishtar said cheerfully. "Maybe we can get one for Gwyn, as well."

Thalion let himself be dragged into examining the swords. Soon enough, they had picked two out and were haggling over the price. When they reached a conclusion, Thalion buckled the sword to his belt with satisfaction. He had chosen one wrapped with gold wire and engraved with cats dancing around multiple suns.

"So, where to now?" he asked, turning to Kishtar. Kishtar had been right; he was feeling more cheerful than he had been earlier.

Kishtar eyed him. "Shall we search for a gift or just wander?"

Thalion swallowed, his throat closing briefly. "Let's just wander," he managed.

Kishtar nodded, and the two of them began strolling through the marketplace. There were all kinds of items, and if Thalion had been searching for a gift, he was certain he could have found one. He turned aside from a flower vendor as his heart squeezed painfully, only to be confronted with an old, tumble-down bookstand. He froze.

The stand was old and shabby. Books lay piled on the counter in a half-haphazard way, and there was no sign of the owner. Nonetheless, Thalion knew exactly who stood in the shadows behind the stand. His mother had told him often enough.

He raised his eyes from the books and met the old woman's eyes. He had never met her before, but her piercing gray eyes stared through his soul as if she had known him all his life.

The old woman grinned a toothless smile. "Welcome, mother's son. What do you wish?"

AeresThonEsia. Thalion swallowed and bowed, elbowing Kishtar to get him to follow suit. "I...I did not intend...greetings to you, Lady," he said.

The crone laughed. "Struggle with words. Poor boy. Filled with pain. But what will you DO?"

Thalion felt cold shivers run down his spine, a feeling that the crone's question was far more important than it appeared. "What can I do?"

The crone gave a harsh cackle that sent chills down Thalion's spine. "What can any of us do?" She reached forward, revealing a withered hand missing two fingers. "Mother's son. The daughter of the broken-hearted one has discovered the truth."

Thalion's eyes widened. "Is the broken-hearted one Saihid?" he asked, barely daring to hope.

The crone merely cackled again and shifted her gaze. "Pained one, young one, daughter's father, yessss...of your blood and not, and not, mother's son. Your blood is much closer."

Thalion followed the crone's gaze over his shoulder. He saw his parents and Gwyn approaching the booth. Vinet's eyes were worried, and his father's expression unreadable.

Vinet smiled a greeting. "It is always an honor to speak to you, Lady."

The crone's visage blurred, and for a moment Thalion swore she looked younger. *Maiden, mother, crone,* he reminded himself. Aeres-ThonEsia, Lady of Leaf and Lake, was a changeable woman.

"Speak much more, we will soon," the crone said. "Snow and ice will come. My northern children should know this." Her gaze fell on Nazir. "Perhaps not you, child of the sun."

Thalion blinked. No one had ever called his father that.

Nazir seemed equally surprised. "I have lived in the north long enough, Lady," he said. "Why call me a child of the sun?"

The crone laughed. "Questions, always questions. A question I have for you," her gaze turned to fasten on Thalion.

He froze. Vinet had told him of the danger of AeresThonEsia's questions.

The crone's gaze was serious. "What will you do when the pained one's daughter seeks you out?"

Thalion's breath caught in his throat. "She…she won't seek me out, not now," he managed. "I said the wrong thing to her, I…"

The crone shook her head angrily. "Mother's son! You do not answer the question."

Thalion nearly took a step back, but the look on his mother's face held him in place. He closed his eyes. What would he do if Serana sought him out? He had told Rian that he would ask her to forgive him. That wasn't the entirety of the truth.

I would ask her to marry me again. I would build her a garden in Ninaeva, where she could be happy and content.

He swallowed. "I would ask her to marry me."

"No matter the obstacles?" The crone smiled.

Thalion furrowed his brow. There were no obstacles to him and Serana getting married, not beside the fact that he had destroyed any such chance. "Yes," he said.

"Ah…" the crone leaned back. "Love. Conquers all. And destroys.

So much pain…" she blinked. "Sky-lord rises, mother's daughter. I will call you soon."

Thalion saw his mother pale, but Vinet said nothing, merely bowed her head. "Farewell for now, Lady." She turned away, Nazir and Gwyn trailing her. Thalion began to follow but couldn't help looking back over his shoulder. The crone stared back at him, an expression of exhausted sadness on her face.

Thalion shivered but stepped toward her again. "Do you need anything, Lady?" he asked.

The crone turned her attention back to him as if she had forgotten his presence. "Need? Need?" she cackled. "Kindhearted boy. Child of the sun indeed! The path is set, the choice is made. Need is done."

"Thalion," Kishtar pulled at his elbow. Thalion had forgotten his presence during the encounter with AeresThonEsia. "Thalion, come on."

The crone said nothing as Thalion let Kishtar pull him away. Thalion shuddered as they caught up to his parents. What had just happened?

"What was that?" he asked his mother.

Vinet shook her head. "She always speaks in riddles," she said. "She sees far more than any of us, but that does not mean she feels the need to speak clearly."

"Why did she call us children of the sun?" Thalion asked his father.

Nazir shook his head. "I am more used to being called child of a demon," he said. "Child of the sun is a new title for me."

Thalion shook his head in frustration. "Why do we serve her if she doesn't give us any answers?"

Vinet laughed. "But she does! Eventually. She expects us to have our own ways of finding things out. Speaking of which," she raised an eyebrow. "The pained one's daughter?"

Thalion cleared his throat. "I think that's Serana," he said.

Vinet just looked at him.

He swallowed. "She didn't know." He hesitated, unwilling to say anymore in the middle of the crowded marketplace. *She didn't know Saihid was her father. She thought I was spreading vile rumors.*

His mother understood without clarification. "What?" Vinet's eyes widened. She stared in the direction of the palace. "Her mother never told her?"

Thalion shook his head.

"I should not be surprised." Vinet pressed her lips together. "Pellalindra always cared more about appearances than feelings."

Thalion shook his head. "Serana won't speak to me now."

"Oh, Thalion," Vinet stepped forward and pulled him into an embrace.

Thalion allowed himself to relax in his mother's arms. "I don't know how to fix it," he mumbled into her shoulder.

"We'll figure it out." Vinet patted his shoulder. "These things take time."

"I wish they didn't," Thalion grumbled.

His father reached out to ruffle his hair. "Patience, my son," he said. "It is a virtue."

Thalion barely refrained from rolling his eyes.

Vinet sighed. "Back to the townhouse," she said. "There is a coronation happening tomorrow, and I am still Lady of the Regency Council. We all have preparations to make."

Thalion smoothed a hand over his finest green and gold silk tunic as he stood near the top of the stone stairs leading toward the palace. The rest of his family gathered around him, all in Ninaevan colors, his mother with her rarely worn emerald-encrusted coronet. He'd forgotten how high Ninaeva was in the order of precedence.

The high priest stood at the head of the stairs, Lord Auriel at his right-hand side. Three burgundy-clad guards stood unobtrusively behind them. Nobles crowded the rest of the stairs, dressed in their brightest and most opulent garb, and all the citizens of the capital crowded the streets. Kishtar stood near the bottom of the stairs with a group of unlanded nobility. Across the stairs stood Pellalindra, Percival, and Serana.

Thalion couldn't keep his gaze from Serana. She had looked up only once to meet his eyes, then lowered her eyes to the ground and refused to cast her gaze up. She still hadn't forgiven him, then.

He forced his attention away as the sound of trumpets heralded the arrival of the prince. He rode at the head of a group of palace guards, dressed in their shining black armor with visors down, marching in crisp precision like animated statues. The prince seemed oblivious to how intimating they were as he smiled and waved to the crowd, causing people to cheer. He dismounted when he reached the base of the stairs, and the palace guard dispersed to either side, forming a wall to keep all below the steps separated. The prince continued up the stairs, his red velvet cloak flowing behind him, his head held high. When he reached the top, he knelt before the high priest.

The high priest nodded and raised the crown of Saemar in the air for everybody to see, his red and gold robes flowing about him like a vision of the sun god himself. He sang the questions of the oaths of rulership in a steady voice. *To protect...to honor...to lay down your life...to serve...to cherish...to guide through all strife...*

The prince sang his answers, pledging to protect and rule Saemar wisely and well, oblivious to the doubts he caused his most powerful nobles. As he finished, the high priest set the golden crown on the prince's head. Lord Auriel stepped forward and placed the scepter into the prince's waiting hands. Thalion was close enough to see the prince...the king, wink at Lord Auriel, and hear the slight whisper, "Don't worry. You'll always be my most trusted advisor."

King Andreas the Fifth rose to his feet and turned to face the people, cloak swirling around his feet. A deafening cheer rose up, nearly making Thalion wince as he joined the applause.

"Thank you, my people!" the king exclaimed. "I will lead Saemar into a new age of prosperity!"

Thalion couldn't stop himself from glancing at his mother. He saw the flash of worry cross her face, quickly concealed into a polite smile. He shivered.

As the people cheered again, the king swept into the palace, trailed by the nobility. Thalion and Niara let themselves fall behind the crush of people, joining Kishtar as they entered the palace. Only those who held land would be required to swear fealty.

Thalion surveyed the crowd, trying to find people he recognized. His mother and father were near the front, since as Lady of the Regency Council she would be obligated to swear fealty first. He found Rian and Niall, ready to swear fealty in their own right, and Percival, ready to swear in his. Next to Percival stood Serana. His eyes fastened on her. Her hair was braided into an elaborate hairstyle crowned with a gold coronet, and her silver dress shimmered with burgundy embroidery. She looked like a princess.

The herald pounded on the floor with his staff. "The king summons Lord Auriel, former regent of Saemar!"

Thalion exchanged a startled glance with Niara. Wasn't their mother supposed to swear fealty first? *Then again, he is the former regent...*

Lord Auriel didn't seem surprised as he knelt before the throne. The king smiled as he sang the oath of fealty. Lord Auriel sang his oath in a clear voice that rang out over the entire hall.

The king nodded as Lord Auriel finished his song. "Rise, Lord Auriel."

Lord Auriel bowed his head as he rose to his feet.

"You have served me well and faithfully as regent," the king said. "I would be honored if you would continue to serve me as steward, as you served my father before me."

Lord Auriel bowed. "I would be honored, my king."

"Then let it be so!" The king waved a hand. Several nobles applauded politely as Lord Auriel walked up to stand at the king's left-hand side.

"The king summons Lady Vinet et-Alim of Ninaeva and Lord Nazir et-Alim of Ninaeva!" the herald's voice rang across the hall.

Thalion watched as the king took his parents' oaths with all due formality. His mother's face was still tinged with worry as they bowed and rejoined the crowd of nobles.

"The king summons Lord Dannan Duatha of Kreutzer!" the herald called.

Thalion shifted his weight, already bored. They would have to go through all of the nobles present for the coronation. Even those who had sworn fealty eighteen years ago would be expected to reaffirm their oaths today.

"Thalion!" Niara whispered.

Thalion's breath caught as he saw where Niara gestured. Serana was making her way toward him, moving slowly through the crowd. His heart leapt in his throat.

Niara pushed him gently. "Go! Talk to her!"

Thalion stumbled forward, only faintly hearing the herald call another noble to swear fealty. He stopped a few feet away from Serana, hardly daring to breathe.

She hesitated, barely meeting his eyes before casting her gaze down. "Lord Thalion," she said, so quietly he had to strain to hear her.

His chest clenched at the formality in her voice. "Lady Serana," he replied.

She looked up, and Thalion's eyes widened at the mix of emotions. Uncertainty warred with fear and regret. He stepped toward her without thinking. "Serana?" he asked.

Before she could answer, another woman came out of the milieu of nobles. "Serana! There you are! Come, you must be seen to support your brother." Lady Pellalindra Auriel took her daughter's arm and swept her away without a word to Thalion. Serana didn't resist, just cast one more glance over her shoulder at him.

Thalion stared after her, disappointment warring with elation. She had tried to talk to him! But her mother had pulled her away without so much as a word of apology…

"Well, that was rude," Niara's voice came over his shoulder.

He turned to his sister. "She probably just didn't notice me there." Even as he said the words, he didn't believe them.

Niara's sniff confirmed his feelings. "Everyone notices you're there, Thalion. It's a little hard not to."

Thalion stared down at his hand. His brown skin did make him stand out in this crowd. The only person who stood out more was his father.

He squared his shoulders. "Well, I'm just going to have to find a time to talk to her alone," he said. "Where her mother won't interrupt us."

"Let me know if I can help with that."

Thalion gave his sister a grateful look. "I'm glad you like her."

"Of course, I like her," Niara said. "My brother is in love with her."

"I'm not sure that's how that usually works," Thalion pointed out.

Niara shrugged and lowered her voice. "She's a half-elf, how could I not like her?" she whispered.

A half-elf like us, Thalion thought. He smiled. It felt entirely appropriate that he, a member of a family of elven blood, should marry a half-elf.

If she wants to marry you, Thalion thought, sobering. *Even if she has forgiven you, she never gave you an answer.* He glanced up as his mother and father approached.

"There you are," Vinet said. "Have you seen Kishtar?"

Thalion shook his head.

"He was keeping Ianna company, I think," Niara said. "In an effort to avoid Dinah."

"I warned him," Vinet said enigmatically.

Niara sobered. "Mother, what did the king mean by placing Lord Auriel above you?"

Thalion glanced at his sister, startled. Niara never worried about the order of precedence.

His mother pursed his lips. "To announce to the court that he trusts Lord Auriel more than me or any of the members of the Regency Council," she said.

"But why?" Niara asked.

"He's flexing his power," Vinet said in a low voice. "He has been straining against the Regency Council for the last few years. He managed to pressure us into approving the Tigrian War, but there was a contingent of us that fought back. He has not forgiven us that."

"Is this a private family conference, Lady Vinet? A bad place for one." Thalion glanced up at the voice. Dannan Duatha approached them, his scarred face and one citron eye presenting an intimidating visage.

"If it was, you might still be invited," Vinet said. "You look well, Lord Dannan."

"As well as ever," Dannan nodded to the rest. "Enjoying the pomp and circumstance?"

Thalion smiled involuntarily. He could see why his mother liked the dark, mysterious councilor, even if he frightened and annoyed half the court.

"As much as you," Vinet said. "And I dare say sharing the same concerns."

Dannan's gaze darkened. "Indeed. We will have much on our hands."

"If he gives us a choice," Vinet's voice was worried.

Niara frowned. "But you're still on the council, right? Doesn't that give you a voice?"

"For now." Vinet's smile was tight.

Dannan's eye flashed. "He wouldn't dare remove us."

Vinet held up a hand. "I am not saying he will," she said. Her gaze was serious. "But be careful, Lord Dannan. There is far more to this king than there was to the last one, and the last one decorated his gates with his first council."

Thalion felt a shiver run down his spine. Why did his mother's words sound so prophetic of late?

Dannan shook his head, and Vinet placed a hand on his arm. "You are always welcome in Ninaeva."

"Why do you say that?" Dannan glared at her.

Vinet shrugged. "Because it's true."

The loud bang of the herald pounding his staff into the ground made all conversations stop as they faced the king. The king rose from his throne and raised his hands.

"My people!" he exclaimed. "Thank you for coming to swear fealty to me as I step into my rightful role. The last eighteen years have been hard, but I am finally come of age. Let there be no more uncertainty as I take my rightful place as king!"

Thalion clapped politely along with the rest of the nobles.

The king held out his hand for silence. "Though I am only now crowned, I am not unaware of the responsibilities of kingship," he said. "My regent advised me through many long years. I am aware that I cannot rule alone."

Whispers began to pass through the crowd, and Thalion felt a faint sense of foreboding.

"Indeed! I am speaking of what you all hope. It is time for me to choose a bride, one who will be Queen of Saemar and stand at my side!"

Out of the corner of his eye, Thalion saw Rian step forward slightly, hope in her eyes. He swallowed and turned his gaze back to the king.

The king smiled, seeming to enjoy the suspenseful silence. "Lords and Ladies of Saemar, it is with great delight that I announce my betrothal to Lady Serana Auriel!" He stepped down from his throne and walked over to Serana, taking her limp hand in his. Her expression was one of complete shock.

Thalion stared at the king, his mouth falling open. This could not be happening.

The king led Serana back to the throne. "We will rule faithfully and well!" he announced, before pulling her into a kiss. She stood stiffly, and Thalion caught one of her hands clenching into a fist before it relaxed.

He instinctively took a step forward before he felt a hand on his shoulder. "Not here," his father whispered. "Not yet."

Thalion swallowed as the king ended the kiss and smiled in satisfaction at Serana. He followed her gaze first to her mother, who was looking on triumphantly, and then to Lord Auriel, who was smiling benevolently. Then her eyes met his. The surprise and suppressed panic on her face was almost more than he could bear, and only his father's hand on his shoulder kept him in place.

He stared back at her, his own pain mirroring hers. He loved her. The king did not. This couldn't happen.

8

FLIGHT

For Thalion, the coronation feast was a nightmare. Serana sat at the king's right, in the place of honor. She had recovered her composure and was smiling politely as the king laughed and chatted with Percival, who had the seat on his left.

"Nothing less than a king for my daughter," Pellalindra said proudly.

Thalion winced. Why in Mazda's name did Serana's mother need to be seated next to the Ninaevans? She had thankfully ignored him most of the meal, focusing her comments instead on Vinet.

"Indeed," Vinet said. She cut a bit of her meat. "And quite an honor to you as well. No doubt you will be doing most of the planning for the wedding?"

Thalion winced. His mother's lack of reference to Lord Auriel had to be intentional.

Pellalindra caught it and cast a reproving glance at Vinet. "As steward, her father will be the one arranging the festivities," she said, emphasizing the word father. "I will, of course, assist with the details, especially the gown. You will attend, I expect, as well as all your family."

Thalion swallowed and stared down at his plate. He'd barely touched his meal.

"We wouldn't miss it," Vinet said. Thalion suppressed another wince. He didn't think he could stomach seeing Serana marry the king.

"Excuse me, my lord." Thalion looked up as a servant appeared at his elbow. He frowned at the small slip of paper the servant handed him.

Thalion,

Meet me in my palace chambers immediately, west wing, third door on the right. Let yourself in. Destroy this message when you get there.

- RL

Thalion blinked at the message, trying to determine its meaning. *RL? Who is RL? Initials, but...*his eyes widened. *Rian Lokris-Pythian. Why does Rian have quarters at the palace? Doesn't she have a townhouse?* He shoved that thought out of his mind. *Why does she want to meet with me? And in such secrecy? There's nothing...*his thoughts skittered to a halt. *Does she have word from Serana? Did Serana entrust her with a message to me?*

"What are your plans when you get back to Ninaeva, Lord Thalion? Since your sister will not, surely, it's time to entertain the idea of marriage?" Pellalindra's voice cut through his thoughts.

He stared at her, trying to process his emotions. It was Pellalindra who'd deliberately kept his chosen bride away from him, who'd arranged for Serana to be wed to another. He felt a lump forming in his throat, and couldn't bring himself to answer. "Excuse me," he said, pushing away from the table and standing up.

He heard Pellalindra's gasp of indignation as he walked away. "Lady Vinet! Your son..."

He ignored the conversation as he exited the main hall. West wing. Third door. The halls were nearly empty. All of the servants must have been in attendance at the feast.

He hesitated in front of the door. Rian's note had said to let himself in, but politeness bade him knock softly on the door, only letting himself in when there was no answer.

He blinked. *I didn't know that Lokrian was this wealthy. Where'd all this luxury come from?* The chairs were lined with embroidered velvet, and the furnishings were made of beautifully carved mahogany wood. Through an open door, Thalion could see a large canopy bed draped in violet silks. He settled himself gingerly into one of the chairs. Rian didn't usually seem to be the sort of person obsessed with opulence.

A small fire danced and crackled in the fireplace. Its presence was fairly useless on a day like today. Although Manyu's Rise was upon them, the air was still hot.

His thoughts danced like the fire. What could Rian want with him? Did she really have a message from Serana? Why would she arrange something so secret?

Secret! He reached into his pocket and pulled out the message. She'd said to destroy the message once he was in the room. He threw the paper onto the fire and watched the flames flare briefly as the paper crumpled into ash.

A knock on the door made Thalion jump to his feet. He hesitated, uncertain about whether to answer. Rian would already know he was here, wouldn't she?

The door creaked open, and a figure stepped into the room. His mouth fell open. Serana's golden hair glinted in the firelight.

"Serana?" he managed, his voice barely more than a croak.

Her eyes flew toward him as she closed the door. "Thalion? Thalion!" Before Thalion could react, she flung herself across the room. He caught her as she threw her arms around his neck and buried her face in his shoulder. "Oh, Thalion, I'm so sorry!"

"Sorry?" Thalion asked. "Serana, I'm the one who's sorry!"

"But it's all my fault!" she exclaimed. "If I hadn't stormed off, I wouldn't…this wouldn't…" she broke down.

Thalion stared at her in utter confusion as she sobbed quietly. Awkwardly, he began stroking her hair. "Hey, hey," he said, trying to sound soothing. "It's not your fault. I sprung the whole thing on you to begin with! I should have tried to figure out if you knew…" he trailed off. *Does she now believe that Saihid is her father? Have I ruined things again?*

She shook her head. "But you were right," she said. "I knew you had to be right. No one would make up that sort of story! But I didn't want to believe it, so I took it out on you. And now I'm engaged to... to..." she tightened her grip on his shoulders.

Thalion thought about the way the king had looked at Serana throughout the feast, how unbearably smug and proud, and his own arms tightened around Serana in reaction. "It's not your fault," was all he could think to say. "Serana, I'm sorry."

"So am I," she whispered. "Now I'm engaged to marry him, when..." she shuddered. "Thalion, I can't bear the thought of marrying him! He frightens me!"

"He frightens you?" Thalion repeated. "But why?"

She pulled away, wrapping her arms around herself. "The way he looks at me, the way he speaks...he doesn't care for me at all, Thalion. And I can't help but think that if he knew who my father really was, he'd discard me in an instant and send me to the palace dungeon."

Thalion felt a flare of protectiveness. "I wouldn't let that happen," he said.

She gave him a quick smile. "You wouldn't have a choice. He's the king." Her face crumpled. "And I have no choice, either. I have to marry him."

"Why?" Thalion tried to suppress his own pain. "Why do you have to? He never asked."

"Because the king gets what he wants," Serana said. "And my mother would kill me if I went against her wishes in this matter."

"What about your wishes?" Thalion asked. "Aren't they important?"

Tears glistened in Serana's eyes. "I wish I had given you an answer back at the hunt," she whispered. "It's too late for that."

Thalion felt hope rising up inside of him. "What answer would you have given me?" he asked, hardly daring to breathe.

She looked up at him. "I was hoping you'd ask all summer," she whispered. "I knew my mother wanted me to be queen, but you...you made me feel like no one else ever had. I could be myself around you, and you never judged." She hung her head. "It doesn't matter now."

Thalion took a step toward her. "I still love you, Serana," he whispered.

She blinked rapidly. "I love you too, Thalion," she whispered. "Oh, I wish I had said yes!"

Thalion could barely speak past the lump in his throat. "Then say yes now," he whispered.

Serana looked at him, her eyes full of love and pain. "Yes," she whispered.

Thalion reached a trembling hand up to stroke her hair. His hand passed over one ear, feeling the sharp angle that no human would have. "May I kiss you?"

"Yes," she whispered.

Hesitantly, Thalion leaned forward, watching her carefully in case she changed her mind. His lips were an inch from hers when she moved, her hand tangling in his hair to pull him to her. Her lips were warm, sending tingles throughout his body. Her mouth opened slightly, and he gasped. She moaned, pulling him closer to her.

They broke apart, panting. Thalion stared wide-eyed at Serana. Her own expression was as unfocused as his own. "Serana..." he whispered.

"Oh, Thalion," she whispered. "I am so sorry."

He stroked her hair. "Marry me, Serana." He spoke without thinking, a wishful hope.

What will you do when the pained one's daughter comes to you? The words echoed in Thalion's mind, as loud as if AeresThonEsia stood beside him. He froze.

Serana looked up at him in confusion. "Thalion, I'm engaged to the king!" she said. "I can't!"

Fear, the feeling of being balanced on a knife's edge. Then he committed, and fear fell away, replaced with excitement. "Why not?" he asked. His mind raced through the possibilities. "You don't want to marry him, he never asked you for your consent. Why can't we just get married instead?"

Her eyes were wide. "You mean elope?" she whispered.

He nodded, his thoughts still whirling. "If we just get married, then there's nothing anyone can do about it!" he exclaimed. "You can't marry the king if you're married to me! If you want to, of course," he stumbled, trying to bring his thoughts under control.

"Thalion..." Serana shook her head. "Thalion, he's the king! I'm sure there's a law somewhere that says a noble can't marry a woman betrothed to the king! Even if there isn't, Andreas would take it as a deathly insult! You might be banned from court. Your entire family could!"

Thalion shook his head. "Not if they don't have anything to do with it," he said. "Mother can pretend to denounce my actions, even though I'm sure she'll welcome you into the family."

Serana caught her breath. Thalion could see the hope warring with fear in her face.

"Serana." He stroked her cheek, marveling yet again at her beauty. "Serana, I love you, and I want to marry you. But I don't want you to do anything you don't want to."

"Oh, Thalion," Serana blinked. "I want to marry you, I do! But there's the king, and...and my mother..." her voice trailed off.

Thalion swallowed. "Your mother?"

Serana looked down. "She has been pushing me toward Andreas for the past few years," she said in a low voice. "This has been what she's wanted for me my entire life. If I betray her plans like this..."

Thalion frowned, trying to wrap his mind around how a parent could plan their child's entire life for them. Vinet never had. Vinet gave her children the tools and education they needed, but their lives were up to them. "Serana," he began. "You don't owe your mother anything. That's what she's wanted for you, but it isn't what you want for you." He frowned, trying to find the right words. "Serana, what do you want?" he finally said.

He could almost see the thoughts spinning in her head. He held his breath, waiting for her to speak.

"I want to marry you," she said.

Thalion felt a huge smile spread across his face. He stepped forward, pulling her to him for another kiss. She returned it with enthusiasm, wrapping her arms around him and pulling him even closer.

He broke away first, his mind spinning. "We need to get out of the capital now, then."

She stared at him. "Now? Tonight?"

He nodded, still thinking. "It's the best time," he said. "It might be the only time. Everyone's still busy at the feast and no one is watching you as queen-to-be yet. If we wait, there will be nobles around you every second as they prepare for the wedding."

Serana shuddered but took a deep breath. "You're right," she said. "So we just…go? Where to?"

"Ninaeva," Thalion said. "We'll be safe there, no matter the outcome of this." He thought for a moment. *Someone will follow us. Even if we leave without a trace, someone will guess and send guards after us. We have to plan for that.* He took a breath. "We'll get married before that, though."

Serana was watching him closely. "Where?"

Despite himself, a smile spread over his face. "There's a roadside temple a day's ride from the capital," he said. "My parents were married there. Would you…would you mind…it won't be fancy, not like a wedding at Ninaeva or at the capital would be…"

"But if someone follows us, then we'll already be married, and all their attempts to separate us will come to naught," Serana nodded and smiled shyly. "I don't mind getting married where your parents did."

Thalion fought the urge to kiss her again. They needed plans, not kissing. "Then we leave now," he said.

Serana's eyes widened. "As in immediately? Without luggage or anything? Thalion, I can't just walk out of the palace in this dress!"

Thalion flushed. She was still dressed in her sparkling silver gown that adorned her like a princess. He looked around. "Do you think Rian will mind if," he blinked. "Where is Rian?" In his shock at Serana's arrival, he had completely forgotten about the note that had sent him here to begin with.

Serana frowned. "I don't know," she said. "She told me to meet her here, but…" she shook her head.

Thalion's mouth fell open in realization. "She plotted this," he said. "She plotted to get us alone together, making us believe we were going to meet her!"

"Why would she do that?" Serana asked.

Thalion shrugged. His heart felt as light as a feather. "She's a good friend," he said. "I don't know if this was what she suspected would happen, but..." he grinned. "I doubt she'll mind if you borrow one of her gowns."

"Thalion!" Serana exclaimed. He couldn't tell whether she was offended or not. "I can't just take one of Rian's dresses!"

He blinked. "Will they not fit?" he asked. "She is a bit taller than you, but..."

Serana shook her head, and Thalion relaxed when he saw she was suppressing laughter. "I'll leave her this one in return," she said. "She can hide it, or sell it, far better than I can."

Thalion watched in bemusement as Serana went into the bedchamber and started going through the closet. She glanced at him over her shoulder.

"Don't watch," she ordered.

Thalion felt himself flush red, and he turned around, carefully not looking. He couldn't stop his mind from imagining, though. She was taking her dress off right behind him. He could hear the rustle of the fabric, and he could almost see her naked body, as the fabric swirled and draped and left her bare...

She coughed, and he jumped, tearing his mind away from where it had been drifting. "I'm ready," she said.

He spun back around and smiled. She had found a simple gown of forest green, complete with a split skirt for riding. "Perfect."

"To the stables, then?"

"You read my mind," Thalion took a deep breath before bowing elaborately. "May I escort you, my lady?"

A giggle slipped out of Serana before she smoothed her expression into a courtier's politeness. "I would be honored, my lord."

Thalion took her arm and led her out of the room. He slipped out, closing the door quietly behind them. "We need to be careful," he whispered. "We can't let anyone see us."

"Follow me," Serana said.

It took Thalion a moment to remember that she had grown up in the palace. She would know the best way out. He nodded, and she led him along the hallway, heading back in the direction of the great hall.

He froze at the sound of voices up ahead. "Where are you taking me?" It was a light female voice, one that spoke of too much flirtation and wine.

Thalion exchanged a panicked glance with Serana. They couldn't be seen, not if they were going to escape!

Serana swallowed, then grabbed his arm and pulled him back toward Rian's room. After two steps, both of them started running. Thalion let Serana take the lead, trusting that she knew how to get out of the palace safely.

"This way!" she hissed, tugging him to the right. He followed blindly, turning down one corridor, then another, until he was well and truly lost. Finally, she stopped in front of a door, breathing heavily.

"Where are we?" he asked.

She nodded at the door, still trying to catch her breath. "The gardens."

Thalion winced. Although everyone should still be at the feast, anyone who wanted a moment of privacy would doubtless be in the gardens.

Serana caught his expression. "I didn't know where else to go!"

He shook his head. "You got us here," he said. "We'll figure it out." He attempted a smile. She returned it.

Thalion took a breath and turned back toward the door. "Right," he said. "Gardens are enclosed on the north, east, and west sides. But this one has multiple entrances." He closed his eyes, trying to remember. "If we can find the entrance that leads to the council chambers, that should do it."

"The council chambers?" Serana looked at him curiously.

"Mother always talks about going to the gardens during breaks in the council sessions. There has to be an entrance close by. And I bet that no one will be near the council chambers right now. Too busy celebrating."

Serana nodded. "Left or right?"

Thalion's eyes widened, and he managed to shrug. "I don't know where we are."

Serana bit her lip. "Then we'll go for it," she said. Underneath the uncertainty and fear, there was steel.

Thalion took her hand and gave it a light squeeze before turning to the doorway. He opened it in one swift motion, pulling Serana into the gardens behind him. He let out a breath of relief as he saw the surrounding hedges. Of course, hedges concealed every doorway except the main entrance. It was part of the illusion.

"Do you know where we are?" Serana whispered.

Thalion shook his head. "I need to see. Come on." He took her hand and peeked around the hedge. He jerked back as he caught a glimpse of two figures walking toward the hedges.

Serana's mouth opened in a question, but he shook his head frantically. She stilled as the figures came close enough to be heard.

"Do you know where Thalion went?"

Thalion froze. It was his sister's voice.

"No," Kishtar's voice was puzzled. "I haven't seen him since the feast."

Niara sighed. "I hope he's alright," she said. "I wish we could help."

It took all of Thalion's willpower not to step out of the hedges. Niara and Kishtar would help him, he was certain of that. But they couldn't. They would be watched and interrogated when his and Serana's disappearance was discovered.

Serana gave him a confused look as Niara and Kishtar moved out of earshot. "Why didn't you call them?" she asked.

Thalion swallowed. "If trouble results from us marrying, then I don't want it to fall on them," he said. "They have to be surprised."

"I don't want to be trouble for you, Thalion." Tears glinting in her eyes.

"No!" he exclaimed. He pulled her into an embrace. "You are worth any trouble, Serana. Any at all." He tried to think of something else to say and couldn't, so he leaned down to kiss her instead. When he broke away, she was smiling.

"We need to get to the stables," he said. "Let's go."

"Not so fast." A figure stepped around the hedge, his arms crossed over his chest.

Thalion instinctively pushed Serana behind him and reached for a sword that wasn't on his belt. He stared at the newcomer, his eyes wide. It took him several seconds to take in the pointed ears and the burgundy livery of Lord Auriel.

"Saihid!" Serana exclaimed.

Thalion blinked as Serana pushed herself forward. "Saihid," he said warily.

"Serana," Saihid's voice cracked. "What are you doing here?"

Serana glanced back at Thalion. "We're...we're..."

Thalion stepped beside her to hold her hand. He gave her an encouraging nod.

She straightened her shoulders. "We're eloping. I don't want to marry the king. I never have."

Saihid's eyes were tired as he gazed at the two of them. "Your mother has worked so hard for this."

Serana's lips tightened. "My mother never asked me if I wanted her to work for it!" she exclaimed. "If she had, I would have told her how I felt about Andreas!"

Saihid closed his eyes, looking even more tired than before. He opened them and turned to Thalion. "And you?"

Thalion swallowed. "I love Serana," he said.

Saihid stared at him for a long moment, then sighed. "Are you certain this is what you want, Serana?"

"I'm certain," Serana's voice was firm. "And if you dare tell my mother about this, I'll, oh, I don't know what I'll do, but I'll think of something!"

A ghost of a smile flickered across Saihid's face. "I'm sure you would." He looked at Serana a moment longer, then at Thalion. "Travel safe."

Thalion nodded. "Of course." He extended a hand as a thought occurred to him. "You could come with us."

"To Ninaeva?" Saihid asked, startled.

"Do!" Serana exclaimed. She took her father's arm. "Come with us."

Saihid shook his head as if he was waking from a dream. "I will think on that," he said. "I think I will stay here and divert suspicion from your absence for now, my child." He smiled at Serana.

Serana pulled her father into an embrace. "Thank you," she whispered.

Saihid met Thalion's eyes, and Thalion could see the unspoken message in them. *Take care of my daughter.* He inclined his head in understanding, and Saihid nodded back.

"You're right to leave now," Saihid said. "I already overheard Lady Pellalindra talking about wedding planning. You need to get to the stables. The city gates will close for the night soon."

Thalion blinked. He hadn't even thought about the city gates! "Can you help us?"

Saihid chuckled. "Easily enough. Come."

They were closer to the stables than Thalion had hoped. Two turns through the hedges, and they were at another gate, this one smelling faintly of horse.

Saihid hesitated. "I can get a stable boy."

Thalion shook his head. "I'll saddle the horses. Thank you, Saihid."

Saihid acknowledged his thanks with a brief nod, then embraced his daughter one more time. "Be happy, child."

"I will, Father," Serana said. "I love him."

Saihid sighed. "Then may this bring you joy." He stepped back into the shadows. "Safe journey."

Thalion swallowed at the jumble of emotions on Saihid's face. Pride and love mixed with fear, pain, and a desperate longing. He suppressed a shudder as he took Serana's arm. "Come on," he whispered.

Serana waved one last time to her father, then followed him through the gate. Thalion let out his breath in relief. They were at the stables. One hurdle passed.

"Hurry, Thalion!" Serana called.

Thalion refrained from answering that he was hurrying. His horse's hooves echoed on the cobblestones as he and Serana galloped toward the gate. Serana clung to her saddle, yielding her reins to Thalion so that she could focus on maintaining her seat. The heavy iron portcullis was visible even from this distance, several blocks away. As he watched, torchlight glinted off the metal bars as they began to lower. His heart sank. They weren't going to make the gate in time.

"No!" Serana exclaimed. "Thalion, what do we do?"

Thalion's mind raced furiously. They couldn't wait in the city till morning. There were too many people, and their absence would be discovered before long. The city would go on lockdown until they were found, now that Serana was betrothed to the king. They needed out tonight.

"Hold on tight!" he yelled. He shifted his weight, urging his horse to a faster pace and slapped the reins of Serana's horse. Serana gasped and grabbed her saddle horn even tighter.

Thalion heard the creak of iron as they drew closer. He leaned down on his horse, whispering a prayer to Mazda under his breath. He wasn't certain this would work.

The portcullis was halfway down, and two guards stood at the opening, torches in their hands. Thalion ground his teeth and leaned further down, urging his horse faster and faster. He could hear the hooves of Serana's horse right beside him.

One of the guards turned around as he heard their approach. His eyes widened. "Halt! In the name of the King!"

"Don't stop!" Thalion shouted. They would make it, if they just kept going!

"Thalion!" Serana shrieked.

Thalion swallowed as he saw the guard draw his weapon. He tightened his grip on the reins and urged his horse to keep moving forward. If the guard didn't get out of the way, that would be his own fault.

Only a few yards separated them when the guard thought the better of his actions. The guard jumped to the side, and Thalion flew underneath the slowly lowering portcullis. He glanced to the right to see Serana right beside him, her eyes wide.

"We need to keep going!" he yelled.

"Thalion! I can't hold on much longer!"

"Just follow me!" Thalion tried to be encouraging, but he knew she was right. They couldn't keep this pace up, not for long. For one, it would exhaust the horses, and second, the faster they went, the more likely it was that one of the horses would trip and break a leg. But they needed to get just a little further from the city walls.

Thalion blessed his elven heritage as they galloped down the path. He could see the path before him, even if his horse couldn't. He guided it down the curves until they were a fair distance from the city gates. Only then did he reign the horses in, patting his horse's neck to help it calm down.

Serana took a deep breath beside him, her green eyes shining in the darkness. "That was...Thalion, what did we just do?" she exclaimed.

Thalion let out a relieved laugh. "Escaped the capital with no one the wiser?"

Serana stared at him a moment longer before breaking into weak laughter herself. "I think we did!" she said. "I think we actually did!"

Thalion grinned at her. "Are you up for riding some more? We have a fair distance to cover still."

Serana nodded. "How far do we go tonight?"

"The temple is a few hours from here," Thalion said. "We should be able to spend the night there, as well. The priest knows my family."

"Then let's go," Serana said.

They set off again, this time at a pace meant for endurance. They rode side by side in the darkness. Thalion kept glancing over at Serana, unable to believe that she was actually there.

She finally caught him. "Why do you keep looking at me?"

He flushed. "You just...I can't believe you're here," he said. The words sounded inadequate as soon as they were out of his mouth, but she smiled.

"I can," she said.

Thalion felt warmth coil within him, and he forced himself to turn his attention back to the road. Just because they were moving at a slower pace didn't mean the horses could see.

It seemed forever until the lights of the Temple of Mazda came into view on the roadside. Thalion exchanged a relieved glance with Serana as they urged their horses the last few hundred yards forward.

"Hail, travelers!" a voice called. "You're out late."

Thalion raised a hand in greeting to the young man approaching them. He was a novice, by his robes. "Indeed we are," he said. "And a long road ahead of us, as well."

The novice blinked as he drew closer. "My lord of Ninaeva?" he asked.

Thalion grinned. Occasionally it was useful to be recognized so readily. "His son," he answered. "Is Father Boilli about, brother? We have business for him."

The novice glanced at Serana and raised an eyebrow, causing her to flush. The novice chuckled. "I'll take your horses, my lord. Father Boilli should have finished evening prayers."

Thalion nodded and gratefully dismounted. He offered a hand to Serana, and she stumbled a bit as she dismounted, falling against him. He caught her, feeling her body warm against his. He hesitated. "Are you certain?" he asked. All at once, doubt filled him. What if she was just fleeing from the king? What if she had changed her mind during their wild flight? What if...

His thoughts were chased away as she leaned up to kiss him. He closed his eyes, savoring her warmth, the feeling of her lips, the tingles that raced through his entire body. He suppressed disappointment as she pulled away.

"Does that answer your question?" she asked, smiling.

He took a deep breath to steady himself. "I...yes," he managed.

"Good," she took his hand and led him toward the temple.

Thalion blinked at the transition from darkness into the light of the temple. A temple of Mazda was never dark. It remained lit all through the night, as a beacon and guide for those who were lost until Mazda's light shone on them again.

He took another deep breath as he saw the priest approaching them, questions in his eyes. He squeezed Serana's hand and pulled her closer to him.

"Lord Thalion?" Father Boilli asked. "What brings you here so late at night? Who is your companion?"

Thalion glanced at Serana. "This is my betrothed, your radiance," he said. "It would be a great honor if you could marry us tonight."

Thalion saw Father Boilli's eyebrows shoot upward. "Tonight? Not at a wedding back in Ninaeva?"

Thalion shook his head. The urge to explain to the priest bubbled up inside him, but he firmly shoved the words down.

Father Boilli gave Thalion a piercing look, then shifted his gaze to Serana. "What is your name, my child?"

Thalion saw her hesitate. "Serana," she said.

Father Boilli's eyes gentled. "And your family name, my child?"

Thalion saw Serana swallow. "I...Auriel," she whispered. "I am Serana Auriel."

"The daughter of the regent?" the priest's eyebrows rose again. "Thalion, are you certain about what you are doing?"

"She's more than the daughter of the regent, your radiance," Thalion said, making the decision in an instant. "She was betrothed to the king earlier today."

He heard Serana's anguished gasp. "Thalion!" she whispered.

Thalion met Father Boilli's eyes steadily, praying that he had made the right decision.

"The king, hmm?" Father Boilli said. "I begin to see." He turned to look at Serana. "Were you given a choice in that betrothal, my child?"

Serana shook her head emphatically. "No, I was never asked! And if they had, I would have told them that Thalion had already asked for my hand."

Father Boilli nodded. "Then you must honor that first arrangement. It is settled, then. Come to the altar, and we shall have a quick, private ceremony."

Thalion released a shuddering breath. He hadn't expected to win the priest over that quickly.

"You will do that for us?" Serana seemed equally startled.

Father Boilli glanced back as he walked toward the altar. "There are times when one's conscience must rise above the dictates of the law," he said. "I fear the temple will face many of those times, in the years to come."

Thalion suppressed a shudder at that enigmatic statement. Instead, he turned to Serana, taking both of her hands in his. "I love you," he whispered.

She leaned forward to kiss him briefly. "I love you too." They walked hand in hand to the altar, where Father Boilli waited for them with a benevolent smile. They had made it. They were going to be married.

The ceremony was quick and simple, a solemn exchange of vows. The priest called in two of his novices as witnesses, including the one who had stabled their horses. He gave Thalion a wink before signing the document that Father Boilli hastily wrote up.

"You will stay here the night, of course," Father Boilli said. "There is a private guestroom you may have."

Thalion exchanged a look with Serana, a shiver of anticipation and nervousness running down his spine. A private chamber. They were married, now.

Serana didn't seem inclined to answer the priest, so Thalion did it for them. "Thank you, your radiance," he said. "You have our heartfelt gratitude."

Father Boilli inclined his head. "A small service to one whose family is so devoted to the temple. May I reassure your father of your safety, when he next passes through here?"

Thalion smiled. "You may tell my father, and any other members of my family, the entire story," he said. "Tell them we will see them in Ninaeva."

Father Boilli nodded. "I will. Now, you must be exhausted, and you have a long ride ahead of you." He gestured at one of the novices. "Show them to their chamber."

The novice led them through the corridors of the temple until they reached a small room. The only furnishings were a bed and wash-basin, and there were no decorations, but to Thalion it seemed perfect.

"You are welcome to join us for the morning meal, though I fear it is not the fare you are used to," the novice said.

Thalion smiled. "Thank you. I've eaten here before, and it will be wonderful."

The novice bowed before he left the room. Thalion shut the door and turned to Serana. She was staring at the bed, uncertainty on her face.

"Serana?" he asked. "What is it?"

She met his eyes. "I...oh, Thalion, it's nothing, I shouldn't..."

Thalion's eyebrows drew together. "It's not nothing," he said. "What's worrying you?"

She stepped forward, and he instinctively took her into his arms. She laid her head against his shoulder, and he felt a moment of relief and protectiveness.

"I'm terrified, Thalion," she admitted. "I just...I have just destroyed any chance of my mother's dreams for me ever coming true. I can't imagine how she will take the news."

Thalion dearly wanted to tell Serana that her mother's opinion hardly mattered, but he knew that was the wrong thing to say. Instead, he stroked her hair. "Well, you may not have married the king, but you've still married a noble, and from a powerful family at that," he said, attempting to sound light-hearted. "She'll come around when she realizes that I'll provide for you."

Serana choked on a laugh. "Oh, Thalion," she said. "You don't understand. The things my mother has said about your family..." she shook her head. "Your mother's position is the only reason she associated with you at all."

Thalion quickly suppressed a flare of anger. "Because of my father," he said.

She nodded. "I think my mother believes the rumors, that he's the child of a demon. But how would the child of a demon be such a devout Mazdian?"

A surge of relief rushed through him. She did not believe his father demon spawn. She did not believe him descended from demons either, then.

"Well, maybe you can tell her that," he said, stroking her hair again. "We'll visit the capital together when everything has settled down a bit. You can talk to her then, and everything will be better."

He felt her smile against his shoulder. "You make it sound so easy."

He shrugged. "Well, it might not be easy," he admitted. "But we'll manage. I promise."

She looked up at him gratefully. "I love you, Thalion et-Alim."

He smiled down at her. "And I love you, Serana…et-Alim," he said hesitantly. What would she think of her new name?

"Serana et-Alim," she said, trying the name out on her tongue. "I like it."

He relaxed in relief. "I'm glad." He stared at her a moment longer. She was his wife. His wife.

"We should probably go to bed," he said. "The priest was right, we have a few long days ahead of us." He shifted as his body responded. Bed. Would she be…did he dare…

Serana flushed. "I…Thalion, I…" she turned even brighter red. "Thalion, I don't know what to do."

He blinked, feeling a surge of heat rush through him. "I…you don't?" he managed.

She shook her head and looked down. "No. Mother thought…it wasn't proper ladies' education."

Thalion felt a surge of gratitude toward his father, who had carefully explained everything that Thalion had ever wanted to know and answered every question Thalion had had. He took a breath. "Well, I think I know, at least in theory," he said. "Do you…do you want to?"

She flushed even brighter but nodded as she reached hesitantly to stroke his cheek. "You are my husband," she whispered. "I want that to be beyond doubt."

He groaned, her words sending a flare of heat through him. He pulled her forward and kissed her. She responded passionately, bringing her arms around him and tangling her hands in his hair.

He pulled away and took a few deep, steadying breaths. Slowly, his father had said. Slowly.

"Let's learn about each other, then," he said. "We have time."

9

NINAEVA

Thalion didn't bother trying to restrain his smile. The gentle clip clop of their horses' hooves was the only sound aside from the breeze blowing through the trees. He could not imagine a more perfect scene. He and Serana, husband and wife, traveling back to Ninaeva.

"Where are we going to stop for the night?" Serana asked.

Thalion shook himself out of his reverie. "I…" he shook his head. "I hadn't thought about it," he admitted, rather sheepishly.

Serana smiled at him, her eyes warm. "Well, we have to stay somewhere between here and Ilhelm. How long will it take?"

"About a week," Thalion was surer of himself there. After all, he had been accompanying his mother on her trips to the capital since he was old enough to walk.

Serana nodded. "Then where will we stay? I assume you and your family have regular stops along the route?"

"Regarding that…" Thalion hesitated. "I don't know if we can stay at any of those inns," he said. "I didn't exactly bring much money with me when we escaped."

Serana blinked. "Oh," she managed. "I didn't even think about that."

Thalion hesitated. "I, ah, don't suppose you had any on you?"

She shook her head, and Thalion felt his heart sink. *Not much money might still be an exaggeration. I hardly have any. Definitely not enough to last a week. Barely enough for food for a week.* At least the priest had given them some provisions, enough for a day.

He thought frantically. "I think we'd better pause at the next village we ride through," he said slowly. "Long enough to buy a few supplies. A blanket, for one. And a tinderbox."

Serana looked dubiously at him. "Why?"

Thalion took a breath. "Because we'll be camping tonight, and perhaps most of the nights until we reach Ninaeva."

Serana's eyes widened. "Camping? Sleeping outside?"

He nodded warily. "Is that…"

"But that's something commoners do!" she exclaimed. For a moment, Thalion could almost hear Pellalindra saying those words to her daughter. She seemed to realize the similarity at the same moment, for she flushed bright red. "Not that that's a bad thing, I just…I mean…" she stuttered to a halt.

Thalion forced a laugh. "Think of it as an adventure!" he said. "We'll have fun together, preparing a campsite, just the two of us." As he spoke, he felt himself warm to the idea.

Serana appeared uncertain. "But we don't have a tent. Or anyone to set one up for us. And what will we eat? And how will we wash tomorrow?" Her voice grew more and more distressed.

"Hey," Thalion kneed his horse closer to hers and leaned over to put a hand on her shoulder, carefully keeping his other gripped on the reins. "Serana, it'll be fine. We'll have an adventure."

"Thalion, are you sure you don't have enough for an inn?" she asked pleadingly.

Thalion sighed and gave her the sparse number of coins in his pouch. It would be enough for three nights, perhaps, but not the entire journey.

She blinked. "Is this a lot?"

"What?" Thalion asked in astonishment.

"Never mind." Serana flushed bright red again. "Don't mind me."

He frowned. "No, what's the matter?" he asked.

Serana looked down at her horse's head. "I never learned anything about money," she said, so quietly that Thalion had to strain to hear her.

Thalion sat up straight in his saddle with shock. "You what?" he exclaimed.

Serana flushed even brighter. "It's not my fault!" she protested. "Mother said my husband would always take care of those details. She said," she paused, "she said I should worry more about my deportment and etiquette."

Thalion stared at her in incomprehension. "But what if you had to travel separately from your husband?" he asked. "Or make a trade deal for your husband's house? Or impress a foreign ambassador?" The more he thought about it, the more confused he got. "Or what if you had gotten lost during your travels from Duskryn to the capital? Or just wanted to go out for a private shopping excursion?"

Serana refused to meet his eyes. "Mother thought it unladylike," she mumbled. "And I was never supposed to be out on my own."

"Never..." Thalion trailed off, stunned. In that instant, he felt a sharp dislike of Pellalindra, who had raised her daughter so perfectly in the image she wanted, without giving her any tools of surviving on her own. "Alright, we're fixing this," he declared.

Her head jerked up. "What do you mean?"

"You're learning about money," he said. "It's a necessary survival skill. I'll teach you the basics, and when we get to the village, you can bargain for the supplies."

Serana's eyes widened. "Bargain? Me?"

Thalion nodded, determination for the idea growing. "Why not?" he said. "Now, you tell me what you already know."

Serana gave him a sideways glance. She obviously had severe doubts about this exercise, but Thalion was not about to back down. *She needs to learn this. What if we get separated on the road? I'll give her half my money when we get to the village; I should have done before this. And she'll need to learn, living in Ninaeva. We're built on trade, she'll come into constant contact with it.*

They spent the next few hours riding with Thalion explaining the basics of currency, mercantile transactions, and wandering into the realm of trade and investments. Serana did not appear to understand the last part at all, but she performed admirably under Thalion's direction when purchasing a blanket, tinderbox, washcloth, and eating utensils. She was flushed with triumph when she concluded the last bargain, and Thalion barely restrained himself from taking her in his arms and kissing her passionately right in front of the entire village.

The rest of the day's riding was also concluded in an equally satisfactory manner. Light still lingered when Thalion found a small clearing off the side of the road to use as a campsite, but it was Manyu's Rise. The darkness would be fast approaching.

Serana glanced uneasily around the clearing. "What do we do?" she asked.

Thalion suppressed his own uncertainty and attempted to appear as confident as possible. "First, we light a fire," he said. "We're going to want one tonight. Would you like to gather some wood while I see to the horses?"

Serana agreed, and Thalion unsaddled both horses and made sure the horses were tethered to a tree with enough lead to graze. He was finished when Serana came back into the clearing dragging a branch behind her. He gave her an approving nod and set about breaking it into smaller bits.

Serana watched him, struggling to get her breath back. "We're going to need a lot more for the night," he said after he finished breaking the branch apart. "Come on."

They went back out into the woods and dragged more branches into the clearing. They had a decent pile of wood before long, and Thalion regarded it uneasily.

"I don't suppose you know how to set a fire?" he asked.

Serana gave him a look that spoke volumes. *No, of course she doesn't. When would she ever have to learn that? I certainly didn't have to.*

"Right," he swallowed, attempting to appear confident. "It can't be that difficult."

Serana greeted his pronouncement with evident relief. "I'll go through the provisions for supper," she said.

Thalion stared at the pile of wood, misgivings rising in him. He had never set a fire in his life. Servants usually had one set up and burning by the time he wanted one.

He grabbed a few of the branches and started stacking them, trying to remember how the wood was laid out in the fireplaces before the maids lit it. Once he produced a satisfactory stack, he opened the tinderbox. He ignored the bit of fluff and took out the flint and steel.

It's too bad I don't have Mother and Niara's ability to just snap their fingers and light a candle, he thought. *That would make this process so much easier.* Sighing in resignation, he bent over the pile of wood and began striking the flint and steel together.

After a few minutes, he sat back in disgust. Sparks were flying in plenty, but even though most of them were landing on the wood, it remained stubbornly unlit.

"What's the matter?" Serana asked.

Thalion shook his head. "Nothing." *I need a fire for her tonight. It's Manyu's Rise, the night is going to be cold, even with the two of us sharing blankets.* He flushed a little at the thought.

He frowned at the bit of fluff in the tinderbox. It seemed a great deal of trouble just to have something to cushion the flint and steel, but perhaps it was so they didn't strike each other and cause sparks when they were being carried around. Though given the way the wood was behaving, it would take a great deal to set something alight. Unless it were something like cloth. Yes, he could see one of these sparks burning right through cloth and burning the clothes of whoever was carrying the flint and steel around themselves.

He nearly hit himself on the head. "Of course!" he exclaimed.

Serana glanced over him in puzzlement, but he ignored her as he dug out a bit of the fluff and placed it under the wood. He struck the flint and steel again, and was filled with momentary elation as the fluff instantly caught fire. The elation died with the flame, however, as the fluff quickly burned to cinders without lighting any of the wood.

He sat back on his heels in disgust. "How do people do this?" he asked aloud.

Serana came over to join him. "I think you have the wood stacked wrong," she observed.

"How would you know?" Thalion asked grouchily. "You've never lit a fire before either." He saw a flash of hurt in Serana's eyes, and immediately castigated himself. *Thalion, you idiot!* "Serana, I'm sorry," he said, dropping the flint and steel and drawing her into an embrace. "I didn't mean that. I'm just frustrated, is all."

Serana blinked as she looked up and smiled tremulously. "I see that," she said. She took a deep breath, and he could feel her spine straightening. "But I am right. The small wood needs to go on the bottom. It lights quicker." He could see the flash of uncertainty in her eyes, the fear that he was going to snap at her again. A lump of guilt rose in his throat, and he leaned down and kissed her soundly before drawing back to examine the firewood. He felt like an idiot. "You're brilliant. How did you think of that?" he asked, shuffling the wood around to a better position.

Serana shrugged, but he could see pleasure sparkling in her eyes. "I've watched a lot of fires," she admitted. "When Mother wanted me to practice my embroidery, or something equally boring. The fire was a way to entertain myself while I listened to ladies ramble on about all kinds of dull things."

Thalion chuckled. "I don't suppose you know any way to get this fluff burning long enough to light one of those twigs?"

Serana frowned thoughtfully. "I don't know," she said. "Maybe some leaves?"

It seemed worth a try to Thalion. "There's plenty on the ground."

Together, they scraped together a handful of leaves and piled them underneath their wood. Thalion took another bit of fluff and struck the flint and steel again. Like before, the fluff caught instantly. This time, he was careful to hold the fluff close to the leaves. To his delight, they began smoldering straight away.

"Blow on it!" Serana exclaimed. "I've seen the maids do it!"

Thalion obediently blew on the smoldering leaves. He had to stop almost immediately, overwhelmed with a fit of coughing. Serana made a worried exclamation and hurried over to him, only to start coughing herself as a cloud of smoke hit her in the face.

Eyes streaming, Thalion managed to move himself and Serana to the other side of the fire. The smoke seemed to follow them, and a few minutes passed before they could get a breath of fresh air. Serana exclaimed gratefully, and Thalion smiled wryly at her. The fire had started to crackle and pop as the wood lit.

"We have a fire!" he exclaimed, pulling her into an embrace.

His enthusiasm was infectious, and Serana laughed. "And we have dinner," she said. "Although I'm afraid it's just bread and cheese."

"With you, anything is a feast," Thalion said gallantly. He drew her close to him as they sat next to the fire, eating their sparse meal. They sat in silence until the sun touched the horizon.

"We should get some sleep." He stood up and retrieved the rough-spun blanket from their pile of belongings. He spread it on the ground, smiling briefly at the cheerful yellow and red plaid, and bowed to Serana. "May I escort you to your chamber, my lady?"

Serana giggled and walked over. The two of them bundled up in the blanket, huddled close to each other.

"Serana?" Thalion asked. "You don't regret this, do you?" *How could she not? I'm making her sleep outdoors, in the open air, and making her do things her mother would never approve of. This isn't the way she's used to being treated. She's a noble lady!*

She snuggled closer to him. "Never," she whispered. "As you said, it's an adventure."

Thalion smiled in relief. "Good," he said. He kissed her forehead. "Goodnight, my love."

He was asleep in almost an instant and had no notion of how much time had passed when a huge drop of water hit him in the face.

The fire had burned low, but there were still coals. He sat up and blinked in confusion as Serana stared at him, her expression pained.

"Thalion, it's starting to rain!" she exclaimed.

Thalion had never felt as much gratitude as he did when they finally reached Ilhelm Castle. Both he and Serana were hungry, cold, grimy, and had no wish to spend another night outdoors ever again. He couldn't quite believe they had survived.

They were welcomed back by Vinet's seneschal. He greeted the announcement that Thalion had married with raised eyebrows but made arrangements for Thalion's quarters to be converted into rooms fitting for a married couple.

Thalion watched Serana throw herself into the redecorating of the rooms with amusement. Together they argued amicably over the layout of the chambers, and their vision slowly took shape together, their living quarters becoming a place that shared both of their wishes.

It was near the end of a week that they found themselves in the garden, plotting out a section for Serana's special use. She was enamored of the northern plants. "Thalion, these are wonderful!" she exclaimed.

Thalion's breath caught as she twirled in delight. She was so beautiful. What had he done to deserve her?

"I can plant anything I want here?" she asked. "You're certain?"

"Positive," Thalion affirmed. They had chosen a section of the garden Vinet had always intended to have the gardeners 'do something' with. Thalion knew she wouldn't mind.

Serana threw her arms around his neck and kissed him. "I love you," she said.

Thalion's head spun with happiness as he returned the kiss. He started as a memory occurred to him and pulled back, removing Serana's arms from his neck. "Wait here," he said.

Serana blinked, startled, but Thalion didn't give her any time to respond as he ran for the seneschal's study. He would know where it had been put.

The seneschal raised his head as Thalion entered. "Lord Thalion?" the young man asked, voice puzzled.

"Do you know where the plant I bought during Dragon's Day is?" Thalion demanded.

The seneschal nodded in comprehension. "In your mother's study, I believe. She didn't know what you intended to do with it once you left to finish the tour."

Thalion stammered out his thanks before rushing to Vinet's study. There, on the table, was the small potted plant with the tiny blue flowers. He picked it up carefully and headed back to the garden.

Serana was still waiting for him, a bemused expression on her face. Her eyes widened when she saw what he was carrying. "Are those veildrops?" she asked, her voice awed.

Thalion nodded. "Consider these a wedding present," he said, holding the plant out to her. "You can start your garden with them."

Serana took the plant from him, her expression still incredulous. "You bought these for me? Thalion, do you know how rare these are?"

Thalion shrugged, trying to appear casual. "They reminded me of you," he said.

Serana set the plant down on a stone bench and flung her arms around him. Thalion caught her as she buried her face into his shoulder. "I love you so much," she whispered.

Thalion tightened his grip around her as satisfaction surged through him. Somehow, he had made her this happy. *I'll do everything in my power to keep you this happy, Serana. I promise.*

He pulled back so he could kiss her. When they broke the kiss, her eyes were still shining.

He smiled down at her. "Well, would you like to get started on the planting, or does that wait?"

Serana laughed. "Well, the veildrops can be planted now, but for the rest we need seeds, or saplings, and we need to turn the soil, and gather supplies..."

Thalion happily let her ramble, letting the sound of her voice wash over him. He obeyed when she put a trowel into his hands and told him where to dig, and together they lifted the veildrops from its pot and into the soft earth. Serana patted the dirt back into place with a satisfied expression.

"Now we just wait for it to grow," she said.

Thalion gave her another kiss. "They're beautiful. But not as beautiful as you."

Serana giggled and allowed him to draw her close. Thalion was just about to suggest retiring to their chamber when he heard an apologetic cough behind them. He turned to see the seneschal standing there.

"Lord Thalion, Lady Serana. You may wish to know that Lady Vinet's party has been sighted." The seneschal bowed.

Thalion felt a surge of apprehension that he quickly suppressed. Whatever the consequences, his mother would welcome Serana into their household as if she was her own daughter.

Serana's apprehension was clearer. Thalion gave her a reassuring smile as he straightened and brushed the dirt off his breeches. "Thank you," he told the seneschal. He offered Serana his hand. "Shall we go welcome them home?"

She took his arm, still seeming uncertain. "Are you certain they'll welcome me?" she whispered.

Thalion smiled at her. "You're my wife." With those words came a feeling of intense protectiveness and love. "That makes you Ninaevan, and Mother protects Ninaeva."

Serana took a steadying breath. Thalion patted her arm but decided that any further reassurances would be wasted. *She'll see when Mother arrives.*

They walked arm in arm through the castle to the gates. They had just arrived when the horses of Vinet's party came into view. Vinet herself was in the lead, riding next to Nazir. Niara and Kishtar rode right behind her. Behind them rode Saihid, looking as solemn as ever, and Gwyn, who gave him a raised eyebrow.

Thalion took heart at the amusement on his father's face. Vinet's expression was more serious, but her expression lightened when she saw him.

"Thalion!" Kishtar exclaimed. He urged his horse through the gates and dismounted, pulling Thalion into a huge bear hug. "Thalion, you rascal! You didn't tell me a word!"

Thalion laughed and pounded his friend on the back. He was

saved from answering as his parents and sister approached, having left their horses with the servants. Saihid came forward as well and gave his daughter a brief kiss on the forehead. Thalion extracted himself from Kishtar's embrace and took Serana's arm again.

"Mother, Father," he said, nervousness rising in him despite himself. "May I present my wife, Serana et-Alim?"

Neither of them appeared surprised in the slightest. Nazir gave them both a broad smile. Vinet said not a word as she walked over and pulled her son into a hard embrace.

Thalion returned the embrace with confusion. "Mother?" he asked.

Vinet only shook her head as she released him and turned to Serana. "Welcome, daughter," she said. To Serana's evident surprise, Vinet embraced her as well.

Thalion took a deep breath. "I assume everyone at the capital knows we're married, then?"

"Oh, the rumors were certainly flying around. But we knew with more certainty than rumors," Vinet raised her eyebrows at Niara, who stepped forward.

Thalion stared at his sister, his mind rapidly comprehending his mother's hints. "You saw us?" he asked, accusation stinging his tone.

Niara shrugged. "You had disappeared! I was worried about you." She shook her head. "That was the first vision I actually managed to call by myself."

Thalion couldn't decide whether to be offended that she had spied on him, or touched that she had been worried.

"Excuse me, saw us?" Serana asked. "How is that possible?"

Vinet turned a questioning gaze to Thalion. "How much have you told her?"

Thalion flushed. Over the course of the two weeks, he had told Serana most of their family secrets. "She knows," he confirmed. He squeezed Serana's hand. "The Sight," he explained.

Serana's mouth opened in a little 'o', and she stared at Niara with wide eyes.

Vinet nodded. "Good," she said. "That saves us an explanation."

Thalion glanced between his mother and father. There was something they hadn't yet said. "Is everything alright at the capital?" he asked.

"Inside," Vinet sighed. "We'll discuss things in the library."

Without protesting, Thalion led Serana back inside the castle. The rest of the family followed, and in short order, they were seated in the library. Thalion sat beside Serana on a small sofa. She leaned against him, and a tingle of warmth ran down his spine.

Vinet smiled as she regarded the two of them. "First, you should know that I approve of your marriage, and of the way you accomplished it. Much as I do wish I could have witnessed it, it was better for everyone this way."

Thalion relaxed. Whatever else had happened, his parents approved. That was the most important thing.

Vinet sighed. "Nevertheless, as I'm sure you're aware, there were complications. The king is absolutely furious. He made a number of decisions that I'm not certain he knows the consequences of."

Thalion felt a surge of foreboding. "Like what?"

"I am no longer Lady of the Council," Vinet said. She held up a hand to forestall Thalion's protest that she had nothing to do with his elopement. "There is no longer a Council to be Lady of. We have all been sent home, except for Lord Percival, who is intimately involved in the planning of the king's next campaign."

"Campaign?" Thalion frowned.

"From what I heard, he is planning a campaign this Manyu's Time. There are no councilors left to tell him how foolish a notion that is. Lord Auriel could, but he," Vinet pressed her lips together. "He is as silent and suspicious as always."

"Suspicious?" Serana exclaimed. She flushed. "I mean..."

Vinet shook her head. "I have been suspicious of Lord Auriel for nearly twenty years," she said. "I have nothing to base that off of, and he has done nothing to warrant such suspicion, but," she shrugged. "He had said nothing about the fact that his daughter eloped rather than marry the king. I know he's not your father," Vinet said to Serana, "but to the rest of the world he still is."

Serana glanced at Saihid, then back down at the floor without answering.

Vinet continued. "For all intents and purposes, we are banished here, as are," she cut off, her eyes wide. The blood drained from his mother's face as she grabbed the edge of her chair. Her eyes stared off into the unknown distance.

"Vinet!" Nazir exclaimed, moving to her side.

"Mother!" Niara was on her feet in an instant, moving to grab her mother's hand. Thalion stood as well, hovering uncertainly. Niara looked up in shock. "It's not working! I can't share it!" she exclaimed.

Nazir held Vinet's shoulders and began murmuring soothingly. It seemed like an eternity before Vinet gasped and nearly doubled over, only caught by Nazir.

Thalion watched, fear rising in him as his mother gazed up at Nazir. Her face was as white as snow. "Nazir," she whispered. "It's time. I need to leave."

The next few hours were a whirlwind. Nazir and Vinet disappeared without explanation into Vinet's private quarters. Thalion tried to ask Niara what such an announcement might mean, but Niara refused to discuss it, turning as pale as their mother at the very mention. Gwyn was restless. Evalynna, Gwyn's fellow bodyguard and lover, appeared and tried to calm her down, but Gwyn refused to listen, watching everything like an anxious rabbit.

Thalion was extremely relieved when his parents re-entered the library. His relief quickly vanished, however, when he saw his mother dressed in a sturdy leather tunic and boots. His father appeared calm, but Thalion didn't dare read the emotions in his eyes.

"Vinet, what's going on?" Gwyn demanded.

Vinet's expression was one of sympathy. "I don't have much time, Gwyn. Please, get the leader of the Thorns."

Gwyn pressed her lips in protest, but one quiet look from Vinet sent her out of the room.

Thalion shifted uneasily. Everyone else stood around, awkwardly waiting.

It seemed like an eternity until Gwyn returned, even though Thalion knew it could only have been a few minutes. She was accompanied by a tall elf, who bowed to Vinet as he entered.

"Good," Vinet said, relief in her voice. "You're here. You need to take the Thorns, and head to Alfheim. As many who can need to come here."

The elf's eyes widened. "This is from the Lady?"

"Yes," Vinet said. "I leave on my own journey as well. My daughter will welcome our people here in my stead."

The elf glanced briefly at Niara and nodded. "As you say." He bowed again and exited the room.

Vinet turned her attention to the rest of the room. "I need to leave now," she said. "It's my Exile. The Lady of Leaf and Lake has called me to become an Eye."

Niara let out a cry, and Thalion felt his own heart contract. He knew in vague terms what the Exile meant, but he did know it was dangerous.

"I'm coming with you," Gwyn demanded.

Vinet shook her head. "No, Gwyn, you cannot come with me." Despite the sympathy in her face, her voice was iron. "Not this time."

"No, you can't go without me." Desperation and stubbornness warred in Gwyn's expression. "You can't leave me, you can't!"

Vinet stepped forward and embraced Gwyn. Thalion blinked as he saw tears forming in Gwyn's eyes.

"You have served me long and faithfully, blood-sister," Vinet whispered. "This is my path, though, and mine alone. You could follow me, but you would die before you set foot on it. Believe me." She smiled, though it seemed forced to Thalion. "Besides, there is one last thing I must ask of you."

"Anything, Vinet," Gwyn said.

"Protect Nazir. He will stay here, while Thalion and Niara have their own mission." Vinet turned to regard her children.

Thalion felt his eyes widen. "We do?" he asked.

"Yes," Vinet's voice was as unyielding as steel. "You need to go north, you and Niara. Find the nephelm and bring a delegation back here to fully repair the passages under the castle. It is of the utmost importance."

"The nephelm?" Niara exclaimed. "Why? Why now? Why us?"

For the first time, his mother appeared uncertain. "I don't know," she said. "I only know you *have* to. For the sake of us all." She walked over and placed one hand on Niara's shoulder, another on Thalion's. "It has to be the two of you. Promise me you'll leave within the next two days."

Thalion couldn't say no to his mother like that. Despite the steel in her voice, he could sense the tremble in her hands, see the underlying fear in her eyes. "I promise, Mother."

"So do I," Niara said. "Mother…"

Vinet turned to fully regard her daughter. "I will return, daughter," she said. "I cannot say how or when, but I promise I will. Nothing could keep me from you." She took Niara's head in her hands and gently kissed her forehead. "You must be Lady of Ninaeva now, my dear."

Niara blinked, tears filling her eyes, but she nodded. Vinet stepped back and surveyed the room again.

Her expression softened as she walked over to his father. "Nazir," she whispered.

His father said nothing, just pulled her into a long, passionate kiss. Thalion felt tears sting his eyes as he watched them.

Vinet pulled away. "I need to leave," she said again. She met everyone's eyes one last time. "Farewell. Look after Ninaeva for me." She caressed Nazir's cheek one more time before walking out of the room.

Nazir stood stock still until she left, then crumpled into a chair. Thalion rushed to his father's side.

"Vinet, wait!" Gwyn called. Distantly, Thalion heard Evalynna call Gwyn back and heard Gwyn's anguished pleas, but his attention was focused on his father. The pain and despair in his father's face was almost more than he could bear.

"Father?" Thalion held his father's shoulders, barely processing his own grief and confusion. It still didn't seem real. His mother was such a fixture in his life. He couldn't imagine the castle without her. But she was gone.

Nazir met his eyes and pulled him into an embrace. Thalion held his father tightly, trying to impart some measure of comfort.

He felt a hesitant hand on his shoulder and looked up to meet Serana's eyes. His heart contracted again. She had been so quiet.

"Do you really need to go too?" she asked, her voice soft.

Thalion swallowed, remembering his promise. "Yes," he said.

Serana took a deep breath and turned her attention to Nazir. "Will you be going with them, Lord Nazir?" she asked.

Nazir shook his head. "No, no. I will stay here, look after," he gasped, "Look after Ninaeva until Vinet returns."

Serana nodded. "I'll stay with you," she said. Thalion drew breath to protest, and Serana met his eyes. "I'm not suited for such a journey," she said. "I would slow you and your sister down. Besides," she moved to whisper in Thalion's ear. "Your father should not be left alone right now. I can take care of him."

Thalion took Serana into his arms and kissed her. She returned the kiss before pulling back with a small smile.

Niara still stood stock still, staring after their mother. "Niara?" Thalion asked.

She shook herself. "Where's that old explorer's journal Mother had?" she asked. "What's was his name, Jimesseran? He went north two decades ago to make contact with the nephelm." She started moving through the library shelves.

Thalion frowned. "Niara," he said, standing up and moving to stand next to her. "Niara, what's the matter?"

"Nothing, nothing, I just," she swallowed. "We need to get moving. If Mother was this adamant, then it's something dreadfully important, even if she didn't know why."

"We will," he said. "But this instant?"

"Your sister's right," Gwyn's hoarse voice came from behind him. "The sooner you leave, the sooner you can return."

"I'll go with you," Kishtar said, moving out from the edge of the room where he'd stood quietly.

Thalion smiled in relief as Gwyn nodded shortly. "You'll need all the information we have," she said. "Niara, find that journal you mentioned. Thalion and Kishtar, start a supply list and give it to the servants to pack. Evalynna…"

"You and I are going to our quarters for a while," Evalynna said, stepping directly in front of Gwyn. "You don't fool me, my dear."

Gwyn stared at Evalynna, then her face crumpled. Evalynna took her in a quick embrace before leading her out of the room.

Thalion swallowed. He'd never seen Gwyn show that much emotion in his life.

"Thalion, let's take your father to his rooms," Serana said. "He should rest, as well."

Thalion seized upon the suggestion gratefully. "I'll meet you in the study," he told Kishtar.

Nazir rose to his feet as Thalion and Serana approached. "I heard you," he said. His voice was hoarse. "There's something you should see, first. Follow me."

Thalion furrowed his brow, but he and Serana followed Nazir through the castle, out into the garden, to the opening to the passage under the castle. The boulder had been completely moved away from the opening, and it was hidden under a veil of vines and leaves.

"You'll need all the information you can find," Nazir said, his voice still raw. He pushed aside the vines, and Thalion followed his father into the darkness. Serana clutched his hand tightly as she followed him.

Thalion blinked as his eyes adjusted to the dim light. Torches had been set up down the long stairway. The flickering light made the carvings and mosaics on the walls leapt out at him, almost as if they were alive. A proper bridge had been built over the chasm, although Serana clung to him as they crossed, and Thalion avoided looking down.

He suppressed a gasp when they reached the elaborate door. It stood wide open, the strange symbols glinting in the torchlight. *The passages under the castle! This is what Mother meant by that. How did they open the door?*

That wasn't the most shocking thing of all, though. Just before the open doorway was a strange statue, one of a monstrous humanoid eight feet tall, but crouched over and bent like a hunchback. The scaly skin and frightened eyes appeared almost lifelike. Thalion eyed it warily.

"How did that statue get there?" Serana whispered.

Nazir barely glanced back. "He's not a statue," he said. "Or, he shouldn't be. He's one of the nephelm."

Thalion's eyes widened even more. "What was he doing in Ninaeva?"

"He was cast out." Nazir sighed. "Your mother was searching everywhere for information, and he was the only nephelm she could find here in the south. He was not sane. He said the cure for what afflicted him is in here, so he opened it, but this happened." He gestured at the statue.

Thalion shuddered.

"And nothing else in here will do that to us?" Serana asked, her voice alarmed.

Nazir shook his head. "Vinet said not." He stared into the darkness. "She was talking about sending someone north, but I didn't think it would be you."

Thalion moved hesitantly forward to place a hand on his father's arm. Nazir gave him a brief smile before returning his gaze to the darkness.

"There are many, many doors in here," he said, "but we cannot open any of them. The nephelm are the only ones with the secret. This was one of their cities."

Thalion blinked. "A nephelm city beneath Ninaeva?" he asked.

Nazir nodded. "Over two thousand years ago. We don't know why they left, why they abandoned it, but they didn't destroy anything, as far as I can tell. Just sealed it off. The few items in the main room seem to work perfectly fine." His voice tightened. "Vinet and

I managed to translate some of the runes, so we know approximately what's here, but we need the nephelm to help us learn more."

"So that's why we're going north?" Thalion couldn't help the confusion in his voice.

"Yes," Nazir said. "Vinet was becoming more and more adamant that this place needed to be explored, needed to be rebuilt. After…" his voice broke, and Thalion tightened his hand on his father's arm. Nazir swallowed, then continued. "Before she left, she told me this place could be our salvation."

Thalion looked around, unable to see anything in the darkness that would lead to their salvation even with his elvish vision, but he knew better to question his mother's words.

"Father," Thalion heard his voice crack, and he drew Nazir in for another hug. "Father, what will we do without her?" he managed.

Nazir's hand ruffled Thalion's hair. "We'll survive. Somehow."

Thalion swallowed as he released his father. Somehow was not comforting.

Serana made a small sound, and Thalion immediately moved toward her, taking her into an embrace. She shivered as he held her, and he tightened his arms.

"Come back to me," she whispered. "Promise you'll come back to me, Thalion."

There was only one answer to that. Thalion leaned down to kiss her as long as he could. "I'll always come back to you," he whispered when they finally had to separate for air. "I promise."

10

———

THE NORTH

Thalion bent over the manuscript in his hands, reading the contents one more time. The record of Jimesseran's expedition north was their only lead to the nephelm city of Utgard.

He, Kishtar, and Niara sat around a table in a crowded Hillsdale inn. Smoke drifted from the fireplace where a minstrel sat playing a bawdy song. Barmaids moved through the crowd, serving mugs of ale and bowls of stew. Thalion had finished his own stew ages ago, but Niara's bowl still sat in front of her, almost untouched.

"So from here, we get a boat and journey northward, finding a landmark called N'Dar's Dagger and then sail through the Channel of Sorrows," he said. "We need a boat with oars because there's apparently no wind in the channel. Then we'll head east and find a road that Jimesseran assumed was the road to Utgard."

"And hope we don't run into his dragon," Kishtar said, furrowing his brow. He was starting in on his second bowl of stew.

Thalion put his head in his hands. "I thought dragons had been extinct for centuries."

Niara glanced up briefly. "I don't think they are." She returned her attention to her soup bowl.

154

Thalion exchanged a look with Kishtar. This had been typical of Niara's behavior since they'd left.

Mazda's light, Mother, why did you have to just up and leave? No warning, no plan, no...nothing. He sighed. *And now I'm stuck on a trip to the unknown with a sullen sister instead of spending the first few months of my marriage with my wife. Mazda's light.* He tried not to blame his mother. If he was honest, she had spoken of the Exile, and he had known that one day she would have to undergo it. But he had thought that day was years away.

"So, boat," he said. "Does anyone know the names of ship captains around here? Did Mother ever tell you any of her contacts here?" He stared at Niara, willing her to answer.

Niara blinked and looked up. "Yes," she said slowly. "I met a few, the last time Mother took me."

Thalion felt a brief flare of relief that his sister was actually answering a question. "Who would be the best one for a trip like this?"

"I don't know," Niara shook her head. "Mother did most of the talking, and we were talking about trade more than traveling."

"That's a start," Thalion nodded. "You must have some idea. Or at least a name so we can get started." *The sooner we get started on this Manyu-cursed trip, the sooner I can get back to Serana.*

"She met with a captain called Finrey Hollstein the longest," Niara said, frowning. "I think I remember where his house is."

Thalion exhaled in relief. "Then we can go there tomorrow morning and attempt to arrange passage," he said.

Niara didn't respond, merely returning her attention to her soup.

Mazda's light, Niara, Thalion thought, *You were outspoken enough during the royal tour. Why are you so quiet now?*

Kishtar met Thalion's eyes sympathetically. "Finrey Hollstein, then," Kishtar said. "Hopefully he'll let us hire a boat so we can get this over with."

"Get what over with?" the bright female voice made everyone at the table jump.

Thalion looked up at the woman standing next to the table. She was short, but with a presence that made her appear far taller than she was. Her red hair was cut in a bob just under her chin, and her eyes were the dark gray of the ocean. She regarded them all with a sparkling smile.

"Pardon, but I couldn't help overhearing your conversation," she said, still in the same bright voice. "I'm afraid if you're searching for Finrey Hollstein, you're out of luck." She gazed speculatively at Thalion. "My, but you're a handsome one. Spent some time on a ship in the south?"

Thalion flushed at the woman's lingering gaze. It seemed like she was undressing him with her eyes.

Kishtar rescued him. "He's a married man, my dear. I'm afraid you'll have no luck there." The suggestion in his voice that she'd have better luck with him was clear. Thalion suppressed a pang at the memory Kishtar's words conjured. Serana, smiling at him in front of the altar, kissing him…

"Such a shame," the woman said before turning her attention to Kishtar. Her smile widened. "If you're free, on the other hand…"

Niara looked up again and frowned at the woman, then stood up without a word, gathered the manuscript up, and headed toward the stairs.

Thalion shook himself out of his memories of Serana and sighed as he watched his sister walk away. He forced his attention back to the red-haired woman. "What do you mean, we'll have no luck with Finrey Hollstein?"

The woman eyed Kishtar a moment longer before returning her eyes to Thalion. "Finrey's dead," she said. "No one'll have any luck with him."

Thalion groaned. *There goes that easy solution.* "Do you know who else might be willing to let us hire a ship?" he asked.

The woman turned her dazzling smile back to him. "I might be willing."

Thalion blinked. "You have a ship? What's your name?"

"Lyra Hollstein." The woman's smile didn't dim. "Finrey's daughter and heir, and captain of the best crew in Hillsdale."

She's a captain? Then our search might be over quicker than we thought!

"What kind of ship do you have?" He asked, trying not to sound too eager.

"Big enough to suit your purposes," Lyra said. "Something about N'Dar's Dagger?"

Thalion glanced guiltily at Kishtar. He'd thought they'd been keeping their voices down. "Yes," he admitted. "Though I wish you hadn't heard that."

"But if I hadn't eavesdropped, you wouldn't have found me! Such a shame that would have been."

Kishtar laughed. "A shame, indeed! Why don't you join us for a drink, and we'll discuss this like civilized people?"

"Civilized?" Lyra slid into the seat next to Kishtar. "What if I don't want you to be civilized?" She raised her eyebrows suggestively at Kishtar.

Thalion frowned as Kishtar leaned toward Lyra in response. *You're engaged, Kishtar. Aren't you?* Kishtar met his gaze and shook his head with a grin.

"So what brings two handsome young men such as yourselves to Hillsdale with...who was that woman?" Lyra eyed Kishtar questioningly.

"Thalion's sister," Kishtar said, gesturing at Thalion.

Lyra blinked. "She's your sister?" she asked.

Thalion sighed at the disbelief in her voice. "Yes," he confirmed. "Ignore her silence, please. She's distracted."

Lyra nodded, then turned her attention back to Kishtar. "Are you going to answer my question, or am I going to have to get it out of you some other way?" The suggestive lilt was back in her voice.

Kishtar grinned, though Thalion could see the tinge of red on his cheeks. "Well, introductions first. My companion and brother-in-arms is Thalion, and I am Kishtar. We seek passage on a ship to go on a daring adventure of discovery, to a land far in the north, untouched by human hands."

Lyra raised an eyebrow. "Land far in the north, hmm? What do you expect to find there?"

Thalion answered before Kishtar could. "What stories have you heard?"

Lyra gave him an appreciative smile. "No tales of treasure," she said. "But strange rumors always come out of the north. Giants, dragons, other monsters…take your pick."

"And what do you think of those legends?" Thalion asked.

Lyra shrugged, and Thalion was struck by the spark of intelligence in her eyes. "There's always some truth to them, I'd say. Something's up there, for certain."

Kishtar leaned forward. "We're seeking the giants," he said. "The nephelm, to be precise."

Lyra blinked but otherwise showed no reaction. "And why are you seeking them?" she asked.

Thalion exchanged a glance with Kishtar. They hadn't ever discussed how much to reveal or hide. "Because of my mother," he finally answered.

Lyra raised an eyebrow. "I don't follow."

Thalion sighed. "My mother is the Lady of Ninaeva, a noble of Saemar," he said. "She found something that the nephelm have the answers to. My sister and I are going there to negotiate with them."

Lyra's eyes widened. "You're a noble's son?" she asked.

Thalion nodded. He wasn't surprised she hadn't immediately guessed. All of them were dressed in sturdy traveling garments rather than noble attire.

Lyra shifted her gaze to Kishtar. "And you?"

Kishtar shrugged. "I have a noble title," he admitted. "But unfortunately, or perhaps fortunately, I'm landless. Far less important than my friend here."

The words seemed to make Lyra relax slightly. "So you're not that much more important than an elder of Hillsdale, then," she said teasingly.

Kishtar smiled. "That would depend on who the elder is," he leaned forward suggestively. "And important to who." His mouth hovered just next to Lyra's ear.

"I see," Lyra was not as all displeased by Kishtar's forwardness. She brought her hand up to stroke her fingers down his neck to where his shirt opened.

Thalion cleared his throat, trying to control a flush. Kishtar pulled back with a grin and a wink at Lyra.

"Will you take us?" Thalion asked. "We have directions and a notion of how long the journey should take. Three weeks sailing, and then at least three weeks for us to contact and negotiate with the nephelm, then transport back. You'd be paid for the entire time, of course."

"Of course," Lyra said. She narrowed her eyes. "Just the three of you?"

"And four guards, and horses," Thalion said. He held his breath. Not all ships were prepared to have horses onboard.

"Easily done," Lyra said. "Seven bodies, seven beasts." She named a fee.

Thalion blinked a little at the steepness of the price, but immediately fell to bargaining. Lyra proved to be no amateur at negotiating. Thalion hesitated a little at the final price but shrugged his doubts away. *Mother said this was important. And knowing her, it's more important than gold.*

"It's a bargain," Lyra said, smiling broadly. "We'll be ready to leave in two days. It'll take me that long to round up my crew and load supplies."

Thalion smiled in relief. "A pleasure doing business with you, Lyra Hollstein," he said.

"You as well," Lyra said. "Though I'm thinking your friend might be able to give me even more pleasure." She raised her eyebrows suggestively at Kishtar.

Thalion decided that it was best if he take his leave before the two of them started outrageously flirting again. "I'll go tell Niara about the arrangements," he said, getting to his feet. "You two enjoy yourselves."

Kishtar laughed. "Oh, don't worry, we will!"

Thalion felt his ears burning at Lyra's husky laugh. *Mazda's light, maybe I should tell Kishtar that he really shouldn't marry Ianna if this is how he's carrying on.* He could never imagine flirting with anyone beside

Serana. When he glanced back, he saw Kishtar and Lyra kissing and quickly turned away, heat rushing through him. He knew very well what Kishtar and Lyra were about to get up to, and his body burned with desire for Serana. But Serana wasn't here. *This is going to be a long voyage.*

The air was as still as the dead. The water was like glass, without a ripple or wave. The rhythmic beat of the oars was the only sound for miles around.

Thalion rested on the deck of the ship, staring at the tip of land to the south. They had passed the jagged cliffs of N'Dar's dagger three days ago, but it was still visible, even from this distance. Two more days and they should reach the beach that Jimesseran's journal described.

"You're looking very thoughtful," Kishtar observed.

Thalion glanced at his friend. Kishtar had adapted to life onboard the ship with alacrity, wearing his shirt loose and tying his hair back like the sailors. He had also been sharing a bed with the captain, causing much speculation throughout the crew.

Thalion shrugged, trying to ignore a feeling of envy. He wished Serana could have accompanied them.

"We're almost there," Kishtar said. "Or at least, almost on land. Then we get to find the nephelm. I'd've thought you'd be excited about that."

Thalion shrugged again. Maybe if this expedition hadn't been foisted on him in such circumstances, he would have been more excited.

Kishtar was persistent. "Come on, Thalion. Just because your sister is all in a huff doesn't mean you have to be as well."

Thalion groaned. "I'm not in a huff," he protested.

Kishtar folded his arms across his chest. "Yes, you are, and it's been getting worse since we've been on the ship."

"I'm surprised you noticed, with all the time you've spent with

Lyra," Thalion muttered. He winced. He hadn't meant that the way it sounded.

Kishtar merely raised an eyebrow. "Thalion! Surely you wouldn't ask me not to flirt with Lyra?"

Thalion groaned. "You've been doing more than just flirting," he shifted toward the railing as his body reacted uncomfortably. He knew what Kishtar had been up to at night, and he was jealous.

Kishtar leaned against the railing next to him. "She's an amazing woman, Thalion."

Thalion shook his head. "And was Ianna also an amazing woman?" He winced as the words left his mouth.

Kishtar drew back as if stung. "What?" he asked.

The pain inside him sent more words out. "At least you didn't promise Lyra anything," he said.

Kishtar flinched. "What does that mean?" he demanded.

Thalion threw his hands up. "I don't know!" he exclaimed. "First you love Ianna, then you sleep with Lyra, and you're doing it while everything else seems to be falling apart."

"Don't think I'm not feeling guilty about that already," Kishtar snapped. He leaned against the railing, and Thalion felt a flare of guilt at the pain in Kishtar's expression.

"Why?" Thalion asked.

Kishtar groaned. "Mazda's light, Thalion, I made a mistake with Ianna, alright? I admit it. I should never have promised to marry her, I should never have slept with her. I'm not ready to settle down, she's not the right woman for me. Satisfied?"

Thalion leaned back, the anger draining out of him. "You don't have to justify yourself," he said. "I'm sorry. I'm not really angry with you. I just..." he shook his head.

"Serana," Kishtar guessed. "You wish she were here."

Thalion nodded. "Not just for that," he said. "But her presence, her company. It would...she would help steady me. After all that's happened..."

"Mazda's light. And I'm spending time with a woman instead of you," Kishtar shook his head. Thalion flushed. He hadn't been going to say it, but he had felt betrayed at Kishtar's abandonment.

Kishtar sighed. "I apologize, Thalion."

Thalion's eyes widened. "You don't have to."

Kishtar shook his head. "Aunt Vinet's departure hit you all hard, much harder than it hit me," he said. "I should have noticed. Niara has shown it the most, but you've had to deal with being away from Serana as well."

Thalion looked down. Kishtar had lost his own mother two years ago to a slow, wasting fever. If anyone knew how he was feeling right now, it would be Kishtar.

"I don't know what to do," he admitted. "It's not like Mother's gone forever, at least, I don't think so. But there's so much uncertainty and mystery about the Exile. Mother said my grandfather was gone for close to thirty years. I'll be an old man by that time! She might as well be gone for good."

Kishtar nodded sympathetically. "And somehow you're the strong one right now."

Thalion shook his head in frustration. "I don't understand Niara," he said. "She understands the Sight far better than I do. Why is she taking it so hard?"

Kishtar raised an eyebrow. "Have you tried talking to her?"

"When haven't I?" Thalion demanded. "She doesn't speak, barely reacts to anything, and acts like a frightened mouse! She's not acting like my sister!"

Kishtar made a sympathetic noise. "Give her time, Thalion. She'll come round."

Thalion shook his head again. He knew Kishtar was right, but it was painful to watch his sister like this.

He prevented himself from rolling his eyes as Lyra appeared from her cabin, red hair shining in the sun. She spotted Kishtar and gave him a sultry wink.

"Ah," Kishtar flushed and looked at Thalion.

Thalion forced a laugh. "Go on," he said. "As you said, we only have two more days."

Kishtar didn't need any more urging. He clapped Thalion once on the back and headed across the deck to Lyra, who pulled him into a passionate kiss.

Thalion sighed and returned to staring at the water. He couldn't wait to be on dry land again. *Serana, I miss you.*

Thalion swallowed as he gazed up at the tall stone structures. They stood easily two or three times as tall as he was, intricately carved with the same kind of figures he'd seen on the door below Ilhelm Castle. Most of them were pillars, perhaps ruins of some kind of ancient building, but one was a statue of a burly woman ten feet fall, dressed in scale armor and helmet and wielding a giant spear. The ruins projected a lingering sadness of fallen splendor and memories that refused to pass, even when the cause of their destruction was long gone. *What kind of beings are these nephelm? Are they peaceful? I do hope they don't attack us on sight.*

The stone road they had followed here continued east, into the snow-covered mountains. The record of Jimesseran's journal lasted two more days, when he'd made contact with *something*. Unfortunately, his physical state had deteriorated so much by that point that his writing became indecipherable.

Thalion observed the four guards setting up camp. His lips tightened as he saw his sister sitting under one of the pillars, knees drawn up to her chest. She had forgotten to wear her hair over her ears, and the long slender points would have shocked anyone who knew her back in Saemar. None of the Ninaevan guards had given her a second look. Then again, they were all Vinet's loyal guards. Surely some of them had to suspect that Vinet's connections to elves were of more than just diplomatic interest.

As he watched, Niara glanced around at the guards. He averted his gaze as she looked at him, not wanting to be caught staring. Out of the corner of his eye, he saw her stand up and slip into the forest.

Niara, you idiot! He shook his head. They were in strange, unknown, and potentially deadly territory. What was she thinking?

Sighing, he set off after her. Surely she wouldn't go far. Perhaps she just wanted some peace and quiet.

He had gone a dozen yards from the camp before he began to worry. "Niara?" he called. "Niara?"

He pushed through the underbrush. The trees here were larger than he'd ever seen before, easily twenty feet around the base, and the giant ferns were just as overgrown. He stumbled as he pushed through a grove of ferns and ended up in a small clearing. Niara stood in the center, her back to him. Her long red-brown hair was unbraided, and she seemed to glow in the soft moonlight.

"Niara?" he asked. "What are you doing? We shouldn't wander off by ourselves!"

Niara didn't turn to look at him. "I'm fine, Thalion," she said, her voice strangely distant. "I'm fine."

"No, you're not!" Thalion said, all his frustration boiling up. "You haven't spoken to any of us since Mother left! You've abandoned the entire planning of this to me and Kishtar, you drift into reveries, refuse to even volunteer an opinion, and act like a skittish cat!"

He saw Niara shiver, but he didn't relent. "You, of all people, had to know that Mother was going to leave one day," he said. "She's taught you all she knows about the Sight, which includes the Exile. You shouldn't be surprised by this!"

"Leave me alone, Thalion," Niara's voice shook.

"No," Thalion had enough. He stepped forward to face his sister. "We're out here in the wilderness, with who knows what out there with us. We need you, Niara. You're going to be the one who needs to negotiate with the nephelm. And what happens if there are other strange beasts here? Jimesseran thought he saw a dragon! If we're attacked, we need you!"

Niara brought her hands up. "No, no, I..." her face went pale, and her eyes glazed over. She opened her mouth as if to scream, but no sound emerged.

"Niara? Niara!" Thalion grabbed his sister's shoulders and shook her. She continued staring, glassy-eyed, into nothingness. He felt panic rising up inside of him. "Niara!"

His vision blurred, and he saw darkness, utter darkness, and then suddenly fire enveloping everything in sight. He caught a brief glimpse of wings, red and glinting, flying through the darkness, jaws opening in a soundless roar.

His vision cleared as Niara let out a soundless gasp and stumbled forward. She clutched at him as if he was the only solid thing in a spinning world. "Thalion!" she buried her face in his shoulder and started crying.

Thalion held his sister, trying to contain his shock and unease. He had never seen his sister cry before. Gently, he lowered them both down until they were sitting on the forest floor. Awkwardly, he reached up to stroke her hair.

She pulled back. "I'm sorry, Thalion," she said, her voice breaking. "I'm sorry. I'm just...I've been terrified. Am terrified."

"Of what?" Thalion asked. "Is it for Mother? Or of this great unknown we're investigating?" Somehow, he couldn't quite believe it.

She shook her head. "No," she whispered. "It's...Thalion, Mother had to leave on the Exile because she's to become an Eye of the Lady. I...I..." her voice broke again.

Thalion frowned, trying to comprehend. "You what?" he asked.

She looked up at him. "I've been training to be an Eye too," she said. "One day, I'm going to have to leave on that journey." The darkness in her eyes was enough to let Thalion know that the very idea terrified her.

He took a deep breath and held her closer. "You don't want to be an Eye, then?" he asked.

She shook her head. "I don't know! I don't have a choice. But I can't call the visions, Thalion, they just happen. And I get visions that..." her eyes widened, and she hurried on. "To be an Eye, I have to have some control over my visions. But I don't! And the Exile... there're only rumors about it. But sometimes the Lady...well, when she doesn't approve of the one she's called, she gets...malicious."

Thalion thought of the woman he'd met in the marketplace. Aeres-

ThonEsia was the name she had given, but to the elves she was the Lady of Leaf and Lake. Thalion was certain she had the potential to be malicious.

"But your Exile shouldn't be for years yet. You've had no warning of it, right?" He was attempting to be comforting but wasn't certain he was succeeding.

"Mother didn't have warning of it either," Niara's voice was bitter. "One vision, and then she had to vanish."

Thalion was at a loss. He wanted to find words to comfort his sister, but he couldn't think of any.

She sighed and pulled away from his arms. "I'm sorry I've been distant," she said. "I'll be better."

Thalion let her go but kept a hand on her shoulder. "I'm here for you," he said, making his voice as firm as possible. "You're my sister. You're going to be an Eye? Well, then I'm your Thorn. Or your Keeper, whichever you prefer." He tried to smile.

Niara managed a weak chuckle. "Please don't try to be my Keeper, brother mine. I wouldn't wish the burden of keeping me on you."

Thalion laughed, feeling stress wash out of him. That sounded more like his sister. "Then I'll be a Thorn," he said. "A warrior. You rule Ninaeva as Lady, and I'll protect it."

"I'd like that," she said.

They sat together in the darkening forest. Thalion felt oddly comforted by the night sounds.

Thalion hesitated before he asked his next question. "You said you just had a vision. What was it?" he asked.

Niara shook her head. "I don't know," she said. "There was intense terror. Darkness, then fire, absolute fire. Something roared. And then a dragon. But the dragon didn't seem...it seemed like it was rescuing me."

Thalion blinked. She was describing what he had seen as his vision blurred. He shook his head. His mind was playing tricks on him, it had to be. "Would that be possible?" he asked.

Niara shrugged. "We know nothing of the dragons," she said. "The only legend I've ever read with any grain of historical truth is King

Enlil and the Dragonriders, and who knows how much that tale has changed over the centuries."

Dragons. Thalion shook his head but couldn't keep the thought from niggling at him. *Why do we keep running into mentions of dragons?*

Niara sighed and stood up, startling Thalion into getting to his feet as well. "We should be getting back to the others before they start to worry," Niara said.

Thalion offered her his arm. "Can I escort you back to camp, sister?" he asked.

She smiled as she accepted. "Thank you, brother." Her tone made it clear she was thanking him for far more than the escort.

Thalion nodded, and they began to walk back to camp. He felt an intense feeling of relief. *Serana might not be here, but at least I have my sister back.*

Thalion stared at the scene before him, his mouth dropping open in wonder. The ancient dark forest had seemed endless. They had seen no sign of civilization since the nephelm ruins two days ago, aside from the stone road they traveled on. But before them...

The forest opened up to reveal a deep canyon. On the other side of the canyon, a mountain rose straight up, high enough that Thalion could barely distinguish between snow and clouds. A crystal blue waterfall fell into the canyon below, drowning all other sounds as it crashed into the rocks. The stone road continued, turning into a huge stone bridge. On the other side of the bridge, facing the small group, were intricate carved giant statues of dragons. Their lifelike eyes blinked in the sunlight. In the center of the bridge stretched a huge arch, fifteen feet tall. A huge nephelm warrior stood above it, her spear pointing at one of the dragons.

"Dragon slayers," Niara murmured. "The legends are true."

Thalion closed his mouth, though a sense of awe still threatened to overwhelm him. How could someone carve something that large and lifelike? The dragons almost looked like they were going to attack them. And the nephelm warrior's very posture spoke of menace and fierceness.

Niara shook herself, as if out of a daze. "Let's keep moving," she said. "We don't have far to go, if Jimesseran's notes are anything to go off of."

That's because Jimesseran's journal ends not far from here, Thalion thought. *We know nothing of what's beyond this point.* He kept that thought to himself.

"Thalion!" a shout from one of the guards made everyone turn. The guard's expression lingered somewhere between fear and disbelief. Thalion followed the line of the guard's pointed finger and felt his own eyes widen. There, far above in the sky, was a shadow of such a distinctive shape…*It can't be. But there's nothing else it could be.*

"Across the bridge, now!" the guard yelled.

It took Thalion a half-second slower to react than Niara and Kishtar. He was still staring at the sky, awe-struck by the shape of the dragon. *How far can they see?* He wondered. *Does it know we're here? Will it attack us?* He suppressed a shudder. How could they even fight such a creature? Even from this distance, he could see its size would easily dwarf the entire party.

"Off the road!" the guard shouted.

Thalion followed his instructions blindly, guiding his horse off the stone road back into the trees. Dimly, he noticed that the trees were nowhere near as large on this side of the canyon. They were still large enough for cover, however. He hunched over his horse, trying to make himself as invisible in the trees as possible, but still couldn't help gazing up at the sky, craning for another glimpse of the dragon.

Kishtar looked at him, eyes wide. "That was a dragon!" he exclaimed, his voice barely above a whisper.

Thalion suddenly realized that he'd been holding his breath and released it in a rush. He felt hyper-aware of everything around him. "It was amazing." He replied.

"Quiet, you two," Niara whispered. "It might not be gone."

Thalion immediately shut up. As incredible as it had been, the last thing he wanted was to deal with a potentially angry dragon.

He caught sight of Niara's expression. Instead of elated, frightened, or awed, she merely appeared thoughtful.

"Niara? What are you thinking?" he asked.

She blinked, shaking her head. "I wonder if this is the same dragon that Jimesseran said he saw," she said. "And if the nephelm are dragon slayers, then why they haven't hunted this one?"

"Maybe it's hiding from them," Kishtar suggested.

Niara frowned. "Perhaps."

"Attack!"

Thalion's head swiveled around at the alarm in the guard's voice. His hand instinctively went to his sword. His eyes widened. Behind them, two of the guards had found shelter deeper in the trees. A giant blur of fur and feathers flew toward them, knocking one of the guards off their horse.

"To Niara!" Thalion yelled. He yanked his cat and sun-engraved sword out of its sheath and moved his horse to block the beast's path to Niara. Niara herself clung frantically to her saddle.

The guard screamed, and Thalion gasped in horror as the beast looked up. Long, razor sharp canines dripped with blood as it stared at him, and its red eyes flashed in a maddened frenzy.

What in Mazda's name is that thing? Thalion's thoughts were a whirl. He'd never seen or heard of a creature like this.

The fallen guard screamed again, and the nearer two guards wheeled their horses around and flanked the beast, attacking it simultaneously with their swords.

It took every inch of Thalion's willpower to remain where he was. *Protect Niara. She's the nonfighter. Protect Niara!*

The two guards' swords cut into the beast, but that only seemed to infuriate it even more. It turned on one of them, tearing a long bloody gash into the horse with its claws and causing the guard to tumble to the ground. The guards rushed at it, trying to distract it before it lashed out at the newly grounded guard. The beast kicked out with its hind legs, knocking both the remaining guards off their horses. It pounced on the fallen guard in front of it, tearing viciously into the guard's legs.

"For Ninaeva!" Kishtar's cry echoed through the trees as he charged the side of the beast, his sword raised high overhead. Thalion let out a cry of horror as the beast whirled toward him.

"No!" he shouted, urging his horse ahead. He could not let that beast get Kishtar!

"Thalion!" He heard Niara's terrified voice.

Thalion ignored Niara as he made for the frenzied beast. He saw Kishtar slash his sword down across the beast's head as Thalion approached. It roared at Kishtar and made to charge. Thalion threw himself forward, driving his sword into the beast's back. It roared again and turned. Thalion was wrenched off his horse, still clutching his sword. He hit the ground hard and rolled.

"Thalion!" He heard Niara's scream. The air tingled, and then the beast howled in pain, the scent of scorched fur on the air.

He scrambled desperately to his feet, every moment expecting the beast's claws or teeth to dig into his back. Instead, he whirled around to see half the beast's face scorched and blackened as it tore into a downed guard in a fury.

Determinedly, Thalion readied his sword for another attack. The beast stared up at him at that moment, red eyes glaring. Thalion swallowed, readying himself for a charge. The beast took two steps, then fell with a howl, a large spear sticking out of its side.

Thalion spun around, sword at the ready. From the road, four giant figures strode toward them. They ignored the humans as one of them approached the dying beast and grabbed the spear, twisting it once before pulling it out. They then stood in a row and regarded the humans.

Thalion took a breath and faced the figures. They stared back impassively. All of them wore the same scale armor as the statues. Their skin was as gray as the surrounding rock, and none of them looked in the least friendly.

"You are intruders," one of them said.

Thalion relaxed his grip on his sword and sheathed it. If these were the nephelm, the last thing he wanted to do was to provoke a fight.

"We have come to speak with you," Niara said as she rode up. Mounted, she was still shorter than the shortest nephelm. "We have come to negotiate in the name of Lady Vinet et-Alim of Ninaeva."

"We are not aware of such a person," the nephelm who had spoken before answered. "And we do not negotiate with humans."

"We are not all human," Niara's voice rang clear. "My brother and I bear the blood of Queen Olvae Oakenspear of the Goldwood Realm."

As one, the nephelm turned to look atNiara. "Which one is your brother?" one asked.

Niara gestured, and Thalion stepped forward, standing as straight as he could. He felt the eyes of all the nephelm upon him, as unyielding as the mountains. Unbidden, a memory from his childhood lessons reached him. *The fourth born from the Mountain-God's hatred of the dragons, his Brother's chaotic creation. The Mountain-God made them in the form of his domain, colossal and strong. It was they, in friendship with the Goldwood-Realm that cast down the Great Burner after her long reign.*

"Fourth born from the Mountain-God," he murmured.

The nephelm's eyes sharpened as they regarded him. "Not untutored, unlike most humans. Though you are a strange one."

Thalion flushed, but me the nephelm's eyes without answering. They met his gaze squarely.

"You will accompany us back to Utgard," one of them said. "You may or may not be as you claim. The Kakkab u Alap will decide your fate."

Thalion glanced uneasily at Niara. She sat tall and proud on her horse, eyeing the nephelm steadily. "We mean you no harm," Niara said. "We will go with you if you swear that none of us will come to harm in your care."

One of the nephelm chuckled. "You will come with us if you do not want to die," he said. "Two of your men already fell to the *Rikandi.* How long will the rest of you last?"

"He has a point," Kishtar said quietly. "We've lost two men, and the others are wounded. Who knows how many more of these creatures are out here?"

Thalion saw a flash of uncertainty cross Niara's face. She turned back to the nephelm and nodded. "We will accept your hospitality. I am Niara," her voice caught. "Niara Sindarilae."

Thalion glanced at his sister, startled. Sindarilae had been their grandfather's name. Their mother had used it in her private writings, but never in public. *Then again, if we're claiming negotiation rights based on our elven blood, then it's probably better for her to use Grandfather's name.*

The nephelm inclined his head. "I am Evikan, leader of this patrol. You will follow us now." Evikan started walking back toward the road, obviously expecting everyone to follow. The other three nephelm waited, clearly not prepared to move until Thalion and the others obeyed.

Thalion looked around. Two of the guards were dead, their throats torn out. The other two were injured. They had lost two of the horses. He moved to help the injured guards remount, Kishtar a half-step behind him. Only then did he remount his own horse.

Niara nodded and ordered her horse forward. Thalion fell in behind her, Kishtar at his side. Behind them came the two guards. The three remaining nephelm followed them, wary not only of their surroundings, but of the group.

To Utgard, then, Thalion thought.

11

UTGARD

The nephelm led them far up the mountain to where the snow piled up in large drifts. Thalion was grateful for the heavy wool cloak he wore. *How do the nephelm not freeze to death? They're barely wearing more than we would during Mazda's Rise.*

He saw no signs of a city until they crested a mountain pass. Below them in a small valley, the fortress towers of Utgard rose high and forbidding. Thalion wanted to stop and take in the scene, but the nephelm kept moving, unaffected by the sight of their home.

Thalion rode up beside Niara and gave her a sideways glance. "What do you think about this?" he asked, keeping his voice low.

Niara shook her head. "I'm trying not to make any judgments," she said. "Mother taught me never to make assumptions going into a negotiation, only to draw on facts and observation."

Thalion nodded reluctantly. "I wish they were a little clearer about where we're going, though. Who do you think this Kakkab u Alap is?"

"At a guess, their leader," Niara said. "But as I said, no assumptions."

Thalion subsided. Niara was right. Until they got to the city and met this Kakkab u Alap, there was no point in worrying.

The city gates were huge, flanked by the same sort of imposing statues that had been on the bridge. One was the same nephelm woman with her spear, while the other was a nephelm male wielding a giant axe.

"I wish I knew who she was," Niara said in a low voice. "She has to be important to them."

Her voice wasn't low enough to avoid the nephelm's attention. Evikan looked back over his shoulder to regard Niara and Thalion. "She is Nehalima, mother of the nephelm. She was one of those who bound the dragons to their forms."

Bound the dragons? Thalion blinked. *What does that mean? Bound them to what forms? The form that we saw flying above us?*

"Bound them how?" Niara asked.

Evikan shook his head. "Is that tale not known to the humans? I would have thought one descended from the Goldwood Realm would know that tale."

Thalion saw Niara's lips tighten. "I am still young, and my blood is mixed," she said. "My grandfather died before he had a chance to teach my mother and I many things."

And before I could even meet him, Thalion thought. He felt a moment's gratitude that Niara was the one handling the talking. The last thing he wanted was an inquiry into his own heritage, especially since he couldn't tell what Evikan thought of Niara's answer.

"If the Kakkab u Alap allows your presence, then you will learn," the nephelm said.

Thalion exchanged an uneasy look with Niara. He did not like the idea that their presence was still under sufferance.

As they approached the gate, Thalion saw more nephelm stationed above it, gazing down at the approaching group. One called out in something unintelligible. It sounded like rocks tumbling down a mountain.

Evikan called something back in the same tongue. The nephelm guard nodded, and Evikan led them through the gates into the city. The path wound in a spiral pattern deeper and deeper into the city, past tower-like houses, built out of the same color rock as the mountains, but engraved with the same geometric designs as the door underneath Ilhelm.

Thalion's eyes widened as they rounded a final bend. The building before them rose straight and tall, with two dragons flanking the female nephelm warrior Nehalima carved above it, her spear striking one of the dragons in the throat. *This isn't a palace, or even a castle. It's a fortress in its own right.*

Evikan nodded to one of the nephelm guarding the door, then turned to look at Niara and Thalion. "You can leave your horses here. Follow me."

Thalion dismounted, and the three nephelm that had escorted them led their horses away. Thalion looked back at Kishtar and their weary but determined guards, who fell in step behind them.

Niara gestured for everyone to follow her, and Thalion fell into step directly behind her as Evikan led them into the fortress.

The doorway opened up into a wide chamber. Curved arches decorated the ceilings, embellished with dragons and other beasts. Thalion thought he saw a carving of the same creature that had attacked them in the forest.

Evikan didn't give them time to linger as he marched through the chamber to a set of wide double doors. He barked something at one of the guards, and the doors swung open, revealing another chamber just as large and elaborate. As they entered, Thalion saw a nephelm sitting on a raised stone throne at the other end of the chamber. Two other nephelm sat in smaller thrones on either side.

The Kakkab u Alap, Thalion thought. *The one who will judge whether or not we will stay.*

Evikan strode confidently up to the base of the dais and bowed low. Thalion followed Niara's lead as she walked to stand beside Evikan and bowed as well. Kishtar and the guards hung back.

"You bring me humans," the nephelm rumbled.

Evikan nodded. "They claim they are here to treat with us."

The Kakkab u Alap turned his gaze on Niara and Thalion. "We do not treat with humans."

Niara stepped forward, and Thalion could see her eyes blazing.

"Not all of us are human," she spoke. "As I told Evikan, I am Niara Sindarilae, great-great-granddaughter of Queen Olvae Oakenspear of the Goldwood Realm. This is my brother, Thalion et-Alim, great-great-grandson of Queen Olvae. We have been sent here by our mother, Lady Vinet Sindarilae et-Alim of Ninaeva, to treat with you about nephelm ruins discovered underneath Ilhelm Castle."

At Niara's words, the two nephelm on the lesser thrones rumbled and looked at each other. The leader remained impassive.

"Humans are deceitful creatures," he said. "The sky-lord created you so, to serve the deceitful dragons. This could be a lie."

Niara pushed her hair back so that her ears were fully visible. "Has any full-blood human ever had ears like mine?" she demanded. "I am of Queen Olvae's bloodline."

"Queen Olvae fell," the nephelm said, unperturbed. "Her line was broken."

Thalion stopped himself from flinching by an effort of will. Another legend their grandfather had never bothered to tell. Their mother had suspected something had happened to Queen Olvae but had never found the truth.

"The line was not broken," Niara's voice remained strong. "My brother and I are proof of it."

"You have offered no proof," the nephelm declared.

Thalion could hear Niara's frustration. "What would constitute proof to you?"

The nephelm didn't answer. Thalion watched as they looked at each other, and then back to Niara.

"Evikan, take the strangers to a guest chamber," the leader said. "We will discuss what is to become of them in private."

Thalion glanced at Niara and saw uncertainty on her face. Would it be better to demand to be included in the discussions, or accept their judgment? Niara looked back at Kishtar and the two guards, and her expression became resolute.

"If you would also send a healer, we would be grateful for your hospitality," Niara said. "We were attacked by a beast in the forest, and two of my men were hurt."

The leader nodded. "It will be done. Evikan, take them away."

Evikan bowed, and Thalion hastily followed his example. Niara bowed as well, and Evikan led them back into the entry chamber and then through a web of stone passages. He stopped beside a wooden door.

"These are your chambers," he said. "The Kakkab u Alap will summon you when he is ready."

"Thank you," Niara said.

Evikan hesitated. "The healer will be here shortly," he said. "I will send another as well. She will find you fascinating." Before Thalion or Niara had a chance to inquire further, he strode off down the hallway.

Thalion exchanged looks with Niara, then turned to join Kishtar in helping the injured guards into the room. It was large and spacious, obviously meant for nephelm. They lay the two injured guards in one of the beds. Niara stood by the fireplace, and Kishtar and Thalion walked over to join her.

"We're in trouble," Kishtar said.

Niara sighed. "I'm afraid you're right."

"I don't like the way they won't take us at our word." Thalion frowned. "And their dislike of humans will be problematic."

Niara nodded. "Agreed. We can use our elven blood, but we can't deny that we're still partly human. And no one knows what part of you is, Thalion. If they place that much importance on blood…" she shook her head.

"I have just as much of Olvae's blood as you, sister," Thalion said. "If they're going to find issue with the unknown part of me, they may as well take issue with the unknown part of you." Unbidden, a thought. *Serana should have come, and Saihid. Having a full-blood elf and his half-elven daughter might have convinced them.*

Niara grimaced. "I wish we knew why they disliked humans," she said. "If we did, then maybe we could negotiate better. We don't have enough information."

"Then perhaps I could help remedy that fact?"

Thalion spun around, unconsciously reaching for his sword at the sound of the unknown voice from the door. The nephelm woman smiled at his reaction. She stood as tall as any of the men they had encountered, just about eight feet, with the same rock-gray skin. Her hair was pure white, and braided in multiple little braids along her scalp that joined a larger braid down her back. Her black eyes twinkled as she regarded them. "Two groups of humans in twenty years. This will be a tale for the records!"

Thalion looked at the nephelm woman warily. "Two human groups?" he asked.

"That explorer," the woman explained. "Though perhaps group is too strong a term, as he was the only one. The rest of his company left him here when it became clear he would not survive the return journey. They were not allowed entrance."

"Jimesseran? He made it here?" Niara asked.

"You know of him?" the woman smiled delightedly. "He was the first human to see Utgard in over three centuries. Too long a time, if you ask me. How are we to know when the sky-lord will return if we do not watch the slaves of his children?"

Thalion frowned. "We are not slaves of anyone," he pointed out. "And while slavery may be practiced in the Jyrian Confederacy and parts of Tigri, it is not the practice in Saemar."

The woman seemed to dismiss his point as irrelevant. "Evikan said you had found ruins of our people under one of your castles? You must tell me about this!" She stepped further into the room.

Niara nodded formally. "I am Niara Sindarilae," she said. "We would gladly tell you our tale…" she hesitated, waiting for a name.

"Where are my manners?" the woman inclined her head. "Zeria of the Nindans, lore master of Utgard. A pleasure to make your acquaintance."

Thalion relaxed slightly. *She certainly seems friendlier than Evikan, at least. Maybe she'll answer some of our questions as well.*

"A pleasure to meet you, Zeria of the Nindans." Niara gestured at the others. "This is my brother, Thalion et-Alim, and our companion, Kishtar. And our guards."

"Ah, yes. Evikan said a healer was necessary." As if Zeria's words had summoned him, another nephelm entered the room. He glared at Zeria before turning his attention to the wounded guards on the bed.

Zeria smiled affably and sat down in one of the large chairs by the fireplace. "Make yourselves comfortable," she invited. "I am certain we have a long discussion ahead of us."

Thalion sat down in one of the other chairs, slightly discomforted by its huge size. Everything here was larger than he was used to.

"So tell me of these ruins!" Zeria's eyes sparkled. "I have never heard of ruins outside our lands."

Thalion looked at Niara. She was the spokesperson.

Niara settled back in her own chair. "I don't know if they are truly ruins, or merely abandoned. But there is an entire city there," she said. "My mother was guided to them by a vision. They are underneath our castle, deep in the earth. The carvings are very much the same as we've seen here in Utgard."

Zeria leaned forward. "Underground, you say?"

Niara nodded. "I do not know why Ilhelm was built on top of them, or if the builders even knew that they were there. We cannot seem to explore most of them, or even unlock most of the doors."

"Of course you can't," Zeria's voice was confident. "We build our doors so that only we can open them. If this place was abandoned, as you say, then everything would have been locked behind them." She frowned. "How did you even know they were nephelm? Our kind are not found in the south."

Thalion glanced at Niara, remembering the new statue in front of the door to the city. The outcast nephelm, his mother had said. Was Niara going to mention him?

He didn't look like these nephelm, Thalion thought. *Their skin isn't scaly like his was. I wonder if that has something to do with why he was outcast?*

"My mother and stepfather are scholars," Niara said, her voice composed. "It took a bit of studying, but they were able to trace the writing they found. My mother also knew Jimesseran, the explorer who set out to find your cities."

"Yes, Jimesseran!" Zeria's eyes lightened. "A pity he was so ill. We could have learned a great deal from each other. The poor man."

"How long did he stay here?" Niara asked curiously.

"A mere month, and for most of that he was not conscious," Zeria sighed. "But he was honored in proper nephelm style. His ashes are scattered at the top of Mount Burgae."

"So humans can be accepted here?" Thalion asked without thinking.

"But of course!" Zeria said. "Jimesseran had broken free of the sky-lord's yoke. If humans prove themselves to have no loyalty to him, then they can gain acceptance here."

"You keep mentioning this sky-lord," Thalion said. "Who is he? We've never heard of him."

Zeria frowned. "No? But he is rising to prominence again. The scouts have sent us worrying reports."

Niara's face was as confused as Thalion felt. "Well, we owe no allegiance to the sky-lord," Thalion said. "How do we prove that?"

"I cannot make that judgment," Zeria said. "The Kakkab u Alap and his advisors must do that. And they will not even attempt to discern your intent until they satisfy themselves that no more of you are arriving."

"How long will that take?" Niara asked. "There is a crew of humans on the coast, but they will not come here. They are waiting for our return."

Zeria shrugged. "I cannot say. It will take longer since you are nobles."

Thalion frowned. "Why would that make a difference?"

"Because the nobles are where the sky-lord will draw his power from," Zeria explained. "Despite your mixed blood, there will always be questions, especially as you come from his kingdom."

Thalion shook his head in confusion. "Saemar is not the sky-lord's kingdom," he protested. "We worship Mazda, God of the Sun. Unless…he's not the sky-lord, is he?" he asked in alarm.

Zeria laughed. "No, Mazda is minor compared to the earth-father and the sky-lord."

Thalion bristled a little at the idea of anyone calling Mazda minor, but firmly told himself not to say anything.

"Do you know of the Lady of Lake and Leaf?" Niara asked.

Zeria nodded. "Of course. Her people helped us cast down the dragons and the sky-lord."

Thalion blinked. "Queen Olvae," he said. "Our ancestress." He exchanged another look with Niara.

Niara's thoughts were running the same pattern as his own. "Then the Great Burner was a dragon?" she asked.

"Is," Zeria's voice was sharp. "And she will rise again, under the sky-lord's rule. That is why we must be ever vigilant."

Thalion wanted to dismiss Zeria's words about the sky-lord and humans being his slaves, but something niggled at the back of his memory. One of his childhood lessons…

Zeria stood up. "I should let you rest," she said. "I will be back, and we can discuss more of the nephelm city. I must consult some records."

Niara, Thalion, and Kishtar stood politely as she left. Thalion remained standing, trying to remember what was bothering him.

"Thalion?" Kishtar asked. "Why the frown?"

Thalion ignored him. "Niara," he asked. "Grandfather's text on the Age of Great Fire. Do you remember it?"

Niara blinked. "Of course," she said. "What part?"

"The races," Thalion said, still frowning. "The first one."

Niara closed her eyes and began to recite. "The first were our kin shorn of the Lady's Gifts. These were made bountiful, but the Great Burner, that dark dragon, also made their lives short to drive them toward servitude." Her eyes flew open. "Do you think that's what Zeria meant?" she exclaimed.

Thalion shrugged helplessly. "Mother was always puzzling over the races, remember?" he said. "The only one she finally figured out was the nephelm, the mountain-god's children. Our kin shorn of the Lady's gifts could certainly mean humans."

"The Lady blessed us with the eyes and ears," Niara whispered, almost as if reliving a memory. "That is certainly what sets me apart from humans."

Thalion nodded. "There's still no mention of this sky-lord, whoever he is," he said, a little grumpily.

"I don't like the idea of being enslaved to anyone," Kishtar said.

"None of us are slaves," Niara said, shaking her head. "That must have ended when the Great Burner fell."

Thalion should have felt relief or satisfaction, but instead there was only a rising worry. "Do you think Zeria's right?" he asked. "That the Great Burner will rise again?"

Niara shook her head, but then her eyes widened. She closed her mouth and frowned.

"Niara?" Thalion asked.

"The Great Burner," Niara whispered. "Is the Great Burner the same as the Great Enemy?"

Thalion exchanged a look of pure bewilderment with Kishtar. "What are you talking about?" he asked.

Niara's brow furrowed. "I don't remember much," she said. "I was barely eight. But at Lady Pellalindra's wedding, a woman was killed because she was carrying a child that would become the Great Enemy."

Thalion remembered the story now. It was because of that incident that Vinet had set out to find Kishtar's mother, and why Kishtar had grown up in Ilhelm rather than in the slums of Venia.

"You think they're the same person?" Kishtar asked, his voice troubled.

"I think it's possible," Niara said.

"But what does any of this mean?" Thalion asked. "If the Great Burner was a dragon, how was it going to rise again from a human child?"

Niara sighed and shrugged.

Kishtar stood uneasily. "The woman was my father's wife," he said. "I...well, I know what my father ended up being. But no one knows exactly what Darkmane was. Darkmane could have certainly carried the spawn of the Great Enemy."

Thalion grimaced. Kishtar's father had been Lord General of Saemar, but in the end he had also been a phantom bandit demon.

"Maybe," Niara's voice remained unconvinced. "But if that's the case, then you should be in the same danger, and Mother was positive she could identify the same feeling."

Kishtar squared his shoulders. "Well, I'm positive I'm not a dragon," he said. "Wouldn't that be great, though? Flying through the air, breathing fire?" he grinned, obviously attempting to lighten the mood.

Niara rolled her eyes. Thalion let out a relieved chuckle.

"Well, I guess now we just wait for the Kakkab u Alap to decide that no other humans are coming and ask us to prove that we're not loyal to this sky-lord," Niara said. "Whatever that's going to take."

"If Jimesseran managed it, as ill as he was, I'm sure we will," Thalion said, trying to sound confident.

Niara didn't seem reassured. "I hope you're right. Mother was so adamant about this trip…"

They spent two more days in Utgard, never being allowed to stray far from their guest chambers. Zeria was a frequent visitor, with more and more questions about the underground nephelm city. She dragged the story about the petrified nephelm from them but appeared entirely unconcerned.

"He was turned to stone because he was cursed," she said. "I know that affliction. It won't happen to any of us, and maybe we can help him."

Other than Zeria's visits, the days went slowly. Thalion and Kishtar grew restless and bored, and passed the time either training, or talking about their respective ladies. Only Niara seemed composed. Several times, Thalion caught her in a meditative stance, and he knew that she was trying to use the Sight. *Mazda's light, I am grateful I am not 'blessed' with the Sight. And Serana isn't either, thankfully.*

Despite his boredom, he was filled with apprehension when he and Niara received a summons to speak to the Kakkab u Alap, alone, without any of their escort. Kishtar wanted to protest, but Thalion shook his head.

"I don't like this," Kishtar grumbled.

Thalion didn't either, but he shrugged. "At least I'm there to protect Niara," he said. He half expected Niara to roll her eyes and protest that she didn't need protecting, but she instead gave him a grateful smile. "Let's go," she said.

Two nephelm escorted Thalion and Niara through the fortress back to the main chamber. Thalion looked at them uneasily. He would try to protect Niara, but he wasn't certain he could even defend himself against one of the nephelm. Gwyn's speeches about overcoming an opponent's size and strength rang in his mind, but he had never faced an opponent so much stronger and larger than himself.

He straightened proudly as they entered the audience chamber. The Kakkab u Alap and the two other nephelm were seated on the same thrones as before. He followed one step behind Niara as she approached and curtsied. He bowed low.

"We have heard Zeria's report of you," the Kakkab u Alap said without preamble. "We wish to hear of your mission from your own lips."

"We have found an abandoned nephelm city underneath Ilhelm Castle," Niara said, her voice calm and level. "My mother sent us to bring back a delegation to repair and explore the passages."

The two nephelm's eyes widened, and they exchanged glances with each other. The Kakkab u Alap's face remained impassive. "You wish nephelm to travel to the human country?" he asked.

Thalion saw Niara straightened. "This mission was given to us as a mandate by the Lady of the Leaf and Lake," she said. "Yes, we do."

The Kakkab u Alap leaned forward, his eyes intent. "Your mission is a strange one, and it comes at a time of many omens," he said. "And yet you claim to have no knowledge of the sky-lord, or any desire to serve him."

Thalion prevented himself from sighing with an effort of will.

"Since we have no knowledge of this sky-lord, it seems quite hard for us to serve him," Niara said, her voice still calm.

"Not so difficult as it may seem," the Kakkab u Alap said enigmatically. "It is possible to serve unknowingly."

"What proof can we offer?" Niara asked. "We came here in good faith, to negotiate an exchange of knowledge, to offer you a chance to learn of your own history."

"So you say," the Kakkab u Alap glanced at the other nephelm, then nodded. "And you will be given a chance to prove yourselves." He stood. "Niara Sindarilae and Thalion et-Alim, you claim to be descended from the Goldwood Realm. Nonetheless, your blood is mixed. Do you deny this?"

Thalion saw Niara's lips tighten. "No," she said.

The Kakkab u Alap continued. "You claim to know nothing of the one who enslaves humankind, and never to serve him. Therefore, the blood of the Goldwood realm must be stronger than your mixed blood. You will face an ordeal that can only be overcome by one of the Goldwood realm."

"What kind of ordeal?" Niara asked.

The Kakkab u Alap didn't blink. "If you knew, then it would be no ordeal," he said. "Return to your quarters. A guard will come for you in three hours." He leaned back in his throne, clearly having dismissed them.

Thalion saw Niara hesitate, and he gently touched her arm. He shook his head as she looked back at him. This was not the time for questions. She grimaced, then curtsied to the Kakkab u Alap. Thalion bowed, and they turned and left the chamber, trailed by their escorts.

"What kind of ordeal can only be overcome by one of the Goldwood Realm?" Niara demanded.

Thalion glanced at the nephelm accompanying them. "Let's talk about it back in our quarters," he said.

12

REVELATIONS

Thalion stared at the passage in front of him. *A maze. This was not what I was expecting.*

He wished he could see through the walls, to get some clue as to what challenges he and Niara might face. He touched the cat-engraved sword on his belt for luck. His shield was slung over his back. He had a feeling he was going to need both.

Thalion glanced over at Kishtar, who observed him with wide eyes. He wished that Kishtar was going into the maze with them, but the nephelm had strictly forbidden any but he and Niara to enter the "ordeal."

"Good luck," Kishtar said.

Thalion smiled, trying to appear confident, and then regarded his sister. She was dressed in a split tunic and breeches but was unarmed except for the knife at her belt. *"Gwyn taught me how to defend myself, but little else,"* she'd said. *"It's far better if I go into this with a weapon I know how to use, rather than one I am unfamiliar with."*

Niara met his eyes and nodded. Thalion turned to Evikan, who stood at the entrance to the maze.

"We're ready," he said.

"Good. Your goal is to make it to the other side," Evikan said. "We will be watching you as you face the challenges."

Thalion felt his lips tighten. None of the nephelm had even breathed a hint about what kind of challenges they would face. *I don't like surprises. Especially potentially dangerous ones.*

"And when we reach the other side, will you accept our word that we and our companions are not slaves to the sky-lord?" Niara asked.

"That is for the Kakkab u Alap to decide," Evikan said. "If you are prepared, then enter."

Niara began to move forward, but Thalion held out a restraining hand. "I'll go first," he told her. She stepped back and they fell into Gwyn's training, guard first, then noble. Thalion took a deep breath and started into the maze.

The walls were tall, at least twice as tall as the tallest nephelm they'd seen, and made of sheer stone. There were no cracks, fissures, or carvings. Nor was there any way to go but forward.

Thalion heard Niara behind him as he followed the path, winding first right, then left. After a few more curves, he began to be concerned. He had been expecting this to be a maze. *A maze implies choices, though,* he thought. *There haven't been any choices so far.*

His worries were confirmed as he rounded another corner and nearly ran head-first into a wall. He glared at it, anger rising in him. He turned back to Niara. "We didn't miss a crossing anywhere, did we?"

Niara shook her head but didn't meet his eyes, staring instead at the wall behind him. "An ordeal only one of the Goldwood can overcome…" she whispered. "But not everyone of the Goldwood has the Sight. It can't be that, can it?" she looked at Thalion as she finished her question.

Thalion shrugged. "You know more about it than I," he said. "But we did tell them we were descendent of Queen Olvae. If they know anything about her," he shrugged again.

Niara gazed intently at the wall, then her eyes widened. "It's on top," she said. "This is the end of the passage, and there are no others. We have to get up the wall."

Thalion turned around and stared in disbelief at the stone wall. It was slick to the touch, polished smooth. "How is anyone supposed to climb that?" he asked incredulously.

Niara ignored his question, staring again at the stone. "Gold-wood realm," she whispered. "The Swaying."

Thalion blinked. "Magic?" he asked. "Is that what this trial is about?" A flare of fear coursed through him, followed by a flash of anger, both of which he quickly suppressed. He had no magical talents, no Sight. A test designed around magic was one he could only fail.

Niara tightened her lips. "Brace yourself," she told her brother. "I'm going to try something."

Thalion opened his mouth to ask what, but Niara had already closed her eyes and was whispering something under her breath. As he watched, he grew lighter and lighter, then swallowed a flash of fear as his feet left the ground.

One look at the fierce concentration on Niara's face made him clench his jaw shut instead of crying out. He stared at the wall, determined to grab onto the ledge as soon as it came into reach. The air around him carried him up faster and faster, and he felt a moment's panic as the ledge appeared before his eyes. "Niara!" he called out, afraid that she was going to lift him far too high into the air.

He dropped, and he grabbed at the ledge. He managed to roll himself onto it just as Niara's spell failed entirely. He lay on his stomach, gasping in relief. No human or elf should float like that. It was just wrong.

"Thalion? Are you alright?" Niara's voice floated up to him, full of worry.

"I'm fine!" Thalion shouted. "Your turn!" He let out another breath as he rolled over, attempting to get a bearing on his surroundings. His eyes widened as he saw the giant lizard stalking right at him.

"Niara! There's a lizard!" he yelled. He scrambled to his feet, grabbing for his shield as he did so. The lizard looked angry. Its orange eyes flashed, and it hissed, forked tongue poking out from between its sharp teeth.

Niara didn't answer, and Thalion shifted all his attention to the lizard in front of him. He drew his sword as it made its way in his direction with slow, ponderous steps.

The lizard stopped barely five feet away and stared at him. Thalion watched it warily, waiting for its next move. The lizard sucked in a breath and then spat. Thalion felt a spike of terror as a ball of fire flew toward him. He brought his shield around at the last minute, protecting himself from most of the blast. His shield hand heated up unbearably, and he reminded himself that dropping his shield was death.

"It breathes fire!" he exclaimed. He dropped into a crouch, ready for the beast's next attack. He started analyzing it, determining its weakness. The scales on its back were thick, but they only covered so much. Its underbelly was entirely exposed.

"Over here!" Thalion felt a jolt of alarm at the sound of Niara's voice. His eyes widened as he glanced at her. She was floating ten feet in the air, almost on top of the beast.

The lizard had heard her voice, as well. It turned toward her, rearing up on its hind legs and sucking in a breath. Thalion reacted on instinct, charging in and driving his sword into the beast's underbelly. It sliced in cleanly, and the beast howled instead of releasing its blast of fire. Thalion rolled out of the way as it dropped to the ground, gasping in pain as the life drained from it.

Niara floated down to the ground beside him. "That worked," she said calmly.

Thalion looked at her incredulously. "It could have breathed fire at you!" he exclaimed. "You don't have a shield!"

Niara smiled at him. "But you were there," she said. "I knew you would kill it as long as I could distract it."

"I," Thalion shut up. He shook his head at his sister. "I don't think Gwyn would approve of you doing that," he finally said.

Niara's expression sobered. "Well, she's not here," she said. "And we need to get through this, for Mother's sake, for all our sakes. Are you ready to keep going?"

Thalion nodded. After a moment's consideration, he kept his

sword and shield out. If there were more monsters, he wanted to be prepared. "Which way do we go?"

He and Niara both looked around. They were still in a passage, with walls on either side. This time, however, they could go either left or right.

Niara stared down the passage, then shrugged and chose the path on the left. Thalion followed.

The first sign that something waited ahead was the increase of heat. Thalion frowned and glanced back at Niara to see if she'd noticed it as well. She nodded, and he kept moving forward, slow and wary.

He rounded a corner and was confronted with a wall of flame. He sprang back, staring at the wall of fire in disbelief. "Do we have to float over that thing too?" he asked.

Niara shook her head. "There's a ceiling," she said. "We have to go through."

With a curse, Thalion realized she was right. The passage turned into a tunnel right where the flame sprouted the highest.

He looked back at his sister. "I think this is where more of the Swaying is required," he said.

She nodded, staring at the fire. "Water," she whispered. She closed her eyes and began chanting something. Thalion felt the air around them grow heavy and humid, and he wiped sweat off of his brow before it could fall into his eyes. The air grew even heavier, and suddenly there was an outbreak of water as it cascaded from the air, falling over the fire. It hissed and spit in an outrage of smoke.

Niara's eyes flew open. "Now!" she exclaimed. "It'll return." She grabbed his shield arm and ran forward. Thalion raced beside her, feeling the heat from the coals pierce through his boots as they crossed. They had barely made it to the other side when the first crackling of flame shot up again.

Thalion stared at his sister in disbelief. "How did it do that? Fire doesn't return that quickly."

"Magic," Niara whispered. She stood bent over with her hands on her knees, breathing heavily. "This entire place is designed by magic."

Thalion glanced back at the leaping flames. "Why?" he asked. "It can't just be to test us. Jimesseran was their last visitor, and I doubt he went through such a trial."

Niara shrugged helplessly. She was still panting. Thalion frowned. "Are you alright?" he asked.

"I'm fine," Niara assured him. "I'm just...not used to using this much magic." She grimaced. "Air is fine, fire is fine, but earth and water..." she shook her head.

Thalion shook his head. He had never been one for magical theory.

Niara saw his confusion and smiled. "The closer an element is to the mental energies, the easier it is to manipulate," she explained. "Air and fire are closer. Earth and water are far more physical."

*And she just used water magic...*Thalion's brow creased in concern. "Are you fine to continue?" he said. "There're probably more obstacles that require magic."

She nodded emphatically. "I'll manage," she said. "Let's keep going."

Despite her words, Thalion deliberately slowed his pace as they continued into the tunnel. Niara didn't say anything, which made him suspect she was more tired than she was letting on. *Not that we have much choice but to keep going,* he thought. *Curse the nephelm and their insistence on this. Why couldn't they just believe us?*

The light from the fire behind them illuminated their course well into the tunnel. It was only at the first turn that Thalion stared into the blackness with dismay.

Niara took a deep breath and chanted a few brief words, and Thalion bit back an exclamation as the sun engravings on his sword began to glow. He looked back at Niara, who just shrugged.

Thalion walked faster through the dark tunnel. If Niara was using magic to keep the light going, he didn't want her to use more energy than absolutely necessary.

This isn't over. There's going to be something else, and we're going to need all of our strength. He didn't know how he knew that, but he felt it in his bones that he was right.

He blinked as he approached the wall in front of him. The tunnel had narrowed, but there was no other passage. This was the end.

He sighed and turned back to his sister. "Another magic trick?"

Niara's face was pale in the dim light. She stepped up to the wall and placed her hands on it. "It's dirt," she said. "Not stone. And…" she frowned, and her eyes went distant. "It's clear on the other side," she said. "I need to move the dirt aside. Air, water, and now earth."

"No," Thalion said. "I can dig through this. You need to save your energy."

Niara shook her head. "It won't work," she said. "It's keyed not to respond to anything but magic."

Thalion ignored her as he placed his sword on the ground and took his shield in both hands. "You need your energy for the fire task," he said. "There's going to be one, mark my words." He brought his shield up, only to have it slide down the wall as if the wall were made of slick stone. He stared at it in disbelief.

To her credit, Niara refrained from saying "I told you so." Instead, she merely closed her eyes and started chanting again.

Thalion felt a lump forming in his throat. *I'm fairly useless during this ordeal,* he thought. *What will the nephelm think of that? I've shown no signs of Olvae's heritage.*

He shoved those thoughts aside and picked up his sword as the wall began to crumble. Light shone through into the tunnel, and he brought an arm over his face to shield himself from the glare.

He dropped his sword again as Niara staggered. He quickly moved to her side and caught her. "Niara?" he asked worriedly.

She shook her head. "I'm fine," she protested. "Let me stand."

"No, you're not," Thalion said. Her hands were shaking, and he doubted she could support herself if he let her go.

She grabbed his arm and her green eyes bored into his. "Thalion, I have to," she said. "The trial of fire is next, it must be. And I have to be there to stop it."

Thalion cursed. "Why did I come with you?" he said. "I'm fair useless!"

Niara managed a smile. "No, you're not, brother," she said. "You dealt with the lizard, remember?"

"Like you wouldn't have figured something out," Thalion grumbled. "Niara, what will they think when you're the only one who's shown signs of Olvae's heritage?"

Niara shook her head. "Don't worry about it, Thalion," she said. "You have just as much of her blood as I. You just also have Father's blood."

Thalion stared at her helplessly. "What does that even mean?"

Niara laughed. "It means you're my brother. Now will you let me stand so we can continue this trial?"

Thalion shook his head but stepped back, allowing Niara to stand on her own feet. He hovered near her until he was certain she wasn't about to collapse again.

Niara steadied herself against the wall with one hand and gestured toward the opening with her other. "Ready?" she asked.

Thalion hefted his sword and shield in his hands and nodded. Cautiously, he stuck his head out, wondering what the fourth trial would be.

The passageway opened into a large, uneven field. Hay bales, walls, and other obstacles stood scattered through it. On the other side of the field, Thalion could faintly make out the figures of the nephelm. *The other side of the course,* he thought. *We're almost there.* He gestured behind him for Niara to follow. There was no immediate danger.

He felt Niara stand at his elbow. "It's a trap," she said.

"Do we have any choice but to walk into it?" Thalion asked.

Niara shook her head. "We have to make it to the other side."

"Right," Thalion took a deep breath. "Slow and steady, then."

They started forward together. Thalion hadn't gone more than ten steps when he heard the whooshing of air above them that signaled something large approaching. His eyes widened in horror.

"Niara, get down!" he shouted. He pulled her down with him behind a small stone wall just as the shape of a dragon swooped down, roaring angrily above them.

Thalion cast a horrified gaze at Niara. "We can't fight a dragon!" he exclaimed.

Niara's eyes were just as wide. "We have to!" she yelled over the roar of the dragon. "That's the test!"

Thalion stared at her in disbelief. "Fighting a dragon is the test?"

"To prove we're not slaves," Niara ducked as the dragon passed overhead. "Thalion, this is mostly your trial. I can make it unable to breathe fire, but that's about it."

At that moment, the dragon came swooping down again, this time from the opposite direction. Thalion grabbed his sister's hand and pulled her to the other side of the stone wall, just as a blast of fire hit the place they had been hiding.

Mazda help me. I don't know if I can do this, Thalion thought. He guarded his expression. Niara needed him. He had to survive, to make it home to Serana. He made sure he had a firm grip on his sword and shield, then ran out of the cover and shouted at the sky. "I'm here, dragon! Fight me if you dare!"

He swallowed as the dragon turned toward him mid-flight. At the last moment, he dove to the side again, barely avoiding a blast of hot air, the remnants of its fiery breath. He leaned against the wooden wall, panting with adrenaline.

Niara can shut it off! For a moment, Thalion was filled with exultation. Then his thoughts dimmed. *But she's exhausted. And its breath is by no means its only weapon.* He looked up at the flying dragon, seeing the long talons and sharp teeth clearly even from a distance. He took a deep breath. *Like the lizard. Look for a weakness.*

The dragon flew toward him again, preparing for another dive. It had apparently figured out that its breath weapon didn't work and instead aimed its claws straight at Thalion.

Thalion's heart almost misgave him, but he stood firm as the dragon dove. He waited until the last minute, then jumped aside, swinging his sword down on the dragon's forearm. He heard a ring as his sword bounced off heavy scales. The dragon roared as it rose up into the air again, but not a single drop of blood dripped from his sword.

Mazda's light, Thalion thought. *How do I fight something with armor like that?* Even if it had an underbelly like the lizard, he couldn't reach it as long as the dragon kept diving and retreating. He looked around, feeling a moment of panic when Niara was no longer behind the wall he'd left her, only relaxing slightly when he realized she had merely moved to a more defensible position, between two small walls, one with a small overhang. He turned toward her, intending to ask her advice. A roar sounded above him, and he flung himself to the side just as the dragon came down in a streaking attack, moving far faster than it had before.

Thalion picked himself off the ground as the dragon launched itself into the air again. He cursed. How was he supposed to fight against that? *I can't dodge forever, I'm going to get tired,* he thought. *I need to ground it somehow!*

"Niara!" he shouted. "I need to ground it!"

"I can't!" Niara's voice was weak, and when he risked a glance in her direction, he saw her face was white and pale. She was running out of energy. *How long will she be able to stop the fire?*

Thalion looked around, frantically trying to determine a way to bring the dragon to the ground. Aside from the various obstacles, there was nothing.

Aside from the various obstacles…Thalion looked around again, this time taking closer note of how the obstacles were placed. He spotted the perfect location just as the dragon dove at him again. This time, he wasn't prepared. The dragon slashed his shoulder as he dove to the side. He yelled as pain flared from his shoulder to the rest of his body.

"Thalion!" Niara shouted.

"I'm fine!" Thalion exclaimed. He picked himself up, ignoring the screaming muscles in his left shoulder, and made his way to his chosen spot and waited for the dragon to dive again.

A roar of anger shook the air and he braced himself. He could hardly lift his shield. Cursing, he dropped it, instead placing both hands on the hilt of his sword.

"Thalion, what are you doing?" Niara's voice sounded panicked.

Thalion ignored her as the dragon dove toward him again, diving between two pillars, close enough to get its wings caught on the stone. This time, instead of dodging, he ran straight forward to meet it, ducking under its slashing claws and driving his sword directly upward. It penetrated flesh, and the dragon roared, louder than before. The very earth shook from the vibration.

He scrambled to the side before the giant body hit the ground. The dragon turned to him, eyes blazing. Blood slowly dripped from its wound.

I have to kill it, Thalion thought, his mind hazy. *It's the only way.* He hefted his sword again, ready to dodge and charge.

The dragon's jaws snapped forward, impossibly fast. Thalion fell backwards, barely avoiding it. His shoulder throbbed, a desperate reminder that he didn't have much time.

"Over here!" Niara's voice called. Thalion's eyes widened as he saw her on the other side of the dragon, standing on top of one of the obstacles, waving her arms frantically.

"No!" he exclaimed as the dragon focused on her, opening its mouth to bite at her. He charged forward, heedless of his injuries.

Niara closed her eyes and chanted something, and a burst of fire appeared in front of her just as the dragon opened its jaws wide. It roared in pain as Thalion reached it, slashing his sword into its upraised throat and tearing a long gash down its neck and to its underbelly. It roared again, weaker this time. Thalion moved back, still wary. It roared once more, then disappeared into a glimmer of air.

Thalion stared at the spot it had been in disbelief. His shoulder still throbbed, confirming that whatever it had been, it had been entirely real. He turned to find Niara and felt a moment of panic when she was no longer standing on the stone wall. He ran around to find her collapsed face-down on the ground.

"Niara? Niara!" he reached her side and shook her.

She groaned, and Thalion gasped in relief. "It didn't like a taste of its own medicine," she managed. "Test of fire, indeed!"

Thalion laughed weakly and started lifting Niara to her feet. She gasped as she moved her ankle, and Thalion froze in fear.

"I fell off the wall," she admitted. "It's hurt."

Thalion nodded and went to look at her ankle. Gently, he examined it. "I don't think it's broken," he announced in relief. "Just a sprain, likely."

"Good," Niara said. "Thalion, your shoulder!"

Thalion winced as her words reminded him of the throbbing pain. He glanced down and saw blood seeping from underneath his chainmail.

"I'll last until the other side of the field," he said. "Come on, I'll help you stand." He sheathed his sword and offered Niara his uninjured arm. She took it, hobbling uneasily on one foot. Slowly, they began moving to the other side of the field.

It seemed to take an eternity before the nephelm came clearly into view. Thalion almost collapsed with relief when he saw Kishtar there with their guards as well. They came dashing onto the field, ignoring the disapproving looks of the nephelm.

One of the guards took Niara from Thalion, and Kishtar moved to support him. "I'm fine," Thalion protested.

"That was amazing!" Kishtar exclaimed, ignoring Thalion's protest. "I wish I could have been there. You'll have to tell me all about it."

Thalion stumbled, and his arm banged against the stone wall, making him cry out in pain.

"Thalion?" Kishtar's voice expressed concern. "Thalion?"

Thalion couldn't answer as his vision started graying. He saw the other guard hurrying toward him, and then the world spun into darkness.

The room hazily came into focus. Thalion was in a bed, as far as he could tell. He could hear the crackling of a fire nearby and feel the warmth of the blankets on top of him. He shifted, blinking away the sleep from his eyes.

"Thalion?" Niara's voice.

He blinked again, the room finally focusing. He was back in the guest chambers. Niara was sitting at the edge of his bed. She smiled in relief as he met her eyes.

The dragon. The trials. The effort to prove themselves. "Did we succeed?" Thalion asked.

Niara laughed. "We did and more!" she exclaimed. "We've been treated as honored guests. We've been promised an audience with the Kakkab u Alap as soon as you awaken. Zeria told me a group has already been selected to travel to Ninaeva, and even Evikan seems to have warmed up to us."

"Then we did it," Thalion sighed in relief. "We fulfilled Mother's wish."

"And all you had to do was fight a dragon," Kishtar's voice came from across the room. Thalion raised his head and saw Kishtar grin.

"Technically, it wasn't a dragon," Niara said. "Zeria told me it was an illusion. It would have stopped short of actually killing us. Same for the lizard."

Thalion started to sit up and grimaced as he felt his shoulder complain. "Some illusion!" he said. "It still hurt me!"

"You'll have scars too," Niara said. "Your chainmail caught most of it, except three slashes. The healer had a time getting your chainmail off without causing more damage."

Thalion winced. Experimentally, he tried to lift his arm. Niara immediately moved to stop him. "No you don't," she said. "If I have to walk around with this cane, you have to take care of that shoulder. The healers left a sling for you."

Thalion rolled his eyes. "I'm fine," he protested.

Niara folded her arms across her chest, and Thalion saw he wasn't winning this argument. He sighed in resignation.

He heard Kishtar's chuckle from across the room. Kishtar grinned as he approached the bed. "This way you can tell anyone who asks that you were injured fighting a dragon," Kishtar said. "Ladies will think you the absolute hero."

Thalion flushed. *What will Serana think of my scars, next time we're together?* he wondered. *Will she think they make me more handsome, more dashing?*

Thalion saw Niara roll her eyes. "It was an illusion," she muttered.

Kishtar ignored her. "That was a fight to watch, Thalion! I wish I could have been by your side."

Thalion managed a smile. "Maybe then I wouldn't have gotten injured!" he said.

Kishtar laughed. "Well, now we can go home. To a place where there are normal-sized people."

Niara's eyes sparkled. "What, you don't want to try to flirt with Zeria?" she asked. "She'll be one of the ones coming to Ninaeva, you know."

Kishtar's eyes widened. "I'd be crushed!" he exclaimed. "Give me a lady like Lyra any day!"

"Well, I'm ready for this audience, if only to take pity on Kishtar and get us home," Thalion said. *Home. To where Serana is.* He swallowed against a sharp pang of longing.

Niara nodded. "Kishtar can help you get ready," she said. She disappeared out the door, hobbling on her cane.

"So how was the fight?" Kishtar asked as Thalion stood up.

Thalion shook his head. "Terrifying," he said honestly. "We knew we had to fight it in order to prove ourselves, but..." he shuddered. "I didn't think we could actually damage it. And now that I know it was an illusion, I'm not sure we could have actually killed a dragon."

Kishtar nodded. "It did seem smaller than the one we saw on our way here," he said. "Not that it wasn't plenty big!"

Thalion frowned, trying to remember. He hadn't spent much time analyzing the size of the dragon as he was fighting it. "No, you're right," he said. He shuddered again. "How big do the real ones get?"

Kishtar helped him into a fresh tunic. "No idea," he said. "Here, you'd better use the sling."

Thalion rolled his eyes. He couldn't deny that his shoulder did feel better when his arm was in the sling.

He knocked on the door to the adjoining room with his good hand to let Niara know he and Kishtar were ready. Together they left the guest quarters and started toward the great hall. To Thalion's surprise, there was no nephelm escort waiting for them outside their rooms.

"We're trusted now," Niara said as she limped along on her cane. "We only need to remember the way back to the great hall."

Thalion snorted. "I think we're good."

The nephelm guards were at the door to the great hall when they found their way to the entry chamber. One nodded a greeting, and the other ducked briefly inside the great hall. "The Kakkab u Alap will see you now," he said when he returned.

To Thalion's surprise, the thrones in the great hall were empty. Instead, a table and chairs had been set up just below the dais. The Kakkab u Alap and his two advisors sat in three of the chairs. One of the advisors stood up and beckoned to the four empty chairs at the table. "Join us, please."

Thalion tried to keep his astonishment from showing on his face as he accepted a seat at the table. He hadn't expected the Kakkab u Alap to give them an informal audience.

The Kakkab u Alap greeted all three of them. "You are welcome here," he said. "I am Harsag of the Nindans. You have been speaking primarily to my daughter. But now there is much that we must discuss."

Zeria, Thalion realized. *I wonder how someone so solemn fathered someone so cheerful.*

Niara was nodding in response to Harsag. "We are happy to discuss things with you. The city beneath Ilhelm…"

Harsag shook his head. "The city will be reclaimed and rebuilt, for use by your people as well as mine. If an Eye of the Goldwood said it must be, then she has good reason for it. What I wish to know is why you have no knowledge of the sky-lord, when he is even now making preparations to rise again in your kingdom."

Thalion knew his expression was as startled as Niara's. "Rise again? In Saemar?" he asked.

Harsag nodded. "We have heard reports and rumors. He is growing more and more powerful, and soon there will be none to stand against him to prevent his ascent."

Thalion stared at Harsag. "Who is he?" he demanded. "You speak as if we should know him."

"I assumed you did," Harsag said. "But perhaps it is not the custom in Saemar to know a man in his position, as it is in ours. Still, the steward is a prestigious position, is it not?"

Thalion froze. The image of Lord Auriel, standing silently behind the king, a small smile on his face, rose to his mind.

"Lord Auriel?" Niara's voice was full of incredulous disbelief. "Lord Auriel is the sky-lord?"

"Then you do know him," Harsag's eyes were dark. "Has he managed to conceal his true nature so well?"

Thalion watched as Niara shook herself. "Mother never trusted him," she said slowly, "but she had no proof, and no one would listen to what she had to say. One does not simply speak out against a steward of the realm, especially with unfounded accusations."

"Your mother is the one who sent you here?" Harsag asked.

Niara nodded.

"Then why she sent you here may well be connected to his presence in Saemar. He is plotting his rise soon. Only the final few rituals remain," Harsag said.

"Rituals?" Thalion asked.

Harsag said, "He was bound, but there is always a way to undo a binding."

"Well, can we stop the rituals?" Thalion asked.

Harsag's eyes remained dark. "All our agents in Saemar have disappeared. The sky-lord is the father of dragons. He has many powers, even bound as he is."

Thalion sat back, stunned for a second time. "Father of dragons?" he asked.

"Indeed," Harsag said. "They all answer his call. He calls them his children. He created the race of humans to serve his children."

"That's why you thought we were slaves," Kishtar breathed. "Because we've done nothing to stop his rise."

Harsag cast an approving glance at Kishtar. "Indeed. And now it may be too late."

Thalion suppressed a shudder. "What do you mean?" he asked.

Harsag shook his head. "We know something of the rituals," he said. "We helped bind him, and there is an artifact here that he may require to rise again. We will keep it safeguarded as long as possible."

Niara glanced over at Thalion. "Can we help?" she asked.

"No," Harsag's voice was firm. "You must return, and build the Ellriheim, the place of refuge. That is what your mother-eye decreed, is it not?"

Thalion shrugged slightly. She had a far better idea of their mother's wishes than he did.

Niara sighed. "I believe it is, yes. Who will be accompanying us?"

"My people will travel overland to you," Harsag said. "We do not travel on boats. Expect us within a few days of your return. When do you plan to leave?"

Thalion looked down at his arm in his sling. He knew that they should wait to recover, but...

"We would prefer to leave as soon as possible," Niara said. "We are very grateful for your hospitality, but we should return."

Harsag nodded. "You will be well supplied for the journey, and a guard will accompany you to the coast." He smiled. "No more encounters with strange beasts."

Thalion relaxed at the offer. He felt a stab of longing as he thought of Serana. It had been too long since he'd seen her.

Serana...Mazda's light, what am I going to tell her about Lord Auriel? She thought the man was her father...but now he's a god.

13

RETURN

They made it back to the ship without incident. Thalion was relieved to see Lyra and her crew still waiting for them at the beach. She greeted them with joy and pulled Kishtar in for a long, drawn-out kiss, causing her crew to whoop and whistle.

Three days later, N'Dar's Dagger was in sight again. Thalion was sitting at the stern of the ship, admiring the evening sunset, when Kishtar approached him.

Thalion smiled a greeting, but Kishtar remained uncharacteristically silent. Thalion raised his eyebrows, deciding to wait for Kishtar to say whatever was on his mind.

Finally, Kishtar sighed. "Thalion, I'm in trouble."

Thalion blinked, taken aback. He had not expected those words.

"I think I love Lyra," Kishtar said. He leaned his elbows on the rail and gazed morosely at the crystal calm water.

"Do you?" Thalion asked, raising his eyebrows.

Kishtar flushed. "I know my last declaration makes this seem unlikely," he said. "But Thalion, she's amazing, and perfect for me, and I want to marry her. But I already promised…"

"Ianna," Thalion refrained from castigating his friend. Kishtar already looked wretched. "Do you love Ianna?" he asked.

Mutely, Kishtar shook his head.

"Then you'd better explain to Ianna that you made a mistake, and you don't want to marry her," Thalion said. He folded his arms across his chest and stared at Kishtar.

Kishtar wilted. "But..."

Thalion didn't back down. "If you don't love Ianna, then you better tell her so," he said. "To not love her and marry her anyway would be doing her a disservice."

"I know," Kishtar admitted. He sighed again. "You're right."

Thalion couldn't help shaking his head. "I knew you were going to get in trouble with women someday," he said.

"I don't even know if Lyra feels the same." Kishtar groaned and rested his head in his hands.

Thalion smiled, enjoying the shift in roles. "Have you asked her? Told her how you feel?"

Kishtar shook his head. "I don't know if I can," he muttered.

"I could tell her for you," Thalion suggested, mischievously.

Kishtar's eyes widened in alarm. "You wouldn't!" he exclaimed.

Laughter broke free. "It's the same threat you made to me with Serana," he pointed out.

"I was wrong, I admit it! I was wrong! Don't you dare tell her, Thalion, please!" Kishtar begged.

"Only if you do," Thalion demanded. "And you do it soon, before we arrive in Hillsdale."

Kishtar groaned again. "I hate it when you're right," he said. "How do you suggest I talk to her?"

Thalion couldn't believe his ears. "You're the expert on women!" he exclaimed. "And I managed to bungle my first proposal to Serana, so I don't think I'm going to give advice on that. No, you just talk to her."

Kishtar stared at him in despair. "Thalion..."

"Kishtar, there you are!" Lyra's voice was sultry as she approached them.

Kishtar looked at Thalion in panic, and Thalion could hardly restrain his laughter. "Kishtar was just talking about you, Lyra," he said, enjoying the alarm in Kishtar's eyes. "I think you should have a nice long talk with him."

"Oh?" Lyra asked, smiling at Kishtar.

Kishtar visibly gathered his courage and offered his arm to Lyra. "Yes," he said. "Perhaps back in your cabin?"

Lyra smiled at him. "Of course."

Thalion gave Kishtar an encouraging wink as they walked away. He turned back to watch the sunset, still chuckling.

"What's so funny?" Niara asked as she approached.

Thalion moved to make space for her on the railing next to him. "Kishtar," he said, without any explanation.

"Oh, has he finally admitted that he's falling in love?" Niara asked. "It's about time. Lyra's been mooning over him."

"She has?" Thalion grinned.

Niara nodded, and they stared at the sunset together. It was beautiful, shades of orange and pink and red dancing across the water.

"What will we do when we get home?" Niara asked.

Thalion didn't need to ask what she meant. She was talking about Auriel. "I don't know," he said. He sighed. "I've already been trying to figure out how to tell Serana. We'll tell Father, of course, but other than that..." he shook his head. "Who would believe us? And who would have the power to do something if he did?"

"No one in Saemar," Niara said. "Perhaps some of the elves?"

"Mother already sent all the Thorns she had to Alfheim," Thalion frowned. "She told them to bring as many as would come back to Ilhelm."

"I've been thinking about that," Niara said. "Do you think the Lady knew about Auriel and gave Mother the tools to prepare?"

Thalion shrugged helplessly. "Can anyone guess what the Lady knows?"

Niara laughed as she shook her head. "No, I suppose not," she said. She stared out over the water. "You believe the nephelm, though, right? That Lord Auriel is the sky-lord, father of dragons?"

Thalion nodded. "They wouldn't lie about that," he said. "And I doubt they're mistaken, either." He couldn't say why he was so certain about that.

"I knew it was true as soon as they said it." She shuddered. "Dragons... do you really think they would return? What would the world look like?"

Thalion gazed up at the sky, imagining the dark form of a dragon flying overhead. "It would be terrifying," he said. "We barely could fight against an illusion of one."

"Would we have to fight?" Niara wondered. "There is the tale of King Enlil and the Dragonriders..."

Thalion snorted. "The nephelm called humans slaves of the sky-lord, created to serve his dragons," he reminded her. "I doubt they'd be content with coexistence. We'd be slaves again."

Niara sighed. "I guess you're right," she said. Her voice sounded wistful.

Thalion put an arm around Niara's shoulders. "I doubt our new king will allow himself to be so easily led," he said, trying to give her confidence. "Andreas is not one to let anyone act above him, even if the man is former regent and steward. Auriel will have a harder time rising than the nephelm think."

Niara sighed again. "I hope you're right," she said. "I just," her eyes widened, and she stared sightlessly out over the water.

Not another vision, Thalion thought. He tightened his grip on Niara's shoulders, steadying her.

His vision went black, and he gasped as the world shifted around him.

Hundreds of trees. Lights flickering in the darkness, revealing longhouses built at the bank of a lake. The lights were torches. Someone screamed. Horses pounded through the forest, carrying soldiers. Elves ran from the soldiers in terror. Some stood and shot arrow after arrow into the attackers, but they were quickly cut down. Blood soaked the ground and the screams... Mazda's light, the screams...elf children ran before the soldiers, only to be cut down or rounded up without mercy. Bodies lay everywhere.

Behind the first wave of soldiers, two men arrived at the scene of the battle. Thalion gasped as he recognized them. The king and Lord Auriel.

"A masterful attack," Lord Auriel said.

The king grinned. "Thanks to your planning," he said. "This land is now part of Saemar."

"As it should be," Lord Auriel said. "A king such as you deserves an Empire."

The king grinned even wider, then spurred his horse forward to join the massacre. Lord Auriel followed at a more careful pace, followed closely by three figures clad in burgundy armor.

Thalion gasped as his vision returned to normal and the ocean swam into view. Niara was still in her arms, tears running soundlessly down her cheeks.

He shook his head, disoriented. "What was that?" he demanded.

"Alfheim," Niara's voice broke. "The king has attacked Alfheim. A massacre..." she cut off with another sob.

Thalion stared at her in disbelief. "That was a vision? A true vision?"

She nodded. Her eyes darkened through her tears. "Alfheim has been massacred," she said. "Saemar has betrayed its alliance. I will not allow Ninaeva to be part of that. When we get home, we are no longer part of Saemar, brother."

Thalion leaned back against the rail, remembering the screams and panicked cries of the elves as the soldiers massacred them. They hadn't even been Eyes or Thorns, he realized. Just common elven citizens. He nodded his agreement. He could not serve a king who would command such a thing.

Thalion could not contain his relief at seeing the towers of Ilhelm Castle rising above the landscape. It had been over two months since they'd set off to find the nephelm, and Manyu's Time was almost over. It would be good to be home.

Though now we're going to have to figure out what to do about Auriel. Thalion shook his head. He would let Niara and his father make a decision on that point. His father would likely want to find everything in the library that referenced the sky-lord.

He glanced over at Kishtar riding next to him and couldn't refrain from chuckling. Their trip had been successful in more ways than one. Kishtar had proposed to Lyra, and she had accepted. She had duties and responsibilities that kept her in Hillsdale for the time, so plans had been made for a wedding in late Mazda's Rise. They would have to discuss their living arrangements sometime before then. Thalion would be sad to see Kishtar leave Ilhelm, but at least in Hillsdale he wouldn't be that far.

He tensed with happy anticipation as they passed through the gates of the castle. He was finally home. *Serana, I'm here!*

He saw Nazir walk out of the castle to greet them, followed by Gwyn and Evalynna. Nazir embraced Thalion first, then turned to Niara. "It is good to have you both home," he said.

Thalion swallowed as he examined his father. He appeared so much older now than he remembered, although his skin was still just as smooth, and his black hair still unchanged. His eyes, however, held a dark sorrow.

"We have much to tell you," Niara said. "But first, did any of the elves Mother sent off to Alfheim return?"

Nazir seemed confused at the insistence in Niara's voice. "Yes, a large group of them arrived a few days ago. They said more would be expected this week."

Niara relaxed. "Mazda give thanks," she said. "They were not all killed."

Nazir's eyes widened. "Killed?" he asked.

Niara nodded grimly. "By Saemarians," she said. "Our own king betrayed his allies and massacred Alfheim, backed by the steward."

Nazir blinked and shook his head. "Why?" he asked.

Thalion let Niara start explaining about Lord Auriel being the fallen god of the sky and father of dragons. He surveyed the courtyard, frowning. Where was Serana? Surely she knew he had returned?

He waited for a break in Niara's explanation. His father was looking more and more revived at the thought of having something to research.

"Father? Where's Serana?" he asked.

His father turned to him. "She went to the capital a few weeks ago," he said. "She couldn't bear being estranged from her mother, so she went to try and mend the bond."

Thalion bit his lip. "A few weeks ago? Did she say when she was going to return?"

Nazir frowned. "Today or tomorrow at the latest," he said. "She went with a contingent of guards and her father."

Thalion felt his gaze drawn back to the road toward the capital. He couldn't shake a feeling of worry.

"I'm sure she'll return within a day, son," Nazir said, laying a comforting hand on his shoulder.

Niara grimaced. "It's not like Lord Auriel is in the capital to cause her any trouble right now, not when he's been off massacring elves."

"Elves," Thalion breathed. "Lord Auriel must know of Serana's true heritage." He looked at Niara. "What if Lord Auriel manipulated the king into that attack for some reason other than simple conquest? What if there's something about elves? They did help bind him last time, didn't they?"

Niara's eyes widened. "The nephelm mentioned an artifact they held," she said. "Do you think the elves held another?"

Thalion shrugged helplessly. "I don't know," he said. "But what if it's just something to do with elves? If so, Serana could be in danger!"

"Thalion," Niara tried to calm him. "Saihid's with her. He'll protect her from anything, including her mother."

"But they don't know about Lord Auriel," Thalion felt certain that something had gone dreadfully wrong. "I'm going after her."

"Thalion, the nephelm will arrive soon," Niara started. "We're needed here."

Thalion turned a pleading expression toward her. "Niara, I have to go. I'm certain of it."

Something in his voice made Niara frown. "You're absolutely certain?" she asked.

Thalion nodded. "If I'm mistaken, I'm sure I'll meet her on the road," he said. "I can feel foolish then."

Niara looked at Nazir for help.

Nazir regarded his son with a strange expression. "You almost sound like your mother right now," he said. "When she was certain she had to do something, but didn't know why." He nodded decisively. "Go then, my son. Return with your wife."

Thalion sighed in relief. The certainty that he needed to leave, and leave now, was only growing in him.

"I'll come with you," Kishtar said.

Thalion blinked as he regarded his friend. A servant had come out in the middle of the conversation and handed Kishtar a letter, and now his face was pale and worried.

"Good. When do you wish to leave?" Nazir asked Thalion.

"Immediately," Thalion said.

"Kishtar? Are you prepared?" Nazir asked.

Kishtar took a deep breath and nodded. Thalion looked curiously at his friend, wondering what had been in that message that disturbed him so much.

"Fresh horses, then, and enough time to pack some provisions," Niara decreed. "It'll save you time in the long run. And maybe we'll see her returning before you're ready to leave."

Thalion could hear the hope in her voice. He walked over and clasped his sister's hand. "Thank you, sister," he said. "I'll be back."

Niara blinked. "You'd better," she said. "I can't secede from Saemar until you return."

Thalion chuckled. "Well, we can't have that." He turned his face back toward the road.

Serana, I'm coming, he thought. *Whatever's happening, just know that I'm coming.*

The closer they got to the capital, the more worried Thalion became. They met a number of people who remembered a noblewoman and her retinue traveling to the capital, but none had seen her returning home. Thalion couldn't shake the feeling that something had gone dreadfully wrong.

Kishtar was equally silent. In a better mood, Thalion would have pressed him about the contents of the letter he had received, about his reasons for traveling to the capital with him, but he couldn't tear his mind away from Serana.

It was in that mood that he saw the temple where he and Serana had been married. He stared at it as they approached, something niggling at the back of his mind.

"Thalion?" Kishtar asked.

Thalion turned his horse toward the temple. "We're stopping here," he said.

The bells for midday services were tolling as they entered the courtyard. Thalion and Kishtar dismounted and tied their horses to a post. Kishtar glanced curiously at Thalion.

"What are we doing?" Kishtar asked.

"Serana and I were married here," Thalion said. "She might have stopped here on her way to the capital. And Father Boilli might know what's going on." He knew something was going on. If they hadn't met Serana yet, then she was still in the capital. *She knew our planned return date. She would have wanted to be in Ninaeva when I returned, wouldn't she? Something has delayed her.*

Thalion entered the temple and waited while Father Boilli finished his final blessing. As the temple emptied, he waited in the very back. As Father Boilli began cleaning up from the service, Thalion walked forward to greet him.

Father Boilli's eyes widened as he caught sight of him. "Lord Thalion!" he said. "My lord, it is good to see you!" He hurriedly put the last of his holy items away and took Thalion's hand. "I knew the rumors they were saying about you could not be true!"

Thalion blinked. "Rumors?" he asked.

Father Boilli shook his head. "Child of demons, kidnapper of princesses, nonsense such as that. I tried to tell them differently when they came here, after all, I was the one who married you, but no one would listen." His voice was full of disgust.

Thalion felt a feeling of foreboding. "Kidnapper?" he asked.

Father Boilli nodded, then his voice rose in alarm. "What am I doing? You must not be seen here! Come, come!" He took Thalion's arm and led him into a small room off the main sanctuary. Kishtar followed.

Thalion stared at the priest. "Your radiance, what's been happening?" he asked. "Has Serana been here? Have you heard anything about her?"

Father Boilli shook his head again. "There are vicious lies being spread about you and your family, Lord Thalion," he said. "Most common is that you, a demon spawn lord, kidnapped Lady Serana against her will, that she has now escaped, and the king is planning to marry her as soon as he returns from campaign. I've heard he plans to exactly vengeance on the northern barbarians who insulted his bride." He raised an eyebrow.

Thalion staggered back a step. "I never kidnapped her!" he exclaimed. "Your radiance, you know that! You saw us here!"

Father Boilli nodded. "Aye, that I know. A couple more in love I never saw. Oh, I knew the obstacles, that she was in name betrothed to the prince, but your wishes superseded that. But the nobles of the land do not see it as such." He paused. "She was also proudly bearing your name when she stopped here last. I do not believe a kidnapped lady would name herself Lady Serana et-Alim."

Thalion felt a surge of relief at Father Boilli's words. There had been a niggling worry that Serana had grown tired of waiting for him and had returned to the capital to leave him.

"My lords," Father Boilli addressed both Thalion and Kishtar. "Please, stay the night here. You, Lord Thalion, cannot enter the capitol without a disguise of some sort. The guards will be on the lookout for you, and given the current mood of the nobles you may be thrown in the dungeons before you can defend yourself. Please, be prepared before you risk such a thing."

Thalion glanced at Kishtar, who shrugged. He turned back helplessly to Father Boilli. "Do you know where Serana is now?" he asked.

Father Boilli shook his head. "She asked for advice on reconciling with her mother, so I presume she went to where her mother resides."

"The palace," Thalion cursed under his breath. The most secure building in Saemar. He sighed. "We will accept your offer for tonight, your radiance," he said. "But in the morning, I am leaving to rescue my wife."

Father Boilli nodded approvingly. "I would expect nothing else from a son of Ninaeva," he said. "I'll show you to your quarters."

Thalion and Kishtar followed the priest to a set of adjoining rooms. As soon as Father Boilli left, Thalion released a string of curses.

"I am not a kidnapper!" he exclaimed. "Or demon spawn! Those are blatant lies, spread by someone who wants to slander me! It must be the king. Who else would hate me so much?"

Kishtar folded his arms over his chest. "Her mother?" he suggested. "Her brother? Lord Auriel, who might view himself as her father?"

Thalion felt a solid weight settle into the pit of his stomach. "So how do I get her out, if all these people are against us?" he asked.

"Well, you find her, and then you leave," Kishtar said. "I'm sure we'll figure out details." He smiled, the first smile he'd worn all week. "After all, the two of us together can take on the world, remember?"

Thalion managed to return the smile. "Of course we can," he said. "And we won't even have to face the king. If Niara's vision occurred at the same time it happened, they'll still be on their way back from Alfheim." He shuddered at the memory of the vision.

Kishtar nodded. "We can rescue her and be gone before they even knew she was here."

There was no doubt in Thalion's mind that they would need to rescue her. Serana would have denied any of the rumors, so someone must be keeping her quiet. And if the king wasn't there, then that left her mother or brother as the most likely culprits.

"How do I get into the city?" Thalion asked. "The priest's right, I can't go without a disguise. But what disguise will cover my entire skin?"

Kishtar frowned in thought. "A monk? Or a priest?" he suggested.

"Some of them wear hooded robes. I'm sure the priest here would be happy to lend you one."

Thalion felt a moment's concern over wearing a priest's robes when he was not entitled to them, then pushed the worry away. Mazda would understand his need. "That will work," he said. "As to where she's being held…" he thought. "Rian," he said. "She'll be willing to help me, at least to tell me where she's being held."

"Rian?" Kishtar asked.

"She helped us escape the first time." Thalion smiled. "Hopefully she'll be willing to do it a second time."

Kishtar took a deep breath. "I suppose we'll have to go to her townhouse, then." He shuddered.

Thalion frowned. "Either that, or her rooms at the palace." He furrowed his brow. "What's wrong?"

"I…I told you I'd promised to marry Ianna?" Kishtar paled.

Thalion nodded. "Are you scared to tell Ianna you're marrying Lyra instead?"

Kishtar shook his head. "No. Well, yes, but it's not just that." He turned his face away and mumbled something.

"Kishtar?" Thalion asked.

He barely heard Kishtar repeat his words. "She's carrying my child."

Thalion's eyes widened. "She's what?" he exclaimed.

Kishtar flushed bright red. "I made a mistake!" he exclaimed. "But she was so kind, so gentle, so different from Dinah, and she wanted me…" he trailed off and stared helplessly at Thalion. "And then I received a message from her begging me to come to the capital and legitimize our child. What am I supposed to do?"

Thalion shook his head. "Kishtar…"

Kishtar turned away again. "I know I should marry her, should do the responsible thing," he said. "I know what happens to women with bastard children! Your mother was one of the lucky ones. Pellalindra married Lord Auriel to hide Serana's parentage. I can't just abandon Ianna to that kind of fate. But I don't love her, and don't want to marry her. I want to marry Lyra."

Thalion shook his head. "I don't know what to tell you, Kishtar," he managed. Kishtar had laid out the entire problem, and Thalion could not help feeling for him. *He shouldn't have slept with Ianna,* he thought, *but I can't blame him for falling in love with Lyra instead. How is he going to solve this?*

Kishtar sighed. "I have to talk to her anyway," he said. "Maybe we can work something out. I'll provide for the child no matter what, of course."

"I never doubted that." Thalion shook his head. He walked over and clasped Kishtar's shoulder. "We'll figure it out. Together we can take on the world, remember?"

That brought a weak smile to Kishtar's face. "Thank you, Thalion," he said. He straightened. "Now, let's work out the details as to how we're going to rescue your wife."

14

THE CAPITOL

Thalion eyed the Lokrian townhouse. "Ready?" he asked.

Kishtar shook his head. "Not really. But let's do it anyway."

Thalion nodded and started walking toward the townhouse. The priests' robes he wore seemed heavy, as if they were dragging him down. Logically, he knew they were no heavier than his armor, but they felt heavier.

Thalion pushed Kishtar in front of him as they approached the door to the townhouse. Since he was disguised, Kishtar would have to be the one to do the talking.

Kishtar swallowed before knocking on the door. It was only moments before a servant appeared and inquired as to their identity.

"Lord Kishtar of Ninaeva," Kishtar said.

The servant looked briefly at Thalion, then dismissed him as irrelevant. "You've been expected, Lord Kishtar. Please, this way."

Kishtar glanced at Thalion before following the servant. Thalion's own heart beat in his chest with nervousness for himself and sympathy for Kishtar.

The servant led them to a small sitting room and then disappeared. Kishtar paced up and down the room, unable to sit still. "He's getting Ianna, I know he is. Mazda's light, what am I going to do?"

Thalion shrugged, unable to think of any advice. He was having trouble focusing on Kishtar's problems. He didn't need to speak to Ianna. He needed to speak to Rian. She would be the one who would help him find Serana.

"Kishtar, you came!" Ianna's voice echoed through the sitting room. Kishtar pivoted, his eyes widening in alarm as Ianna strode forward, moving to throw her arms around him.

"Ianna," he managed, taking a step back.

Ianna stopped an arm's length away. "Did you get my note?" she asked, worry in her voice.

Kishtar swallowed. "Yes."

I need to ask her about Rian before they talk any further. Thalion cleared his throat, and Ianna glanced at him, startled. She had been so focused on Kishtar's presence she hadn't even noticed him in his priest's guise.

"My pardon, I didn't see you," she said, her voice suddenly formal. She looked back at Kishtar. "Will you introduce me?"

Thalion saw Kishtar open his mouth, and he intervened again. "I'm a simple priest, my lady," he said, lowering his voice. "I have a message for your sister, Lady Rian, and Lord Kishtar was good enough to escort me here."

Ianna's expression cleared. "Rian's not here," she said. "She's at the palace."

Thalion suppressed a curse. The palace was the last place he wanted to go until he was ready to rescue Serana. "Would it be possible for you to summon her here?" he asked. "The message was quite urgent."

Ianna shook her head. "I'm sorry," she said. "She was quite adamant she was not going to leave until the king arrived, and he's expected back any day now."

Mazda's light. Thalion took an involuntary step backwards. The king was expected any day? *I have to get Serana out of here. When the king gets back, she'll be even more closely guarded. I need to get her out!*

Ianna continued, oblivious to his reaction. "You can visit her in the palace, though, if it's that urgent. Unless…" she hesitated, turning to Kishtar. "You'd be willing to witness something first?"

"Ianna…" Kishtar whispered.

"What?" Ianna turned toward him, her expression confused. "Kishtar, what is it?"

Thalion saw Kishtar struggle with his words. "Ianna, I'm sorry," he managed. "I can't marry you."

"What?" Ianna demanded. "You got my note, and then come to tell me that?" her voice shook. "Kishtar, you promised me!"

"Ianna, I'm sorry," Kishtar repeated. He took a step backwards. "I made a mistake. I enjoyed our time, really, I did, but I want to marry for love, and I'm sorry, I just don't love you. I'll support you and our child, I'll acknowledge them, I'll do anything you want me to, I just can't marry you." Kishtar seemed to realize he was babbling and shut up, breathing hard.

Ianna's expression was blank as she stared at him. "Get out," she whispered.

"Ianna," Kishtar's voice was broken.

"Get out," Ianna said again, her voice louder. "I can't deal with you right now, Kishtar, just get out!" she turned away, her shoulders shaking.

Kishtar swallowed. "I meant what I said about supporting you," he said.

"Manyu curse you, Kishtar," Ianna said.

Thalion put a hand on Kishtar's arm, cutting off whatever further protest or apology Kishtar was going to make. "Write her later," he said, shaking his head.

Kishtar looked like he was about to protest, then deflated. "I'll write you," he said to Ianna's back.

Ianna didn't respond, and Thalion tugged Kishtar's arm, pulling him out of the study and to the exit. They made it halfway down the street before Kishtar groaned.

"Mazda's light, Thalion, what have I done?" he said.

Thalion grimaced, unable to offer any comfort. "She didn't seem to take it well," he said.

Kishtar shook his head. "She didn't even want to talk! What if she hides the child from me? What if she never allows me to see them?"

Thalion blinked. "Do you want to see the child?" he asked. He didn't know how Lyra would take that, another woman and child being part of Kishtar's life, but he supposed that was Kishtar's problem, not his.

Kishtar groaned again. "I hadn't even thought about it before, but yes," he said. "And now I might've just lost my chance at that."

Thalion hesitated, then moved over to clap Kishtar on the shoulder. "I'm sure we can discover them," he said. "Ianna can't hide the child's existence from everyone, especially since we know they exist."

Kishtar nodded but didn't seem comforted.

Thalion frowned and waited for Kishtar to say something.

"I just...Thalion, I feel like I made a dreadful mistake somewhere, but now I don't know what to do to fix it," Kishtar said. "I thought...I thought Ianna would make a good wife. She was sweet, kind, and lively, and not demanding like Dinah. But then I met Lyra..." he shook his head. "Thalion, am I doing the right thing?"

Thalion held out his hands helplessly. "Did I do the right thing when I eloped with Serana?" he asked.

Kishtar's eyes widened. "What do you mean?"

Thalion shrugged. "I love her, and she loves me, but it's caused Ninaeva no end of trouble. I think it's worth it, but if my parents were anyone else, they might not agree."

Kishtar blinked. "But you love each other," he said.

"And you love Lyra," Thalion pointed out.

Kishtar sighed. "It's not the same situation."

"No," Thalion agreed. "But you can't know what the right choice is, just like I can't. You just have to take a chance."

Kishtar straightened. "You're right. I'm sorry I'm distracting you with my own problems."

Thalion managed a smile. "That's what brothers are for, right?"

A ghost of a smile flitted across Kishtar's face. "Well, we failed to find Rian," he said. "Any ideas of what to do next?"

Thalion took a deep breath. "Actually, yes," he said. He looked in the direction of the palace, the large building rising up over the rows of townhouses. "I'm going to have to do it alone, however. You go to our townhouse and prepare for an escape, alright?"

Kishtar raised his eyebrows. "You're sneaking into the palace?"

"I'm not going to sneak." Thalion grinned. "I'm going to walk right in."

Thalion had always thought the palace intimidating. Staring at it now, dressed in his Mazdian priests' robes with a hood that hung low over his face, it was more intimidating than ever. The black-armored guards stood like statues, their spears at the ready to deny anyone entry.

He shook himself as he realized he stared at the main palace entrance. That wasn't the way he was going to enter. The stables were around the right, as was the servant's entrance. Servants couldn't share the same entryway as the nobles, of course. *Though they probably do more of the actual work of running the palace than the nobles.*

Thalion made his way over to the stables and stood for a moment, watching. Far too many people crowded around. Stable hands milled about, all on alert for something.

Thalion squared his shoulders. *You're a priest giving blessings. Mazda will forgive you for pretending to be his priest. It's the only way to get into the palace without arousing suspicion.*

A huge commotion caught his ear just before he stepped into the stable. Every stable hand leaped to attention, and a few seconds later dozens of horses and men were arriving in the stable. They were loud, tired, and sweaty. The stable hands rushed to work unsaddling and rubbing down the horses, while the men got in their way and talked at the top of their lungs.

Thalion couldn't believe his luck. *Now!* he thought. He stepped forward, taking advantage of the commotion to walk quickly through the stable.

"Priest!"

He froze at the barked voice. Keeping his head bowed, he turned in the direction of the voice. *I have to brazen this out, I have to...Mazda help me!*

"Yes, my son?" he asked, keeping his voice as low as possible.

The man facing him was a soldier, dressed in the uniform of the king's guard. He hesitated as he regarded Thalion. "Might I ask for your blessing, your radiance?" he asked. "I think I'm in sore need of it."

The words froze in Thalion's throat. Somehow, he nodded and walked over to the man. He had seen the priests give blessings enough times to mimic the stance. He raised his hands above his head to call on the sun-lord, then brought them down on either side of the soldier's head as he sang the traditional blessing. As he did warmth spread through him, enveloping both him and the soldier. It tingled through him like lightning, and he nearly gave away his disguise by staring at the soldier in shock.

The soldier had no such worries, and his gaze was as astonished as Thalion felt. The soldier fell to one knee and bowed his head. "You are a blessed priest," he whispered. "Thank you, your radiance."

Thalion barely managed to mumble out a proper response. He still shook. What had happened?

Still tingling, he turned away from the soldier and made his way through the stables. Everything seemed sharper. His sight pierced through the shadows, saw the mice scurrying through the straw on the ground. He moved quickly, staying as quiet as possible.

At the entrance of the gardens, he took a deep breath. With the frantic coming and going of servants, he had been unnoticed. Now he had to make his way to the west wing.

He wished he had Serana's knowledge of the passages of the palace. All he had to guide him were memories of their desperate flight the first time. *I wish I knew where Serana's quarters were. Then I could see if she's there and leave without worry. If she's being held there. If she's not being guarded.* He felt his lips tighten. *I'll get you out, Serana, I promise.* Remembering the path Saihid had led them out the first time, he made his way through the hedges.

"Has she come around at all?"

Thalion froze as he heard a voice, low and male. He ducked behind the hedge. He recognized the voice: Percival Duskryn.

"Not yet. She will." That second voice belonged to Percival's mother, Lady Pellalindra.

"She's married, Lady Mother. Don't you think the king would prefer a legitimate marriage? Only if both Thalion and Serana agree can the marriage be dissolved." Despite his words, Percival did not sound concerned.

Pellalindra sniffed. "A marriage performed on the run, in a forsaken roadside temple? It never happened. I have been assured that the king will see things our way. She was kidnapped and remains as virtuous and innocent as before."

Thalion felt his breathing get quicker. They were talking about Serana, his wife, and dismissing the very idea that she was married!

"What about Thalion? What if he comes forward?" Percival asked.

Pellalindra laughed. "The man who kidnapped the king's intended bride? He would be a fool."

He could hear the frown in Percival's words. "Lady Mother, the Ninaevans are not without power."

"There has been absolute silence from Ninaeva," Pellalindra said, her voice calm. "And I have it on good authority that Lady Vinet and her children have not been seen there for over two months."

Thalion held his breath. What else did she know?

"What does that mean?" Percival asked.

Pellalindra chuckled. "It means, my dear son, that by the time anyone from Ninaeva hears about it, Serana will be Queen."

"If she decides to marry the king," Percival said in a wry tone.

"Oh, she will. Trust me, my son, she will." Pellalindra's voice faded as they moved away.

Thalion fought to get his breathing under control as they left.

Pellalindra sounded so certain that her daughter would marry the king. Did she have a plan? Something to change Serana's mind?

Does she not care for her daughter's happiness? Or does she think being queen will make up for anything Serana could want? Thalion shook those thoughts aside. He couldn't be distracted, not now. He still needed to make his way through the palace to Rian's quarters.

He paused at the door that he remembered coming through with Serana. The memory of their flight was a blur. Serana had led the way. He didn't know if he could remember the exact passages she had taken.

It doesn't matter. I have to try. Resolutely, he took a breath and opened the door. To his relief, the corridor was empty. He started walking, trying to be confident in his directions.

Within five turns, he knew he was lost. Still, he kept going, going deeper and deeper into the palace. He stopped in despair when he realized that by some mischance, he was in a passage that he'd already been in. *Or this one looks so alike that it could be the same passage.*

He heard a giggle behind him and only barely prevented himself from whirling around. Instead, he turned slowly, in time to see two female servants holding hands and giggling together. One of them raised her head and saw him. She blanched and pulled her companion to a stop, dropping her hand.

"Forgive us, your radiance, pay us no mind…" she babbled.

Thalion made himself smile. "Nothing to forgive, my child," he said, keeping his voice low.

The servant smiled, relief evident in her face. "Thank you, your radiance. We weren't neglecting our duties, I swear."

From the uneasy glance the other sent her, Thalion knew she was probably lying. He relaxed slightly. If they weren't where they should be, they were less likely to report a priest where he shouldn't be.

"Perhaps you could help a poor, confused, priest?" he asked. "I am supposed to deliver a message to Lady Rian in the west wing, but I fear I have been turned around."

The servant giggled. "Oh, that's fine, your radiance. Just keep straight, then left and up the stairs. You're almost there."

Thalion nodded his thanks. As he turned to leave, he heard the other servant clear her throat.

"Forgive me, your radiance, but could we ask for your blessing? I think my friend," she shot a glare at her companion, "is in sore need of it."

Thalion cursed to himself under his breath, but there was no way to back out of it without arousing suspicion. *You should have chosen a better disguise.*

He forced a smile as he raised his hands to call upon Mazda and brought them down first on the one girl's head, then the other, singing the chant as he did so. Once again, he felt the strange tingling, sharpening sensation as before.

The girls stared at him, both their mouths dropping open. As one, they curtsied, then rapidly backed away. "Thank you, your radiance!" one called. As they left, Thalion heard one of them whisper to the other, "That was a real holy man! Blessed by Mazda himself!"

"Then you'd best behave now that you have his blessing..." their voices trailed off down the corridor.

Thalion took a deep breath and leaned against the wall, vowing to leave an appropriate offering to Mazda as soon as he was out of the capital with Serana.

He swallowed to steady himself against the sharpness of his perceptions. Following the servant's directions, he made his way down the corridor, stopping once as he heard a door opening and closing. He frowned. That door was well past the distance he could normally hear even with his elven heritage. He shook his head and continued, finding the flight of stairs that led up.

He breathed a sigh of relief. The west wing. It took him only one glance to locate Rian's quarters. He braced himself as he knocked quietly on her door. *What if she's not in? What if she screams loud enough to alert the palace? It would certainly gain her the favor of the king if she reported me...*he didn't have time to worry anymore when Rian opened the door, a wide smile on her face. The smile quickly turned to horror as she saw him.

"I...uh..." Thalion stammered.

Rian grabbed his arm. "What are you *doing* here?" she demanded. "Now, of all times?"

Thalion blinked, confused by her words. "I..."

"Never mind," Rian snapped as she dragged him through her rooms. She looked around frantically, then shoved him toward the bed. "Get under there now, and for the love of your life, do not make a sound!"

Thalion stared at her in confusion, but she only shoved him again, more urgently. He crawled under the bed, hurrying as he heard a loud knock on the outer door. He heard Rian's footsteps as she moved to open it.

She was expecting visitors! Mazda's light, how long am I going to have to stay here?

"Your majesty, welcome home!" Rian's voice was low and seductive.

Thalion froze. *The king? In Rian's quarters? Mazda's light, please, get me out of this, I swear I'll repay you somehow...*

"Lady Rian," the king's tone was smooth. "How could I fail to return home when such a beautiful lady awaited me?"

Rian chuckled. "Such flattery, your majesty."

Thalion could barely breathe as he tried to remain as quiet as possible. He strained his ears for some sound, some hint of what was occurring. Why was the king visiting Rian's private chambers, and right after his return?

The next sound he heard was the king's gasping voice. "Mazda's light, Rian, but you tempt me."

"Successfully?" Rian asked in a playful tone.

The king groaned. "Temptress." A long silence fell again.

Thalion's eyes widened, even though he had nothing to stare at in the darkness. *Rian...and the king? She's sleeping with him? The king?*

"Now, your majesty, don't you have an important meeting with your generals?" Rian laughed. "A debrief? Or perhaps a meeting with your steward?"

"Manyu take my meetings," the king said in a growl.

Rian's voice was low. "I would never want to come between you and the duties of the crown," she said. "Not that you don't sorely tempt me, your majesty."

"Mazda's light, woman," the king breathed. "I said Manyu take the meetings."

Thalion's breath quickened. *They're not...oh Mazda's light, please no...*

"Manyu take the meetings, indeed." Rian laughed lightly. "Then perhaps you would enjoy a bath first? You must be terribly sore from that long ride. A bath, and a nice massage, and then..." her voice trailed off suggestively.

"You, my dear, are the most brilliant woman in the court. Accompany me?"

"I cannot be seen accompanying you just yet, your majesty," Rian said in a disappointed voice. "But I can meet you in your chambers?"

Another intake of breath from the king. "Don't be late," he growled. Heavy footsteps, followed by the sound of the door opening and closing.

Thalion's breath released in a rush. He heard Rian's footsteps as she entered the bedchamber again.

"Thalion, out, now," her voice was sharp.

Thalion scrambled out from under the bed to meet her blazing eyes. "Don't you breathe a word about what you just witnessed," she hissed.

Thalion raised his hands in surrender. His mind was still whirling, trying to process the scene. *Rian is the king's mistress. No wonder she was willing to help me. Me marrying Serana got the competition out of the way...*

"Rian, I don't care what's between you and the king," he said. "I just care about Serana. Do you know where she is? Where she's being held?"

Rian stared at him a moment longer, then nodded shortly. "She's here in the palace," she said. "In her quarters. People saw her arrive but haven't seen her since."

Thalion's lips tightened. "Where are her quarters?" he asked.

"East wing," Rian said. "She shares with her mother. Thalion..." her voice trailed off. "You can't just go march up and demand she be returned to you. The guards will throw you in the dungeon as soon as they know you're here."

"I know," Thalion said grimly. "Don't worry, I'm not planning on doing that."

Rian frowned. "Then what are you planning?" she demanded.

"I'm planning to rescue my wife," Thalion said simply.

Rian shook her head. "You know, I didn't really expect you to be able to convince her to elope," she said. "I thought I was giving you a chance to say goodbye."

Thalion managed a crooked smile. "I'm sure you were pleased with the result anyway."

Rian's eyes darkened. "Serana doesn't want to be queen," she said. "I do." Unspoken were the words that she would do anything to achieve that goal.

Thalion took a deep breath. "Well, when you do become queen, I would appreciate it if you could ask the king not to ravage Ninaeva in revenge. My mother and sister, not to mention the common people, had nothing to do with our elopement."

Rian smiled. "I'll be sure to mention it. Now, I have to go. Can you make your way out of the palace?"

Thalion glanced down at his robes. "I'm sure getting out will be easier than getting in."

Rian nodded. "Farewell, then. And Thalion… good luck."

"There you are!" Kishtar's voice was a hiss of relief. "I was getting worried!"

Thalion threw the hood off of his head, glad to be rid of the confining disguise. The hall of the Ninaevan townhouse seemed unfamiliar after being away from the capital for so long. "Sneaking into and out of the palace takes a while," he said.

Kishtar snorted as he led Thalion deeper into the townhouse. Thalion stopped short when he realized they were in his mother's study. He blinked. They were not alone. "Saihid?" he asked.

Saihid nodded. "I thought you would come. You're not a moment too soon."

"Saihid, what happened?" Thalion demanded. "Why did you come here?"

Saihid's eyes were dark. "Serana was lonely," he said. "And distressed she'd heard nothing from her mother, despite several messages. She decided to visit in person. Your father seemed better and made no protest."

Thalion made an inarticulate sound. "I wish she'd waited."

Saihid glared at him. "You were not there," he said. "She was alone in a strange land. I could not gainsay her wishes."

Thalion wanted to protest that he'd had no choice, but he kept his mouth shut. "I assume you haven't been able to see her since she went to the palace?" he asked instead.

Saihid nodded, his eyes dark. "I did not dare go to her mother myself," he said. "Luckily, I do not believe Pellalindra is aware of my presence in the capital, otherwise she would have sought me out by now."

Thalion let out his breath in a rush. *Her former lover and father of her child. She would probably love to ensure his continued silence about Serana's parentage.* "But you'll help us get her out?"

Saihid's eyes flashed. "My daughter is being held against her will. I will do anything to protect her wishes."

Thalion sighed in relief. Having his father-in-law help them would make the rescue easier.

"We have to move fast," he said. "The king returned today. I heard Pellalindra say that he's planning on wedding Serana immediately." He could hear the fear in his own voice.

"I did some eavesdropping in the marketplace, and heard the same," Kishtar said. "Never mind that she's already married. The nobility is split in opinion. Some believe that her elopement has forever tarnished her, while others think that the king should not let a rebellious noble prevent him from doing what he wants." He paused, opened his mouth, then closed it again.

Thalion frowned. "What else?"

Kishtar sighed. "The rest think that your elopement was a direct result of you being descended from demons, as only a demon's influence could convince her to abandon being queen. The rumors about your father's heritage are stronger than they've ever been."

Thalion prevented himself from cursing by an effort of will. He pushed the thought about the rumors to the side. "We'll have more to worry about than rumors of my heritage, if what the nephelm told us is true," he said.

Saihid's eyes widened in question.

Thalion stared at him, searching for the right words. How to explain? "Lord Auriel is more of a danger to everyone than he seems to be," he finally said. "My sister can explain the details when we get back to Ninaeva."

Saihid inclined his head in acceptance.

"So how do we get Serana out? Did you discover where she is?" Kishtar asked.

Thalion nodded. "We can't get her out during the day," he said. "There are guards outside her door, patrolling the gardens, and everything. However, I think I figured out which window is hers from the garden." He managed a grim smile. "And if I'm right, they will have to let her leave her room tonight. Pellalindra wouldn't let her daughter miss the king's return feast. Her room should be unguarded then."

"Then we'd best get rest before this evening. We have a long night's work ahead of us." Saihid gave Thalion a long, penetrating look. "I am glad you arrived," he said before walking out of the room.

Thalion collapsed in his mother's chair. "So am I," he said. "Mazda's light, will we pull this off, Kishtar? With Ianna threatening you and everything?"

"Ianna won't betray you to get to me," Kishtar said, but his voice sounded uncertain. "Besides, she doesn't know our plans. We can risk it."

Thalion groaned. "I wish we had taken Serana with us up north. Mazda's light, I wish we had never gone!"

Kishtar clapped a hand on Thalion's shoulder. "We'll manage, Thalion." He summoned a smile. "We'd better follow Saihid's advice and get some sleep. Can't have the rescue of your wife going wrong because I fell asleep, right?" He started toward the door, whistling as he went, a clear effort to cheer himself up.

Thalion smiled until Kishtar left the room, then sat down in his mother's chair. He stared broodingly at the wall.

We can take on the world, yes, but can we take on a god? Will Lord Auriel let us get away with rescuing Serana, or will he interfere? And will he actually rise as a God again and awaken the dragons?

15

ESCAPE

Thalion breathed a sigh of relief as he spotted the door to the quarters Rian had said Serana was being held in. There were no guards. His guess had been right; Serana was at the feast.

Cautiously, he slipped through the hall, the hood of his priest's robe hung low over his head. All the servants had been frantically busy preparing for the feast, too busy to pay attention to a humble priest making his way through the palace. Most probably assumed he was part of High Priest Ellil's entourage. But if someone noticed him entering the quarters of Lady Auriel, they would likely report it to the steward. He couldn't afford that.

The hall was deserted. Silently, he turned the handle and slipped inside. He blinked, his eyes adjusting to the dim light. He stood before an elaborate sitting room, designed to perfectly showcase the owner's influence. It was as opulent as the sitting room in Rian's quarters but far more tastefully decorated.

Of course, now I know why Rian has opulent quarters in the palace. She's the king's mistress. Thalion shook his head. He had never guessed, not even suspected.

Slowly, he made his way further into the room. He needed to

find Serana's room, the one place where she'd have some privacy while being under guard.

He exited the sitting room and made his way down a small hallway, where he opened one door to find a study and shook his head in frustration. *Why do Lady Auriel's quarters have to be the most extensive ones in the palace?* He made his way further down the hallway, pausing in front of the next door. He leaned against it, straining his ears. If it was Serana's bedroom, would there be a maid waiting?

He almost decided that no one occupied the room when he heard the sound of a chair scraping across a wooden floor. He heard a muttered curse and hastily backed away, looking at the final door.

If one of them has a maid, it will be Lady Auriel, he decided. *Serana didn't bring one, at least, Saihid and Father didn't say she did. Unless her mother assigned her one.* He shook his head. Before he could think better, he opened the door and slipped inside as fast as he could.

He closed the door behind him before he looked around. It was a bedroom, a large canopy bed in the middle of the room, a fireplace over on the left, and a desk on the left. No maid in sight. He felt his shoulders relax as he noticed the row of plants by the window. This was definitely Serana's room.

Now I just need a place to hide, he thought. He sighed. *Back under the bed for me.*

He crawled under the bed and lay there, staring at the wooden undercarriage. This was the tedious part of the rescue plan. Unfortunately, it also gave him plenty of opportunity to reflect on what might go wrong.

What if she doesn't want to come with me? What if we get seen? What if... his thoughts went in circles, spiraling further and further into doubt. There were so many ways this could go dreadfully wrong.

He was so wrapped up in his thoughts that he jumped when he heard the door to the outer chamber slam. Dimly, he heard voices, two female ones, arguing. *Serana!*

"I won't marry him, Mother! I'm already married!" Serana's voice was strong.

"Nonsense," Pellalindra. "This is the best thing for you, child. You'll see, in time."

"No! I won't!" Serana exclaimed. "Haven't you listened? I'm married to Thalion!"

"A mistake that will be remedied," Pellalindra remained calm. "But you will be married to King Andreas tomorrow."

Tomorrow! Thalion suppressed a gasp. *Mazda's light, we got here just in time!*

"I won't, Mother." Serana was calmer now, but no less determined.

Pellalindra ignored her daughter's statement and addressed someone else instead. "Ivette, go with my daughter and make sure she does not leave her room tonight. She needs to be rested for tomorrow."

"Yes, my lady," another female voice, this one quiet and submissive.

"Mother," Serana's voice again.

"No," Pellalindra cut her off. "There will be no more discussion of this matter. You disappointed me once, daughter. Do not do so again."

Thalion listened, his heart clenching in sympathy for Serana. There was silence until the door to the bedroom opened.

"You don't have to help me," Serana said sharply. "As Mother said, I'm not going anywhere."

"I have my orders, my lady," the maid's tone was no longer submissive. "I will stay here all night."

Serana sighed but didn't protest. Apparently, they'd had this argument before.

Thalion peeked out from under the edge of the bed, trying to determine which set of feet belonged to the maid. One pair of feet wore satin slippers, while the other sturdy leather shoes. He stared at the satin slippers, seeing the small, pale ankles. Unbidden, his mind remembered running his hands up and down those legs.

Firmly, he tore his thoughts away from those memories. *Plenty of time for that later,* he scolded himself. *First, you have to figure out how to deal with the maid.*

Patience, patience was key. Patience, and hoping

that Kishtar and Saihid wouldn't be spotted, hoping that they'd be in the stables, that…

He shook himself and took a deep breath, trying to be as quiet as possible. Serana and the maid were moving about the room, the maid presumably helping Serana get ready for the night. *You'll have to get dressed in a hurry again, my love.*

Where was the maid going to sleep? Thalion frowned as the thought occurred to him. There was no second bed or a trundle bed for a maid. Was Pellalindra so heartless as to make the maid sleep on the floor? Or did she expect the maid to stay awake all night? *If she does, then maybe I can catch her as she drifts off.*

He saw Serana's feet by the edge of the bed and had to restrain himself from reaching out to touch her, just to let her know he was there. He heard the bed creak above him as she got in and felt a pang of longing. *Soon, my love.*

"Goodnight, my lady," the maid said sharply. Thalion followed her footsteps back to a chair by the fireplace. Soon, he heard a steady clicking of needles. *Knitting. She's knitting. Pellalindra does expect her to stay awake.*

Thalion tried to measure how far it was from the bed to the fireplace. Could he roll out, grab the maid and subdue her before she screamed?

He waited. The clicking of the knitting needles remained steady. Above him, he heard Serana shift on the bed.

Patience, Thalion, patience. Maybe she'll relax when she believes Serana has gone to sleep.

He waited, listening to the steady click-clack of the needles. He was in no danger of falling asleep himself. He was tense, as tense as a wire strung on a harp.

Finally, he heard the clicking stop. The fire had died down, enough that he could barely see the chair the maid sat on in the dim light. He heard a sigh, and the maid stood up and moved over to the fire.

Thalion saw his chance. As silently as he could, he crept from under the bed. The maid was crouched in front of the fire, preparing to throw another log on. He crept up behind her. When she threw the log on the fire it hissed and cracked, and Thalion grabbed her, holding a hand firmly over her mouth, cutting off any possible screams.

"Stay quiet," he hissed.

The maid struggled, and he tightened his grip around her waist. He looked around for something to tie her up with.

"What's going on?" Serana's voice came from the bed, striking relief into Thalion's heart.

"Serana!" he turned to her. "Serana, it's me!"

"Thalion!" Serana pushed herself out of bed and came toward him, stopping a few feet away with an uncertain expression on her face. Thalion cursed the struggling woman in his arms.

"Could you get me something to tie her up and gag her with?" he asked.

A smile spread across Serana's face. "With pleasure." She opened the closet, and a few seconds later emerged with several sashes. "Will these do?"

Thalion nodded. Working together, they had the hapless maid gagged and tied to the chair in seconds. She glared at them both, fire in her eyes, but the only sounds she could make were inarticulate mumbles.

Serana flung herself at Thalion as soon as they had secured the maid. "Oh, Thalion!" she whispered. "I'm so sorry!"

Thalion held her firmly against his chest, feeling the warmth of her body as it trembled against him. "It's not your fault," he said. "I'm here to take you home."

"Thalion, they want me to marry the king tomorrow!"

"I know," he placed his hands on her shoulders. "We have a plan, trust me. We're leaving tonight."

A ghost of a smile spread across Serana's face. "Another midnight escape?"

Thalion smiled back. "Hopefully with a bit more planning this time." He glanced at the maid. He didn't want to tell Serana their plans where the maid would overhear them. "Trust me. Get dressed, and let's go."

Serana hesitated. "Thalion, there're guards at the door."

Thalion's lips twitched. "Who said we're leaving by the door?" He moved to the window, fumbling around until he found the latch. It opened into the cool night air, and he turned back to Serana.

"We're on the second story," she said, her voice still uncertain.

Thalion nodded. "Get dressed, and help me get the sheets from your bed."

Serana's eyes widened in realization, and she went back to the closet, stripping off her nightgown and pulling out a plain, dark dress.

Thalion had to catch his breath as her pale skin was revealed, and he firmly told his body to behave itself. When she was finished changing, they quickly stripped the sheets and tied them together, forming a long rope. Thalion secured one end to a bedpost and gestured to Serana. "Ladies first?"

"Only if you're right behind me." She smiled and pulled him in for a long kiss.

Thalion felt his breath catch. "Always."

Serana nodded and moved to the window. She hesitated as she looked down.

Thalion placed a hand on her shoulder. "You can do it, love," he said. "I'll be right behind you."

Serana visibly gathered her courage before taking the sheet rope in hand. Thalion held onto it to steady her as she worked her way down the wall.

He glanced back once more to make certain the maid was still secured. Her eyes blazed in the darkness. He couldn't help winking at her before following Serana down into the garden, landing lightly on his feet and turning to Serana. She smiled at him, a fierce joy in her eyes.

Thalion pulled her into an embrace before he could think better of it. Never mind that they needed to move, needed to get out of here as quickly as possible.

"You murderer!" the shout cut through the garden, and Thalion pulled Serana to the ground, hiding behind the hedge. His heart leapt in his throat as he recognized the sound of swords clashing together.

Serana huddled next to him. "Please tell me this isn't part of the escape," she whispered.

Thalion shook his head, but couldn't do more to reassure her as the sound of clashing steel came closer. He pulled Serana around the hedge, trying to get further from the sound.

He heard a laugh and felt his blood turn to ice. The king sounded cocky as he fought. "Murderer? What do you know about murder, Lord Dannan?"

Dannan! Thalion swallowed. The king was fighting Dannan? The man who had been his mother's friend and ally on the regency council?

"You're a traitor," Dannan's tone was almost a growl. "You betrayed them!"

"You're the traitor, Dannan!" The king's voice grew louder. "You're the one fighting me!"

Whatever response Dannan had was lost in the clash of steel. Thalion's heart dropped as he realized that the fight was placing the men near the stables. He tightened his grip on Serana's hand. *We need to get out of here.*

Slowly, he edged his way around the hedge, trying to see if they could make a dash for it. It was dark, after all, and they were both wearing dark clothing...if they could look like they were fleeing from this fight...

Thalion froze peered around a hedge and caught sight of the two figures. Both were still dressed in their finery from the feast, but they had been scuffed and dirtied. Dannan's eyes flashed, one bright citron eye like fire. As he watched, Dannan brought his sword around in a complicated attack, and Thalion held his breath, certain that the king was going to be stabbed through the heart. He felt a moment's shame as he recognized the hope leaping in his chest.

The king laughed, destroying that hope as soon as it was acknowledged. The king twisted, throwing Dannan's attack off balance and binding his sword. Thalion watched, horrified, as Dannan's sword went flying across the garden. Serana stiffened beside him, the same horror on her face.

"Now you die like the traitor you are," the king said, walking slowly toward Dannan. Thalion's pulse thundered in his throat. He hadn't brought his sword. It would be madness to go to Dannan's aid.

Dannan looked up and grinned. Thalion's eyes widened as he began to glow brighter and brighter. As the king approached, raising his sword high, Dannan burst into flames.

Thalion barely stifled a yell as he fell back. The king didn't need to hide his yell, staring at the fiery tower with rage. Dannan moved forward, reaching toward the king with his flaming hands.

Thalion knew they couldn't linger. The fire only made it more likely that the garden was about to be swarmed with guards. He squeezed Serana's hand and led her through the hedges, sticking as close to the palace wall as he could. Out of the corner of his eye, he saw the king dodge Dannan's attack and square off again, sword against fire.

Thalion cursed as he heard shouts of alarm. He stumbled to a halt as soldiers ran out of the stables, stopping in horror as they saw the king fighting a flaming demon.

Serana whimpered next to him, and he squeezed her hand tighter, trying to reassure her. They would get out. They had to.

They started moving again, creeping slowly toward the exit. Thalion's heart stopped as one of the soldiers saw them. *No! Not now, not when we're so close!*

The soldier's eyes widened, and he strode forward and took Thalion's arm. "Get her out of here! Fast!"

He doesn't recognize us! "Yes sir," he said, quickening his pace. He heard Serana's rapid breathing beside him. They were almost at the door.

A loud, piercing scream distracted him just as he reached the stables. He tried to usher Serana through the door as he turned to see the king's sword driven through the chest of Dannan's flaming body. Blood poured from his wound, mixed with fire that dripped down like a living thing. The king laughed, a triumphant, evil sound.

Thalion swallowed and pushed Serana through the door, following right on her heels. He felt bile rising up in his throat as the king's laughter echoed into the stables.

"There you are!" Kishtar's voice was full of relief. "Mazda's light, Thalion, we were getting worried!"

"Father!" Serana caught sight of Saihid, standing in the shadows next to Kishtar. She detached herself from Thalion and flung her arms around him. "Father, I was so worried!"

Saihid managed a chuckle.

Thalion smiled in relief. "You have the horses?"

Kishtar nodded and gestured to four horses, saddled and ready to ride.

"Then let's go," Thalion said. "While everyone is distracted."

"Not so fast," the voice made everyone turn toward the front door of the stable. Thalion's eyes widened as he saw Percival Duskryn standing in the doorway, his sword drawn.

"Percy!" Serana exclaimed. "Percy, what are you doing?"

Percival's expression didn't change. "Stopping you from making another mistake." He walked forward, sword pointing straight at Thalion. "You will not abduct my sister again."

"He didn't abduct me!" Serana exclaimed. "Percival, I love him!"

Percival ignored Serana as he continued advancing on Thalion. Thalion cursed, wishing for the second time that evening that he had brought his weapons along with him. Never mind that they would have been impossible to get to underneath the priest's robe...

"Percival, stop," he said, trying to keep his voice level. "Listen to your sister. We're just going home. We don't want trouble."

Percival's eyes flashed. "You have brought trouble to my family," he said. "You will receive trouble in return." He raised his sword overhead, preparing to strike. Thalion tensed, ready to dive out of the way, when the clash of steel made him flinch. Saihid's greatsword flashed out, intercepting Percival's strike.

"Get her out of here," Saihid said before turning his full attention to Percival. Percival's eyes lit as they began fighting.

"Father!" Serana's voice was filled with fear. Thalion grabbed her arm, urging her to one of the saddled horses.

"Come on!" Kishtar exclaimed. "We don't have much time!" As if to underscore his words, voices sounded outside the stable, alerted by the ringing of weapons as Saihid and Percival danced around each other, dodging in and out of empty stalls and making the horses whinny in terror.

"Stand down," Saihid said. "I taught you everything you know, boy."

Percival simply laughed and brought his sword down for another attack. Saihid dodged aside, but it seemed to Thalion that he was surprised by the intensity of the attack.

Thalion boosted Serana up into the saddle and mounted his own horse. He turned toward Saihid, wishing that he could interfere in the fight. "Saihid! We're ready!" he shouted.

"Get her out of here!" was all Saihid shouted back as he danced around Percival. To Thalion's eyes, he was becoming more and more desperate.

"Father!" Serana exclaimed again. Thalion moved his horse closer to hers, ready to lean over and grab her horse's reins. *She won't leave without him. Mazda's light, I don't want to leave without him!*

"You told her she was your daughter?" Percival asked in a low voice. "Why would you invent such a lie?"

Saihid's eyes flashed. "It is not a lie!" he exclaimed. "Your mother forced me to keep the secret these twenty years!"

"Ha!" Percival attacked again, missing Saihid and hitting one of the wooden stable posts instead. He pulled his sword free and advanced on Saihid. "My mother would never betray her husband."

Saihid's smile was grim. "No, she wouldn't. But she didn't have a husband at the time. I was the only one!"

"Liar!" Percival exclaimed. He brought his sword down again, and Thalion's heart stopped as he saw Saihid miss the parry. Saihid dodged, only just avoiding Percival's sword, and brought his sword around, sending Percival's blade flying out of his hand.

"No!" Serana's voice was barely a gasp.

"Give up, boy," Saihid said in a harsh tone. "I don't want to kill you."

Percival's eyes were dark. He stepped forward, raising his hands as if in surrender. In one quick, fluid motion, he withdrew a dagger from his sleeve and plunged it into Saihid's chest.

"NO!" Serana screamed. "Father!"

Thalion's mouth fell open in horror. Saihid crumpled to the ground, disbelief in his eyes as blood poured onto the dirt.

Percival stared down. "I learned some new things since you taught me," he rasped. He looked up to meet Thalion's horrified expression, and his face darkened.

Thalion's heart started beating again, faster than ever before. They needed out of there, now. He reached over and grabbed Serana's reins as he kicked his own horse into motion.

"Guards!" Percival shouted. "Guards! Serana Auriel is being abducted!"

Thalion ignored Percival's shouts as his horse picked up speed. As they reached the entrance to the stables, two soldiers appeared. Thalion ignored their startled shouts as he charged straight forward. He heard the sound of Kishtar's horse right behind him.

Thalion's face was set and grim as he glanced sideways to see tears streaming down Serana's face. She had grabbed her saddle horn, at least, and was holding on with all her might.

He and Kishtar had thought to return to the Ninaevan townhouse first, but Thalion knew that was no longer an option. Percival was right behind them raising the alarm. They needed to get out of the city as fast as possible. The gates should be open for a little more time. He urged his horse to a gallop, knowing that Kishtar would follow him without question. People on the streets shouted in fear as he barreled toward them, not caring about anyone in his path.

"Thalion!" Serana's voice was filled with fright.

Thalion's eyes widened in fear as he saw the cart pull out into the road in front of them. "Serana, right!" he shouted. He dropped her horse's reins and slapped its neck, and it veered right as ordered, but he knew he wasn't going to have time to avoid the collision. He bent over his horse's back, trying to relax as he urged his horse to jump.

For a moment, he didn't think the unfamiliar beast would obey him. Then its muscles gathered together as it prepared to leap. They flew through the air, and for a glorious moment, he thought they were going to clear the cart. Then he felt the collision of impact as the horse's back hooves caught, and wind rushed past his ears as they fell sideways. He threw himself out of the saddle, desperately seeking to avoid being crushed.

"Thalion!" Kishtar shouted.

Thalion didn't have any attention to spare. He hit the ground hard, feeling his hip complain from the impact. He rolled away, hearing the sounds of terrified horses and splintering wood behind him.

"You idiot!" the driver was screeching. "Guards! I want damages paid! Now!"

*No, not more guards. We can't afford this, we need to get out...*Thalion scrambled to his feet, hoping against hope that his horse was uninjured. He saw it rear in a panic, and then gallop down one of the side streets. He cursed.

"Thalion!" Like an angel, Serana appeared next to him. He swung himself up into the saddle behind her and they set off at a gallop again.

"Come back!" the driver yelled. "By Mazda's light, I demand compensation!"

Thalion tried to force his breathing back into a normal pattern as they galloped on. He saw Kishtar pull up beside them, a look of intense concentration on his face.

"So much for a subtle escape!" Kishtar yelled.

Thalion couldn't help the small chuckle that escaped him. He leaned forward to wrap his arms around Serana, shifting his weight to be in balance with hers. Her hands were clutched on the reins, and he wrapped his hands around hers, so they were leading the horse together.

Before them, he saw the gates of the city before them. He felt a flash of deja vu as he heard the bells tolling the end of the day. The gates would be closing in a few minutes.

"Same as last time," he whispered in Serana's ear. She nodded and hunched over, and he shifted his leg muscles, urging her horse to greater speed. The beast's muscles strained to obey her. They weren't going to be able to keep this pace up for long. This horse wasn't used to carrying double.

He heard the shouts of alarm from the guards as they saw the two horses galloping toward the gate. Serana ignored them. Thalion saw Kishtar's pale face beside them as he followed their lead.

"Halt!" the guard screeched. Thalion heard Serana's strangled gasp as their horse charged straight at him.

The guard jumped aside as the last second, and Thalion felt a moment's relief. They were through!

Kishtar gave a cry, and Thalion glanced back to see a second guard right in the path of Kishtar's horse. His heart leapt in his throat as he saw Kishtar's horse barrel right over the guard, producing a sickening crack. The guard fell to the side, screaming in agony.

"Keep going!" Thalion shouted. He could see the green in Kishtar's expression, but they couldn't stop now. They needed to outdistance their pursuers.

In front of him, he heard Serana's choked sobs, but she didn't try to slow their pace at all. She trusted him. They would escape.

His chest contracted. *I'm sorry, my love. I'm sorry. I will make this up to you, I swear it. I just wish I knew.*

<hr>

Thalion lost track of how long and far they went. They stopped their headlong charge as soon as they were out of sight of the city's walls, but they continued at a trot for hours thereafter. Only when Thalion was close to falling out of the saddle from exhaustion did they guide their horses off the road and into a small grove of trees.

Serana collapsed against Thalion as soon as they dismounted. Sobs shook her entire body.

"I'll get camp set up," Kishtar said before disappearing into the trees.

"No fire," Thalion called after him. "We can't risk it."

He didn't hear Kishtar acknowledge his words as he turned his full attention to Serana. He held her close, trying to think of something, anything, he could say. He had never felt so helpless.

"I'm sorry," he whispered. The words sounded so inadequate.

"My brother," Serana whispered, her voice shaking. "My own brother!"

Thalion held her tighter to him. "I'm sorry," he said again.

"He killed my father," Serana's voice was harsh with disbelief. "Why would he do that?"

Because your mother told him not to let you escape under any circumstances, Thalion thought. *Because both he and your mother cared more about you becoming queen than your happiness. Oh Serana, I am so sorry.* He didn't voice his thoughts. If Serana hadn't thought of how her mother must have influenced Percival, he didn't want to be the one to tell her. He didn't know how she would handle such a betrayal.

"He killed my father," Serana whispered again. "My father...oh, Thalion..." she buried her face in his shoulder.

Thalion held her close as he stared out into the darkness. He remembered the suddenness of the act. Saihid had been the better fighter, there was no question of that. Percival had used trickery to win, to stab Saihid when Saihid believed him unarmed. *For a supposedly honorable noble, he certainly had no honor,* he thought. *Then again, maybe honor is just for other nobles. Bastard.* He forced those thoughts to the side. Serana would not appreciate hearing his cutting thoughts about her brother.

She started to settle in his arms, and he drew her down to sit on the ground beside him. He kept her close to him as she calmed, the sobs drying.

He waited, uncertain what to say. If he hadn't come to the capital, Saihid would probably still be alive. Then again, Serana would also be facing marriage to the king tomorrow.

"I haven't thanked you yet," Serana whispered.

Thalion blinked in surprise. "What for?" he asked.

"For rescuing me," Serana's voice was soft. "If you hadn't..." her voice broke.

Thalion swallowed past the lump in his throat. "You're my wife, and I love you," he said. "I would always come for you."

"I know," she whispered. "We're never going to be able to go to the capital again, are we?"

Thalion hesitated as he remembered Niara's resolution. If she had her say, Ninaeva would not be part of Saemar for long. "I don't think so," he said. He paused. *Do I tell her what we found out about Auriel now? Or do I wait until she's calmer? When is the best time? Is there a best time?*

"What is it?" Serana's eyes flashed with worry in the darkness. "Thalion? What's the matter?"

He sighed. "Niara and I found out some things during our trip north," he said. He tried to think of a way to be subtle, but he couldn't. "Lord Auriel is the god of the sky and father of dragons," he said bluntly. "And he's looking to rise to power and release his children again."

Serana went utterly still, and for a long moment, Thalion wasn't certain she believed him. It sounded outlandish to his own ears.

"He's the father of dragons?" she asked. He couldn't read her voice. He nodded.

"That..." Serana shuddered. "That makes far too much sense. He has a penchant for dragon items, and his bodyguards...they've reminded me of dragons on more than one occasion."

"Have they?" Thalion encouraged her to continue, trying to distract her thoughts from Saihid for just a little longer.

"There's three of them, a woman and two men. She calls them her consorts, whatever that means. But the way she looks at everyone...at me...she makes my skin crawl."

Consorts, Thalion frowned as something jogged his memory. He set the thought aside for now. "They may be dragons bound in human form," he said. "Lord Auriel was bound, with his dragons, thousands of years ago. He's attempting to break those bonds."

Serana shuddered. "He's going to return dragons to the world," she whispered. "Father would have hated to see dragons...he hated the stories about them."

Thalion pulled her close as she shuddered again.

She got herself under control. "I'm sorry," she whispered.

He shook his head. "I'm sorry," he said. "If we hadn't come…"

"Then I would still be locked in my room," Serana interrupted. "I don't know what I would have done. I had vague plans, ideas…but I doubt any of them would have worked."

"I'm sure you would have thought of something," Thalion tried to sound encouraging.

Serana managed a weak laugh. "Maybe," she conceded. "But I'm glad you came."

Thalion hesitated, then leaned down to kiss her. She responded immediately, twining her fingers into his hair and pulling him insistently closer.

He pulled away, gasping. "Serana…" he whispered.

"Thalion…" Serana's voice broke again. "Don't let me go. Hold me." He could hear the desperation in her voice.

"I'll always be here," Thalion promised. "As long as you want me."

"I'll always want you," she whispered as she nestled into his arms. They sat together in silence until Kishtar came back. Kishtar looked warily into the clearing until he spotted the two of them on the ground.

"There you are," Kishtar said. "May I join you?"

Thalion felt Serana stir in his arms. "Of course," she said.

Kishtar made his way to one of the horses first and fumbled with the saddle. "We still have most of the supplies we packed," he said.

Saddlebags. Thalion had completely forgotten about the saddlebags in their headlong flight.

"Not quite like last time, then," Serana said. She giggled. "We have supplies this time, and…" her voice broke again, "my father…"

Thalion pulled her close again. "It's alright," he whispered. "Cry as much as you need."

Kishtar finished fumbling in the saddlebags and walked toward them, stopping awkwardly in front of them, a large blanket in his hand. He draped it around Serana's shoulders, moving stiffly and uncertainly.

"Thank you, Kishtar," Serana said. She swallowed. "Thank you for being part of my rescue."

"Ah," Kishtar seemed flustered. "I couldn't let Thalion charge after you myself now, could I?"

Serana glanced at Thalion, and his face flushed. "You would have?" she asked.

Thalion's face heated even more as Kishtar chuckled. "As soon as we found out you weren't at Ilhelm, he was ready to charge after you. We must have left a few hours after we got home."

"That soon?" Serana asked, wonder in her voice.

Thalion shrugged. "I had a feeling," he managed.

She embraced him, pulling him in for another kiss. Thalion didn't resist, as another type of heat rose in him.

Kishtar cleared his throat, and Thalion and Serana broke apart. Thalion breathed heavily.

"Now I know how you felt on the boat," Kishtar muttered. "Should I find a clearing of my own?"

Thalion suppressed a chuckle as Serana stiffened in his arms. He tightened his embrace around her. "No, not tonight, Kishtar," he said, firmly ignoring the ache in his body. "We're not safe yet. We don't know how much of a search party they're going to send out, and whether or not they'll continue through the night."

Serana sighed and relaxed in his arms. "You're right," she said reluctantly.

Thalion's heart leaped at the reluctance in her voice, and firmly told his body to stop reacting. "We'd better get some rest," he said. "We have a long ride ahead of us."

Serana sighed again. "I thought last time would be my last long ride for a while," she said under her breath.

Kishtar snorted as he pulled another blanket around himself and lay down. "Don't ever think that. As soon as you think you're never doing something again, you'll have to."

Thalion smiled as he heard Serana's muttered grumbling. He pulled her to his chest as they lay down on the ground, their blanket wrapped around them both. He held her close as they drifted off into sleep. "I love you, Serana," he whispered, right before sleep claimed him.

16

―――――

ASCENT

For the third time in the course of six months, Thalion greeted the gates of Ilhelm Castle with relief. Beside him, Kishtar and Serana seemed equally relieved and overjoyed.

Thalion's relief was short-lived, however. As soon as they rode through the courtyard, he knew something was up. It was a flurry of activity and organized chaos. Servants and soldiers were moving everywhere, carrying bundles of supplies, moving crates, setting out on patrols, and training and drilling. Thalion exchanged a look with Kishtar.

He didn't have long to wait to find out what was happening. As soon as they dismounted, Niara came flying out of the castle and threw her arms around him.

"You're back!" she exclaimed. "Mazda's light, Thalion, when you arrived at the capital, I was worried sick!"

Thalion blinked as hugged his sister. *The Sight. Did she manage to call a vision?*

Niara pulled away and turned to Serana, pulling her into a hug that was just as intense. "I'm so sorry," she said.

Serana paled, and Thalion felt his chest knot at the sorrow in her eyes. She returned Niara's embrace fervently.

Thalion frowned as another patrol of soldiers marched past. "Niara, what's going on?" he asked.

Niara pulled away. A wry smile spread over her face. "Easier to explain inside," she said. "Besides, I'm sure you want to rest."

Thalion couldn't disagree with that sentiment. Although they had managed to stay in inns for the second half of their journey this time, they had still pushed themselves each day, well beyond what most people would consider a reasonable traveling distance.

The three of them followed Niara into the castle. Thalion's throat caught as Niara walked straight for the library, exactly like their mother would have.

Niara stroked one of the bookshelves as they entered, and Thalion could tell she was also thinking about their mother. Then she sighed and squared her shoulders.

"We're evacuating," she said without preamble. "Or preparing to, at least. All the excess supplies are going underground. The nephelm delegation arrived, and they've been making the place habitable. We can fit thousands of people there, far more than the population of Ilhelm. Everyone from the surrounding area has been getting messages to prepare."

"Why?" Thalion asked. *Evacuation? Abandoning Ilhelm?*

Niara's eyes grew dark. "Because there's an army getting ready to follow you," she said. "They began mustering the day after you left the capital."

Serana gasped, and Thalion saw the pain in her expression. He drew her close. None of this was her fault, and he didn't want her to think that for an instant.

"Are we certain they're heading for us?" Kishtar asked. "Knowing the king, he could also be heading out to conquer the free cities."

"That's part of his plan," Niara said, her tone not changing a bit. "But first he's coming for Ninaeva. We've defied him too many times."

Thalion felt Serana begin to shake in his arms, and he held her tighter. "It's not your fault," he said.

"No," Niara's voice was strong. "You might be the excuse they needed to justify it to the nobles, but this would have happened anyway. Auriel has to know about our heritage. After the massacre of Alfheim, this was the inevitable next step."

Thalion stared at his sister. "What have you seen?" he asked instead.

A shadow passed over Niara's face. "Auriel is the one in charge, completely," he said. "He controls the king's every movement, by word and subtle manipulation. He is preparing something, something big."

Thalion looked away from his sister to exchange glances with Kishtar and Serana. After what they had learned from the nephelm, *'Auriel is planning something big'* could only mean one thing. He was going to attempt to break whatever bindings had been placed on him long ago.

And that means the dragons will also have their bonds broken. Mazda's light. Could Ilhelm stand against an attack by dragons? Thalion didn't know. Now Niara's orders to prepare an evacuation made a great deal of sense.

He frowned as a thought occurred to him. "Where's Father?" he asked.

"Down below," Niara answered. "He's organizing the underground city, with the help of the nephelm and elves."

Thalion took a deep breath. "How long do we have until the army gets here?" he asked.

Niara shrugged, appearing uncertain. "They move slower than you did," she said. "And they needed time to prepare. But they'll be here in two weeks at most."

Two weeks. Thalion shook his head, his mind still not fully comprehending the series of events. "I'll go help Father, then," he said. "Sounds like he's going to need all the hands we can spare."

"I'll go with you," Serana said. Her voice shook, but there was an underlying steel in her voice that made Thalion give her a quick smile and kiss.

"Thank you. I was going to ask you to." Niara blinked, her eyes turning distant. "I need to be up here. To prepare."

Thalion nodded in understanding. He stood and began heading toward the underground city.

Can we truly withstand an attack by dragons?

"How does it do that?" Thalion stared at the blue lanterns in amazement.

Serana shook her head. "Niara said it's some nephelm magic," she said. "The elves had never seen anything like it before, either."

They were in a small underground chamber, deep under Ilhelm, with only a table and some stone chairs as furnishings. Thalion wasn't certain how deep the tunnels went, but they were far enough down that no root from any tree could be found. He sighed and returned to staring at the map spread out before him. The blue light provided some illumination, but his elvish heritage allowed him to see the map clearly. This was their current task, mapping out the outlying areas of the city in order to organize best for when the evacuation actually started. If it started.

It'll start. Niara has the same gifts as Mother. If she says something's going to happen, we trust her.

"How many people can we fit in this main compound again? Comfortably?" He rubbed his forehead, trying to ward off a headache. *How many days have I been down here? It's Papsukkal, isn't it? My name-day. I should be up above, preparing for a celebration. Instead, I'm down here planning an evacuation. Day out of time, indeed. I'd never be doing this if things were normal.*

"Over five thousand," Serana said, her voice confident. "Don't worry, Nazir and I have already allocated housing sites for families, for single folk, and so on, at least for the main compound. What we need to figure out is the outer areas. We can fit the entire population of Ilhelm down here, and still have more for the surrounding villages."

Thalion regarded her in admiration. In the last few days, Serana had done far more to help organize this plan than he had. He reached out a hand, drew her down to sit beside him, and kissed her.

She returned the kiss fervently, then pulled back. "Thalion, we need to focus," she said. "If Auriel does attack…" her voice trailed off.

Thalion sighed. "He will," he said. He looked up as Niara entered the room, Mar a shadow at her side. The boy had attached himself to both Niara and Serana, becoming a constant help in running the errands needed for organization. "Another vision?" he asked.

Niara's lips tightened. "The army's getting closer," she said. "Auriel's not with the army, but…" she shook her head. "His mark is all over it."

Whatever that means, Thalion thought. He didn't know enough about magic to know what Auriel's mark might mean.

Niara joined them at the table. "Making progress?" she asked.

Thalion let Serana begin to explain the details of how the people inside would be organized, where everyone would live, and so forth. He was more involved with the initial evacuation, how they were going to handle the thousands of people entering the city at the same time. Some, most notably the nephelm and the refugee elves from Alfheim, were already living here, but if everyone from Ilhelm was also supposed to live here…he shook his head. It was a logistical nightmare. At least he didn't need to worry about them sustaining themselves. The nephelm, led by Evikan and Zeria, were in charge of lighting and food. Though how they were going to grow food underground was a mystery to Thalion.

Will we really be hiding here long enough to need to grow food? He shook his head. Niara hadn't said anything about that. Hopefully, once the attack was over, they'd be able to come out and return to normal. *Just a precaution, Thalion.*

Niara sighed, jolting Thalion out of his thoughts. "That all sounds good," she said. "Thank you, Serana. I don't know what we would do without you."

Serana flushed, but Thalion could tell she was pleased. "Oh, you'd manage, I suspect," she said. "There's enough people here."

"Yes, but you're organized," Niara said. She smiled. "You'll make a capable administrator if you ever want to be."

Serana flushed even more. Thalion knew why. This was a newly discovered talent for Serana. Her mother had never taught her anything about administering an estate, assuming that her husband would provide for her. Serana had taken to organization like a fish to water, and now the people of Ilhelm Castle turned to her at least as often as they came to Nazir, Niara, or Thalion.

A good thing, too. Or we'd all be so busy we couldn't see straight.

Niara stood up. "Well, I'd better get back to work. Unless—" she cut off, blood draining from her face, and her eyes turned sightless. Thalion jumped to his feet.

Another vision. Not again. She's been having two or three a day.

He reached her side in time to steady her. As soon as he touched her arm, the world around him faded.

Mazda's light! Not again!

It was the capital. The palace. The gardens. Someone had cleaned up from Dannan's fiery inferno. The first blooms of Mazda's Rise were just starting to appear.

Auriel stood in the center of a circle of hedges, dressed in his full burgundy finery. His three guards stood behind him, the woman with eyes like fire and the two men who always stood right behind her.

"Why are we here, Usumgal?" Lady Pellalindra asked. She was dressed in full burgundy colors, as well. There must have been some kind of event at the capital. Percival stood slightly behind her, dressed in just as formal clothing.

Auriel took Pellalindra's hand and escorted her to one of the benches. "It is a momentous day, my dear." His eyes seemed sad as he gazed at his wife. She smiled back, oblivious.

"What, Papsukkal?" she asked, her voice light and playful. "You've always known my thoughts about that."

Auriel smiled but didn't answer.

Thalion felt an intense feeling of foreboding. Something was going to happen, and he, as a mere witness to Niara's vision, was powerless to stop it.

His eyes widened as the king entered the circle of hedges. *Wait, if the king's here, then who's leading the army?*

"Why did you summon me, Lord Auriel?" The king's voice was testy. "You know I want to reach the army as soon as possible. I trust Niall and my generals, but I want to be there to teach Thalion a lesson."

Thalion flinched. Despite knowing what Niara had said was true, that his actions were the excuse Auriel needed to attack the north, hearing the king say that...*For Andreas, it's personal. He's a terrible king if he can't separate personal feelings from politics.*

"All in good time, my king," Auriel said in a calm and unwavering tone. "We are all assembled. It is time." He gestured to his three guards. "Izila, you know what to do."

The woman nodded shortly and moved to stand behind Pellalindra. The two men moved to lead the king and Percival to opposite sides of the circle of hedges, across from each other. Auriel gave his wife a brief kiss on the cheek before walking across the circle himself.

He's in the north, Thalion thought. *North, south, east, west...Mazda's light.* He felt his throat tighten.

Auriel extended his hand, and Thalion saw that he held a small figurine, carved in the shape of a dragon. It moved and writhed, as if it were trying to escape its tiny form.

"Long have I awaited this day," Auriel said, his voice quiet. In his other hand, he produced a knife and sliced the palm of one of his hands. In the next breath, his three guards did the same.

Thalion watched, feeling trapped. He wanted to stop this, he had to stop this...

Pellalindra gasped. "My lord! Are you alright?"

Auriel stopped her from moving toward him with a raised hand. He nodded, and his three guards stepped forward, each dropping a bit of their blood on his dragon figurine.

"Blood of the bound," Auriel said, his voice suddenly ringing across the garden. "What the Goldwood Realm and Mountain-folk sought to bind shall now be unleashed. Let what they stole from us be returned!" He threw the figurine to the ground, where it shattered against the stone.

Immediately the air filled with a red haze so powerful that Thalion could barely see. He only knew Andreas was dead when he heard him gasp and slump to the ground, blood spilling out of his throat. The guard standing next to him wiped his knife clean on a handkerchief before sheathing it again.

Percival managed to cry out, but that was all that he could do before the second guard slit his throat with the same efficiency. He slumped to the ground, blood spilling over the stone and grass.

Pellalindra stared across the circle at Auriel, her eyes wide with horror. "Usumgal?" she whispered.

Auriel crossed the circle, moving purposefully toward Pellalindra. Thalion wanted to shout, to urge her to run, but he was voiceless. All he could do was watch.

Pellalindra took one step backward before Izila grabbed her arms. Her eyes filled with tears as Auriel drew closer.

"Percival..." she whispered.

"The blood of the son of a traitor," Auriel said, gesturing to Percival. His voice was calm, although his eyes were filled with sorrow. He gestured briefly at Andreas's slumped body. "The blood of a king." He turned to Pellalindra.

"I'm sorry, my love. It was not supposed to be you." He leaned forward, ignoring Pellalindra's startled gasp, and kissed her. Pellalindra made a noise of surprise before relaxing into his arms.

No! Thalion wanted to scream. He could see the knife Auriel drew out again, although Pellalindra could not. *Pellalindra, run!*

It was too late. As he broke the kiss, Auriel reached up and drew his knife across Pellalindra's throat. He held her as the life died from her eyes, taking with it her expression of pain, betrayal, and confusion.

"And the blood of one who lies about their blood," Auriel said, laying Pellalindra gently on the ground. "If only you had never married into the nobility, dear." He stood up, the sadness gone from his eyes. He regarded his three guards. "Now."

The three guards raised their hands toward the sky and began chanting, some arcane tongue that Thalion couldn't hope to understand. The red mist intensified, until Thalion swore he could feel his eyes stinging. But he couldn't look away.

The chanting reached a peak, and Auriel raised his hands to the sky. A bolt of lightning flashed down, striking the center of the circle. Thalion cried out, blinded by the sudden light. Thunder roared from the heavens, although there was not a cloud in the sky. The world felt like it was full of fire. He couldn't breathe!

The air cleared, and Thalion wished desperately he could pull out of the vision. Terror filled his heart as he took in the sight.

Four dragons stood in the center of the palace gardens. One was burgundy, and much larger than the others. He roared a challenge skyward in triumph.

A large red dragon roared a stream of fire toward the palace. Screams erupted, and people starting running out in a panic, covered in fire and debris. As one, the four dragons took off from the ground, the air from the wing beats flattening what was left of the garden. Thalion tried to scream, but no sound would come out of his mouth.

His vision went black, then white. He was curled up on the ground, and Serana was shaking him. "Thalion! Thalion, Niara, please, wake up!"

Thalion gasped, sucking in huge gulps of air. *A vision. It was a vision. You're not there.*

He sat up, barely noticing that he was shaking. Niara was still curled up in a ball on the floor, her face white. Mar crouched beside her, his face a mask of terror.

"Niara!" Thalion reached for her. When he touched her shoulder, she looked up into his eyes. They were as fear-filled as he had been.

"He's done it," Niara whispered.

Thalion couldn't answer, only stare at her as the implications of what they'd just seen started to click. *Auriel. The sky-lord. The sky-god, father of dragons. He broke his bonds, he's now...Mazda's light, he's now a god, with all of the dragons unbound and at his beck and call.*

"Who's done what?" Serana asked, her voice shaking.

Thalion shook his head, unable to answer. Niara turned to Serana, her face still ashen.

"Auriel," she said. "He's risen. He's become the sky-lord. And the dragons are on their way here."

"Civilians this way!"

Thalion stared at the courtyard of Ilhelm Castle from a stone balcony. Serana stood next to him, her hand clutched in his. He had thought it had been busy when he'd first arrived back. Now it was packed. Everyone from the city was here, it seemed, coming into the castle in a steady stream. Ninaevan guards guided them to the entrance to the underground city, where clerks and administrators waited to show everyone to their new living quarters.

He felt Niara's presence as she moved to stand next to them. "They're listening," he said. That had been his biggest fear, that the people of Ilhelm wouldn't believe that there was an attack coming until too late.

Niara sighed. "We have Mother to thank for that," she said. "People were used to her making pronouncements that turned out to be true. I'm using her authority, really."

Thalion nodded and turned his attention back to the milieu of people. Gwyn and Evalynna were in the thick of the planning, walking around, making certain that families were together, that everyone had supplies. He'd been doing his share of that earlier this morning, as had Niara.

"You're going to have to make a speech at some point," Thalion told her.

Niara's eyes widened. "What?" she asked.

Thalion gestured down at the crowd of people. "How long do they think we'll be underground? What were the details of the evacuation message?"

Niara looked down guiltily, and Thalion nodded again. "They think it's going to be just for the attack, don't they," he said. He had thought that himself, before the vision of Auriel rising. There would be no escaping the dragons once they conquered Saemar.

"I didn't think people would come if they thought it was forever," Niara said.

Serana's eyes were dark. "I don't know if I would come if I didn't know about the dragons," she whispered. She shuddered, and Thalion wrapped his arm around her.

Niara shook her head. "I hope it's not forever. I couldn't stand to live down there that long."

Thalion thought of living in the underground forever and shuddered. "But it'll be longer than a few days, or weeks," he said. "They won't be expecting that. Once everyone is down there, and the initial assault is over, you're going to have to tell them the truth."

Niara sighed. "I know," she said. "Though Mazda alone only knows how they'll take that."

She was right to worry, Thalion knew. If they weren't careful, they'd be dealing with riots and revolts once people got tired of living underground and in the dark.

"Play on their patriotism," he recommended. "To both Ninaeva and Saemar. Tell them what we saw, that Auriel killed the king, that he's leading the army here, that he'll destroy both Ninaeva and Saemar as we knew it."

Niara made a face. "It sounds like you should be the one making the speech," she said.

Thalion shook his head. "You're the Lady," he said. "Not me. I'm just your Thorn, your right hand."

Niara sighed. "Sometimes I think we should switch roles," she said, sounding slightly mournful.

Thalion snorted. "You're the one raised for this," he said. "Don't worry. The people love you. You'll do fine."

She sighed again and shook her head. "I hope you're right."

Serana tightened her arms around him, and he gazed down into her face. "You'd do fine too," she whispered.

Footsteps behind them made Thalion look up. He smiled weakly as Kishtar stepped through the door onto the balcony, his face pale and worried. "What's up?" he asked.

Kishtar joined them, staring down at the mass of people below. "How long will we be down there, Niara?" he asked.

Niara bit her lip. "I don't know, Kishtar," she said.

"It could be forever," Kishtar whispered.

Thalion leaned down to kiss Serana's forehead, ignoring the drop in his stomach. Could they live underground, in the dark, forever?

Niara shrugged. "As I said, I don't know," she said.

Kishtar gazed out across the mountains toward the sea, his eyes distant. Thalion swallowed as he realized what was actually bothering Kishtar.

"Are you thinking of Lyra?" he asked.

Kishtar nodded. "I promised I'd be back to marry her," he whispered. "Mazda's Rise is here, and I haven't gone. And if we're forced underground..." he took a deep breath. "I may never see her again."

"We'll all leave people behind. The world is changing." Niara's voice was dark. "The capital's in disarray. More dragons are arriving there every day. The palace is in ruins, the king's guard destroyed. I don't know what has happened to any of the nobles who were in the capital. The dragons' influence has been slowly expanding."

Thalion stared at Niara. "Why haven't you said anything?" he demanded.

She shrugged. "We knew it would happen," she said. "Did anyone really need confirmation?"

The darkness of her tone made Thalion bite his tongue. She sighed at his silence and cast her eyes down at the stone beneath their feet.

"I can barely bear to see it," she said. "The townhouse has been destroyed, Thalion. The trees burned to the ground."

The pain in her voice made Thalion instantly forget his frustration that she hadn't shared her information earlier. Serana made a small sound of sympathy and left his arms, placing her hand on Niara's shoulder.

"How many dragons are there?" Kishtar asked, his voice low.

Niara shook her head. "More every day," she said. "Dozens by now, at least. Maybe even a hundred. And they keep coming."

"How many are heading here?" Thalion asked. "With the army?"

Niara shook her head. "Not all of them. They'll join in the attack, and the generals will cheer to believe that they are the dragonriders reborn." Her voice turned hard. "And they will be, for a while. Until the news that the king is dead reaches them, and the dragons take command of everything."

Thalion could almost see it as Niara spoke. It was a masterful plan, and if Auriel hadn't been aiming to destroy Ninaeva and their elven bloodline, then Thalion might have even applauded him.

Kishtar cursed. He looked down, then at Thalion and Niara, and then down again.

"Thalion. Niara..." he started.

Thalion exchanged a glance with his sister. Niara just shrugged, clearly at a loss.

"Do you truly need me here?" Kishtar asked. "I feel like I haven't been that much help in the past few days."

Thalion wanted to exclaim that of course they needed him, but a sharp look from Niara silenced him.

"What do you mean, Kishtar?" Niara asked. "You can tell us. We won't feel betrayed."

Kishtar took a deep breath. "I'd like to go to Hillsdale," he said. "To marry Lyra. I don't know whether she'll want to come back here. I'll try to convince her, but..." his eyes filled with pain. "I don't want to abandon her out here. I don't want to live without her."

Thalion swallowed as he realized exactly what Kishtar was asking.

"Kishtar..." Niara's voice held the same realization. "You realize if you stay above ground, the army is going to go to the free states after they conquer Ninaeva, and Hillsdale will probably be first on that list."

"I know," Kishtar said. He shook his head. "Hopefully I can convince Lyra to hide instead of fight, and maybe flee...somewhere, I don't know where. But I can't...Niara, I'm sorry. I can't."

Thalion and Niara exchanged another glance. Thalion knew

without either one of them saying a thing that neither would stand in Kishtar's way.

Thalion reached out to embrace Kishtar. "You're like a brother to me," he whispered. He stepped back against the balcony railing, taking Serana's hands. "You helped me win my love. I would never stand in the way of yours."

Kishtar smiled. "Thank you," he said. He raised an eyebrow at Serana. "Take care of him, will you?"

"I'll try." Serana managed a laugh.

Niara was next. "Be careful," she said. She sniffed. "That's an order, as your liege-lady. Try to convince Lyra to return here, but if you see dragons in the sky, don't. It'll be too late. Hide, and if you need to, work with whatever demands the dragons give you."

Kishtar nodded, looking slightly overwhelmed. "Do you know what those will be?" he asked.

Niara shook her head. "I've no idea," she said, regret in her voice. "I wish I did."

Kishtar shrugged. "No matter," he said. "I'll take your advice, liege-lady, and sister of my heart." He bowed extravagantly.

"You'll need to leave as soon as possible," Niara said.

"I already packed," Kishtar said. "I just...I couldn't leave without your approval." He blinked rapidly.

Thalion felt his own eyes stinging. "Go, before we keep you here forever," he said. "And say goodbye to Gwyn before you leave. Otherwise she'll likely kill me."

"And we can't have that." Kishtar grinned. He gave all three of them one more quick hug before leaving the balcony.

Thalion gazed down, swallowing the lump in his throat. *It's always been him and me against the world. When will we ever see each other again?*

Serana seemed to know exactly what he was thinking, for she just leaned against him comfortingly, not saying a word. Until she gasped and stiffened, staring at the sky.

Thalion followed her gaze. When he finally saw what had caught her attention, his heart started pounding in his chest.

Several small black spots, far in the distance. They could have been anything, they could be a trick of the light, but Thalion knew what they were.

They stood there, gazing out across the hills of Ninaeva. The spots grew larger until they began to take form.

Thalion stared at Serana, his eyes wide. Her expression mirrored his.

"The dragons have come," she said.

17

ASSAULT

Thalion stood on the ramparts of the castle walls, gazing out at the army. He shivered at the number of men. *Even if everyone in Ilhelm were armed and ready to fight, I don't know if we could withstand this force. Even disregarding the dragons.*

Since their first sighting, the dragons had remained in the distance, far enough away that the army ignored them, but close enough that all of Ilhelm knew them for a distinct threat. At least there hadn't been any complaints about the evacuation since the dragons had been spotted.

Beside him, Niara shuddered. "The entire army of Saemar," she whispered. "All to attack us."

Thalion turned to place a comforting hand on her shoulder. She ignored him as she continued to stare at the army.

"Two-fold purpose," she whispered. "Eliminate the line of Olvae and send a message to the rest of Saemar. This is what will happen if you stand against the dragon overlords."

Thalion bit his lip. He squeezed Niara's shoulder. "Niara," he said. "Stop dwelling on it. They're here. We have a plan."

Niara blinked as if she were coming out of a daze. "Yes," she said. "A plan. Where's Gwyn?"

On her words, Mar emerged from one of the towers, leading Gwyn their way. Niara had sent the boy to fetch her.

"They're starting to construct the trebuchets, Niara," Gwyn said without preamble. "You'd best be getting below soon."

Niara swallowed and nodded without protest. "Where're Serana and Father?" Thalion wanted to know.

"Waiting in the garden," Gwyn said. "They'll go below as soon as Niara arrives."

Niara took Thalion's hands. "Are you sure..." she began.

Thalion nodded without waiting for her to finish. "Some of us need to be up here," he said. "And someone needs to make sure that door gets closed. It's best if it's me."

Niara didn't make any more protests. "Let's go, then." She turned her back on the army.

Thalion, Gwyn, and Mar followed Niara down the stairs and through the castle. Thalion blinked tears away as they walked through the corridors. It hadn't just been people who'd been evacuated. In the past few days, the entire castle had been stripped bare, from the library to the tapestries. Niara had sworn that no one other than Ninaevans would lay their hands on Ninaevan treasures. Thalion agreed with her, but now the castle seemed empty and lifeless. He could almost imagine that there were ghosts lurking behind doorways and in corners.

There will be ghosts after this battle, Thalion thought. *Some of us are going to die. All of them volunteers, but still...*He shook off that morbid thought. *It's a necessary sacrifice. Otherwise, they'll level the castle until they break through to the underground sanctuary.*

It still left a bitter taste in his mouth. He'd talked to each of the volunteers, to make certain they knew what they were getting themselves into. All of them had been willing to die for Ninaeva.

I feel like I should be one of them, he thought. *I'm not lord of Ninaeva, I'm Niara's right hand. I should be the one leading the last defense.* But he had Serana to think of. Serana, who had just lost her father, and whose elven blood condemned her as surely as it condemned him and Niara. *And I am going to be out here. I'm the one shutting the door.*

His thoughts vanished in a flash of smoke as they entered the garden and Serana ran up to him. She didn't give him a chance to say anything as she threw herself into his arms and kissed him.

Thalion wrapped his arms around her and kissed her back with all the passion he could muster. His armor had to be hurting her, but she didn't seem to care.

She finally drew back, breathing heavily. "You be careful, Thalion," she demanded.

Any notions of guilt Thalion had felt about not being one of the men sacrificing his life for Ninaeva vanished at that demand. "I promise," he said. "Nothing could keep me from you." He kissed Serana again, then turned to his father.

Nazir had abandoned any pretense of lordly clothing in exchange for a plain scholar's robe. His dark eyes were shadowed with pain.

Thalion swallowed. He couldn't begin to imagine what Nazir was feeling right now. "I'll see you soon, Father."

Nazir managed a smile. He embraced his son. "Come back safe, son," he said. "Otherwise, I don't know what I'll tell your mother."

Thalion blinked. *What would Mother think, knowing that her home was about to be ravaged by the armies of Saemar and dragons?* He swallowed again. *She knew. Or at least, she wouldn't be surprised. It was due to her visions that we even have an escape plan.*

"I will, Father," he said. "I just promised my wife, didn't I?" he sobered. "Take care of her until I'm back?"

"Of course," Nazir said.

"You too," Thalion told Mar. The boy gazed up at him solemnly and nodded. Of all of them, he had the best idea of what was coming, having already seen the destruction of his first home.

Thalion turned to his sister. She surprised him by giving him a smile before she hugged him.

"I have perfect faith in you, brother," she said.

Thalion squeezed her tight, glad of her words. He needed all the confidence he could get.

A loud boom made everyone jump. Gwyn grimaced. "They've started," she said. "They must have constructed those trebuchets faster than I expected. You get underground, now."

Thalion's heart constricted at the flare of fright that passed over Serana's face before she masked it. He restrained himself from dashing after her as she entered the underground passage with Nazir, Mar, and Niara.

Gwyn sighed and closed her eyes, only opening them when another collision shook the castle. "Let's get to the men, Thalion," she said. "Put up our last defense."

Thalion nodded, swallowing the fear in his throat. *Mazda's light, I don't know if I'm ready for this.*

He followed Gwyn through the garden until they reached the courtyard of the castle. A small group of Ninaevan guardsmen stood there, grim expressions on their faces.

Gwyn gestured to Thalion, and he felt his mouth dry, realizing that she meant him to address the crowd. *How do you talk to a group of men who are going to die for you?*

He had to, though. He straightened consciously before he opened his mouth. "Friends," he said. "Guards of Ninaeva." He blanked, wondering what should come next. He blinked as he saw a dark figure rise into the sky in the distance. *A dragon. They're going to join the attack.*

He stiffened his shoulders. "You all know what we're facing," he said. "Auriel has betrayed our king, released the dragons from their bonds, and now seeks to reign death and destruction down upon us. Well, we are not going to let them!" He raised his voice, seeing some of the guardsmen straightening in response to his words. "We're Ninaevans! And we've outwitted them! All we need to do is one more thing!"

He was caught up in his own speech now. He took a deep breath before continuing. "All our friends wait down below, hidden from the dragons, from the army. We have to protect them. And we will do so with our lives! No dragon shall ever conquer the people of Ninaeva!"

He released his breath in a rush as the guards started spontaneously cheering. He turned to Gwyn, realizing he was shaking with adrenaline. "Your orders, Aunt Gwyn?" he asked.

Gwyn stepped forward. "Archers to the walls!" she ordered. "Let's make them pay for every inch until they reach the gates! Pikemen at the gates, and the rest behind them!"

Another cheer, and the guardsmen began to scatter to their assigned positions. Gwyn remained standing next to Thalion. "Good speech," she said.

Thalion managed a smile. "Thanks," he said. He raised an eyebrow. "You're helping me close the gate, right?"

Before Gwyn could respond, her face turned pale. Thalion followed her gaze and blinked in surprise. Approaching them, dressed in plain guardsmen's armor, was Evalynna. Gwyn's lover.

"You were supposed to be below!" The pain in Gwyn's voice made Thalion flinch.

Evalynna stood unmoved. "Do you really think I'd let you do this alone?" she demanded. "I'm standing with you until the last, Gwyn, my dear. Don't even think about ordering me otherwise."

Gwyn looked on the verge of opening her mouth to object. Thalion elbowed her hard in the side.

Evalynna has as much right to be up here as Gwyn. And if both of them help me with the gate, I'll have that much more chance to close it safely.

Gwyn glared at him, but relaxed as she turned back to Evalynna. She sighed. "Alright. But stay safe, no charging in, alright?"

"Yes, dear," Evalynna smiled before she saluted Thalion. "At your service, Lord Thalion."

Thalion grinned at her. "Glad to have you, Evalynna."

Another boom shook the castle and made the three of them glance up at the wall. Thalion's heart constricted to see a section of the wall completely blown away.

Gwyn cursed. "New plan!" she shouted to the men at the gate. "Be ready to charge that hole they're making in our wall! Remember, make them pay! Kill two or three of them for every one of us!"

Something made Thalion look upward. He blanched. The dark

spots in the sky were coming closer, and now bore the distinct shapes of dragons. He could even make out the colors. Bright blue and green, the two dragons roared in triumph as they approached, making the ground shake.

Gwyn's eyes were wide. "Thalion, fall back to the garden," she ordered. "We need you there. We may have to close that door sooner than we thought."

Thalion hesitated a moment too long. Before he could reply, another boom shook the courtyard. The gate splintered, and a large boulder rolled through the courtyard, kicking up dust and debris. Thalion fell backward into the dust. He scrambled to his feet, trying not to cough from the dust. *They hit the gate. They hit the gate directly.*

Several of their men were down, taken out by falling debris from the boulder. Thalion stared in horror as Saemarian regulars poured through the gates.

"Thalion! Now!" Gwyn shouted.

*This wasn't how this was supposed to happen! I was supposed to have plenty of warning...*Thalion pushed his thoughts away. *No plan survives first engagement with the enemy!*

He started to turn when he caught sight of the man at the front of the charge. Anger rose up in him. Niall MacTir ran straight for him, his sword raised in triumph.

"I told you Ninaeva would be mine, Thalion!" Niall screamed.

Thalion drew his sword and moved to counter Niall's wild swings. Around him the battle raged, men screaming and dying.

Thalion parried Niall's blows easily. "You'll never have Ninaeva," he promised. He glared at Niall. "I'll kill you first."

"Ha!" Niall swung again, forcing Thalion to dodge out of the way. "There are dragons on my side! I've been promised a position as one of the king's dragonriders! You shall never stand against me!"

"The king's dragonriders?" Thalion taunted. "Don't you know the king is dead, Niall? Killed by one of your precious dragons! They're on no one's side but their own!"

Niall's face grew dark. "You lie!" he screamed. He swung again, and Thalion's arm shook as he barely managed to counter the blow.

I need to get out of here, he thought. *I need to get below. The gate is still open, I need to hide it...*Why hadn't they closed the door before the assault began?

Because we still held out hope that some of us would escape the assault. Sentimentality. It better not kill us all!

He swallowed as Niall came at him again, swinging more and more wildly. Thalion backed up, trying to figure a way out of this fight. Much as he wanted to kill Niall, he had more important responsibilities. Serana was below!

"Running, Thalion?" Niall taunted. "Like the coward you truly are? There's nowhere for you to hide. And your wife, the one you kidnapped? Maybe I'll see what's so attractive about her myself before I take her back to the king, like I did with your sister."

Anger flared up in Thalion. He charged forward, bringing his sword up to strike.

Niall parried, a twisted expression of satisfaction on his face. "You didn't know that, did you? Know that I got a taste of Ninaeva's heir? A proper man could bring out the woman under that ice exterior of hers."

Thalion felt the fire in his blood blazing, and he swung wildly. He saw the gleeful expression on Niall's face too late. He tried to backpedal, tried to avoid the trap that Niall had set for him, but he knew he wasn't going to make it.

Niall's sword came down, sending Thalion's sun engraved sword flying out of his hand. Thalion scrambled backward to avoid the blow he knew was coming.

"I think I'll take your sister as my wife," Niall said. "Or maybe a leman. Teach her some respect. Too bad you won't be around to see it."

Thalion narrowed his eyes, remaining impervious to Niall's taunts. He crouched low, keeping his eye on Niall's sword.

He dodged once, twice, keeping well back of the blade. Niall smiled lazily, and anger rose up in Thalion again. Niall was toying with him!

"You can't run," Niall promised. "You do, I'll kill you slowly. Right now, I might just let you have a quick death."

Thalion's breath caught in his throat. At the moment, he couldn't see any way out of Niall's promise. All around him, men from Ninaeva were falling, overwhelmed by the sheer number of Saemarian regulars charging through the gates.

Niall swung his sword, and Thalion took a chance, diving forward instead of dodging away. Niall's sword passed over his head, and Thalion collided hard into Niall's side. He grabbed for Niall's sword arm, gripping Niall's arm with both hands as he slammed it down into his leg.

Niall shouted in surprise as he dropped his sword. Quick as a cat, Thalion picked it up and thrust it into Niall's throat. Blood spurted out, choking off whatever cry Niall might have made before he died.

"My lord!" a Saemarian Regular stared at Niall's body in horror. He charged at Thalion, who backpedaled, Niall's sword still clutched in his hand. He pushed aside a brief pang of regret for his own cat and sun engraved sword that had served him so well.

A fury dressed in green and gold appeared to his right, and he caught his breath as Gwyn cut down the Regular in one fluid motion.

"Thalion! Run!" she ordered. "Evalynna and I are right behind you!"

Thalion gasped and ran for the garden, hope rising inside of him. Maybe they would survive this!

The garden was still deserted. Thalion pounded up to the entrance. The rope he had to cut was still there, ready. One cut and the rocks would come pounding down. Between that and the destruction the trebuchets would wreck, the entrance to the underground city should remain a secret.

His throat closed as he turned. Gwyn and Evalynna were nowhere to be seen. He hesitated, wondering if he should go back. *I can't leave them!* He thought frantically. *I can't!*

He heard the sound of fighting right outside the garden, and his heart leapt. Moments later, Gwyn and Evalynna appeared with a small group of Ninaevan guards, fighting desperately against a group of

Regulars. They retreated together, step by step heading toward the garden.

"Thalion!" Gwyn shouted. "Cut the rope *now!*"

Thalion shook his head, even though he knew she couldn't see him. He stepped forward, intending to help the two women fend off the Regulars.

A shadow passed overhead, followed by a gust of wind. Thalion gasped in fear as a blue dragon swept down into the courtyard, scattering Regulars and Ninaevan guards alike.

"Thalion! Now!" Gwyn screamed.

Thalion caught his breath. He knew he should follow Gwyn's orders, but...

"Gwyn! Get over here!" he shouted back.

Gwyn continued fighting as if she hadn't heard him. He saw her kill two Regulars, then three. The dragon was advancing on her, its eyes flashing like fire.

"Gwyn!" Thalion screamed.

The dragon reared back, and Thalion felt a heart-wrenching lurch as he realized what was going to happen. It sucked in air as it prepared to unleash fire on Gwyn and the remaining Ninaevan guards.

"Here, you beast!" Evalynna's shout caused everyone, even the dragon, to look up for a moment. Her shout had not come from the garden.

Thalion's breath caught. Somehow, she had managed to scale one of the garden walls and now stood triumphant, a spear in her hand. As the dragon turned toward her, she jumped, spear aimed at the dragon like some hero of legend.

"Evalynna!" Gwyn cried.

The dragon unleashed its breath of fire, and Thalion screamed as Evalynna was consumed in a mass of fire. Her agonized screech made him want to clap his hands over his ears. Instead, he stared in mesmerized horror. Evalynna's burning body hit the dragon with a loud crunching sound. The dragon roared in pain as her spear dug into its neck. It shook itself, and Evalynna's body fell to the ground, broken and burned.

"No!" Gwyn's voice shook with rage and grief. "You beast, no!"

Thalion blinked back tears of his own. Hands shaking, he started cutting the rope. He had no choice. "Gwyn!" he shouted desperately. "Gwyn!"

Gwyn didn't hear him as she charged the dragon, her sword raised high. Thalion watched in horror as she slashed at the beast, her sword hardly making any impact on the dragon's scales. He remembered his own battle against an illusionary dragon. He had barely made it through that with the help of magic...

The dragon roared, and Thalion gasped as he realized Gwyn's sword was caught in the wound Evalynna's spear had made. Gwyn jerked hard, tearing it wider. Blood poured out of the wound, and the dragon hissed, flailing wildly.

She's going to do it! Thalion thought. His hand froze, knife hovering a hair's breadth from the rope. Maybe, just maybe...

The dragon swung around, throwing Gwyn to the ground. She scrambled to her feet, eyes still wild with rage, and charged the dragon again. It reared back, sucking in a breath.

"Gwyn!" Thalion shouted in fear, trying to warn her. In his heart, he knew it was too late.

Gwyn reached the beast just as it opened its mouth to breathe fire. Gwyn leapt, ramming her sword down the dragon's mouth. It coughed and spat, fire flying everywhere, landing in the trees and grass. It flailed wildly, sending Gwyn flying again as a clawed hand ripped open her chest.

"Gwyn!" Thalion screamed as he saw the blood begin to pour from her chest. Behind her, the dragon lay choking and dying, but Thalion didn't have eyes for anyone but Gwyn.

This time, Gwyn raised her head. He couldn't hear her over the roars of the dragon, but he could read her lips well enough.

"Close the door."

Behind Gwyn, Regulars ran forward, swords in hand. Eyes blurring with tears, Thalion raised a shaking hand to the rope. Quickly, he sawed through the rope. He heard the stacked boulders above him start to give way, and he began running into the darkened tunnel.

"Follow him!" He heard pounding feet behind him, and he sped up the pace. He nearly tripped going down the steep stairs. He needed to be fast…

The entire tunnel began to shake as boulder after boulder fell to seal the door shut. Thalion slipped as the step underneath him trembled, and he fell down the stairs, grabbing desperately at anything that looked remotely stable, trying to stop, or at least slow, his fall. He kept tumbling, collecting scrapes and bruises as small rocks tumbled down with him.

Finally, everything stopped moving. Thalion lay at the bottom of the first long flight of the staircase, breathing heavily. Tears streamed down his face, blurring his vision. *Gwyn. Evalynna.* His mentor, his aunt, his friend, lay outside, her body burned and broken by one of Auriel's dragons.

I hate him! Thalion thought in a rage. *He will pay for what he did!*

He choked on another sob. He had no idea if they were ever going to make it out of the underground city, much less if he was ever going to have the chance to make Auriel pay.

He will. Someday, somehow, I don't know how, but he will pay for Gwyn's death. Mazda's light, how am I going to tell Mother?

Vinet would be heartbroken. Gwyn had been her best friend since childhood.

Thalion shook his head, trying to stop his tears. He wasn't safe yet. It was still a ways down to the underground city.

He sighed as he realized he could see nothing other than pitch blackness. *A flaw in the plan,* he thought. *Maybe there was a torch by the entrance, but I'm not about to go back there and try to find it.* He sighed again and settled himself on one of the tall stairs. Sooner or later someone would come searching for him. They had to have heard the door close, after all. And Serana would make someone come look.

Thalion blinked, feeling his eyes start stinging again. *Mazda's light, at least she's safe,* he thought. *I couldn't bear it if anything happened to her.*

Another boom sounded above him, and he shuddered. It sounded like the trebuchets were still hard at work.

Boom! Boom! Boom!

Thalion shuddered again and wrapped his arms around his head. They were destroying the castle. Right above him, they were destroying the only home he'd ever known.

Serana, please send someone soon, he thought. *I don't know how much more of this I can handle.*

ELLRIHEIM

People of Ilhelm." Thalion faced the assembled crowd, trying to disguise how nervous he was. "Thank you for listening to me."

Only Niara and Serana were near enough to see Thalion's hands clenched tightly into fists. He had tried to convince Niara that this should be her duty, but she had adamantly refused, leaving the duty to him.

"We all heard the destruction above us," Thalion said. "I'm sure you have all guessed what it means by now, but let me make it clear for everyone. Our home has been destroyed. Ilhelm City is no more."

Thalion watched the reaction of the crowd carefully. No one seemed surprised, although several of the human families held each other tightly as his words sank in.

"The entrance back to the surface has been cut off," he continued. "We cannot escape the way we came in. Even if we could, I would not recommend it. The dragons have come back, and they will soon rule the entirety of Saemar. We would be immediately pressed into service, as slaves of the new overlords."

Thalion took a deep breath at the bleak picture his words painted. Niara was the one who could have told him how true they were. She was the one who had been observing the dragon's conquest.

"But all is not lost!" He raised his voice. "Thanks to the nephelm, we have a whole city at our disposal! We have food, water, and light! We have tools for every craftsman, a library for scholars, and a military to defend us. We will survive down here, and we will prosper! And we will have a better life than anyone on the surface because we will be free!"

A halting cheer spread through the crowd, although many of the humans looked unconvinced. The nephelm said nothing, only regarded him grimly. Then again, they had a much better idea of what they were facing than any of the humans.

Thalion waited until silence fell again. He took Serana's hand in his, drawing him closer to him for comfort as he continued. "There's more," he said. "I'm sure you've all heard rumors of a new god rising. The god that controls the dragons, the one in whose name they rule. He is our enemy," his voice was flat. "He means to enslave us all to his whim. We are Ninaevans! We will never submit!"

This time, the cheer was slightly louder. He glared fiercely at the crowd. "Will we submit?" he shouted.

"No!" The call came back strong, but not enough for him. He needed them behind him, devoted to the cause.

"Will we submit?" he shouted again.

"No!" The call was stronger this time, filling the entire cavern with a low roar.

Thalion nodded in satisfaction. "Down here, we are not just the people of Ilhelm," he said. "We are the humans of Ilhelm, the nephelm of Utgard, the elves of Alfheim. Some of us may have differences," he glanced at Evikan, standing with the nephelm in the back of the crowd, "but down here, we all have one goal. To survive. And we need everyone to do that. We cannot survive without each other."

Silence reigned over the crowd. Thalion held his breath. What he was asking them to do was beyond anything they'd ever asked of the people of Ninaeva before. He took a deep breath. "To that end, I ask that you set aside your notions of races, of places of origin. All of our homes have been destroyed, or soon will be. That binds us together more than anything else."

Thalion relaxed. The people, even Evikan in the back, were nodding thoughtfully. Most of them had heard about the massacre of Alfheim by this point, and they all had heard the destruction happen above them.

"This place is now our home! All of ours! Be we human, elf, or nephelm! And we shall defend this home to the death!" Thalion squeezed Serana's hand as he raised his voice. "In years past, this place was Ellriheim, a sanctuary for the nephelm people. Now, it is our sanctuary from the outside world. We are not people of Ilhelm, Alfheim, or Utgard. We are all people of Ellriheim!"

"Ellriheim!" Someone shouted. Thalion caught his breath as others took up the cheer.

He held up the hand unclaimed by Serana. "I have one more pledge to make you," he said. "The entrance under Ilhelm Castle was not the only way into Ellriheim. We have mapped out only a fraction of the tunnels surrounding the main compound. Somewhere, there is another entrance to the surface. And I pledge you we will find it." He thought of the destruction outside, and his expression turned fierce. "And when we find it, we will take back our homes! We will take back our land from the dragons and make them pay for the destruction they've wrought!"

This time, the cheer was far louder, far more honest. Thalion felt his own heart beat faster.

He raised his and Serana's joined hands to the sky. "For Ellriheim!"

"For Ellriheim!" the crowd cheered.

Serana smiled at him, pride shining clearly from her eyes. "For Ellriheim," she said.

ACKNOWLEDGMENTS

This book is where I went off the rails. *A Mother's Secrets* was easy to write, as most of the material was fresh in my mind from our role-playing game that was definitely not an excuse to not work on our theses. But the first book ends right where our game ended, and it definitely didn't seem finished. So I jumped forward eighteen years to find out what happened to this world we invested so much time into.

Josh, my wonderful husband and game master, is the one who encouraged me the most. He provided his view of the world, including the secret identities of Auriel, and I ran from there. I also have to thank the other members of the game, Jonathan, Megan, Neil, Nathan, and especially Rose, and beg pardon for the liberties I took with their characters. Especially Pellalindra and Serana.

I feel like I've inevitably forgotten someone, but thank you to Sally, who was the was the first person to edit this book. And a huge thanks to the editors at Falstaff Books, who caught so many errors and inconsistencies to give you this finished product. And thank you to Melissa for designing the cover, and John and Erin for taking the lead and getting everything published!

ABOUT THE AUTHOR

Tuppence Van de Vaarst has long been obsessed with history, writing, fantasy, the ocean, and magic. She taught herself to read at the age of three and read every single book she could get her hands on. At the age of eleven, she started creating her own stories. As she grew, her passion for stories never faded.

When she was eighteen, she decided to pursue her love of the ocean by enlisting in the United States Coast Guard. Although she decided military life did not suit her, she views it as a useful experience that she can now insert into her own writing. She has an MA in Medieval Studies and an MA in Library Science from University College Dublin. When she's not writing she's still surrounded by books as her full-time job is that of librarian.

FRIENDS OF FALSTAFF

Thank You to All our Falstaff Books Patrons, who get extra digital content each month! To be featured here and see what other great rewards we offer, go to www.patreon.com/falstaffbooks.

PATRONS

Dino Hicks
John Hooks
John Kilgallon
Larissa Lichty
Travis & Casey Schilling
Staci-Leigh Santore
Sheryl R. Hayes
Scott Norris
Samuel Montgomery-Blinn
Junkle
Vickie DeSantos
Quincy J. Allen
Allison Charlesworth

Thank You for Supporting Independent Publishing!

We believe that you should be able
to read your books, your way.
That's why this Falstaff Books
print edition includes a digital copy
at no additional cost!

Just scan the QR code with your device,
follow the directions on Prolific Works,
and enjoy!
You can also join our newsletter when prompted,
and never miss an awesome Falstaff Release!

9 781645 543428